THE OLD
FAMILIAR
PLACES

Published under licence by Brown Dog Books and
The Self-Publishing Partnership Ltd, 10b Greenway Farm, Bath Rd, Wick,
nr. Bath BS30 5RL

www.selfpublishingpartnership.co.uk

ISBN hardback book: 978-1-83952-504-9
ISBN paperback book: 978-1-83952-505-6
ISBN e-book: 978-1-83952-506-3

Cover design by Kevin Rylands
Internal design by Andrew Easton

Printed and bound in the UK
This book is printed on FSC certified paper

THE OLD FAMILIAR PLACES

'A joyful, funny, moving journey.'
'The story of Sonny and Ruby, a rollercoaster of a ride.'

SAM EMONY

BROWN
DOG
BOOKS

To Patricia Emony
For making the sun shine in my familiar places.

To Anne
For your continual belief.
And to our familiar places, especially Crete.

TRAGEDY

I stare at her grave. I'd give anything to talk to my sister. I'm all alone as usual. I listen to the rumble of engines as the church car park fills up.

Footsteps approach. 'You ok, Sonny?'

'I guess so.'

'How's your hand?'

I look at the red swollen mess. 'Sorry about the wall, Mum.'

'Don't worry, but you must stop lashing out.' How many times has she told me this?

'You're at the church now, you may as well come in.'

'Where's Dad?'

'He's in the car, waiting. He's sorry.'

'Why can't he come here and say it then?'

'He can't, darling, he can't bring himself to ever visit here.' She sighs. 'He's different your dad, he doesn't know how to ...'

'Mum, those things he said about me being a waster, dreaming my life away ...'

'Don't worry about that now, let's just get through today for Ruby's sake, she's lost her husband.'

Why am I even at the funeral of Freddie Wilson?

I don't know how Mum and Ruby Wilson became best friends, She is just part of her life. Coffee mornings, choir, dinner parties and shopping. Dad thinks she's a bit hoity-toity, but he never refuses a dance when they come to ours. Sometimes I watch from the top of the stairs as they boogie in the lounge to 'Yeh Yeh' by Georgie Fame or 'The Twist' by Chubby Checker. I came back late one Saturday from band practice, and Mrs Wilson tried to get me to dance, I was so embarrassed. After a few drinks Freddie gets his trumpet out and joins in. I like Freddie. I mean I liked Freddie. He would always talk to me about music, especially jazz, which he loved. He said, 'Jazz is where it's at, Sonny. Play jazz and you can play anything.' Now he's dead.

I turn to Mum knowing I'm about to hurt her but unable to stop. 'I'm leaving after my A levels, I can't stand him screaming at me every day.'

She takes my hand, she's shaking. 'Let's not talk about this now, Sonny. I've got to help Ruby.'

'I'm still leaving. I'm going to be a musician.'

'For God's sake, don't tell your dad that, it will only make things worse.'

'Can things get any worse? Unless he has a drink of course.'

I know Mum is holding back tears. She fumbles with her hankie and sniffs.

'Why can't he be proud of me like other dads?'

'Let's just give it time.'

'His moods are doing my head in, he's so angry. I'll show him. One day, I'll make him eat his words.'

'I know you will, darling. We'll be fine. We're a good team, aren't we? You and me.'

She bear-hugs me. Her tears wet my face. 'Please come to the service. For me?'

I nod.

'I'll see you in there, it starts in fifteen minutes. We're right at the front.'

I watch Mum as she kisses her fingers and taps Maisie's headstone and shuffles across the graveyard. She's always the peacemaker.

A copy of the Mirror has been left on a bench. It says Maurice Gibb from the Bee Gees is getting married today, and he's a Manchester lad, so there's hope for me, Jack and Karen. We've just got to finish our A Levels and we'll be off. I mean it. This claustrophobic, semi-detached suburban life. I'll shed it like a skin.

Chrysanthemums

The hearse is pulling in as I duck under some tress and reach the car park. Mum is waiting at the door, there's no sign of Dad. Mrs Wilson steps out in her high heels, and pulls the creases out of her skirt. She's dressed all in black, wearing a veil, but I still recognise her. I can see her bright red lipstick. Mum manages a discreet wave and points me inside.

I walk into the church, and my best mate Jack is there handing out the order of service. I mutter a quick hello.

He looks embarrassed. 'My mum's in the choir with Mrs Wilson, so she's dragged me in to help, but it's worth it for the day off college.'

'We need to have a meeting about our escape plan.'

'That bad?'

'He went off his head again at me this morning, I ended up hitting the wall.' I show him my swollen knuckles.

I walk to the front. Dad huffs. I can smell the flowers and the candles and the perfumes and aftershaves. It's a mixture of sweet sickly candy floss and alcohol. I read the order of service, Freddie's picture is on the front with his full name, Edward Wilson. It's a formal photo with a shirt and tie, and I've never seen him like this. I flick over and on the back cover is his wedding photo, and he looks the same, but Mrs Wilson seems so young and glamorous in a very short white skirt. I shiver in my seat, thinking about poor Freddie and what being dead means, and what happened to him.

The church organ screeches. We stand as one, and I swear the coffin takes ten minutes to arrive. It goes on forever, loads of the adults flicking their heads backwards but I can't, I'm locked in, I just stare at the altar until Mum and Mrs Wilson are in front of us. Mrs Wilson begins to weep, I hear her gasps, and I see her shoulders heaving up and down. Mum leans across, puts her arm around her and passes a handkerchief.

I can't stop looking at the coffin. It's so weird to think that Freddie is in there lying still when just a few weeks ago he was at ours drinking and dancing and blasting out his trumpet. A string quartet play 'Chrysanthemums' by Puccini. It is beautiful. I can't tell you how or why but I am overwhelmed with sadness and salty tears stream down my cheeks. My hand is killing me. Mum slips me a tissue. The sounds reverberate around the church, and I am so moved by the music, I really can't explain it. I look up, and everybody else is looking down. The sun peeks through the stained-glass dome high above us, the coffin handles sparkle and I look at Freddie's photo, he's too young to die. I think of Maisie and realise I'd have loved a sister, someone to look after, to talk to, to share my NME with and visit Decoy Records together in Manchester. Maybe Dad wouldn't be like this if Maisie was still here and I can't stop crying now as the violins make me think about things I'd never considered before. Mum leans back, holds my hand and I let her. I make a promise to talk to her about Maisie when this is all over. I know she'd like that.

We have the final blessing and the strings play Freddie's favourite tune called 'Time After Time' as he is carried out. A trumpeter joins in. It is haunting, the notes echoing around the church, and again I find myself spellbound by music. I'm dreaming about running away, escaping this humdrum existence until Dad nudges me out, the bastard, and we follow the coffin down the aisle. As I leave the church, Jack gives me a thumbs-up. I hope he doesn't see my tears.

Shelter from the Storm

It is pouring down. The graveyard is a sea of umbrellas, and the rain bounces off them. Mum goes to the graveside, but we stay at the back. She's going to the reception with the funeral cars. We are going home and then catching the train to town. Dad fancies the free beer. We arrive at Oxford Road, it's stopped raining, and we splash our way across town dodging the puddles. We don't say much. What is there to say?

Manchester feels different on a Friday. I usually come in on Saturdays with Jack and Karen. Today everyone is rushing, heads down, carrying their brollies and dressed more formally. Dad marches us to the Midland, we run up the steps where uniformed men greet us and tell us where to go for the Wilson funeral reception. The place is huge, it's like stepping into a cathedral, and I didn't even know it existed. We head towards a dining room.

'The management refused to let the Beatles in here, you know,' says Dad as we go through massive wooden doors.

'Really?' I guess he's winding me up, but the waiter who gives us a glass of Champagne confirms it.

'It is true,' he says in a French accent. 'They were not dressed correctly! It's a fact.'

Dad is smirking. 'Ha, told you so. You should listen to your old man a bit more, shouldn't ya?'

He hasn't said anything about me drinking today, but this is my first glass of Champagne ever, and I gulp too many bubbles and snort and splutter and have to fake a cough to recover. We squeeze forward, through more doors, and then it opens up into a vast dining room set with tables. I see Mum chatting to Jack's mum, and head over with Dad following me for a change.

Jack's mum winks at me. 'Jack's gone home. He was just helping out at the church.' She leans in close. 'I've told your mum how good you are on the piano when you rehearse at mine.'

Dad does his stupid laugh. 'Are we talking about Sonny, here?'

Arsehole. I sit down at table seventeen with other local families, and I'm the only one on my own. Dad tells Mum he is going to look for the buffet table. She shouts a bit too loud, 'Don't be stupid, Pete. We are in a silver service restaurant.'

Dad looks disappointed. 'Ooooh, how the other half live.'

Mum orders him to pipe down. He raises his hand to ask the waiter for a beer, to be told it is wine only at the table. He wanders off, and Mum moves next to me and asks if I'm ok. 'If you look at the tables at the front you might see some stars from the music scene. Ruby says they are here.' When Dad returns with a pint, I tell him that I think I've just seen Bob Dylan at the front of the room.

He almost spills his beer as he stands up for a look, and then he catches me smiling at Mum. 'Got ya,' I say. Dad loves Dylan and I make a pledge to wind him up more.

'Let me tell you a story, Sonny, about a night next door at the Free Trade Hall in 1967.'

Mum smiles at me. How many times have we heard this story after Dad has too many whiskies?

'Just a few hundred yards from here, Bob came out for the second set and...'

'Judas,' me and Mum yell together, and we burst out laughing and the atmosphere in the room changes and the afternoon becomes a celebration of Freddie as we tell stories and drink and laugh. Mum relaxes, we let Dad finish his story about Dylan going electric, and they even hold hands at the table. The food is amazing, Dad sneaks me a beer, and I guess I realise at my very first funeral that they're not really that bad. Once we were over the mumbo jumbo at the church, and everyone has had a drink or two the stories about Freddie and his good times are fun to listen to. All involve too much alcohol. I guess I just don't feel like a teenager at a party. It's better than that.

The reception winds down and people begin to leave. We get invited back to the house for the wake. Mum says she'd love to, Dad smiles at the prospect of more free drinks, raises his glass and says, 'Cheers.' Mrs Wilson lets me know that I am invited too, she says, 'I've got something to show you.' Dad sniggers, and Mum says the wake is going to feature some of the London lot who are staying over so that could be fun. We stagger back to the station, and Dad falls asleep before we've set off. Mum holds my good hand tight and says it's been a great day in the circumstances, and I agree. At home, we get changed, have a brew and then set off for the Wilsons, just a short walk away.

Paint It Black

As I come out of the downstairs toilet, I catch a glimpse of Ruby Wilson. She looks fantastic, a bit like Dusty Springfield, nothing like the girls in college. She descends from the top of her grand staircase with a landing in the middle and a sofa. And a table. In our house, you bang your elbows on both walls as you run up and down. These stairs are immense. She doesn't notice me as I stare at the wide flares on her tight flowery trouser suit and halfway down she checks herself in the landing mirror. She adjusts her top, pushes her boobs up, and I swear she winks to herself. She really is quite something with her blonde hair held up high. You'd never think she'd just come from her husband's funeral. I tiptoe across the hall to avoid detection. I fail.

'Hello, Sonny sweetheart. How are you?'

Shit.

'Hi, Mrs Wilson… Err, I'm okay, thank you.' What do I say? What do I say? My pause lasts forever as she sashays towards me. 'I'm sorry about Freddie's accident,' I mumble.

'Now, don't you be worried about that, we've had enough tears for one day. And please, call me Ruby.'

I don't know how to continue. I'm trembling.

'Sonny, you're studying music, aren't you? Your mum told me

you were very talented.'

'Yes, I am. Studying I mean. Music, English and history.'

'Do you want to be a musician?'

'I think so. But Dad says…'

'Don't you worry about what your dad says. Come and see this.'

She shimmies past me, grabs my sore hand and leads me to a set of ornate sliding doors. I'm blushing as she unlocks the right-hand door. There is scratching and barking as she turns the key, and pushes me into a room as grand as the foyer in the Midland Hotel.

'Ringo, sit. Ringo – good boy.' Ruby quietens the Afghan as I gaze in amazement. This room is stunning. I am mesmerised. It seems larger than the whole of our downstairs with a grand piano, a drum kit, double bass and walls covered with silver and gold discs. And Freddie's trumpet. Photos of Freddie with pop stars and royalty, every photo labelled and dated. And sofas, one with a fancy back and no arms. And a drinks cabinet. It's like being in the movies.

Ruby comes close, too close, stumbling a little. I can smell her perfume. And the drink. Even though I am taller, she makes me blush again and whispers, 'Welcome to Waverly, Sonny, this is Freddie's music room. It's his pride and joy. He doesn't usually like visitors, but I think today is a good day to break some rules.'

I try using her first name as instructed, and it feels weird. For some reason I speak very slowly, 'This is amazing, Ruby. It's so bloody amazing. Did Freddie really know the Beatles and the Stones?'

'You bet he did, Darling. We always used to be in London at the 100 Club with the boys. He wanted to be a musician himself in the early days. In fact, he earned enough money for this house and music room from writing just one hit song himself, "Mama's Coming Home". Then he became a music lawyer.'

'Wow, just one song? That's incredible. He wrote that song, really?' Even I'd heard that song. Even my dad had listened to that song.

Ruby waits until I am facing her. 'If you become a musician, Sonny, this is what you could have. Freddie's good fortune was that one tune.'

I am on a high, I can taste success, in London with Mick and Keith, I'm on piano jamming away, and then Ruby snaps her fingers, and brings me back down to earth and asks me to take Ringo around the block. She has to get back to the wake. She shows me to the back door, gives me Ringo's lead and sets me on my way. 'I'll tell your mum and dad you'll be back soon, don't worry.' And she's gone.

As I stumble towards the garden gate, someone shouts. I jump out of my skin. I snap the lead tight. Through a cloud of cigarette smoke, I see a scruffy, unsteady man in the shadows of a dull outside light.

'Taking Ringo out, are we?' he snarls.

He must know Ruby. He knows the dog, and he's a guest at Freddie's funeral, so I'm not scared. I just reacted like I was, and I feel the need to get away fast.

'Yes, Ruby asked me to.'

'You do that, son. One thing you need to learn in this life is,' he takes a long, long drag on his cigarette, 'what Ruby wants Ruby gets. Bitch.'

He stubs it out and disappears. This is my introduction to Jimmy the Drums.

Time After Time

Ringo is no trouble at all, just a quick walk around the block and I head back to the house. No one is lurking as I let myself in the gate and take him to the kitchen. He gulps grub down from his bowl, and I leave him on his own so I can rediscover the music room. I'm fascinated about what I'd seen earlier. It's been a long day, but the cold night air has woken me up. I slide the door open and let myself in. This room is just perfect. I could stay here forever. I creep around, feeling a little guilty and looking at the photos to see who I can recognise. All the time Freddie has been coming to our house and I just didn't know, he seemed an average guy like Dad. Give him a few drinks, and he became louder and funny for sure, but he wasn't a name-dropper. Yet here he is with the Beatles in Liverpool, the Rolling Stones at the Marquee in London. There's a Royal Variety section, a photo of Freddie and Ruby with the queen mother at the Palace Theatre in 1959 alongside the Northern Dance Orchestra and Cliff Richard. Then ten years later, Freddie, Ruby, Cilla Black and Tom Jones at the London Palladium. And wow, in 1970 Freddie with Peter Noone and Herman's Hermits with the queen.

So many more, so many of the people I'd read about in NME and then seen on TV. I play a few scales and muck about dreaming of being at the Palace or even the Palladium. I only get to play grand pianos when I do my grades in town, so it's nice to have some time on this one.

The door opens, and a head pops through. 'Alright, mate, thought I heard someone on the old Joanna, mind if I come in?' I don't get a chance to answer. He sneaks in and closes the door.

'I'm Charlie, pleased to meet you.'

'Hello, I'm Sonny.'

'After Sonny Rollins?'

'No, Sonny Clark. Dad had a thing about him the year before I was born. Dial S for Sonny.'

Charlie looks impressed. 'Your dad knows his shit. Louis Hayes was on the kit in '57 on that album. Anyway, cool name. You a pianist then?'

Nobody has ever asked me that before. 'I guess I'd like to be. I'm in a band.'

'Good lad. We all want to be in bands, don't we? I'm in a band, you're in a band, Freddie would have loved to be in a band, but he was better behind the desk if you know what I mean? God rest his soul. You know Freddie?'

'Ruby is Mum's best friend and sometimes he would come to our house for parties. He used to bring twenty or more LPs and we'd read the liners and stare at the photos together.'

'That's my boy.'

'He would bring his trumpet and tell me about all about jazz.'

'Yeah,' says Charlie, 'I've collected jazz records since I was a nipper with my mate Dave Green. Taught me all I know. Listen, you hang on here, keep tinkling the ivory, I'm going to get a drink, and I'll bring someone to meet you.' He turned and hurried out of the room.

A few minutes later he's back with a smartly dressed man carrying a case.

'Sonny, this is Syd. You may have heard him in church today. Syd, this is Sonny. He's a pianist, and he's in a band. Right, let's have some fun.'

Syd opens the case, and that beautiful trumpet that we heard in church emerges. He unfolds a piece of music and sticks it on my piano. 'Syd, I'm only grade five. First time I heard this song was today.'

Syd shrugged, 'Don't matter. Just go for it.'

Charlie is searching Freddie's room for drumsticks, Syd starts oiling his valves, and no one is listening to me.

'Sonny,' says Charlie, 'we're just gonna play some jazz. Play the chords on the sheet, not the notes for now, just to feel your way in, Syd'll handle the tune. As soon as we're in the groove, throw a few notes in, either off the page or whatever you fancy.' Charlie lifts up the brushes, counts us in and we're off.

I am so out of my depth it's untrue. I just sit and listen for a while. Syd wanders over whilst playing, pointing to the score with his left hand. I'm following the melody with him as he finishes the first verse, and he shouts over to Charlie.

'Back to the top, here we go...' Two bars of drums and then I hit a C major chord bang on time, followed by an A minor two beats later and on and on and on I go, just basic chords every two beats or for a whole bar sometimes. It sounds simple, but it sounds beautiful too, that trumpet just rings around the room. I don't take my eyes off the music, I can't stop counting, and then

Syd shouts, 'Breathe, Sonny!' and Charlie bursts out laughing as my bright red face relaxes.

We break for a minute so the guys can have a drink.

Charlie leans over his kit. 'Jazz is all about feel and composing on the fly, it's improvising. Just feel your way in, keep looking at your bandmates but most importantly, keep listening.'

We're off again for one more run-through. I get a bit more hopeful and throw some little riffs in, Syd takes a verse out, stands next to me and urges me on, building my confidence. This is so much fun. And then it's over.

'That's it,' says Syd. 'Sorted. See you later. We'll play that for Ruby – she'll love it. It's one of Freddie's favourite tunes, especially that Chet Baker version from '54. Well played Sonny, great chops. Put that score in your back pocket and don't lose it.'

Then they were gone, back to the wake, leaving me on cloud nine. I guess my piano lessons with Miss Wolstenholme hadn't been a waste of time. Holy shit, that was fun.

I jump up and have another look around the room and feel guilty as I see Freddie with John Lennon looking at me. 'Sorry Freddie,' I mumble. 'I wish you were here.'

In the kitchen, Ringo is asleep in his basket. He doesn't move as I splash water around the sink and I fill my glass. I walk through the house. The front room has about twenty people in, and you wouldn't guess that they had all been to a funeral that day. The music is playing and the people are swaying, including Dad, who is in danger of bumping into the Pioneer turntable which tops a stack of electronics. Two substantial wooden speakers with black fronts sit either side of the room and the tunes are pumping out. I see Charlie and Syd, heads nodding in unison, flicking through Freddie's music collection. Clouds of smoke billow around two massive stained-glass lights, Mum says they are Tiffany's, but I haven't met her yet. She had been chatting with Ruby but popped over to check on me as Dad trips over an orange pouffe and she scuttles back and gets help to manhandle him onto a sofa. The guy I saw in the garden is on his haunches checking over the sound system, still smoking. He catches my eye, and he's in my face in seconds.

He scowls. 'Alright, dog boy, you back then. How's Ringo?'

'He's fine. He's sleeping in the kitchen.' The thing about pissed adults is they're not very funny.

'It's quadraphonic, mate. The amps are quad although silly old sod Freddie's only got two speakers.'

Ruby comes to my rescue, grabs his arm and leads him away. She turns her head and winks at me and whispers, 'Jimmy's jealous. Don't worry.'

Mum comes back and says Dad's out for the count, but I can see that already. It's nothing new. Poor Mum, she's funny when she's tipsy, but he's a nightmare. She chats away, and tonight she's hanging on to me to stop her from falling. We walk arm in arm to the kitchen to get her a glass of water, and we talk more tonight than we have done in ages, no snarky comments from Dad, just Mum and me.

Ringo barks as I am about to tell Mum about Maisie and how I was thinking about her in church. I pat the dog and settle him down, and the chance is missed as Ruby wobbles in and cuddles Mum.

'We're going to the music room,' she shouts. 'Follow me you two.'

Mum looks at me. 'You've made yourself at home. Ringo doesn't like strangers.'

I tell her that I've already walked and fed him tonight. 'He's my new best buddy.'

Charlie puts his head around the door. 'Oi Sonny, you're wanted. Come on.'

Mum looks shocked. Syd runs in, fill his glass, clears his throat for effect and announces, 'Sonny, warm up those fingers.'

Mum's face. 'Sonny, how do you know all these people?'

'It's a long story, Mum, and you've been busy with Dad.'

Even though she has visited Ruby's quite a few times, she surprises me when she says, 'I've never been to the music room, Freddie doesn't allow it.'

'Follow me, it's fantastic.'

'How the heck would you know?' And she shuffles after me.

We sit on the floor in front of the sofa, Ruby's there and Mum chats to her as she weeps. A few of the guys are playing a tune, and we all listen. Dad's taken me to a few jazz gigs. He teases me about his heyday when he would catch the Yanks down at Club 43 or the Free Trade Hall. Bird, Dizzy, Miles, they have all played in Manchester, and he's seen them live. He still has the records and sometimes I put them on at home.

Jealous Jimmy is on the drums, he looks a mess, and there is a pianist and a bass player. I glance around the room, and everybody seems so tired, it's been a long day.

Mum smiles at me, and I turn to Ruby as she bends down. 'I love this room, Sonny. I always told Freddie to let people in here but he wouldn't have it.'

Mum agrees. 'It's a beautiful room, Ruby, and it's been a

wonderful day, you've done him proud.' The two of them are off again with the sniffles. Ruby rubs my hair from behind, just like Mum used to when I was younger. Charlie walks over and has a word with Ruby.

Autumn Leaves finishes, and Charlie stands up and tells the musicians that's a wrap. Then he shouts, 'One last tune,' and he sits at the drums and Syd takes his trumpet out of its case. Charlie looks around the room and calls a guy called Eric up.

Eric says, 'Here I go again.'

Everyone claps and cheers.

Syd hushes the room. 'And on the piano we have Sonny.' He points at me. I don't know who is more surprised, me or Mum. 'Come on, Sonny,' shouts Syd. 'This is the last song, and we all know why we are playing it.'

I am carried to the piano on a wave of applause. I remember the music is in my back pocket and I place it on the stand.

The room goes quiet, Syd clears his throat. 'Ladies and Gentlemen, this is the last tune of the day, and I am very privileged to be here and to have played this in the church earlier with the strings. Freddie was a true gentleman, and he became a good friend to many of us here in Manchester and in London. As did Ruby, that goes without saying. This is Freddie's favourite tune. God rest his soul.' Ruby stands up and tries to say a few words too but only manages a brief, 'Thank you,' and sits down in tears with Mum holding onto her on the sofa.

Charlie counts us in, Syd looks across at me, mouths, 'Start with the chords,' and we're off.

And my life changes.

BROWN EYED GIRL

I lie in bed dreaming of last night, going through it over and over again. I know it's only one song, but it has changed my outlook on everything I understand about music. All the practice, all the exams, the heartache, the turmoil and out of the blue it all makes sense. I have the skills to make my dreams come true. I just couldn't see it. But today, my mind is clear. I'll show him. I'll bloody show him. I leap out of bed. I need some toast and a brew.

Mum's in the kitchen already, and I smell the burned crusts, and the steam drifts like clouds from the teapot.

She looks up. 'Morning, son, pot's still hot, get yourself a mug.' I hug Mum, and she pulls me in, ruffles my hair and asks, 'Are you alright?'

I fetch the milk, and tell her, 'Last night was so exciting.' I can't quite explain it all, but many, many dots have been joined.

She brings me straight back down to earth, 'I don't think Ruby will see it like that.'

'Oh shit, sorry Mum. I don't mean it like that. It's just that after Dad had a go at me in the morning, I was doubting myself, and then these guys turn up, and show me a route I didn't even understand.' I take a sip of my tea, bang my mug down and spill it. Mum wipes up the mess. 'Do you know how good I felt last night?'

'I could see it, Sonny, you were beaming for the whole tune. I didn't even know you understood jazz.'

'That's the thing, I don't. Some of it I was making up as I went along, improvising if you like, and it felt so good, but I couldn't have done it without having had my lessons. I knew it, but I just didn't know I knew it. Does that make sense?'

Mum makes more toast, and we talk for ages about music and dancing, big bands she's seen, live music, when she'd first got a TV. Mum believes in me even if Dad doesn't, and it feels good. 'I want that feeling again, the one I had last night.'

She smiles the biggest of smiles. 'I'm going round to Ruby's house in half an hour to help her tidy up, why don't you come along?'

I jump in the bath, fix the showerhead on the taps and have a quick wash. I'm smiling like a village idiot, singing 'Time After Time' and clicking my fingers. I comb my hair, brush my teeth, splash on some of Dad's Old Spice and it's not even 11 am.

As I come out of my bedroom, I hear Mum shouting at Dad, telling him off for drinking too much. I race down the stairs, jumping the last six. Boom. Leather jacket on, shoes on. I'm ready to take on the world.

Yesterday's rain has given way to today's dry but cold Saturday. We walk together, not saying much at all, laughing at Dad falling asleep, chatting about Ringo and the fantastic music room. I remember my tears for Maisie yesterday as I listened to

Puccini. I grab Mum's arm, and we change direction, turning left. She resists a little, but I pull harder and she and murmurs a surprised, 'Oh, I see,' and she tags along. I am taller than Mum, I have been since I was fourteen, and this is me taking charge for the first time. I know she understands the church is at the end of this winding road. It's a path we should have walked a long time ago. We march together in silence, our strides synchronising and I can feel her gripping me tighter the nearer we get. Without asking, she leads me through the churchyard. We are here, in front of Maisie's grave, which looks beautiful after Mum tended it yesterday. We cling to each other, tears rolling down our faces. Minutes, maybe hours pass. Neither of us speak, yet we say everything we need to say. A hundred apologies and a thousand 'I wishes.' A downpour breaks the spell and we rush into the church, to where we sat just twenty-four hours ago. It's empty and unlit. Some of Freddie's flowers remain around the edges. Churches smell. Musty, smoky, damp and foreboding but I've come this far, and there is no going back now.

I hold Mum's hand, take a breath, turn my head. 'Tell me about Maisie.'

Another thousand tears fall and flow as we ebb back and forth, mother and son, mother and daughter and the forever unknown brother and sister. 'You should have seen her, Sonny.' She drifts into another world. 'Maisie walking, dancing, talking and giggling. She was so beautiful. People stopped in the street just to meet her or cross her palm with silver or to see her smile. She had the biggest brown eyes.' Mum says I looked like her as a baby.

I tell Mum about my dreams yesterday as the music played in church, about how I was thinking about Maisie being my big sister, playing her own music. 'Would she have loved the Osmonds or the Bay City Rollers?'

'The Osmonds, I think.' Mum laughs at the thought.

'She could have come with me to Decoy Records in town and we could have gone out together on a Saturday night.' We laugh thinking about it and Mum says she has thought about Maisie every day for twenty years. I know now why she spends time in Maisie's room; it's her sanctuary.

'It broke your dad's heart too. Don't be too hard on him, Sonny. He's never been the same since Maisie died. He's not the man I married. He feels so guilty.'

I stare at the altar. I could never believe. 'Why would he feel guilty?'

Five minutes pass, maybe more. The rain continues to pour, chiming off the roof tiles. Mum speaks without lifting her head, 'I guess he thinks he should have checked in on her instead of passing out drunk.' She pauses. 'The doctors said it didn't make any difference.'

'And what do you think?'

She takes her time. 'It wouldn't have made a difference, the post mortem proved it, she just stopped breathing. Your dad can't let it go. He's been like a stuck record for twenty years.' Mum looks up. The rain stops, it's a sign. 'Time to go, Sonny.'

We wander hand in hand through the graveyard and say bye to Maisie on the way out. Mum opens her purse and gives me a passport-sized photo of my sister. 'She'd have loved you so much.'

We head off to Ruby's for the second day running, dodging the puddles. Mum says she feels lighter and that she's proud of me for last night. We stop at the florist on the way. Mum says,

'It will be nice to get Ruby some flowers, something she doesn't have to associate with the funeral.' She and June, the florist, choose dahlias, pinks and purples and some greenery to make a large bouquet. They have a chat about how the funeral went and Mum thanks her for her help.

She looks at me. 'And who's this lovely young man then?'

'This is Sonny, my youngest. He's going to be a musician.'

'Really?' says June. 'Well, just remember your roots. You started here in Manchester. Don't forget us, will you?'

'I won't, I promise.' I can't stop smiling.

We leave the shop and Mum hands me the flowers. I tell Mum she's never called me her youngest before. 'Well,' she says, 'we've never spoken about Maisie, not properly, and she was... She is my eldest, so that makes you my...'

I squeeze her. I've always felt like an only child but the penny dropped and I realise it's different for Mum. 'And you told June I was going to be a musician.'

'Sonny, I am so proud of you, and now that you've played music with a Rolling Stone, I do think you're going to make it.'

The flowers hit the floor. I stop walking. I can't even think about my sister. Everything goes blank. 'What did you say, Mum?'

She laughs and says, 'I wasn't going to tell you till later and you mustn't get a big head but your mate Charlie on the drums last night, that's Charlie Watts from the Stones.' It all makes sense. Charlie coming to the funeral, he's on the photos on the wall in the music room, and I didn't recognise him. He said he's in a band. He loves jazz, which I'd read about in the NME. Bloody hell, my thoughts race around my head, and Mum's shouting at me, but I don't hear a word. If I'd been asked to the play piano with a Rolling Stone I couldn't have done it. Mum picks up the flowers and waves them in front of my face like smelling salts, and I regain my focus.

'Why didn't you tell me last night?' Mum admits she didn't even know who he was until Ruby whispered it to her when I was playing. A dog barks and interrupts our chat and as we turn the corner, Ringo is coming towards us, pulling a scruffy man smoking a fag.

I smirk. 'Hello Jimmy, how are you today?'

He looks embarrassed to be recognised and mutters something about doing Ruby a favour.

I seize the high ground. 'Well, what Ruby wants, Ruby gets.'

Mum rings the bell. We are both still smiling.

Ticket to Ride

Ruby answers the door looking nothing like she did last night. Blue cowboy boots under wide jeans and a sweater, she shows Mum through. Then she looks at me for far too long and makes me blush for the third time in two days. 'Hello, Sonny, after last night everybody is talking about you. You had better come in.' I am stumbling again…

'Hello, Ruby, these are for you.'

I hand over the flowers, and she leans in and kisses my cheek. 'Mmmm, somebody smells good today.' I attempt to escape, she pulls me back in and kisses the other cheek. 'Continental.' There is a pause as I try to work out what she means. 'Continental. I kiss like an Italian.'

I follow Ruby through to the kitchen. There are quite a few people around, including a group of guys in the corner with smoke rising. Syd turns rounds and recognises me. 'Hey, Sonny, come and join us.' He introduces me to everybody and tells them that I am a pianist. No one questions it. They are all playing later tonight, and they invite me to come along and sit in, I make some excuse about having a date at the Odeon in town. I think they can tell I'm nervous. 'What you going to see then?' says Syd, checking out my story.

Luckily I had been last weekend with Jack, but they weren't to know that, *The Return of the Pink Panther*. This gets me off the hook, and I promise to come and see them soon. Mum and Ruby have moved to the lounge for a coffee. Ruby waves me in.

'Thanks for coming yesterday and especially for playing last night.' She's been chatting to Mum, and they've cooked up a plan between them.

'Sit down, Sonny,' Ruby pats the cushion next to her. Freddie has paid a piano teacher in advance for some lessons and Ruby doesn't want them to go to waste. She needs some help walking Ringo and gardening. 'Could we do an exchange?' I glance at Mum, who nods approval. I accept before anyone changes their mind. I am still high from yesterday, and Ruby says the lessons can be on the grand piano in the music room. 'I also have a little surprise for you, Sonny. Alphonso from the London Jazz College was here last night. He listened to you playing and thought you might like to apply for your degree there. He's dropping by in about an hour.' I look at Mum, I look at Ruby, and I don't know what to say, I lose the power of speech. Although I always tell everyone I'm going to be a musician I haven't thought of studying to get there, it was just going to happen.

Mum's smiling at me, urging me to answer. 'But we're going to Germany,' I blurt out and they look even more shocked than I did.

Mum's mug of coffee hits the table a little hard. 'Who's going to Germany?'

I tell them about our plans, Jack, Karen and me, following in the footsteps of so many bands including the Beatles. We're going to finish college, get a job for a few months to save some money and then we're off. Mum looks aghast as she realises I'm nearly eighteen and will be leaving home when college finishes. Ruby calms her down and says it's good to plan, but I should also speak with Alphonso to keep my options open and Mum agrees. I can tell she hates the German option. After the turmoil of the last few days I pretend to back down. 'Listen, Mum, it's only an idea, and it's months away.'

Alphonso arrives, and we head off to the music room for a chat, he seems a nice guy. I think Mum will like him, he looks like Charles Aznavour. We sit on the sofa and talk for ages. He is sophisticated, well dressed with a waistcoat and jacket, his jet black hair swept back. He says, 'Sonny, jazz is in the bones,' and he knows I've got it because he heard me last night, he was amazed how I fitted in with so many pros. He knew Freddie from way back, including gigs all over town, and he would be delighted to invite me to London to see the college and to talk about studying there. I can't get a word in as he speaks so fast and with his Italian accent, but I am carried along on a wave of enthusiasm as he explains how much music means to him and he can tell I'm the same. 'Keep your head down, study hard, play every day but most importantly listen to the greats. They tell you all you need to know.' He opens the piano, plays some incredible classical music with jazz overtones for a couple of minutes, smiles at me and says, 'See you in London in December. It's in your bones. I just know it.' And he leaves, that's it.

I sit there, taking in the last few minutes as if a whirlwind has struck. Did I say anything? I don't think I did, I just accepted everything, nodded in the right places and agreed to go to London. I've only been once, and that was with the school to see the museums.

Jimmy appears at the door and strolls in. He slides along the wall taking in the photos. He stops. 'See that one, there's me and Freddie with Gerry Marsden and Cilla, what a night that was.' I join him and stare, him and Freddie in bow ties and black jackets, looking cool with cigarettes in their hands. He notices too. 'Everybody smoked then, although Ruby hated it of course. You never saw Freddie smoking when Ruby was around.' It's true. I check out the other photos on the wall. Everybody has a fag, but not Freddie and Ruby when they are together. 'Let me tell you some tales.' His eyes light up and he recounts how he and Freddie used to go to all the swanky dos, drinking Champagne and having the finest meals, how Freddie ended up in some private gardens near the Savoy, face down in the grass after drinking too much. How security escorted the two of them out of Greenwich park after they failed to make it up the hill to the observatory at four in the morning and how Freddie came to be arrested for outraging public decency in Kensington Gardens after a night out with him and Princess Margaret. Jimmy was misty-eyed when telling these tales. 'And that's only the 'alf of it,' he said as he blew his nose and wiped his eyes.

I tell Jimmy that Alphonso has invited me to London in December and his demeanour transforms to best mate.

I am to go and stay with him as Freddie always did. He will show me the bright lights, and we will visit some of the jazz clubs. This grumpy, scruffy man is animated beyond belief and sells London to me as this utopia for having the most fun. He promises, 'I'll introduce you to all of the VIPs, except the Kray twins, they've gone away now, but all the bookers, hookers and the razzmatazz. You'll be a star, I'm sure. I'll show you the ropes,

Sonny.' He gives me a business card with Jimmy the Drums written on it, and I promise to call him before I visit. Everyone is so nice to me today. He gets up, kisses his fingers and touches a photo of him and Freddie. He must have really liked him. 'Ta ta now. I'm off to the big smoke.' And he's gone.

Mum and Ruby look pleased when I return. They seem secretive, as if they are plotting again. There is a pile of LPs on the coffee table, and Ruby says Alphonso has had a look through Freddie's collection and I am to listen to these. There must be over thirty. It'll take me forever. Ruby sees the disappointment in my eyes, and says to just take the top five for now. 'We can play the rest later.' I thumb through them, Chet Baker is on the top, of course, then Bill Evans at the Village Vanguard, Herbie Hancock's *Maiden Voyage*, *Dial 'S' for Sonny*, that will please Dad, although I know he already has a copy and Miles Davis's *Birth of the Cool*. I skim off the top five and hang onto them.

'How is Alphonso?' asks Ruby. I explain that he's lovely, that he talks very fast and that he assumes I am already a great pianist. He wants me to visit London in December.

'He is lovely,' says Ruby. 'An absolute gentleman. And steeped in history, he knows his music. In fact, he taught Julia in London too. She's Freddie's piano teacher, who you'll meet soon.' It was as if these secret forces were beginning to control my destiny, so many names, so many connections. I like the sound of London, and I do feel different after the last two days, a little more confident. Ruby asks if I am worried.

'No, not really. Jimmy said I could stay with him when I go down so I'll be fine. He said he'd show me around.'

It's like a bomb has gone off in the room. Ruby jumps up and shouts, 'Jimmy. Jimmy. How the fuck does Jimmy know you're going to London?'

Ruby looks stunned, and Mum is shocked as she never swears. I tell them that he came into the music room after I'd finished with Alphonso and I told him I'd been invited to London, and he said I could stay with him and he would show me around. Ruby paces the room. She is on the verge of speaking three or four times but can't. Mum and I look at each other but dare not interrupt. And then she regains her composure and sits down. 'Sorry, Jess, Sonny … I shouldn't have cursed like that. I'm so sorry. It's just that with Freddie's funeral being yesterday, I'm still on edge. Look … Jimmy used to take Freddie away from me all the time, and they used to fight each other and drink and get into trouble. Freddie would say it's the scene. That's no excuse. I wouldn't want you to suffer the way I suffered, Sonny. I shouldn't have even invited him here but Freddie said I had to … I'm sorry.'

Mum smooths things over, Ruby calms down and we prepare to leave. We had come to help tidy up the house and had done nothing. Mum says she'll pop over tomorrow when all the visitors have gone, and Ruby says she'll call Mum to arrange a time for my first lesson.

We say goodbye and walk arm in arm down the drive. Mum speaks out the side of her mouth. 'What was all that about?'

'I don't know. Very weird. How did Freddie invite Jimmy to his own funeral?'

'I'm sure Ruby just got confused.'

I can feel Mum clinging on. She's desperate to talk. As soon as we are out of sight, she says she's got something to tell me, and Dad's not going to believe it. I'm worried. I think the German question is the bone of contention, but she's forgotten about that already.

Mum is excitable and says Ruby has filled her in on the blanks from last night. Not only was I playing music with Charlie Watts from the Rolling Stones but 'That was Syd Lawrence on trumpet, he's from the Northern Dance Orchestra, and Eric Haydock was on bass, he's from the Hollies.' She skips along. We pass the florist, Mum waves to June. 'Ruby loved the flowers, thank you. And by the way, did I tell you? My son is going to London to study music.'

June gives me a double thumbs-up. 'Don't forget where you came from.' We pick up our pace, Mum's almost running.

'Wait till I tell your dad.'

S FOR SONNY

We giggle as we slow down and get closer to home, me carrying Freddie's albums and Mum invading my dreams by saying she's coming to London too. She says she'd fit very well into London life, afternoon teas and walks along the Thames. All I can think about is how I'm going to tell Jack there may be a Plan B, when for the last few years there has only been Plan A, Germany. Mum says not to worry about that for now, just enjoy the rest of the weekend, listen to my new music and let's tell Dad about my life-changing performance. Mum says, 'We'll tell him at tea time, let him settle first and I'll cook his favourite meal, or we can get fish and chips as we're celebrating.' Talking about food makes me realise how hungry I am, and as soon as we are through the front door, I put the kettle on and make a ham sandwich for us both. Mum takes a tea upstairs to see if Dad's recovered from last night, she's soon back. 'He's not there, he must have gone out.' I wondered why the kettle was still warm. He must have had a brew before he left. She says, 'I'll kill him if he's gone to the pub.'

We walk into the front room, and I use Dad's new turntable. I put on *Dial "S" for Sonny*, and we sit down. It is strange being told you're named after someone. Dad says he used to love music and wanted me to have an American name. Anyway, my love of jazz starts right now, the piano kicks in and transports me to another world. The cover is signed 'To Freddie, from one trumpeter to another, Art', and I begin to learn all about the players who visit these shores. This signature is Art Farmer and the drummer that Charlie mentioned, Louis Hayes, is featured too. Mum looks over. 'You look just like your dad poring over that album, he used to do the same thing.' She looks happy this afternoon, and we finish our late lunch in silence. Mum puts a cushion behind her head and nods off, I cover her up with her throw, and sit back and listen. Every instrument is talking to me. It's as if I have a different pair of ears. I close my eyes and I'm playing along just as I was last night, listening, playing, listening, responding, listening, improvising. I can hear the notes, the tempo changes. The love between the players. I'm smiling, and my fingers are whizzing up and down the keys, I can smell the jazz club and the customers within touching distance, I can see through the smoky basement to the bar where the bartender mixes my drink, and I hear the applause as we reach our magnificent conclusion. Oh, jazz piano, you have got me. You have infiltrated me, and I know there is no going back.

'Someone's happy.' Yes, I am. Yes, sir. Yes I am.

'Someone's happy,' comes through a little louder. Thank you, thank you. You're very welcome.

'Oi, Walter bloody Mitty.' What?

Dad's shouting, 'I said, someone's happy,' and it brings me back to Manchester from my New York basement gig in my head.

I'm embarrassed as I straighten up and 'Loved Walked In' begins on the record player. Dad turns it down. Mum coughs and opens her eyes. 'Oh hello, love, where have you been?'

Dad mumbles, 'It's Saturday. I put a few bets on. I've got myself a little accumulator on the ITV Seven.'

He turns the record off and switches on the television. I get the vinyl from the turntable and put it into the sleeve and gather the rest of them ready to go to the back room. Mum gets up, and I can smell the tension, she hates him changing channels and ruling the roost. As he sits down looking at his form guide in the Mirror, she switches off the racing. He jerks his head up, his eyes swivelling and his face contorted, snarling on the bit, waiting for starters orders. And she's off. Mum approaches the first hurdle, the bit between her teeth. 'Pete, do you know which album Sonny was listening to when you came in?' He looks shocked at the question, opens his arms wide and shakes his head. 'Show him, Sonny,' Mum spurs me on, and we approach the second hurdle in unison. I show Dad the top album cover, and he's defeated before we've even reached the third. I don't often see Dad back down, but he looks at Mum and then at me.

He's crestfallen. 'Oh God. I'm so sorry, Sonny, I didn't realise. I'm just not thinking today. Sonny Clark, bloody hell, I wasn't concentrating. I saw Art Farmer the trumpeter in '68 at Club 43 in Manchester, so many memories.'

After this morning's emotional chat with Mum, I now have Dad looking on the verge of tears. He says sorry over and over again. I am just a bystander as Mum lets him know about how he's changed, how he doesn't listen to his family anymore, how he's forgotten to talk to me about what I want. She sends me off to make another pot of tea for all of us, and I can see Mum gaining strength for the home straight. I leave them alone for five minutes and take my time brewing up. I load up the Coca-Cola tea tray, pile on some rich tea biscuits and saunter down the hall. Dad looks sheepish, Mum smiles at me and nods, all is going to be ok for now.

'Right son, your mum says that you've got some news for me.' I look at Mum. I need a clue. Is this the news news? The German news, the London news or the playing the piano news?

'Start with the music at Ruby's,' says Mum. 'Everything else can follow.'

I begin by saying that I met Ruby in the hall that she took me to the music room and left me there. 'This guy called Charlie came in, told me he loved jazz and asked if I was a pianist. When I said "Yes" he fetched his mate called Syd, the one who played the trumpet in the church, and we had a quick practise, and that was that. Later on, everybody went to the music room and played some jazz, and they finished with the same tune Syd had played with the strings, except this time it was with drums, bass and piano. And I was the piano.' I see Mum itching to get to the punchline, but I have one last surprise. I leg it up to my bedroom and return with the sheet music for 'Time After Time', with all the chord markings on. How could I forget? Syd had got the boys to sign it, and I hadn't even read it. I hand it to Dad.

It reads 'To Sonny, congratulations on your first gig. Well played and all the very best from Syd Lawrence, Charlie Watts and Eric Haydock', and there are their autographs. Dad reads it again, looks at Mum, then me and then says, 'No bloody way, you're joking. I never saw these guys.' Well, he'd certainly seen Syd, he was in the church. Mum swears to him it's true, and he makes me tell him the story again. I think he's checking me out to see if I can remember the details. I repeat it in full. 'Charlie bloody Watts, Eric bloody Haydock.'

Mum nudges me and says, 'Tell him about London.' Dad is shocked as I go through today's activity, how there was a guy at Ruby's from London Jazz College who saw me play last night and has invited me to audition in December. I tell him about working for Ruby in exchange for piano lessons so I can get up to speed and that I may fancy doing a music degree next September. I don't mention Germany, and as I think about it, Plan A seems a million miles away. Dad looks at me, still shaking his head. All this happened whilst he was asleep.

He asks me how I even know the tune. And I tell him that I didn't, but Syd played it, and I just played the chords to start with. He looks dumbfounded. I am not quite sure if he doesn't understand or thinks I'm not capable, so we run through to the back room. I put the music on the piano and tell Dad to hum the tune. He does better than that, he follows the words, and as I hit the chords, he sings out loud. Mum joins in, and we are all laughing together belting out 'Time After Time', we finish with 'You'll hear me say, that I'm so lucky to be loving you'. I try a very fancy ending and almost get away with it. As I turn around, Mum and Dad are kissing, both looking tearful and Mum is holding a photo of Maisie. In the end, I think Dad believes that I can play the piano.

Mum blows her nose. Dad wipes his eyes and shakes his head. 'Charlie bloody Watts.'

Mum is laughing and crying, 'Fish and chips tonight, boys?'

'Yessssss.'

Satisfaction

Saturday 1 November 1975

Over the next few weeks, Mum and I visit Ruby several times, and I get to know the music room well. They leave me to it and have a coffee and catch up and I play the piano, listen to Freddie's albums and immerse myself in jazz. I still haven't had 'the chat' with Jack yet about Plan B, but I'm meeting him and Karen tonight for our first practice in ages. This music catches me right in the heart. I feel it talking to me. I can listen and play for hours. It is so hard to explain to anyone. It takes over my thoughts, and I have dropped everything else, going out with mates, talking poetry with Debs and reading. It has improved my relationship with Dad too. He's gone back to his old albums, and sometimes we listen together, and he fills me in about the scene in Manchester in his teenage years when the jazz clubs were the place to get into. Some of the people we listen to now were often in town. He saw Stan Kenton, Dave Brubeck a month before I was born and Oscar Peterson at Belle Vue in Feb '55. Even when I was a toddler, he said he nipped out to a few gigs such as Count Basie in 1960. He comes alive when he remembers these gigs, and I guess I have been listening to this music all through my childhood without noticing it. Some of these musicians are now my idols. I asked Dad why he stopped going to gigs, and he said they made him melancholic and that he prefers to listen to his LPs at home. I think he meant they made him think about Maisie, but I wasn't sure and didn't ask.

Ruby and Mum come into the room. I carry on playing Waltz for Debby for a few minutes, I have fallen in love with Bill Evans as a composer. They clap as I finish the tune. I wouldn't have played in front of anyone a few weeks ago, I'd have shut myself away. I ask Mum if I can have our piano tuned at home as it is so bad and this one feels so good. Ruby jumps in. 'Sonny, your mum and I have just been chatting, I'm happy for you to come and visit anytime and play here. You're eighteen soon, you already walk Ringo for me, so I'll give you a key. All agreed?'.

Mum looks on and adds, 'And we'll have the piano tuned at home too, but I don't hold out much hope for it.'

I can't believe it. 'Are you sure?'

Ruby says it's fine and that she has arranged for Julia to come and meet me tomorrow if I'm free about midday. It's going to be so much better practising here, peace and quiet.

'One more thing,' says Mum. 'You must keep up with your schoolwork, no slacking.' I agree. I know my exams are just around the corner. 'Me and Ruby will be keeping a close eye on you. Music and studying; both are important.' Mum always says education is crucial. It was drilled into her by Granddad. He used to call me his little book worm, and he would read to me whenever he stayed. Ruby says she is speaking with Alphonso tonight and will get a date for me in December in London. Mum is beaming at me. It seems like their plans are coming together.

We leave Ruby alone, and I promise to return tomorrow for a chat with Julia and to sort out the key. It's November, and it's cold, Mum takes my arm, and we head home. She whistles a tune, which is her way of telling me she's got something to say. 'Sonny, can I tell you a secret?' This is a first, and she confides in me that she is thinking of going to college. She says she's been inspired by me having a plan. She's thinking of doing a social work degree so she can help young mothers. She says she's always hated the factory, even though it's now only three days per week, and it's about time she thought of her future. 'I'm only thirty-seven for God's sake.' She has an interview on Monday evening, and she asks me to cover for her as she's not telling Dad until she's sure. We can tell him we're going to Ruby's on Monday evening and she can get to the college from there. Mum says she still has doubts, but she's going to try, as she wants to be erudite like me.

I keep a straight face and ask her, 'What does erudite mean?' She's about to answer when my smile gives it away, and she clips me around the ear. But I do know exactly how she feels, and I tell her that deep down I have doubts too and I'm not sure I'm good enough to pass the audition in December. She refuses to let me believe it. 'Sonny, just think back to a few weeks ago when you played with those guys, you were amazing. Hang on to that.' And I do, I keep dreaming about that night over and over again. I just need to keep practising and perform more. I'll see what Julia has to say tomorrow.

I head to Jack's, knowing that I have to tell him about the German problem. It's our first session for weeks as Jack's dad has been in hospital, and they've been visiting every night. I knock on, and Mrs Hammond comes to the door. She whispers, 'Come in, Sonny. They're in the front room. Jack's dad is upstairs so we're keeping quiet.' Jack and Karen are on the sofa looking glum, and this is not our usual practice room.

'Change of plan,' says Jack. His dad only got out yesterday so we can't rehearse anymore. 'Sonny ... I'm thinking of leaving college.' Jack's mum comes in with ginger beer and biscuits and tells Jack not to make up his mind too soon. She explains to me that Mr Hammond had an accident at work and he won't be earning for a long time, so it's going to be hard to keep up with the rent. Jack looks devastated and says he might have to get a job to help out. He's speaking to the college before he makes his mind up, but he's going to have a word with his dad's company too in case they can let him work on the building sites. 'Or maybe the factory.'

Mrs Hammond snorts. 'It hasn't come to that yet, Jack, we'll get through it. I don't want you in the factory at your age.' Karen holds hands with Jack, and she's teary too.

Jack looks at me. 'I'm so sorry, mate. After all these years I don't think Germany's going to happen.' I almost let out a little cheer, but manage to stifle my relief at not having to be the one to raise doubts.

'Ah, don't worry, mate, the most important thing is your dad.'

Mrs Hammond looks at us all. 'You three and your German dreams that you never told us about, you daft bunch.' And with that, she sends us out saying enjoy your youth, and you don't want to be stuck inside on a Saturday night. I give Mrs Hammond a big hug. She has always been the best at helping us out. The friendliest, coolest parent.

I know I should say something and turn as we are leaving. 'I hope Jack's dad improves soon.'

'He'll be fine, let me worry about that.' She wipes away a tear. 'Off you go, Sonny.'

We head to the local park even though it's freezing. 'One more thing,' says Jack, and he raises his hand, and Karen is still holding it. They are both smiling like mad. 'We're going out.' My life is changing before me: first of all playing with Charlie Watts, then the offer of piano lessons and an audition in London and now my best mates have hooked up. We all scream with delight and have an awkward cuddle. I am so happy for them. Karen says she's going to be there for Jack whatever happens. I always knew they suited each other, but it's difficult when you have been friends for so long.

I give Karen a quick look, grab her hand and whisper, 'Good luck, you know I mean it.'

She squeezes me back. 'I know you do, Sonny. Thank you.' We did kiss once when we were about fifteen, and we spoke for weeks about if we should we go out formally but she is a friend more than a girlfriend.

Jack shouts, 'Leave my girl alone,' and we burst out laughing and they hold hands and kiss. I look at the darkest of skies as we stroll along, these two chirping away in front of me. I decide not to say anything tonight, as it will just ruin their moment. We pass the chippy. The music is blaring out. Jack turns to me and sings along, 'I Can't Get No Satisfaction', and Karen joins in. I catch up and I wedge myself in between them. Jack says, 'Remember when we used to play that song together. We loved the Stones, didn't we?'

Karen puts her arm around me. 'Sorry about Germany, Sonny.'

'Don't worry,' I say. 'You can't always get what you want.'

I will tell them about my audition soon, very soon. I promise.

Under Milk Wood

Sunday 2 November 1975

It's Sunday morning, and I'm not wearing my favourite pants, but I don't think it's a problem. I got soaked last night on the way home from the park, and I put all my clothes on the washing pile. I'm up and showered ready for my big day. Dad's in the kitchen doing a fry up, and I am starving. I tell them about Jack's dad coming home after his accident and that he can't work for ages so Jack thinks he's going to have to quit college to help pay the rent. Dad pontificates about home ownership, as usual, saying it offers more protection, but Mum says not everyone is as lucky as us. Mum adds, 'It's so important to get an education,' and winks at me. 'I hope Jack doesn't have to leave before his exams. You are both so close now.'

'And one more thing,' I say. 'Jack and Karen are going out together, who'd have believed that?' Mum cheers.

'Missed the boat there, Sonny.' Dad smirks as he starts piling bacon on the plates. I'm not getting drawn in today.

'Not my ship to sail, Dad. I'm happy for them both.' Mum is too. She likes Jack. I tell them that practices are off for now, so I am concentrating on piano only. Dad's fry up is just what

I need, and he asks me if I fancy Club 43 this weekend. Stan Tracey is in town. Dad fetches an album for me called *Jazz Suite*, inspired by Dylan Thomas's *Under Milk Wood*. I can't believe it. 'I'm studying this book at college at the moment.' We agree on Friday night, and I rush off to play the album, I haven't got long.

I'm lost in the music when Mum interrupts me. 'It's half eleven, Sonny, better get a move on.' I jump up, needle off, coat on. 'Good luck,' is ringing in my ears from Mum as I leave the house. I half run as I'm excited to get going.

I scoot up Ruby's drive and ring the bell and Ringo barks to welcome me. Ruby lets me in, we go to the kitchen and she puts the kettle on. Ruby looks like pop star Lynsey de Paul with her long blonde hair, tight jumper and jeans with bell bottoms. We could be on the TV together, and I'm daydreaming again about being in London, 'Sonny, Sonny!' Ruby invades my dream. 'Here are your keys. I'll show you around.' Ringo stalks me as we visit every room. When Ruby's not in I am to check on Ringo straight away, let him out into the back garden or take him for a walk. I have to do that before I play the piano and he's allowed to sit and listen if he wants to. 'Leave the hall light on if you are practising, so I know you're here.' She trusts me already. 'I'm going away for a few days soon so you'll be responsible for Ringo, and you can practise as much as you like, but not too late please.'

'Are you sure?'

'You'll be fine, honestly. I know it's early days,' says Ruby, 'but I think we are going to get along.' We head back to the kitchen for our tea, Ringo jumps into his huge bed, right up against a door. Ruby looks at Ringo and then at me, and says, 'And please, never go into the garage behind Ringo's bed, that is off-limits.

House rules.' The doorbell rings as I am about to ask why not and Ringo charges off, followed by Ruby.

I hear her chatting on the doorstep, and Ruby looks worried when she returns. She hands me some books and a file of handwritten music. 'Julia has sent these for you to work through for your audition.' Ruby begins to cry. 'Lessons are off for now. I knew Julia had been ill, but I thought she was better. I am so sorry, Sonny, I thought I had this all arranged.' I tell her not to worry and that I will still put the work in. We walk through to the music room, and I set out the music on the piano and read it through. It's so different to the classical pieces I play every week. Julia's handwritten notes give me an idea of where to start and a rough six-week plan up to the audition. An envelope slips out with Ruby's name on the front, and I pass it over. Ruby cries again and rushes out of the room. I sit for a while not knowing what to do. Should I carry on and play? Or just let myself out and not mention it? I'm sure Mum would know what to do and say, she always does, but I'm lost. After a few minutes I decide to play the piano. I was meant to be having a lesson, so I just carry on. Over the next hour, I work through a couple of tunes and some scales and exercises that Julia has left me. I can feel the improvement from a few weeks ago but daren't tell anyone as they wouldn't understand. I'm in my own little bubble. If I tried to explain, my mates would think I was a smart arse. Anyway, I'm hoping there will be some people in London who will understand me.

I finish my practice and decide today is the day I'll tell Jack about London. I search for Ruby to say goodbye, but she's not in the kitchen or the lounge. I open the doors into the garden thinking she'll be letting the dog out but no sign of her there.

Ringo's basket has moved from the garage door, and I creep towards it. 'Hello.' I listen at the door and can hear Ruby murmuring.

'Hello?'

The door bursts open, I scream, and Ringo charges through and knocks me over. Ruby follows, still in tears and clutching the envelope. She tries to pick me up, which is impossible, and we end up laughing together for ages as Ringo licks me whilst I am on the floor, and I have to roll onto all fours to clamber up.

Ruby laughs and asks, 'Why did you scream?'

'Because I was scared,' which seems stupid as I am the biggest person in the house. 'Who were you talking to?' I regret it as she sobs again and waves the letter around.

'This, this set me off. Julia was telling me all about Freddie and his lessons and how she loved teaching him and about a special song he was learning for me. I just wanted to say a few words to him.' She looks at me but doesn't explain. She recovers. 'Anyway, I'll see you tomorrow. I hear we are covering for your mum's interview.' She shows me out. 'Pop round anytime to practice and don't worry about London.' I wish I had her confidence.

I take a detour on the way home and call in on Jack. I tap the door, in case his dad's asleep, and Mrs Hammond opens up. 'How's Mr Hammond?'

'He's looking good today, but you always sleep much better in your own bed, don't you?' Since I always sleep in my own bed, I'm not too sure what she means. She shouts 'Jack' and says she's surprised I am here as we were all up so late last night. Jack's behind her, finger on lips telling me not to let on. He gets his stuff, and we mooch over to the precinct.

I ask him why he was out so late, and he laughs.

'Wouldn't you like to know?' He finally ends up telling me of course, we've had this pact about telling each other the truth about girls since high school, and it remains unbroken. He went out with Karen and managed to get into a pub, even though they are seventeen. He said it wasn't that good, but at least they had each other to chat to, and he thinks he's in love. He's meeting her later tonight.

I explain where I have been today and that I was so nervous I couldn't tell anyone about my last three weeks, including playing with you know who. He doesn't believe me at first, and he says he's going to check with my mum. 'Look at this.' I get the key out of my pocket. 'You'll have to come over one night when Ruby's away.'

I tell Jack that I am going to audition for a jazz music degree in December in London. 'Jazz, why the hell would you want to study jazz?' he asks, and I find myself repeating Freddie's mantra. 'If you can play jazz, you can play anything.' If I get selected, I'll be off next year. Of all my mates at school, Jack knows me best.

'You'll walk it, mate. If anybody deserves it, you do.'

Love Me Do

Sometimes Ruby just sits on the sofa listening to me practising. I've got used to it. At first, it was strange having someone hear my mistakes over and over again, but Ruby said, 'Just concentrate, you've got to get used to people being around.' I work so hard. Playing music is exhilarating. All I do is listen to music, play music, walk Ringo and sleep. I am intoxicated by the music. Julia's exercises are exhaustive.

Ruby insists I invite my friends over and they can't believe the music room, Jack repeats 'Wow' about two hundred times, and I play a few tunes for them. They sit and listen as I concentrate. It feels good to show off a little, I've progressed so much since we stopped band practice. Afterwards, we sit in the kitchen having a few snacks and Ruby quizzes us all about college, music, friends and families. The telephone rings and Ruby rushes off to take it in the lounge.

'Bloody hell, mate, you have fallen on your feet,' says Jack.

'It's amazing isn't it? Can't believe I get to play here whenever I want to.'

Karen says, 'Ruby seems a lovely lady, Sonny, I hope you appreciate her.'

'Of course I do,' I think about it. 'I'm sure I do.'

'Well make sure she knows. This set up is wonderful.'

Ruby rushes back into the room. 'Right folks. We have a plan.'

She asks us about next Friday, checks if we are free and tells us we are all going out to a little club she knows where some of her old friends are playing. 'That was Syd on the phone, he'll be there, and he asked me if Sonny was coming.' Jack and Karen are excited. They hold hands all the time and can't stop looking at each other.

Karen asks if she's allowed in. 'I'm only seventeen.' But Ruby says she knows the club manager, so it's not a problem. 'Next question,' says Karen, looking worried, 'what do I wear?' Ruby laughs and drags her off of Jack, and we can hear the giggling as they go upstairs.

Jack looks at me. He is wide-eyed, with a broad grin spread across his face. 'Sonny. Sonny, have you got something to tell me?' I turn away and take the dishes to the sink. 'Sonny, remember our pact.' I turn around, blushing, and he's on me. 'Sonny, you little devil.' I deny everything, but he doesn't believe me, and he's strumming his imaginary guitar and singing 'Love Me Do' way too loudly. He grabs my shoulders, holds me so tight I can't escape and gives me his serious face.

'Jack, I swear nothing has happened. Right. Nothing. It's not like that. She's my mum's best friend.' He lets me go. He knows the pact is still in place. 'And how about you?'

He gives me that look again and smiles. 'Second base, ok. And don't tell Karen I told you.' We have half an hour chatting about the old times, the footy, the junior school, about kiss chase in the playground. And about the time Jack had a massive boil on his arse. He had a doctor's appointment on the Monday but he burst it when he crashed his bike in the park on Saturday. He was screaming so much we all thought he'd broken his leg, so smelly Kelly rushed off to get his mum. She came back and pulled his shorts down in front of all of us, and we saw the remnants of the boil splattered and oozing on his arse cheeks. He had to walk to the chemist straight away for some iodine, and his mum gave me the job of taking his bike home. 'Good times, eh?' says Jack. 'I've still got the scar, and that was nearly ten years ago.'

We are still laughing when the girls come in. Karen is drowning under a pile of clothes and Ruby says, 'What are you boys laughing about?'

I ask Karen, 'Have you seen Jack's scar?'

Far too quickly she says, 'You mean the one on his bum?' Poor girl, it is her turn to blush. We have to retell the story for Ruby's sake. Karen and Jack are still holding hands, and they walk off with the clothes piled into bags.

We wave them off at the front door. 'Thanks, Ruby, thanks for letting my friends come round.'

Ruby gives me an enormous hug, and I hear her trying to stifle tears and be strong. She lets me go and looks at me. 'I need to thank you, Sonny. Thank you so much.' She leans in and kisses me on one cheek and then the other. 'Continental.'

She steps back and fixes her eyes on mine. 'Now, Monday night, I'll introduce you to Johnny at "Kendals." Freddie went there all the time. We'll get you a lovely suit for Friday night, and for your audition in two weeks.'

'Ruby, that's really … You can't …'

'Me and Karen are going to look a million dollars, so you

and Jack better shape up too.' She takes my arm and leads me down the hall. 'In fact, tell Jack to come on Monday at four pm as well. Freddie left some money on account. We can stretch to two suits, I'm sure.'

I was about to protest when she places a finger on my lips.

'Shush. This is how it's going to be.'

Love for Sale

Jack and I rush into town after college and we stand out like sore thumbs as we sit on a sofa in menswear. I spy one of the staff looking us up and down. 'Jack, to your left.'

'What?'

'He thinks we're taking the mick.'

'Well, it's not every day two schoolboys come to "Kendals."'

'That's true, my last jacket was from "Stolen from Ivor".'

'Have you ever bought a suit, Sonny?'

'No. First time.'

'Mum said it's a huge thing. Apparently, Dad got his first suit for the wedding.'

I couldn't believe Jack had told his mum what we were doing. I'm keeping everything under wraps.

We hear a commotion, and Ruby emerges from all the chaos, so many staff and Johnny treating her like a princess. There are mumbled words about the funeral and then Johnny descends on us. Nobody asks us what we want, we are told. Jack ends up with a plaid two-piece, and I get a three-piece in black with straighter legs, not flares.

Ruby smooths down the lapels, then whispers in my ear, 'It always looks good when the pianist takes his jacket off after a few songs, as though you are relaxing into the groove.' She runs her hand down the back of the jacket. 'It makes the audience feel good too. You'll learn.'

Johnny holds up two white shirts. 'Classic look, boys. Now take a stroll up and down the aisle, let's see how they hang.'

We start to giggle and take a few paces up and down the aisle.

'Perfect,' says Ruby, then grabs Johnny's arm to lead him away to another part of the store.

Jack elbows me. 'Did you see the price tag?'

'No, I was busy adjusting my crotch, it was so uncomfortable.'

He winks. 'I think Ruby was after a tight fit.'

'Well don't tell your mum any of this, especially the price.'

'She did say …' Jack stops as an assistant passes by.

'What?'

'She said she thought she'd be the person buying me my first suit.'

'Oh shit, I never thought of it like that. Sorry.'

'Don't worry, she'll get over it.'

Ruby and Johnny flounce over, staff in their wake. He hands Jack a huge bag.

Johnny looks at me. I swear I can see a tear in his eye. He hands me my suit. 'This is a big thing, a man's first suit. Enjoy.' He pulls me in for a hug and whispers through his tears, 'Freddie would be so pleased.'

We are escorted to the stairs and all the staff wave us off, and as we make our way to the front doors, Ruby sprays us with aftershave from the counter. Jacks starts coughing.

Ruby laughs and slides her arm through mine. I feel and smell like a million dollars.

Night and Day

Jack and Karen arrive at Ruby's house to get ready. Ruby appears
with a bright orange soda siphon. 'This calls for an aperitif.' She
squirts it on top of Campari, and we toast each other. She leads
us upstairs to get changed. Ruby and Karen disappear to her
dressing room, and Jack and I go into a spare room. Our suits
are hanging in a wardrobe, and we pull them on. I've never worn
a suit, and it feels great. Jack looks fantastic, and we do funny
walks, making sure we have enough room to move. All is good,
and we make ourselves another drink downstairs and wait for
the girls. Karen saunters in, and Jack's eyes pop out of his head.
She has this fantastic pink jumpsuit on with high boots, and
looks stunning with full makeup. She loves Jack in his natty suit
and they do a twirl for each other and end up snogging. Karen
says, 'Mind my lipstick,' and Jack wipes it off.

Ruby looks at me. 'Well hello, Sonny. You are starting to
look like a musician.' She makes me give her a twirl too, and she
surprises me by taking my hand. We're almost at eye level with
her heels on, and she tells me to have a quick warm-up on the
piano as Syd is bound to ask me to sit in. I'd forgotten I'd told Syd

that one day I would join him. A shiver runs through my body. She senses my worry and leads me through to the music room, still holding my hand. She sits me down and hands me a gift box. 'This is a good luck charm for your first gig.' I open it, and inside there is a gemstone. 'It's a real ruby. Freddie gave it me for my first gig, it's there to remind you …' She can't finish her sentence but places it in a cloth bag and hands it back to me. 'Keep it in your pocket. Rubies are the stones of love, passion and motivation.' She leaves the room wiping her eyes and then calls back, 'And Sonny, don't worry, just be yourself. That's all you need to do. Taxi is in thirty minutes. I'll leave you alone now.' I rub the stone and wish I'd told her how gorgeous she looks.

We arrive at the George, down the stairs into the basement. The greeter makes an enormous fuss of Ruby and shows us to a table in the middle of the room. A bottle of Champagne arrives with four glasses, and Jack and Karen get the giggles as they take their first sip. Jack leans in. 'Have you ever had real Champagne before?'

'Of course,' I say, and then remember where I had my first and only glass. 'Just the once.' It feels wrong, I rub the ruby in my pocket and think of the funeral. The club fills up as a pianist runs through tune after tune, with polite clapping between songs. As we are finishing our glasses, Syd comes over and says hello. The ladies get kisses, and Jack gets a handshake.

Syd greets me like a long lost friend, and says, 'Green room, let's go.' I follow him to the front of the stage, and we dive left through a fire door. It's not actually a room, just a corridor with chairs. Syd introduces me to everyone as a local pianist on his way to London.

'Nice whistle,' says the bass player.

'Eh?'

'The suit. Whistle and flute, suit. You'll have to get used to that in the big smoke.' They all laugh, although I'm not in on the joke. Syd gives me some music sheets. 'Three songs, Sonny, okay? End of the first set. We'll start with "Time After Time", which you know, then "Lester Left Town" and finish with a Bill Evans arrangement of "Night and Day". Just follow the chords, play your way in, keep listening and look at me. You ok?'

I feel out of my depth, but I know I have to get through this. 'That's cool, Syd, thanks for letting me in.'

He looks at me for a moment. 'Ruby says you are doing just fine, that's good enough for me. When are you going to London?'

'Two weeks.'

'Just enjoy tonight, very soon you'll be in clubs like this every night of the week.'

Back at the table, the second bottle of bubbles has arrived, and Jack and Karen are holding hands and smiling.

Ruby nudges me. 'Sonny, you okay?'

'Not really.'

She laughs and places her hand on my arm. 'You'll be fine. You've nailed it in practice, and the band will look after you. When Freddie used to get nervous or lost, he used to stop playing and just listen, and he'd always find his way back.'

I take the music out of my jacket and flick through. It's clearly written with the chords stated everywhere above the piano parts. I put them back in my pocket and take a sip, then have another read through. Ruby's hand moves to my thigh, and she gives me a little squeeze.

'All will be fine, don't worry.'

'But what if it's not?' I blurt out, and my heart races.

'Breathe, Sonny, breathe. Here comes the band now.'

I swear the first set passes in a blur, and the music goes in and out of my pocket a hundred times. Syd begins talking about me, and my breathing slows down. Maybe it's because I know there is no escape now, I have to play. The room goes deathly quiet, and I hear Syd announcing me on, welcoming a home-grown talent to the stage. Ruby presses her lips to my ear. 'Sonny, just listen. Listen. You'll always find your way back.' I get to my feet, hand in pocket caressing the ruby, and walk to the stage dodging the legs and the bags. In slow motion, I see everyone turning towards me. I'm nearly there, and the smoke is in my eyes and as I start to climb on stage the band count in and they're away. It takes the pressure off me, and I sit on the piano stool and tune in for the first time tonight. All eyes are on Syd and he sounds magnificent. I remember the music, put it on the piano and pick up the beat in my head and then in my feet, I can remember how this felt just a couple of months ago, and yet it seems a million miles away. I have played more piano and listened to more albums than ever before.

The verse finishes, Syd eyeballs me, removes his trumpet and mouths, 'To the top, Sonny.'

I hit my first chord hard, the room explodes in a crescendo of noise, whooping and hollering and I am home. This is my home. I lap it up, every single note. As we finish the first tune, I stand up for a bow, directed by Syd, and remember to take off my jacket. Even this gets applause. Ruby was right of course.

I am relaxing, and so is the audience. I play less on the next song but listen more. Syd carries the whole tune, and I just add little flicks and stabs here and there. I turn the page to 'Night and Day', and I look at the music and it's all a blur, just a maze of hieroglyphics. I don't know what I'm looking at.

I am failing, failing in front of an audience, falling into a pit of despair of my own making. I don't hear anything and can't see anything. An arm brushes my shoulder and breaks the spell, and Syd whispers, 'Bass solo, you've got sixty seconds to breathe.' I look up, startled. Where am I? Who was I kidding? I feel lonely in a room of a hundred people.

Syd remains next to me. 'Take a deep breath, Sonny. Ok, look at the music, look above the line. Just hit the chords, I'll take the lead.' We're off again, and I do recover, and I manage to listen and even to read the chords. I remember to breathe, just. And I make it, or fake it, to the very end. I sit on my piano stool as we finish the set, and I'm drained. The guys make me stand up for a bow and all the way back to the table hands reach out to pat me and clap me and shake my hand. Flat cap man pulls my sleeve. 'Not bad, Jackson, not bad.' I look down, and it's my music teacher Mr Potter. He says, 'We'll chat Monday, I'm sure.' I can't believe he's here. I'm sure he hates Jack and me, he's always deriding our input.

I fall into Ruby's embrace.

'I am so proud of you, Sonny.' She kisses me on one cheek and then the other. 'Continental.' Then she's off, meeting and greeting old friends who she hasn't seen for ages and I can hear the shouts of 'Congratulations' on discovering a new talent.

Jack gives me the biggest hug he's ever given me. 'Mate, that was awesome. I'm blown away. Can we come again? Jazz is brilliant!'

Karen tries to stand, but needs Jack's help as she's had too much Champagne.

'I think I might be back if Ruby's got anything to do with it.'

Ruby waves at me from the back of the room, she's holding my jacket, which I'd forgotten. I go over to get it, and she introduces me to a few of her jazz buddies. She's showing me off tonight, which feels uncomfortable. She puts an arm around me and whispers, 'Sonny, I've got one last surprise for you. Look who I invited.' She points to the back of the room, and Mum and Dad are sitting there. Mum starts crying as I walk over, Dad puts his thumbs up.

Ruby pushes me in. 'I've been telling your mum all about your hard work, Sonny.'

Mum can't stop crying, 'I'm so proud of you, son.'

Dad's not quite so enthusiastic though he does take credit for introducing me to the music 'from a very young age.' He says, 'You've heard this all your life, it must be in your bones.' He sounds like Alphonso and Mum lets him have this one.

Ruby holds my jacket up for me. 'Set two is about to kick off. Anyone for Champagne?'

Dad raises his beer glass, 'No bloody way,' and Mum shrieks with delight. Ruby goes to get her a glass and Dad leans into us and the mask drops. 'Who the fuck does she think she is? Lady bloody Muck.'

Mum looks daggers at him. 'Pete, for heaven's sake, she's just asking if you would like a drink.'

'Well, look at her … Champagne, in a jazz club. And buying suits for the boys, I mean …' He picks up his beer as Ruby returns. Mum's bubble has surely burst. She looks so sad as Dad stares into his pint.

'All ok?' Ruby asks.

Mum manages 'Cheers' and raises her glass as the band start set two. Ruby takes my hand as we make our way back to Jack and Karen. I turn round, wishing I was brave enough to retaliate.

Dad glares at me, wagging his finger. 'Be careful, Sonny. Just be careful.'

WE'VE ONLY JUST BEGUN

FRIDAY 19 DECEMBER 1975

I'm sitting at the railway station, got a ticket to my destination.
We are bound for London, and my audition is at 3 pm. Ruby
spoke to Alphonso last night. They had a long chat about my
practice regime, my gig in Manchester and the old days. She
didn't mind me listening whilst she was chatting. Ruby says the
audition will be very informal, and Alphonso always has the last
word, so I'm not to worry. I don't think she realises. 'Ruby, the
more you say don't worry, the more I worry.'

'I'm sorry.'

We are on the InterCity leaving Manchester Piccadilly at 11
am. We're an hour early. My brown suitcase is battered from so
many family holidays to North Wales. Ruby has a fancy case with
her initials on it and a matching bag. She says they are Jaeger.
She has persuaded Mum that I can stay overnight in London as
Ella Fitzgerald is playing live at Ronnie Scott's and she wants to
introduce me to some old friends. Dad has been moody since
he was so rude at the George gig. Every development seems to
be upsetting him lately, my music certainly, Ruby's interference
as he sees it and doesn't stop mentioning it, and now Mum has

announced she's doing a degree from January. I need this break from all the tension.

'What are you thinking about?' asks Ruby.

'Families. Parents spend all their time wanting kids, then all their time shouting at them.'

'It's tough, isn't it? Growing up is hard work, looking at the disappointment in your father's eyes every time you leave the house. I remember that, I was fifteen when me and my mate Trish started going out regularly and he couldn't handle it, just a look of disdain as we left our boring houses to find fun. Then he died, no warning signs, and I was on my own, and he never saw me grow up or get married. All I remember is that look.'

'Do you miss him?'

'Some days I do. Some days I'd love to have tea with him and tell him I'm ok.'

'Where was your mum?'

'She passed away when I was ten, and it was just Dad and me from then on.'

'I'm sorry, I didn't mean to …'

'Don't worry,' says Ruby, 'it was a long time ago. Mum was …' and she drifts off in thought.

'Well, you haven't got a boring house now, have you?'

Ruby glares at me. 'You're right, I haven't. But I haven't got the man who paid for it either.'

I had forgotten. I guess I've only ever known the house with just Ruby in it, I never see Freddie walking around the rooms I have come to know so well.

'I'm so sorry, Ruby, I never meant to …'

'Don't worry, just think of your parents, about what they

have gone through. You men are funny creatures, keeping it all bottled up and not letting us girls in. I'm sure your dad's finding it difficult to see you becoming a man and I know he's not best pleased with your mum getting an education.' She assures me it will all end up just fine. 'It just takes time.'

I tell her about my fears for today, 'I'm not sure I'll pass the audition. I don't think I'm ready.'

The announcement comes over the Tannoy, and we rush to the front of the train. Ruby says we are in first class so I can relax on my big day. We put our cases in the racks and get to our seats. I am so excited as we pull away, heading to a very different world. Ruby sits back to relax, and I get my music out of my satchel to have a read through. I turn to tell her about my first piece, and tears are cascading down her cheeks. 'Ruby, what's wrong?'

'I was thinking of my first trip on a train with Freddie. I was in love, of course, and excited to be leaving Manchester. That's when my new life began.' She told me so many stories we forgot about my music. Ruby was only seventeen, not yet married, and being taken to London town. Freddie had already written his hit song, and the money was rolling in. He knew all the right people, and she was introduced to them. She learned about couture, she dressed at Biba in Kensington, purchased carpets and furniture at Liberty's, drank Champagne in Mayfair and dined at the Ritz. A uniformed waiter serves us tea and sandwiches, and we carry on talking about her nights out in underground bars, visits to the 100 Club for rock, the Marquee Club for rhythm and blues and jazz and of course the old Ronnie Scott's in Gerrard Street before it moved. The artists she's seen are like a who's who and she knows them all.

'It sounds amazing.'

'It was, I loved it.'

'Why didn't you move to London?'

She thinks for a while. 'We did talk about it, well I did. But Freddie was very forthright, said he needed to keep his two worlds apart.' Ruby rolled her eyes, remembering. 'He always said Manchester was his real world and that London was his fantasy world in which he liked to dip in and out. We were going to start a family, but it all went wrong and ...' The announcement interrupts her flow. We tidy our table, I put my music away and grab our cases. As we get our things together on the platform, Ruby rubs her eyes with a tissue. 'Sonny, that was then, and this is now. Let's enjoy moving forward.' We jump into a black cab and head to our hotel in Mayfair for a quick wash and change. The hotel room is massive, twice as big as my bedroom and it even has a sofa and desk.

We walk around to London Jazz College in Marylebone. I am a bag of nerves. I'm in my suit, hair combed, polished shoes, satchel with music in the right order. Ruby straightens my tie and says not to worry again. She says, 'You are on your own now. Remember Alphonso has picked you, not the other way round.' We walk into reception and Ruby says she is off to see some old friends in the teaching department. She blows some dust off my jacket and kisses me on the cheek. 'Good luck.'

She turns to go, and as I call after her my voice catches and sounds like I am about to cry. She rushes back and grasps my hands. I clear my throat. 'Thanks, Ruby. Thank you for the opportunity today and for believing in me.'

She looks at me, wets her thumb and wipes some lipstick off

my cheek. 'Good luck, Sonny.' She pushes me towards reception.

I check in, and a young lady is called to assist. Donna introduces herself as a year one student who has been studying for three months. 'I'm your buddy.' The college allocate a student who is in the year above to help new students settle in. Donna says when I get in, not if, she will be here to greet me when she is starting year two. She shows me around the college, the common rooms, the practice rooms, each of which has a grand piano, and the performance space. 'We have an hour together so ask any questions, and I'll try to answer them before you have to play your pieces and chat with the faculty.'

It turns out an hour isn't enough. I have never had a friend like Donna, who knows so much about music. She can't believe I met Alphonso at a funeral, and when I tell her who I played with on the night, she is star-struck. I insist it was pure luck, just the right place at the right time and that if you'd told me in advance I would never have joined in. She says the jazz scene is like that. Sometimes you just get a call when someone is ill, and you just drop everything for a gig. Donna is cool. She doesn't look like any of my college mates in Manchester, more like a young mod. This place is ace, we have tea in the common room, and so many people come and say hello, including Frank, who is Donna's buddy.

He's from Newcastle and is in year two. He explains how learning works, says it is not strictly about the lectures, but more up to us to go and find out about the history and the influences. There will be a few formal lectures, some group and big band ensembles, but the onus is the students to practise, form bands, rehearse and perform. 'What grade you up to?' says Frank and when I tell him I am working on six, he says, 'That's fine, I came in on grade five and was just about ok.' Donna tells Frank that Alphonso has already heard me play so I'm on to a winner and then she lets on about Charlie Watts. 'Jesus,' says Frank. 'I'd love to play with that man, he's a hero of mine.'

I joke, 'I'll introduce you,' and his eyes light up as he at looks at me until I break into a smile.

Donna taps her watch. 'Time to go.' We're off for a fifteen-minute practise.

'See you next September,' shouts Frank.

'If I'm lucky enough.'

'You will be,' says Donna. 'Frank's the main man for social gatherings. He's introduced me to everybody around here.'

'Are you two an item?'

'Not yet …'

I sit alone at the piano. I so want to study here. This place is impressive. I'm all over the place, my head is far away, but my fingers understand the exercises well enough. The door opens with a whoosh. 'Sonny Jackson, please follow me.' I stuff the music into my bag and begin the walk to the promised land. I convince myself that my years in the wilderness are over, that I will buckle down, and come out a better man whose hard work will be justly rewarded. I have images of me performing with singers, bands and orchestras. The double-height door swings open and I am in a room with one piano and one chair facing a panel of three.

'Take a seat, please,' says the lady in the middle. The corners of her mouth twitch upwards, an attempted smile designed to put me at ease, but it has the opposite effect. She asks why I am here, which other conservatoires I am talking to, which big bands I practise with, who my teachers are and after I have answered all of the questions, she asks again, 'Why are you here?' I think she wants me to beg to get in.

I look at Alphonso for help, and this time he comes to my rescue and explains that for him, jazz music comes from the heart and the college must understand this. She tuts. He talks about seeing me at a gig in Manchester, he doesn't mention the funeral, and that there were many famous musicians there and that they invited me to sit in and play. Everyone was astounded with my natural ability. He name drops Charlie Watts and Eric Haydock, and the other two seem to relax. And then he adds with a flourish, 'But the most impressed was the trumpeter Syd Lawrence who was in the trio. Just two weeks ago Syd invited Sonny back to perform with him again.' Their faces light up, and I sense if I am good enough for Syd, I am good enough for them. We set off on a musical merry-go-round from Lester Young to Art Farmer, to Bill Evans and Miles Davis. All the album names, all the musicians stick in my head, and I say all the right things. After all this time I am relaxed, talking about jazz in front of other people. And then ... they ask me to play.

I'm not at my best. The exercises are fine and I nail them. I am not so good on the pieces, my chosen pieces, my timing drifts a little, but I get through. All in all, just fifteen minutes action after thirty minutes of talking. Mrs Challinor, the lady in the middle, asks me how I plan to improve in the nine months up until entry.

I am about to answer when Alphonso saves me again, 'Sonny is starting lessons in January with Julia Betteson, who used to be a student here. He is sure to improve under her eye, no?'

Mrs Challinor agrees, and her face softens. 'Ahh Julia, what a talent she was.'

They ask me to wait outside whilst they have a chat. Ruby appears from nowhere. 'Hello and how did it go?' I shrug. She looks through the glass strip in the door. 'Give me five minutes,' she says, and slips into the room. I am on death row. Four people are talking about me, presiding over my fate. I start to sweat and to relive all my mistakes. I have failed, I know I have failed, and Germany is off too. Dad's right, I'll be a good for nothing working in the factory dreaming of what-ifs and maybes. I should have worked harder, been more dedicated. Ruby is in front of me, I stand tall. 'Sonny, we're going. Come on.' Alphonso appears, looking sad.

'Well, what's happening?' I'm sure that comes out louder than I expect it to.

We race out of the building to a waiting taxi with Alphonso waving us off. 'See you later, Ruby. See you later, Sonny.'

Ruby looks at me and smiles. 'There's good news, and there's bad news.'

The Very Thought of You

'Don't worry, don't worry. I said don't worry.' Ruby looks at me, and I swear she is enjoying the moment, she's teasing me. 'I will tell you everything in five minutes in the hotel bar when we are alone. I have a plan.' The taxi pulls up, and I rush into the bar and find the quietest of corners. Ruby speaks to the barman and wanders over, still smiling.

My stomach is doing somersaults, and she's smiling. 'Bloody hell, Ruby, what's the bad news?'

She thinks about how to let me down. I can read her mind. How am I going to tell Jack that I have failed? What about Mum? She was willing me to succeed. And Dad? The purveyor of doom was right about his layabout son. As Ruby opens her mouth to break me in two, the barman arrives with a martini for her and a beer for me. This is agony. He's too bloody happy for my liking, making small talk and asking me how my day has been. Ruby takes a sip. 'Listen, Sonny, you need to understand the politics of the board at the jazz college. They find it very hard to make decisions based on personal recommendations, even from their leading jazz teacher. Especially from their own teacher.' This is going nowhere, and I'm not sure what Ruby is saying.

'Have I got in or not?'

'Well, let's put it like this ...'

Alphonso appears out of nowhere. Ruby stands and the exchanges two kisses, cheek to cheek.

I have to stand. Alphonso grabs both my hands and we exchange two air kisses cheek to cheek. This doesn't happen in Manchester.

The barman arrives, Alphonso lets go of me and orders a large glass of Italian wine. 'Only the best. And some olives. Please.'

I take a seat and drown my sorrows in beer. I am a little lost boy in a strange town, with strange people who blow kisses at each other. Continental. All goes quiet.

Ruby looks at me, 'So, as I was about say ...'

Alphonso interrupts, 'It's just the hoops, only the hoops, Sonny. Don't worry.'

'What he means,' says Ruby, seeing my hopes dashed, 'the answer is yes, you will be studying at London Jazz College next year. But, you just have to jump through a few more hoops to get it confirmed.'

Alphonso stands up as his wine arrives. 'Congratulations Sonny and *salute*.'

We all raise our glasses. '*Salute*'

Even the barman joins in. '*Salute*.'

I look at Ruby. 'So the bad news is?'

Ruby dithers. 'It's just that we have to wait for the final confirmation in March and have another visit to London to play again. They need to see your progression.' She can see my disappointment. 'The good news is Alphonso says you're in and not to worry.'

'No problema, no problema,' he agrees. 'It's not audition, Sonny, just progression.'

Ruby packs me off, orders me to call Mum from my room. She has a few things to discuss with Alphonso before we go out tonight. I slope away and hear, 'Don't worry,' one more time.

I sit on the bed, beer in hand, and think that the one person I'd like to talk to now is Donna. She was so helpful. She'd know all about the politics of the board for sure. I think I'm in, I think I have succeeded today, I just have to jump through a few hoops. I kick off my shoes and lie down. It's been a long day. The phone rings and pierces my dream. I gasp for air, fight to open my eyes. The phone's on the desk, which means I have to get up to answer it. It's Ruby checking on me and reminding me that we are going out tonight. I agree to meet her in one hour. I shower and change, put on my new trousers that Mum bought me and my suit jacket too. I've borrowed an overcoat from Dad as its freezing but it's too small to do up. I splash on some Denim aftershave that I bought. Jack says I'm going all poncey since I started going to gigs, but I like it.

Ruby takes me to a small restaurant in Chinatown, and we sit in a booth.

'I'm sorry about earlier. Alphonso wasn't meant to arrive so early.'

'What did you mean, the politics of the board? That's not fair …'

'Life's not fair, Sonny, but I'm doing my best, alright?'

'Sorry, I'm wound up. I worked so hard for this.'

'Me too.' She explains about the board and how he upsets them with his favourites and that he always has to buck the system. So they are saying yes but making him justify his decision. 'You're caught in the crossfire, that's all.'

'And the good news is …?'

She says sorry over and over again. 'Anyway. You're in. Take it from me, you're in. So tonight we will be celebrating. Now, about a little plan I have. Would you like to move to Waverly after Christmas?' My glass slips though my fingers and crashes into the table.

Ruby grabs the glass. 'Saved you. Again.'

'Waverly? I mean why?'

'Sonny, we have just three months to jump through the hoops.'

I rub my eyes.

'Julia can come round for lessons, Alphonso can visit now and again to help and you can focus on college and piano without the pressure from your dad.' It sounds exciting. She even says that Jack and Karen can visit regularly, and Mum too, of course. Actually, it sounds amazing, I mean, I think I would like to but it's just so weird, thinking of moving out. 'You're nearly eighteen, and your dad had to do national service at your age, so it's not such a big deal.'

She has a point. She sees my shock and says, 'Look, no rush, it's just a thought, but I like having you around the house.' I like it too, but still, it feels like a big step.

The meal is gorgeous, Mum and Dad have never had a Chinese, and so everything is new to me. It's different from anything I have eaten before. The smells, the spices, being able to see into the kitchen and hearing the chefs shouting and joking. Ruby says Manchester has a growing Chinatown and we must go there sometime. I like Ruby. She just says things and you know they will happen, there's no edge, and I feel more grown up in her company. 'You look as though you are starting to relax now after your busy day.'

'I'd just like to have got a definite answer today.'

For the hundredth time Ruby says, 'Don't worry, Alphonso loves me. He won't let me down.' Ruby's on my side, I know that, and she gets my nervousness mixed with my ambition.

Four guys walk in and take another booth and Ruby stares at them. Three black men, one white, suited and booted. Ruby smiles. She realises who they are and whispers to me. 'That's Ella's band. We'll be seeing them play later.' Ella's new album was recorded last year here in London. Freddie has got a copy, and she loves 'The Very Thought of You'. We finish up, we're waiting for Alphonso to meet us here, and then we are walking round to Frith Street. He comes in with the most outrageous suit on and wide-brimmed hat, waves at us from the entrance and orders a whisky on the way to the table. The four guys stand up when they recognise him, and it seems as though everyone knows each other. It's all hugs and kisses and handshakes and pats on the back. Once again, I'm the pianist from Manchester. No questions, just an immediate acceptance that I'm in. Ruby knows them. She's seen them perform many times. She pushes me towards Tommy Flanagan and introduces me. I have the best half-hour talking Coltrane, Giant Steps, and Wes Montgomery's Incredible Jazz Guitar. That intro on 'In Your Own Sweet Way'. Tommy Flanagan played that, and I'm speaking to the man. I pinch myself as he talks me through recording sessions and the characters involved.

When I tell him that I'll see him at the gig, he says, 'I'll make sure we get to hang out later.' Wow, Tommy Flanagan asks me to hang out, I'm in heaven. We head off, Ruby and Alphonso arm in arm along the hallowed streets of Soho. They are playing my tune, and I'm all ears.

The gig is brilliant, and Ruby keeps grabbing my arm and whispering, then Alphonso does the same to her. Tommy knows just how to accompany Ella. That's a trick I need to learn, how to play less and make it sound so much more. I can see his hands, but at times he just kicks back and listens and drops a few notes or a chord in. At half time Ruby is meeting and greeting like royalty again when the band come to the bar for a chat. Tommy recognises me, and we are deep in conversation when Alphonso makes his way across the room with a lady with very long dark hair. I remember her from somewhere. He introduces Eloise to Tommy, and she gushes, says she's loving the gig and could she possibly meet Ella? Tommy says not at half time, maybe later, but he winks at me and says he could introduce her to a fine young pianist. 'Eloise, meet Sonny, a lovely young man from Manchester.' She looks at me with pity. 'We've met already. He auditioned for me today.' It all falls into place. It's Mrs Challinor, the lady in the middle this afternoon. I couldn't place her with her hair down, but I recover quickly, shake her hand and thank her very much for the earlier opportunity. She warms up a little and smiles at me before she leaves. 'Pass on my very best to Julia, you'll be in fine hands.' And she's gone, leaving a whiff of sour perfume hanging in the air.

The second set is sublime. I can see Ruby loves the music, and the atmosphere is electric. We don't get to see the musicians after the gig, but I don't mind, I am on such a high from meeting them earlier. Tommy, Joe Pass and Keter Betts, amazing. And then watching them play, and Ella Fitzgerald singing. There is an atmosphere of reverence when audiences watch these people, even when I go to gigs with Dad and I can't wait to dig out the LP when we get home. The three of us hit a bar and talk late into the night. Alphonso lets me know he is looking forward to having me in his college next year. When Ruby disappears for a minute, he grabs my arm a little too hard. 'She is a lovely, lovely woman. One of the very best.' He lets go. 'You have fallen on your feet, do not waste the opportunity.' He says Ruby has confided in him about her offer for me to move in. 'Take it, young man, it will be like going to college six months early. No problema. You can jump through the hoops easily.' We say goodnight to Alphonso, and we see him into his taxi after many double kisses. Ruby and I walk arm in arm through the cold night back to Marylebone. What a day. What a bloody day.

We wobble through the lobby and up the stairs to the second floor. We reach my room first, and I fumble in my pocket to get my key out. 'Good night, Ruby. Thank you again.' She lets go of my arm, and we head for the final cheek-to-cheek of the night. She looks at me and I am not sure if it is with pity or excitement. I think the drink is playing tricks with me. For a brief moment I think she's going to kiss me and I am excited, but her eyes lose focus and she slurs, 'Sleep on it, Sonny. Three months, no distractions. Good night.'

It is some offer, a chance to escape, a chance to recreate myself and define my future. I don't sleep all night.

CHEEK TO CHEEK

SATURDAY 20 DECEMBER 1975

I drag myself into the bathroom at 9.55 am. Breakfast finishes at 10. The face in the mirror tells a story, at first one of tiredness and exhaustion, but then I break into the broadest possible grin. I don't have the vocabulary to describe how I feel, but I know yesterday was a momentous day. I am so lucky. I've thought about it all night and it's the first big decision in my life, but I feel ready. I am going to move out.

I miss breakfast of course, but I don't care. I don't care at all. I pack my case and I can't stop smiling, I'm going to do it.

The phone rings, it will be Ruby repeating her offer in the cold light of day.

'Hello.' It's reception. 'Good morning, your taxi has been booked for half-past ten and your train leaves at eleven. Thank you.' I'm straight back down to earth. She's changed her mind. She must have changed her mind. Why has she got reception to call?

We meet in the lobby. We don't talk, Ruby looks worse than I feel. As the train pulls out of Euston, Ruby puts on her sunglasses, takes some tablets and says she has a headache. She is asleep within minutes, and I pass the time rehearsing my lines for Mum and Dad later on. I go over and over my life a hundred times, the bickering, the tiny house, the sarcasm and now I have this opportunity before me. Positive people like Donna and Frank and Alphonso want me to succeed. And of course Ruby, my Ruby, whose house the chance meeting with Charlie Watts took place in. Since that night, everything has changed.

We pull into Piccadilly. I pluck up courage.

'Ruby, you know last night?'

'Sonny, I'm sorry, I just …' She looks withdrawn.

'You haven't changed your mind, have you?'

'About what?'

'You asked me to move in with you for three months to practise without the pressure. I want to … I mean … I'm saying yes if the offer is still there? I was going to tell Mum and Dad when I get home.'

She looks surprised. 'Really? I thought you were going to say no. I thought I'd made a mistake. Been too pushy.'

'I couldn't sleep,' I tell her. 'Yesterday was just full of highs and lows, and then I had to play and …' tears run down my face.

'Oh, Sonny, I thought I had frightened you off, and that was the last thing I wanted to do.' She gives me a big hug. 'I wanted to make sure you knew you could have a safe space if you needed it.'

She wipes away my tears, I feel like a big kid. 'It's just that you are the only one that understands me.'

Ruby pulls away. 'I think it might be better if I tell your mum.'

'No, it's something I have to do. If I am to become a professional musician, I need to take it seriously. I'll tell them.'

Over three hours since our awkward meeting in the lobby,

she smiles for the first time today. We're back, walking arm in arm towards the taxi rank laughing and joking and discussing the gig last night. The cab pulls up at Ruby's house, and I jump out to help her with her case. The engine idles away, blowing its diesely breath into the cold December afternoon. She takes my left hand, and says goodbye to me as I climb in.

'Good luck.' She lifts up her dark glasses. 'Well done for yesterday, Sonny, I'm so proud of you.'

'That was some gig, wasn't it?'

She leans in and kisses me on one cheek, and then the other. We look in each other's eyes and laugh. 'Continental.'

JULIA

MONDAY 12 JANUARY 1976

Julia sits on the sofa in the music room, pats the cushion, and I join her. Ruby introduced us in the kitchen and then sent us in. Julia seems sweet. I lean in to catch her words. 'So, what brings us together?' I'm off. I tell her about my piano lessons with Miss Wolstenholme and my dad's record collection. I told her what I listened to as a kid, either consciously or in the background, my band project with my best mate Jack, my studying music at college, everything. 'How did you know Freddie?' she asks and I tell her about Mum and the parties and how he used to turn up at our house, drink too much and blast out his trumpet. 'That's Freddie,' she says. 'Always on a high.' She pauses. 'No one ever saw the lows.' She goes on, 'Now what people don't know is that Freddie was a very accomplished pianist and I was helping him with that, although sometimes we chatted more than we played. I've heard through the grapevine that you may have already played in public yourself?'

I deny it. 'No, not yet. Not really. Well, only to Mum and Ruby when I come here to practice. Oh and once in Manchester.' Julia says that's funny because she was on the phone to Alphonso yesterday and he mentioned something about meeting me at the funeral. How had I forgotten? And we can't stop talking again. I tell her all about Charlie Watts, then Syd, who gave me the music and showed me the chords and then how Eric joined in.

She asks me how I felt, and I say, 'It was one of the best feelings ever.'

'I get that. Alphonso said you were a natural, someone who understands the music from the heart.'

'He said that?'

'And believe me, coming from him, that is a huge compliment.'

Julia reels off her story. She is only eight years older than me, and she also had Miss Wolstenholme as a teacher from a very young age. She loved classical music, and did all the grades and then her mum took her to see Blossom Dearie. She gets a little emotional. 'I can still see her on stage, it was January fifteenth, 1966, and she sang, "What Kind of Fool Am I?" And I was hooked. Instead of people politely listening they were standing up and cheering, the atmosphere was electric. I got the sheet music the next week, then the LP and then I couldn't stop listening.'

I tell her, 'Yes. Finally someone who understands. The Stan Tracey gig was like that too,' and I let her know how Syd had asked me to sit in a few weeks ago and I got so much attention. She asks me about the Ella gig at Ronnie Scott's, and we go on and on about how brilliant she is.

We talk about me playing music for a career. She puts her cup down and examines me. 'Sonny, if you want to do this, you can do it. But it takes over your life, your relationships, it can lead to some very dark places, emotionally and financially, but it can be the most rewarding of times too.' I agree I do want to do it, I have always wanted to be a professional but have only just realised that I have to work so hard at it. We talk about only having ten weeks until I go back to London, so the onus is on me to put the hours in and I will meet Julia twice a week in the music room. Mondays and Thursdays.

'Let's play,' says Julia and we have half an hour of fun together on the piano stool going up and down the scales and then some tunes. We are laughing and joking, and I begin to realise just how much I know. She is chucking things at me, and I am coping, just. She is stretching me, but it doesn't hurt. I am failing, but with a smile, because I know I'll come back stronger. We collapse onto the sofa, and I say I can't believe Miss Wolstenholme would ever sit on the piano stool with one of her pupils. Julia says, 'No she wouldn't because she's old school.' And then she looks serious. 'But don't ever disrespect her for that. She has given you all the building blocks you need for the future. She's quite a legend in these parts you know.' She reminds me that I am still having my classical lessons too. Mum and Dad have booked those for years for me, and it's always been a bit of a bribe. 'Keep going for the grade six lessons and concentrate on the pieces and scales as you'll need all of them in the future.'

She flicks through the stack of albums that Alphonso chose and picks out another three for me, *Blossom Dearie Sings Rootin' Songs*, John Coltrane *Live at Birdland* and *The Real McCoy*. She says just to listen, listen, listen. Read the liner notes, learn the musicians, research who they play for and what influences them. I look puzzled. 'For instance,' she says, 'The McCoy Tyner album I've given you was recorded just after he left the John Coltrane

Quartet, which you also have, so he has all that experience at his fingertips.' You can hear his progression. That is what jazz is, decades of experience wrapped up into tunes, most of which are composed, or improvised, on the stand right in front of the audience. 'For example, when Syd Lawrence gave you the lead sheet did you know what you were going to play?' I admit I didn't. 'Did you know how to play the chords?'

I think out loud. 'Yes, I did.'

Julia hits home. 'Did you play anything, did you invent anything on the night that wasn't written in front of you?'

'Yes, definitely.'

She is as excited today as I was on the night. 'So, Sonny, you are a composer. You knew some rules, the chords, you understood the tempo, you then listened to your bandmates and then, and this is the important bit, you wrote something in your head and played it. That is your composition.' I was ecstatic. 'And that is what Alphonso heard so clearly.' It's tiny, just a snippet, but he saw it and heard it. 'If you work with him and the other teachers in London, then after three years you'll be a professional, as long as you don't get blown off course or fall prey to the scene.'

I remember Ruby mentioning the scene a few weeks ago when she was angry. 'Julia, do you know Jimmy the Drums?' Her face goes ashen, and all colour drains from it. The small talk is over. So is the lesson.

When Ruby arrives she looks worried. 'What did you say to Julia? She seemed so upset. I tell Ruby that we were getting on well until the very end when I asked her about Jimmy. 'Oh. I see.' She explains that for a short while, Julia was in some sort of relationship with him, but that it went wrong, terribly wrong. 'Make sure you clear the air with her on Thursday before the next lesson. Tea is in fifteen minutes.' It has only been a week, but we've settled into this domestic arrangement of sorts. I don't usually see Ruby in the mornings. I'm off and out to college after I walk Ringo and feed him. Any free periods I stay at college and get back around half-past four. It's so calm here, no neighbours shouting, no cars bombing past and no Dad screaming at me. In the first week, I missed Mum, but she popped round, and we spent loads of time together on Saturday. The weirdest thing is no one says when to get up and go to bed. Ruby just assumed from day one that I had it all under control. When I first told Mum I was moving she was upset, but when I explained that I would be leaving in September anyway, she kind of understood, and I did tell her Ruby said she could come round anytime. All three of us met at Ruby's for a chat, and we sorted it out. Dad is off the planet. He said if I'm moving out then I have to survive on my own and there's no way back. He'd be happy to buy me a pint when I was eighteen but no more favours. Mum said, 'Don't you worry about him. He'll come round in time.' Ruby and Mum agree we will have a meal together once a week and Mum suggests I should cook it as part of my agreement to stay. I hope they know what they are letting themselves in for. I also agree to go round to Mum's on Wednesday nights after my lesson with Miss Wolstenholme, then that gives Ruby a night off. What started off as a plan already seems so comfortable. When we get to the top of the huge stairs, I turn left, and Ruby turns right. I have my own bedroom and a bathroom next door, or the guest bathroom as it's called, and Ruby has hers at the end of the house. There is a room for washing and ironing and another bedroom that remains locked.

Life is different. It's only week two and Ruby and I are starting to spark off each other. She still wanders in and listens to me playing all the time, if it's late at night she brings in a brew and sits and writes and I carry on playing. She has started this lovely little routine of writing out some lyrics for me, suggesting songs I should learn. I go and find the albums and try and understand the tunes. After an evening meal, I wash up and practise some more. I am really busy with music and college work but so relaxed.

And every single night wherever I am in the house Ruby comes to find me to say goodnight with those two kisses. Continental.

You've Got A Friend

Thursday 15 January 1976

I walk into the kitchen after an hour practising, and Ruby is chopping veg. She looks up and smiles, that's all. It makes me happy to know that she knows this is all she needs to do. No words.

I have been at Waverly for a fortnight, and it suits me. I am a bit of an introvert, and I am beginning to realise it's not such a problem despite what Dad has said over the years. Sometimes I lie on the bed just thinking, and no one interrupts me. The tales of my life, the songs in my head, the books I am reading go around and around and then around again. It's bliss. I think of Mr Mog Edwards writing his letters to Myfanwy Price hoping for love or Mercutio encouraging Romeo in his pursuit of Juliet, the stories I am studying. I see Jack and Karen all the time of course, and Deborah never stops talking to me in English. I am not boring, as Jack sometimes ribs me, but I love my own company and my thoughts. This is why I am happy at Ruby's.

Last night at Mum's we had steak and kidney pie with mash and it was obvious Dad was under orders to behave. First of all, there was no Newcastle Brown Ale at the table, and secondly, he kept asking me questions about college. I don't think he understands stories and plays and dramas the way me and Mum do. We loved Penda's Fen on Play for Today, but he got up and left us to it. That was last year, and he hasn't changed. The meal was nice, and there were no bad words between us, so it counts as a win.

Ruby looks at me. 'You ok, Sonny?' I tell her I was dreaming. She smiles. 'Again.' She has a little giggle. 'There's nothing wrong with dreaming, look where it got me.' I ask her what were her dreams before she met Freddie. Steam escapes from the oven as she puts the veg in. 'Life was straightforward. I'd started working in a shop but me and Trish, we lived for dancing and live music.' She goes on about how there was a post-war feeling that you had to make every day count. 'Then the Beatles came along, and the world started screaming.' We chat whilst the dinner cooks, she's just so matter of fact, life goes on, and she has an attitude of if it happens it happens. She says she just got lucky. We eat together most nights, Ruby says she's not very good at cooking, but I love it. One day, she says, she'll start going out again but for now 'it's just you and me.' As we finish our meal, the doorbell rings, and Ruby reminds me to say sorry to Julia.

We go through to the music room, and Julia seems quiet. 'Julia, I'm sorry about the other day. I didn't mean to poke my nose in.'

She looks at the floor. 'It's okay, I need to toughen up. I haven't spoken about it to anyone. It's a period of my London life that I'm not proud of, even after all these years. Everyone calls it the scene.' Julia says she was the straight-laced one, the student who did extra practice and didn't even drink until she met Jimmy and began going to gigs. Jimmy was two years older and was already taking drugs, and one thing led to another, and she got involved too. At first, she didn't know it was a problem, it just became normal, but Alphonso stepped in and saved her. He ordered her back to Manchester for three months rest, and she weaned herself off everything, including Jimmy. When she returned to finish her studies, he was abusive, but she held her ground and graduated and escaped back up north as soon as she could. She says Alphonso is a lovely man, and she is forever grateful to him for his intervention. 'When he asked me to help you, I was delighted to be able to return a favour.'

'Are you happy now?'

'Of course.' She explains all about her son Michael, who is two, and her husband Stephen and how she is loving life with her boys. Julia says she has been quite ill recently and she blames London and the drugs she took. I see the tears in her eyes. 'I think I'm paying the price for my poor decisions.' She begs me not to go down the same path if I make it to London.

'Let's play.' And she pushes me just a little bit harder tonight, an hour of to and fro and pieces that stretch me. It feels like her frustrations are coming out in her words, but I match her intensity with concentration. She jumps on the stool at the end of the lesson, and we play together for ten minutes. She is so bloody good. We finish with a flourish and go through to the kitchen.

Ruby joins us. 'Hello, you two. How did it go?'

Julia is quick off the mark. 'The lesson or the chat?' she says, smiling.

'I meant the lesson,' said Ruby. Julia is lightening up a lot. 'Well, I have told Sonny all about the dangers of you know what.'

'And you know who, I hope,' adds Ruby.

'Indeed,' says Julia. 'But we all make our own mistakes don't we? He is warned.' I have to tell them I am still in the room, but they just keep on talking about me and not to me, laughing and teasing me along the way. As Julia is going she says to me, 'And don't let that head get too big.' She gives me a big squeeze by the front door.

Ruby is in the lounge, and I take her a mug of tea in. I tell her that although it is only week two of the lessons, I am going to get along with Julia just fine, she's such good fun. 'Alphonso says she could have been one of the very best pianists in the country, but she lost her confidence and left London.'

'Julia said she is so grateful to Alphonso.' Ruby smiles. 'In fact she told me he's one of the best, a real dapper gentleman.'

Ruby listens, and I'm sure tries to hide some blushes. She says she's going to invite Julia and her family over for tea one weekend as she was so good to Freddie. 'And Sonny, ask your friends over whenever you want to, don't to be too reclusive even though you are studying hard. You've got to have some fun too.'

I guess it's true, and I do need to keep in touch with everyone. 'What about you, Ruby, when are you going to have some fun?'

She looks at me like it's such a daft question. 'Well, I'm going to London next week. I have some business to attend to, and Alphonso has invited me out to a concert.'

'Fantastic,' I shout and raise my arms.

'Don't be too happy I'm going, will you? You are on Ringo duty.' She says she has so much to understand now that Freddie has gone. She has got a new lawyer and an accountant in London to see. She's not interested in any of the management contracts but she has to get her head around the royalties and Alphonso is helping, but Jimmy is getting in the way as usual.

I sidle over to the turntable as Ruby sips her tea and makes notes. I sneak the Ella vinyl on, find track six and 'You've Got A Friend' begins to play. Ruby looks up and smiles, no words. I sit beside her, and she snaps her diary shut. 'What are you writing?'

'You'll have to wait a long time to find out.' We listen for a while.

She finishes her tea. She leans in and holds me a little longer than usual tonight and kisses me on both cheeks. 'Goodnight, Sonny.'

CROCODILE ROCK

I'm on my own in the house as Ruby went to London yesterday and it is heaven. I have managed to skip Miss Wolstenholme's lesson on the promise that I do some extra work. It's a horrible day. I've been soaked through twice already, taking Ringo out for his walks. Jack's coming round soon, and I'm cooking a meal. There's a loud knocking from the hall, and Jack's silly face is grinning at me as I open the door. We go through to the kitchen and Jack towels himself dry. He looks around the place. 'Bloody hell, mate, I've said it before, and I'll say it again, you have well and truly landed on your feet.'

It's weird how quickly you get used to something. Before Christmas we'd just been mates messing about together, and now I'm in this beautiful house studying to go to London. It's become normal to me, and I have to pinch myself. Jack is good about it, he just keeps winding me up about Ruby, but I know he loves visiting. He brings me back down to earth. 'Oi, Fanny Craddock, what about you taking the mickey out of Potter in music today?' I'd already forgotten about that. Ever since Mr Potter had seen me at the gig at the George, he is relentless in lessons. He hasn't said it, but he thinks I'm above my station and he delights in getting me to demonstrate anything he is teaching us. The trouble is I always can, so he should stop asking me and pick on someone else. Today I went a bit too far and moved on from the basic chord structure we were working on to a full rock and roll version of Crocodile Rock. I was on the new synth, and I swore to him I'd hit the button by mistake as we moved from piano to psychedelic pitch-bending funk and then, to make it worse, Jack snatched a Fender and joined in, everyone else stood up and sang along and then as we all screamed the ending the principal walked in. I'm sure I saw her smile.

She looked at Potter and muttered, 'Working on the next show I see.' She dragged him out for some reason, and we laughed for ages.

I tell Jack he should keep up the guitar. We could have so much fun together but he looks down in the dumps. 'You'll be in London hobnobbing, and I'll be stuck here.' The good news is Jack is going to finish college as his dad's company is paying him for six months, but after that, he's going out to work. 'Actually, I start at the factory in two weeks,' he says. 'Part-time. Then in June, I'll probably go full time, so that I can help Mum out.'

'How's your dad doing?'

'He manages the stairs now we've put an extra rail in.'

It sounds like it will be a long road. 'At least you've got Karen to cheer you up when I'm away. I'll be back every holiday, of course.' Jack asks me how I am going to afford music college, and I may be stupid, but I haven't even thought of it. 'Bloody hell, Jack, I don't know, I think there are grants and things. I'll have to ask Mum and Dad.'

The doorbell interrupts us, Ringo goes crazy. We rush out of the kitchen together, and it's Julia hiding from the rain under the eaves, silhouetted against the dazzling headlights. She comes in and says she has been searching everywhere for a bag she's lost, and the music room is her last chance. I introduce her to Jack, and we all go through, and there it is sitting on the chaise longue. She looks relieved. 'Thank God for that, I only got these on Monday. I thought I'd lost them.'

Jack has no shame. 'What are they?'

Julia looks at me and then Jack. She doesn't seem sure she wants to give up the information. 'My meds from Christies.' She gives them a shake. 'Can't get along without these.' Now Jack is embarrassed. 'See you boys, and watch out for the storm, it's coming soon. See you tomorrow, Sonny. Keep practising.' Stephen and Michael are waiting in the car, and she's gone.

'Who's that?' says Jack. I tell him it's a long story. After the night with Charlie, and then the day I met Alphonso, and the invitation to London and … I forget the correct order, but Julia was Freddie's piano teacher, he had pre-paid for lessons, and I am using them up. That's it. Simple.

Jack looks at me, squinting and shaking his head. 'Yes, but how many had he paid for?' For the second time in ten minutes, I have to admit I don't know. Jack thinks he's Columbo. He opens his arms and then taps his forehead. 'Just one more thing,' he says in his best American accent, 'I think someone is winding you up.' We burst out laughing.

We're in the kitchen, and I'm watching the spuds when the phone rings, I pick it up and hear the soft Italian tones of Alphonso. 'Hello, Sonny, how are your lessons going with Julia?'

I tell him it is only week two but very, very well and she is a brilliant teacher. He replies, 'I taught her everything she knows, you know, I'm very happy for you.' He asks a question that baffles me, 'Can I speak to Ruby please?' My head spins, has Ruby changed her mind about meeting him? I hope she hasn't had an accident.

'She caught the train to London yesterday, I think, that's what she told me.' Alphonso said he was expecting her last night for drinks and tonight they were due at a concert, but he hadn't heard from her, and she's not at her usual hotel. I can't help him, he says goodbye, and he hopes to see me soon. Jack looks at me, and I tell him about Ruby not showing up last night. He makes a joke of it like I'm some sort of jealous boyfriend.

We let Ringo out in the garden before dinner. It is bucketing down, and he skirts around the edge trying to avoid the rain, it sounds like a waterfall. We are tucking into dinner when the lights begin to flash, and the thunder rolls in. Ringo quivers in his basket and howls in distress and as I go over to comfort him the room lights up from outside and we lose all power. We plunge into darkness, Jack screams, and there are more thunderclaps and the windows rattle. 'Jack, are you ok?'

I can hear his heavy breathing. 'Yes, where are you?' The lightning cracks and we see each other across the room, he's standing up holding onto the table, and I'm on the floor with Ringo. In under a second, the thunder belches, the storm must be overhead.

'We might have to sit this one out,' I say.

Jack is getting nearer to me. 'Do you know where a torch is or a candle?' I don't know where anything is in the house. How often do you need these things? The lightning flashes again, like a thousand paparazzi cameras at the Oscars. Ringo panics and escapes my clutches, and as my eyes are blinded. I hear Jack crash into the kitchen stools and hit the floor hard. He's moaning, Ringo's running wild bumping into walls and seats and Jack. This room is chaotic, and I don't know what to do. I think for a minute, I'm fully in charge of a house for the first time in my life.

I gasp for air. 'Jack, we have to get Ringo out of this room, somewhere where he can't see the lightning. It's frightening him. At the next flash, one of us grab the dog. I've got the lead down from the shelf.' We only have to wait thirty seconds and the room lights up from an almighty flash, bluey white zig-zags in the sky and quite terrifying. Jack lunges towards the dog and pushes him towards me. I grab him as the light fades and the three of us sit down panting.

'What next?' croaks Jack. I creep on my hands and knees towards the door and tell Jack I'll try to find the lounge as the curtains are drawn in there. I drag Ringo into the hall, feeling my way along the skirting boards. It's pitch black, and I headbutt the hall table, knocking something off that shatters on the floor.

'Shit a brick this is difficult.'

Jack shouts, 'You alright, Sonny?' and I guess he knows from the cursing that I'm far from alright.

'Nearly there.' I take my jumper off and I inch forward, sweeping glass to the left and keeping Ringo safely behind me and one more flash lights up the hall. I see my target, speed up and reach for the handle. The door flies open, and it's pitch black. I take off the lead, push Ringo in, and reverse out. My knees are sore. I crash against the wall, and I can hear the blood pumping around my body. I start crawling again, my jumper in my right hand pushing any glass away, only a few yards to go now. I know the door is open into the kitchen so I shout to Jack, 'I'll be back soon, promise.'

He laughs. 'Dinner is on the table, darling,' and as he finishes joking the biggest electrical flash you have ever seen lights my path. I rush through the door, and Jack is still there by Ringo's bed.

'You haven't moved?' It goes dark again.

I can't see him, but I can tell he's looking at me. 'And where do you expect me to go?' The thunder follows. It seems like the storm is drifting away as it takes a few seconds to roll in.

We sit there for ten minutes, and more lightning continues to light up the black sky and the thunder booms in the distance. 'Well, what are we going to do?' Jack asks me, and I'm not sure. If the power doesn't come back, there isn't much we can do. I suppose we could both go to our parents' houses, but I'd have to take Ringo. We decide to light the gas burners, and for the first time in ages, we have a little glow from the far end of the room. We both sit down at the table and drink some water. Jack has a massive bump on his head, and I have blood from lots of little cuts on my hands. We are a mess. We eat some cold chicken and wait, and wait. The phone rings, and we both scream like we've seen a ghost. It's Mum seeing if we are in the dark and she explains that everyone in the area is in the same boat. I tell her that I have put Ringo in a dark room as he is scared and that we are just sitting in the kitchen waiting for the electricity to come back on.

'Search for a candle or a torch as you may have a long wait.'

Jack calls home and explains the same, and his mum says to search for a torch too. We start opening every drawer and cupboard, feeling our way in the dimmest of light. Jack suggests the garage and convinces me that every home has a torch. He finds the key on the highest shelf above the dog's bed and puts it in the lock. I know I am not meant to go in here, but I don't say anything as he is so sure. The door opens, Jack inches forward, finds a light switch and puts it on. 'Duhhh. Why am I surprised this doesn't work?' He trips down a step, hitting something hard and cursing again. I follow slowly, I don't know how we are going to find anything in here as none of the glow from the kitchen is coming in. There is a rustling by the garage door, the lights flicker and come back on, and we both look up and are blinded. A frightened bird flies up and around the garage, screeching. We jump out of our skins, and we both scream out loud again. As our eyes get used to the light, we look into the centre of the room and there is an immaculate red Jaguar Series II. The garage door creaks and begins to open. We hold onto each other shaking, not knowing what is happening. We hear the rain first, wet spears of water crashing onto the drive and then a lady steps out of the shadows.

'I thought you were in London,' I say to Ruby.

'I thought I told you to never come in this garage.'

La-La Lies

The three of us sit in the kitchen, Jack and me are still in shock. The lights are on, and the place looks like a bomb site, stools on their sides, blood on the floor and my screwed up jumper covered in it. Glass shards form a trail from the hall door to the garage. Ruby looks at us, but her focus remains on me. She looks so disappointed in me, as if I have broken the bond of trust when given my very first chance. I can feel Jack shaking. Ruby breaks the silence and fetches two glasses of water. 'Do you want to start at the beginning?'

I decide there is no point in lying. The evidence is laid out like before us. 'We were having tea when the storm arrived, which at first seemed quite fun. But then Ringo ...'

Ruby's eyes show the fear as she realises he's not here. 'Where's Ringo?' she shouts. 'Have you lost him in the storm?'

'No, listen, Ringo is safe in the lounge ...'

Ruby stands up to go and check on him.

'Don't leave the room,' I squeal. 'There is glass on the hall floor.' I raise my hands to show Ruby the cuts.

'What happened in the hall?' Ruby peers around the door and bursts into tears. 'Oh no, my Waterford vase, that was a wedding present.'

I pull her back into the kitchen. 'Ruby, sit down. Ringo is fine. The vase isn't. But we need to tell you how we got into this mess.' It's her turn to have a glass of water.

I am about to start the story again when Dad walks into the kitchen from the garage, followed by Mum, who's looking worried. This night is going from bad to worse. Mum says, 'Why is the garage open with all the lights on?' Dad is not the master of tact, asking Ruby if she's had a party. Mum said she'd tried calling. I look at the phone. It's hanging off the wall, no wonder she couldn't get through. My ability to tell the story melts away, and we look like two naughty schoolboys in front of the head. All eyes are on me. Eventually, I get through the kitchen episode, I explain how Ringo knocked over Jack, how we managed to get his lead on him to try and calm things down. About how it was so dark we were waiting for each lightning bolt to give us a little bit of light. Jack helps me out by saying we were scared and trying to make the best decisions and we thought we'd put Ringo somewhere safe and that his mum had told him to find a torch.

Ruby looks at me. 'But what about the vase?' I'm not sure she is convinced about my being on all fours story and inching down the corridor, but she gets up and fetches a broom, and we follow her into the hall. We creep behind her as she sweeps any bits of glass to the side and as we get nearer Ringo gives a loud bark and doesn't let up. She opens the lounge door, and he launches himself at her, knocking Ruby over and into the wall. He lands on top of her, and she is winded, and he's still yelping and licking her face. Dad helps Ruby to her feet, and just when you think things can't get any worse Mum switches the light on and another scene of utter devastation is in front of us. Ringo has cut his paw, and there is blood all over the carpet. He has knocked over the table lamp, the side table and jumped on the sofa. You can see the bloody paw prints. Ruby bursts into tears again, Mum takes her to the couch, and Ringo follows whimpering. Mum orders Dad to put the kettle on and then whispers, 'Drive Jack home if you can, please?'

We go back to the kitchen and do as Mum told us. Jacks picks up the stools, I throw the food away, and Dad fills the kettle. It doesn't take us long to work our magic, and the kitchen looks much better. I search for a mop and find myself back in the garage. Dad says, 'That is some car isn't it?' We all admire the red Jaguar in front of us. It is a thing of beauty.

Dad pulls the garage door shut as Jack shouts, 'Found it.'

We turn around, and he's holding a big black torch high above his head. It works perfectly.

Dad sniggers. 'It's a bit late now.'

Thankfully the bird is nowhere to be seen. Dad says we better get out of here and I take one last look at the leaping jaguar on the bonnet and notice something dangling from it. I step back in. It is black and yellow tape marked 'Crime Scene'. I grab a mop, turn the light off and lock the door quickly.

Tea is delivered, and Dad leaves with Jack to take him home. I finish tidying the hall, picking up the glass and then mopping through to the kitchen. Ten minutes later the doorbell rings and I let Dad back in. We stay in the kitchen out of the way, and conversation is stilted. He asks me how I am getting on, and I say, 'I was doing ok until tonight.'

'Don't worry, storms like this are rare, and you were just unlucky with the power going off,' he says. 'It's all Ringo's fault really.' If he hadn't panicked there wouldn't have been any mess. We laugh at that, blaming the poor dog, and he says if you know where everything is it's easy. He had the candles out from under the sink as soon as the storm started, and he reminds me that next time I'll be prepared. 'We all learn from experience, don't we?' I was about to retort with, 'Does that apply to your drinking?' but I managed to keep it in. There's no point any more. I look up at Dad, and he's smiling at me. 'I hope you are happy here, Sonny, I really do. I can't give you all this.' He sweeps his arms around the rooms and indicates the whole house. I think about what Mum told me about his guilty feelings and how he was devastated by his loss.

'Dad, it's just for a few months whilst I get my head down on the piano …' We look at each other, we know that's not entirely true, but there's not going to be any fighting tonight. 'How's work?' He gets quite excited as he reveals the latest regeneration plans for Manchester, saying I won't recognise it in five years. He's in the middle of discussions right now with all the interested parties on the project, and for the first time in my life, I see real passion in his eyes.

Mum comes in with two empty mugs and tells us we're off and adds, 'You too, Sonny.' I look surprised, and Mum adds, 'Ruby needs some time on her own, let's just leave her be. Come on, you two. Sonny, we'll come back tomorrow, you can have the day off college.' We try to leave quietly, but Ruby comes down the hall to say bye to us. I can see she's been crying. Dad opens the door and waves, Mum gives her a big cuddle, and I say sorry again and squeeze her tight. As we are walking to the car I look over my shoulder and then remember something and run back,

'Ruby ...' She interrupts me with two kisses cheek to cheek, but that's not what I came back for. 'Ruby, was everything alright in London?'

She lies to me. 'Yes, of course, why do you ask?'

'Because Alphonso phoned earlier, he said he'd missed you last night. You were meant to be going to the concert tonight. He sounded worried, and he didn't know where you were.'

She looks at me. The look that says I know you know I'm lying but I can't go back.

Ruby stares right through me. All her energy has departed. The doubts creep in. Will I ever return to Waverly? Will I even make it to London?

'I'll phone him now. Goodnight, Sonny.'

HEAVEN'S DOOR

We drive in silence, it's not that late, but it feels like we have been up all night. Dad dodges branches and puddles as the storm subsides and we are soon home. Mum makes the family brew, and we sit around the table like we used to with steam rising from our mugs. 'Toast anyone?' Dad hits the spot, and within minutes we have butter coated fingers and messy chins as we wolf down our toast and slurp our tea. 'Better than your chicken dinner, Sonny?' asks Dad.

'Miles better,' I agree. And it is, warm and welcoming. It's good to be back home. Dad takes the mick about how scared we were, and how I knocked the vase over and soon we are all laughing about Jack's and my incompetence. It's funny repeating the story, but it wasn't funny at the time, we were terrified.

I tell Mum and Dad about the moment when the power came on, first we were blinded because we looked at the light and then this bird launched itself and went crazy flapping around our heads. 'Then the garage door creaks open, we hear the rain pouring, and we see a shadow. I thought we were about to get murdered!'

Mum asks, 'Who was it?'

'It was Ruby.' I'm sweating just thinking about it. I shiver a little and swig my tea. 'The weird thing is she was meant to be in London.' Mum says not to worry. She will explain everything tomorrow when we go round. I think, 'If I go round more like,' but I don't say anything. Dad wipes his hands on his thighs, gets told off and goes to watch the late news.

Mum puts the kettle on again, says 'More toast?' and I know it is going to be a long night.

I have missed my chats with Mum, the late ones in the kitchen. She sits down and looks at me. 'I have missed you, Sonny, you do know that?' She seems sad, and she wipes away a tear or two. 'I know you're growing up and moving on with your life, but you're still my little boy.' I reach across the table, and we hold hands, look into each other's eyes, and silently acknowledge that Maisie never had the chance to grow up.

'How's college?'

Mum is so enthusiastic. She is a different woman. 'It's only been two weeks, but I have the five years mapped out already. Foundation studies to get back up to speed and then I'm diving deep into social work, working in the field and then a degree and a job.' It's lovely to see her this animated. She has chosen the right course for sure. 'So, we'll both be students together,' she says.

My heart skips a beat, and I tell her, 'After tonight I'm not sure London is on any more.' I'm not sure Ruby will have me back either.

Mum says I'm talking nonsense. We have to remember that Ruby has only been widowed since October and although every day she seems strong to us, she is bound to have moments of complete meltdown. 'She had a difficult day yesterday with someone who is causing her trouble.'

'Jimmy?'

Mum agrees. 'Yes it was, he seems a nasty piece, trying to claw money from Freddie even after he's died.' Then she clams up, says we shouldn't be speaking about other people's affairs. Mum tries to reassure me that all of the talk in the lounge was about Ruby, Freddie and London; Ruby didn't mention the house or me. I ask Mum about how are we going to pay for my degree, and she says she's not sure, but we'll find a way. Mum says that she'll phone the council and find out about the available grants. 'But don't you worry about it, me and your dad will sort that out for you. I promise.'

'How well do you know Ruby?' She puts her mug down and asks me why I am asking her that question. 'The speed of all this, from Freddie dying to me living there.'

Mum begins to tell me how they met, when Mum was at one of her lowest points, years after Maisie had died, and that Ruby had been the one person who had picked her up. She had shown her that life still contained meaning, that talking about Maisie was comfortable with Ruby. They became best friends as adults and always support each other, which is why we need to go round tomorrow and finish tidying up.

'Do you think I am safe at Ruby's house?'

She can't believe I am asking the question.

'Do you feel safe, Sonny?' I tell her that I love being there and always feel safe, but I had seen something earlier that I ...

Mum looks at me, and I know that I have to tell her now even if it means my dreams are finished.

'Sonny, what did you see?'

I can't say it. My mouth goes dry, and I sip my warm tea.

'Sonny, please tell me, you're frightening me.'

Dad almost takes the door off the hinge as he barges in, 'Right you two, I'm off to bed, some of us have got work in the morning.' He looks at us and senses the tension. 'What's wrong?'

Mum seizes her opportunity. 'Nothing too much, Sonny was worried about London and how he was going to pay for his degree, but I told him we would sort it out. It's not every family that has a child going off to study, is it?'

He ermms and aaghs and says, 'We'll sort it, don't you worry. Goodnight, don't stay up too late.' Mum is so bloody clever. She has hijacked my current dilemma to force Dad into a corner.

We look at each other, and we know there's no way back.

'Mum. The police have been in Ruby's garage. I saw the crime scene tag hanging off the Jaguar. I'm not being funny, but Ruby told me never to go in there, I mean that's weird, isn't it? I can go everywhere except the one room where a crime has been committed. Something is wrong, I know it is. And that's what is scaring me.' My heart is racing, my mouth is like sandpaper, and I can only see my future in the factory with Jack.

'Hang on, Sonny, slow down, slow down …'

'But Mum, it's a crime scene, do you know what that means?'

She takes my hands and faces me. 'I know all about the garage.' I thought my secret would be the biggest surprise, that she would say that I can't live there anymore and I would have to return to my boring and normal life. It's like they've teased me with this new way of living and thinking only to bring me rudely crashing down. My mind is scrambled. What crime Ruby has committed, who has she hurt or tortured, is she a spy for the secret service, maybe that's why she goes to London so much? I am all over the place, reading everything into her travels, the hotels, the fancy photos, the European cities and trips to America. I have been deceived, or maybe I am being set up myself.

Mum looks at me. 'Sonny, you know I said we shouldn't talk about other people's affairs. Well, I can tell you that I trust Ruby one hundred per cent, I wouldn't have let you live there otherwise. Now I am going to tell you something that is nothing to do with us, but it may help you understand the police tag and why Ruby didn't want you in there.' She takes a deep breath. 'Freddie killed himself in the garage.'

We stare at each other for minutes. Mum gets up and paces around the room and puts the kettle on for the third time and goes for a wee. This news lets Ruby off the hook. All those thoughts that flashed through my mind were a million miles out. It wasn't Ruby being devious or criminal as I imagined, it was Freddie's self-sabotage, and now she was living with the consequences. I try to wipe those thoughts from my mind, and I apologise to Ruby for thinking them. Bloody hell, he killed himself. Why did he do that? Mum walks over to the kettle and makes two fresh teas.

'You ok, Sonny?'

'Why?'

She sits down. 'Whatever I think, whatever Ruby thinks, we are all guessing. No one but no one knew what was going through Freddie's mind when he sat in his car in his garage after taking a mixture of drugs.' She says it is possible that it was an accident, but he had written letters for Ruby. 'She is left to sort out the business, the house and her future alone.' Mum says we will all help her as much as we can. The best thing we can do is to be there for Ruby, just be there. And talk about Freddie, don't be afraid to talk about him. Mum lets me know that she got help with grief counselling when Maisie had died, and that is one of the reasons she wants to do her social work degree. She adds, 'Ruby has always been there for me, especially when I needed to talk about your sister and now we need to step up for her.'

I think back to the funeral. None of this was mentioned. Even Dad said it was a car accident. 'Do you think Jimmy and Julia know that he killed himself?' Mum says she doesn't know. She says to ask Ruby when the time is right.

We sit in silence, lost in our thoughts. This morning I was in my own space, no adults. I was cooking for Jack, playing music, dreaming of London. My eyes sting. Tiredness envelops me. I look at my hands still marked with cuts and grazes and feel my knees, sore from crawling up the hall, what a day it has been. My thoughts turn to Mum, who always knows what to say and what to do, even in times of crisis.

'Will Ruby be all right?' Without a moment's hesitation, she says she will. There is no doubt in her voice.

'Goodnight, Mum.'

'Goodnight, Sonny.'

'And Mum, if you ever want to talk about Maisie, you know you've got me to talk to.'

Mum stands up and hugs me tight. 'You're growing up so fast. I love you.'

'Love you too.'

I sneak a look back as I leave the room, Mum is wiping away her tears.

Melancholy Man

Today I am at Julia's house for a lesson as she is prepping students for exams, and this makes her life easier. Stephen lets me in as Julia is running late. He makes me a drink as little Michael runs wild. I didn't realise two-year-olds can be so much fun, chasing me around the kitchen and making me pick up his toys. Stephen puts him in a high chair and gives me a spoon and shows me what to do. He prepares dinner. Julia arrives in a fluster apologising for being late. Stephen gives her a cuddle and makes Julia a tea and Michael stretches his arms out too. Stephen tells Julia, 'He's a natural so he is, that wee young man has kept the boy entertained and fed.'

Julia looks at me, surprised. 'Maybe we have our babysitter fixed then, we can go out on the weekend?'

Stephen, who has the softest of Irish accents, agrees. 'Sure thing, are you up for that, Sonny?'

I squirm. 'I have zero experience in the baby department.' They both laugh. I think they are teasing me. Julia wolfs down a sandwich and tells little Michael that Mummy has to go to work, and after many goodbyes and waves, we head to the music room.

Julia says take a few minutes. She goes for a quick change. I don't mind as I need to let my college stress subside. Potter was on at me again, asking me this and that. Why can't he see I'm serious about becoming a musician? He knows I have an audition coming up but couldn't be less supportive. Julia is the complete opposite, pushing me on and encouraging me, and she has become someone I can rely on to give me honest feedback. She says she sees her younger self in me, young and hungry to learn and so open to opportunities. She comes back into the room and apologises that it is so small and she only has an upright piano. 'It's not quite Freddie's music room is it?' It's not a problem for me. I'm just happy to be playing. Julia asks me if I mind having my Monday lessons here as it is closer to her previous client, and it means that Ruby won't keep wandering in. She sees my surprise and asks me, 'Is that ok?' I'm fine with it, but I didn't realise Ruby was an issue. Julia explains that it is a difficult situation because Ruby is paying, but I am the student and sometimes after the lessons, Ruby questions what she is doing and how she's doing it.

'Ruby said Freddie had pre-paid for everything.'

'Not quite everything, he used to pay for a month at a time.'

'Sorry. I didn't know that.'

'Not to worry, I know Ruby has the best of intentions. She wants to protect me and my income, and she loves having you around the house too. She is a control freak, but her heart is in the right place.'

I already know this. After Mum had told me about the support she had given her, and after the garage incident, we had a long chat about everything. I was scared to go back and thought I had blown it, but Mum visited first and then Ruby called me at home to invite me round. When I got there, the house was spotless, and it was like nothing had happened. We talked about Freddie and his accident, as Ruby called it. We spoke about how Ruby couldn't imagine ever letting anyone in the garage because it was too personal to her. She did want me back, she forgave me for smashing the vase and we could go on as before. Mum said it was my choice. She was continuing to work on Dad and he was getting better and less argumentative. Ruby took control, convinced me to stay and told Mum that she would send me home more often. After Mum left, Ruby took me out for lunch and spoilt us both, and she said she was so happy we were together again. She gripped my hands. 'I'm serious, Sonny. I've lost Freddie, I refuse to lose you.'

It brought Julia's comments back to mind.

'What was Freddie like?'

Julia smiles. 'He was the sweetest of men, deeply into his music.' He regretted that he hadn't studied it when he was younger and although everybody knew him as a trumpeter, he was becoming a fine pianist.

'Did he tell you about his one hit song?'

'Not really, but if he missed a lesson because of business, I would sit with Ruby and chat, and she would mention it. Not to show off, more to say how lucky they were. She was so grateful to escape her hell hole.' Julia says that Ruby's mum and then her dad had died when she was very young, so she got moved to an uncle's place, which she hated. Her escape route was Freddie, a very wealthy man. 'But he always told me that she saved him more than he saved her. They were well suited.' I can't believe what Julia is telling me.

'Why did Freddie need saving?'

Julia takes a deep breath. 'He had his demons. He was quite low sometimes, drowning in melancholy and someone was pursuing him for a share of those song rights.'

'Don't tell me this story involves Jimmy?'

Julia looks at me. 'How did you know that?'

'Jimmy called her a bitch at the funeral and Ruby said he was jealous.'

'Freddie admits playing the song to Jimmy in its early form,' but he insisted it was all his work. She adds that money corrupts and Jimmy always needs money, 'if you know what I mean.' I look at Julia, and I tell her I can't believe Jimmy trapped her. 'Nor can I. Look at me, miss goody two shoes.' She lowers her voice. 'Please don't tell Stephen, he doesn't know about my London life. That's one of the reasons I didn't go to the funeral, just too many people knocking around. Ruby understood.' Julia says she doesn't believe Freddie meant to kill himself, and she thinks it was an accident. I tell her about the letters left for Ruby, but she says he was always writing notes. Julia said that on the day he died he'd had a piano lesson with her in the afternoon, and he was distracted by something in London, he mentioned Jimmy causing trouble, but when she left, he said see you next week, and he meant it. 'I know he meant it.' She grabs both my wrists. 'Sonny, I will help you achieve your dreams but promise me you will never, ever take drugs. Promise me on your mum's life.'

'I promise. On Mum's life.'

'Let's play.' And we transport ourselves to another world. We leave our worries behind as we blast through scales, exercises and tunes. Julia is a joy to work with. She forces me along at a furious pace, and my brain aches with all the hard work. It is so much fun. There's a knock on the door. Michael has come to say goodnight to his mum. Julia pops out to put him to bed, and Stephen says he'll make two teas. I follow him to the kitchen, and he asks me how I'm getting on.

When I tell him I am playing and practising about twenty-five hours a week he is amazed. 'That's nearly a full-time job, so it is.' I say I hope it's going to be one day. He lets me know a secret, that when Julia is on her own, she also sings and, 'Sure she has a lovely voice, you know.' He asks me if I could get her singing more. 'That would be grand. Michael loves it when she sings.' These lessons are for me, not Julia. He goes on about the building trade and the jobs he is working on at the moment, before I am whisked away to finish my lesson.

'Will you ever perform again?'

She surprises me. 'Probably not. That part of my life is in the past. I'm just concentrating on staying healthy.'

'How are you, Julia? Really?'

She smiles and says, 'How come a smart arse kid can ask me that question when so many of my friends and even my husband can't?'

I smile back. 'Because my mum taught me always to ask the tough question. It's usually the right one.'

Julia leans back on her chair and puffs out her cheeks. 'At the moment I'm cancer free, and I feel amazing. But I know it's one day at a time. It's been a nightmare, but I am just starting to think this could be an excellent year. And Sonny, thanks for asking.'

I stand up to leave. I tower over her. Julia gives me a cuddle.

'You're not a kid. I didn't mean that bit.'

'But I am a smart arse?'

'Yes, that bit's true.' She laughs.

I pull out an invitation to my eighteenth birthday party. Mum and Ruby insist I do something and they have cooked up this idea between them. It's at Ruby's house in the music room. 'Ahhh, I see,' says Julia. 'We may as well play a few tunes in preparation for your second audition then?'

I knew this was coming. 'You sound just like my mother.'

Julia says mothers are the voice of reason, and that includes her. 'Do we have a deal or not?'

'Kind of, but if I have to play then so must you. And sing with me too.'

She looks pleased to be asked. 'Who put you up to this?'

'I'd love it if you could, I need to learn how to accompany amazing singers.'

She smiles at me and offers her hand. We shake on it.

What Kind of Fool

I am at Waverly. Ruby has gone to London to finalise a deal with her lawyers and get Jimmy off her back. She doesn't let me know too much, but now and again I get a snippet after Alphonso has phoned her. My birthday party is coming soon, and my three mates are coming round tomorrow to discuss it, Jack and Karen and Deborah too. She's kind of worked her way in and made it a gang of four. Debs is cool, very academic and going to university to study English, so we go on and on about Shakespeare and sonnets and the Romantics. Ruby says she loves having my mates round.

I open the door to Julia for my Thursday lesson. She looks fabulous, and I say 'Wow' far too loudly, she apologises, saying she has to go out straight after my lesson, Stephen's company has an awards night. It doesn't bother me that she's all dressed up, but then she mentions it again. 'Julia, you look stunning. You're beautiful, and you don't have to apologise.'

She bursts into tears and fetches a tissue out of her handbag, mascara running down her face. She takes ages to compose herself. 'I'm sorry, this is the first time I've felt normal for years.

In fact, it's the first time I've dressed up for more than two years, and Stephen didn't say a bloody thing.'

'Men.'

'Exactly. I do feel amazing, and yes I do feel beautiful, and you're not even eighteen, and you know exactly what to say and …'

I interrupt her and kiss her on one cheek and then the other and then hold her tight and whisper, 'You are beautiful.'

She weeps into my shirt for ages and eventually squeezes me and says, 'Thank you. I so needed to hear that.'

I lead her to the sofa and say I have a little surprise for her, but she must keep it a secret until my party. I have listened to Blossom Dearie, and I begin to play 'What Kind of Fool Am I', the song that first got her into jazz. I look across at Julia, still wiping her eyes and after a couple of verses where I see her mouthing the words I say, 'Your turn to help me now,' and she begins to sing. It is difficult to concentrate and keep playing as she has the purest and most emotional voice. We do go wrong, we go back and forth, but we never stop, this is not about perfection, it is about getting to the end and surviving.

And we do, and we cheer and we dance around the room and Julia says, 'Sorry, I can't stop crying.' She kisses me, she properly kisses me on the lips, and says whoever ends up being my girlfriend will be one lucky lady. She rushes off to the loo. 'To fix my makeup.'

She meets me in the kitchen, and I hand her a glass of white wine. It's something Ruby has got me into. We would never have had it at home. Julia says 'Cheers' and we both know the lesson is over even though Stephen isn't picking her up just yet.

We decamp to the lounge, and I feel like the master of the

house. Julia says, 'Let's chat.' And we do. She speaks about the skill of accompanying singers, a very different thing to playing solo or instrumental. Tonight was probably my first real attempt, but she praises me and says it won't count for much at my audition but will stand me in good stead for the future, especially commercially. She says, 'We've got a few weeks, so we can practise a few more songs together for the party if you like?'

'Can we get Jack and Karen involved? I used to play with them, but our practices were cancelled as Jack's dad had an accident at work.'

'You are so empathetic. Tell them to come round next Monday.' She promises to call Alphonso and give him an update before I have to go to London, and then she asks me if I'm sure this is what I really want out of life.

I've been flitting over the last few months, but in the end I say, 'I do want to be a musician, of course I do, but I just want to make my dad proud. He's so old school.' Julia says she'll help me. There are two weeks to my party and three weeks to my audition. When Stephen arrives, I go out to the taxi as Julia pops to the loo again to use the mirror. He gets out the car and shakes my hand and apologises for looking like a dick in his tuxedo.

'What is it with you boys?'

'I'm at the awards you see. I hope I'm on to a winner tonight.'

'Stephen, you are already a winner in my eyes. Have you seen how gorgeous your wife looks? After all she's been through, she is stunning.' He beams with pride. Sometimes it is hard to see the beauty in front of us.

'Thanks, mate, that means a lot.' Julia's on her way out, so I whisper, 'It doesn't mean a thing if you don't tell her, so make sure you do.' He gives me a thumbs-up, and Julia does air kisses with me so as not to ruin her makeup.

She holds on to me and says, 'Thanks for being bloody brilliant.' As the taxi departs, she is wiping her eyes once again.

I run inside and call Jack. He's round as quick as he can be, guitar on his back and ready for action. I pour a glass of wine for him, and he takes the piss out of me for being a hooray henry, but he still drinks it. We go into the music room, and I can't wait to tell him my news.

'Is this about your party?' Jack says as he hoists the guitar off his back and swigs his wine.

'Kind of,' I say. I can't hold it in any longer. 'She kissed me.'

Jack high fives me. 'I knew it, I bloody told you didn't I?' Jack does a silly dance around the room and finishes by singing, 'And then I kissed her.' He looks at me laughing my head off and repeats, 'I bloody told you didn't I, Romeo? What was it like?'

I have to think to make sure I get the right words. 'Well, it was so unexpected but exciting and I know it was because I told her she was beautiful ...'

Jack interrupts. 'That always works, I've read about flattery in Karen's Jackie magazine.'

I shut him up. 'I think this counts as my first proper kiss, but it was friendly, and she's married, but I thought I'd tell you anyway.'

Jack looks at me. 'But her husband is dead, so you have a pass mate.'

I knew what he'd been thinking, and I loved winding him up. 'No, it was Julia that kissed me, not Ruby.'

Jack is stunned. 'The piano teacher? How many girls are you leading on?'

Now it was my turn to enjoy it, singing, 'And then she kissed me.'

I explain to Jack about Julia's tough few years and how she just collapsed when I told her she was looking gorgeous. He says, 'You've got a way with words and it will get you into trouble one day.' I tell him all about the lessons, going to Julia's house and meeting the family and the singing tonight. I persuade Jack to help me out at my party, and we agree to practise next week with Julia, just a few songs for old time's sake.

'None of that bloody jazz,' says Jack. I tell him it's top-secret, as a surprise for the family.

We spend the rest of the night on guitar and piano mucking about playing pop songs and drinking another bottle of wine. It's getting late, and we are both a little drunk. Jack says he can't believe I am going to be eighteen soon and planning on going away.

I remind him we met at infant school. 'We've been mates forever.'

'That seems so long ago.'

'It was, but it was so much fun. Do you remember Miss Jones, the head?'

Jack does. 'Of course, I got taken into her office about the mud incident, remember?'

'Oh bloody hell, I'd forgotten about that. You were only about six, and you rubbed mud down the back of Alfie's pants and called him pooh bum.'

'I was a bully, wasn't I?'

'You were. A little bit … No Jack, you weren't a bully, just looking for fun, as you still do.'

'Yeah, life's still fun, isn't it?' He burps and hiccoughs. 'And now you are here, in this little palace and nearly eighteen.'

'I know, how did this all happen? And where will we be in ten years' time?'

Jack sighs. 'Eighteen, that's bloody old, isn't it? Do you remember when we went to high school, in the first week your old man went mental when he found out we'd bunked off to buy some new records?'

'Oh shit, that was a serious bollocking.'

'I was always scared about visiting your house after that.'

'You were scared. I had to live with him and all his ex-army crap.'

'Why was he always so angry?'

The words spew out of my mouth. 'Because my elder sister died.'

We are silent, and we sober up in seconds. It has taken me nearly eighteen years to admit to my best mate I even had a sister. Tears fall from my eyes, and I can't stop them. I think of Maisie. She'd love to be here with me now, drinking and making music and having fun. She would love Jack and Karen, and she would have her own gang, and we'd go out together every weekend drinking and dancing. I am crying for so many lost opportunities.

'Sonny, you never said. I'm sorry, mate. What's your sister called?'

That feels so good, someone asking me her name in the present tense. 'Maisie.'

'Maisie, that's a beautiful name.'

I fumble in my wallet and bring out the photo that Mum gave me. I realise she's about the same age as little Michael running around the house at Julia's.

'She's gorgeous,' says Jack

'Yep, and I never got to meet her.'

Jacks hugs me, a real matey bear hug and after a few minutes says, 'Sorry, mate, I don't know what to say.'

I agree. 'Neither do I.'

He packs his guitar away, and I take the wine glasses to the kitchen and start to tidy up.

'Tonight went considerably better than the last time we were on our own in the house.' We laugh about how scared we were when the bird attacked us in the garage. We both shiver at the same time. He asks me if I like being alone and I have to agree I do, it suits me.

I open the door. 'See ya, Jack and seriously, thanks for being my best mate.' Another massive hug.

'Maisie, that's a beautiful name.' He ambles down the drive.

After a few yards I shout at him, 'Oi Jack, you've got a something on the back of your pants.'

He turns his head, trying to see and rubs his hand up and down.

I shout, 'Pooh bum,' as loud as I dare, and he laughs and flicks me the V sign.

Outward Bound

Friday 20 February 1976

I race back from college, and I don't know why, but I am more excited to see Ruby than ever. She greets me in the hall as I open the door and we bump into each other. She looks dazzling. I think she's had her hair done. 'How was London?'

'Amazing, so much better than last time. I think Alphonso has forgiven me.'

She asks me if I am ready to go buy tonight's nibbles for my friends and I say, 'Give me ten minutes,' and I rush up the stairs to shower and get changed. I always need to get out of college clothes as soon as I am in: it's a habit I've had since my school days. As I am leaving the bathroom, towel around my waist, Ruby surprises me.

'That was a quick shower, Sonny, you eager to get going?' She passes me my washing basket, and adds, 'You smell nice,' as she hands it to me and our hands touch.

I want to say, 'You look gorgeous,' as I did last night to Julia, but it just doesn't seem right. As I turn to go to my bedroom my towel slips and falls to the floor. I am holding the basket in front of me, and I don't know whether Ruby has gone or not. I creep to my room naked and unscathed. That was close.

We jump in the car and hit the shops. Ruby looks different, she's glowing. She tries to take me to an upmarket deli, but I insist on Sainsbury's, and we buy a mountain of stuff and it's not until we reach the till I realise that this is wrong, so wrong. I can't get past that it's my mates coming round, it's my mates eating all the food, but it is Ruby who is paying the bills. I must look glum as Ruby goads me as we empty the trolley. 'Sonny, what's wrong? You were full of life when you got home, and now you look like you've swallowed a wasp.'

'I don't think this is fair, Ruby,' I stumble. 'I'm having the time of my life, and you're paying for it.'

We get in the car, she holds my hand and says, 'I think you need an aperitif before tonight, young man.' She drives to a pub and gets a table.

Two glasses of wine arrive, and Ruby sits opposite me. She looks serious, 'Now you listen to me. Life isn't fair, Sonny, it's not fair for millions of people. I lost my husband at thirty-three, and that's not fair for me. I have told you about that lucky break for Freddie with the hit song, so I have enough money to last me a lifetime and every six months more rolls in, it's fucking unbelievable.' I snigger, I love it when Ruby swears. It's so out of place.

'Cheers.' I raise my glass,

'Cheers.' She just carries on. 'So, you coming to mine, and me spending my money on you, that is my choice, borne out of unfortunate circumstances I admit, but still, it's my choice. And how else would I get to see a naked man walking along my corridor?' She's giggling and drinking and holds her glass up high. 'Come on, come on, toast me.' And I can't be sad around her, I just can't. 'Cheeky cheers.'

I tell her that I know she is paying for my music lessons and she shakes her head and laughs. 'Do not worry.' She asks me would I like to start going out to more gigs? And would I want to have a lovely flat in London? Of course I answer yes to all of her questions. Her positivity seeps from every pore, this lady who only a few months ago was at her lowest point is now lifting me up. As we sip our wine, I think of Julia and how the power of my words lifted her. But her husband, who saw her every day, had missed the transformation. I raise my eyes and see a different Ruby, with her new fringe and manicured hands and a spanking new, fashionable coat. I can even smell a new perfume.

'Ruby ...' She meets my gaze. 'You look ...' I pause for far too long. 'I mean ... I'm so grateful for all your help, and I'll make you proud I promise.'

She finishes her wine and takes my hands. 'Sonny, it's not a problem, and your journey is only just beginning. Now, what were you going to say?' And she raises her eyebrows.

I look at her. I know exactly why she's asking because I bottled it. She caught me. 'I was going to say, I noticed your new hair, and you look different. I think ... I think you are beautiful.' I look down. 'Inside and out.'

She grabs me. 'Come on, let's get you home, that would have been so nice without the caveat of the last three words.' I am left to worry about how I got it so right last night with Julia and so wrong tonight with Ruby. We drive home in silence.

I take Ringo for a walk, and when I get back, Ruby has laid everything out for us. It's informal with salmon and pork pies, cheese on sticks, crisps, ham and French bread. There are some sausage rolls and chicken bites in the oven for later. We would never have done this at home. Mum would have said keep things simple and cooked a hotpot. Karen and Jack arrive first, and we pour some drinks in the kitchen. It's weird seeing them here after being in college all day. Deborah rigs the bell, and it's at this point I realise that I have forgotten to mention our third guest. Ruby looks up, 'Who can that be?' and Ringo charges out.

'It'll be Debs,' says Karen. 'She's at school, and Sonny and her are as thick as thieves when it comes to English.' Ruby's face changes in an instant, and I let her know Debs is in our gang and is coming to my party.

'Sorry, I should have said,' and I feel like a naughty schoolboy again. Ruby says not to worry, and she greets Debs politely as Jack brings her in. I am aware that five is not as fun as four, and even though we all drink and eat, the conversation is difficult. Ruby is keeping an eye on Debs as she talks, but I feel tension when we speak about the party. I am only inviting a few friends, Mum and Dad, of course, and Jack's mum and dad too. This is to be one of his first trips out. Ruby doesn't know about the music plans. We are trying to keep them secret.

She mentions that Alphonso says he might come and I say that will be awkward as I am seeing him the following week in London and she snaps, 'I do need to have some of my friends here you know.'

Jack chips in, 'What about Mr Potter?' and this gets boos all round.

'Who is Mr Potter?' says Ruby, and it only highlights how tight our little group is. She doesn't laugh at any of our in-jokes, our college stories or silly phrases. It's like she's in a different world.

Debs asks, 'Where is the party going to be?' and now Ruby is in her element, controlling the story. 'Come on, I'll show you,' and she takes the girls to the music room with their drinks.

Jack looks at me, and when he is sure they have gone, he says, 'Awkward.' We get a beer out of the fridge and sit on the stools that Jack knows so well. 'She's jealous, mate, I'm telling you … she's jealous.' For the first time, I think it may be a possibility, but I don't really get it. Jack asks me has there been any signs, any come-ons. I say I can't think of any. She is very tactile, we do have fun but not in that way. 'For instance,' says Jack, 'Last night you told Julia she looked gorgeous. Have you ever said that to Ruby?'

Jack is getting forensic with me, and I admit that, 'Yes, earlier tonight in the pub I told Ruby she was beautiful. Inside and out.'

He looks shocked. 'Why did you say inside and out?'

'Don't know. Ruby said it was a caveat.'

'Well,' he says, 'that was stupid.' He asks why we were in the pub, and when I say we often call in after shopping, he snorts that we are like a married couple. 'This is getting worse, Sonny,' says Mr voice of bloody reason. 'You two should apply to Derek Batey for a spot on Mr & Mrs.' Now that is funny. Mum would like that. He puts on his best TV voice and says, 'Sonny, this is your final question. 'When did Ruby last see you completely naked?' We laugh together, and I think it's over, but he insists I have to answer the question. I start to go red, and he says, 'I knew it, I bloody knew it.' The look he gives me, he is invoking the pact. 'Your final answer please?' I know how this is going to sound, but I am honour bound.

'Tonight, just before we went shopping.'

Jack whoops and runs around the room. 'I knew it, I bloody knew it.' He swings his air guitar high, strums hard and hollers, 'And then she kissed me.' I am about to explain the towel falling when the ladies return to the room. Karen threads her hands into Jacks, and those two look sickly sweet. Ruby looks much more relaxed, chatting to Debs and pouring some more wine and she asks us, 'What are you boys so happy about?'

I stare at Jack, my eyes imploring him not to tell tales and he is the master of discretion. 'Just getting in the party mood for the birthday boy.' Ruby says we have one more guest if that's ok. We all nod.

Debs looks at the three of us, Karen is smiling. Debs breaks her news. 'Guys, I know I haven't told you this before, but I'm bringing my girlfriend, if that's ok?' Jack and I exchange glances. We'd never have guessed Debs was gay. I thought she was a shy, lonely English nerd, a bit like me. I don't think I know anyone who is gay. I love Debs to bits so if she wishes to bring her girlfriend to my party that's fine by me and I tell her that.

'Who is she?' Jacks asks. 'We need to know.'

Debs laughs. 'It's all pretty recent, so don't mention it at college, and if you ever meet my parents don't say a thing, not yet. She's called Linda, and we met doing Outward Bound.'

Ruby looks at us. 'No jokes you two. It's more popular than you think, as you'll discover in London, Sonny.'

I look at Jack. 'Outward Bound is popular in London, blimey.'

Ruby has to explain as we manage to keep straight faces. 'No, you know what I mean ...'

Debs sees Ruby getting stuck and saves her. 'I think she means

lesbianism. You can all say it if you wish to. It's not a problem.'
Jack and I break into 'Outward Bound' to the tune of Simon and
Garfunkel's hit tune.

My party is getting bigger by the minute, but we are all
back in friendly territory and so hungry that we demolish the
food. We run through likes and dislikes for the night and agree
that Ruby can get the dinner brought in – no one wants to be
cooking. She says she will conspire with Mum. They know the
chef at a pub, and they'll get some ideas from him. Jack and
Karen will do the balloons on the day, and Debs and Linda are
going to make some bunting. It sounds like a plan. The guys call
it a day around eleven and take forever to get coats and scarves
and boots on. I put an excitable Ringo out the back for a few
minutes, and we all say our goodbyes in the hall. Ruby thanks
everybody for coming. She loves showing off her magnificent
home, and we all kiss and cuddle and shoo them out. As we are
watching them walk away, Ruby puts her arm around my waist.
It feels good, and my mind wanders to thoughts of appearing on
'Mr & Mrs' We stand there for ages, watching the snow start to
fall, sparkling in front of the streetlights.

Ruby pulls me round to face her, takes a deep breath and says
she has forgotten to tell me something. She looks worried as she
weighs up her options.

'Alphonso called. Your audition has been brought forward to
Thursday.'

TWENTY-FOUR
LITTLE HOURS

THURSDAY 4 MARCH 1976

I don't stop yawning as we take a seat at the station. The lights are harsh, the noise brittle. Last time we were here seems a lifetime ago; I hadn't had a lesson with Julia, and I hadn't yet moved in with Ruby. I struggle to do the maths, but I'm pretty sure I have played the piano for more hours since November than my entire life. Statistically it's impressive and kind of bears out Dad's stroppy missives that I was a lazy sod, although I'm not sure I'll tell him just yet. Ruby pulls out a card like Ali Bongo, and says, 'Open it.' It's handmade and has a squiggle from Michael on the front. Two pages of perfect handwriting from Julia are inside. She knew I went into panic mode when the jazz college brought my audition forward, but she calmed me down and got me set. She has written me a beautiful note saying all of my hard work and practice will be worthwhile, and my dreams can come true. Julia has been my absolute rock, guiding me musically and helping me discover new composers and easing my fears when I am down. She said it was better for the audition to come before the party, so we just ramped up the practice. After today I can look forward to my birthday without any pressure.

'A penny for your thoughts.'

I scan the card and reread the last paragraph. I pass it to Ruby in silence. I let her digest it before sighing. 'It reads like a goodbye letter, doesn't it? The lessons are over once I'm in.'

Ruby wipes her eyes and looks at her watch and then up at the departures board. 'It doesn't have to be.' The destinations rotate, click clacking. The London train is moving upwards but still no platform. Ruby taps my leg with the letter. 'Let's just keep the lessons going. That's what Freddie would have wanted.'

I smile. 'Are you sure?' She smiles back. 'Thanks Ruby.' And I read the letter again.

'You get on well with her, don't you?'

I nod. 'There's something extraordinary about Julia. I'm not quite sure how to put it into words.'

'Freddie was the same. He said it was like having an hour of therapy. He came out lighter and feeling invincible.'

'That's a brilliant description.'

The London Euston train is allocated platform seven, and we march together, satchel and suitcases.

I feel different this time. I have come to terms with leaving Manchester, Mum and Dad, Jack and Karen and college too. I feel ready for a new life and new challenges. Julia said to me last week that there is progress every day, small bite-size chunks of progress, and when you add them up over three months, you notice you have made giant steps forward. We went back to do some of the first exercises she had given me, and I was so confident. She said, 'Imagine what three years does for you when you get to study full time.' She's prepared me very well. Ruby opens her file and starts reading, she fumbles in her bag and puts on some reading specs with red frames. I sneak a look across. She looks groovy. Her eyes flick up, mine go down, I hope she didn't catch me peeking. The tea trolley rattles into the carriage and invades our peace, but it is a welcome distraction for me. Ruby closes her papers, and the glasses go up on her head. 'You feeling good, Sonny?'

I have to admit, 'I am actually, last week's panic has given way to modest stillness.'

She shifts in her seat. 'Where do you come up with these phrases?'

'Shakespeare mostly, if you must know.'

She laughs. 'Is your English as good as your music?'

'Not any more, but I still love it. If things had been different what would you like to have studied?'

She sits up straight. 'What I love is sculpture. I used to adore art at school. Mum was brilliant at it and left me loads of pieces around the house. I used to clean them every week and move them from room to room, and in the school holidays I would try to copy them if I could get some clay.'

'Where are they now?'

'After Dad died, my uncle cleared the lot out. Bastard.' She seems chirpy. 'I'm thinking of studying next term at college, but I haven't done anything for years. I may even do it in London.' I think this would be brilliant and she lets me in on more about her family life and her struggles after her mum died. I didn't know it had been so hard. She bangs the table. 'Touch wood, it all works out. I've always been an optimist, and I'm sure it will.' We finish our tea and biscuits, and Ruby says she's going to finalise the deal with her lawyers today. 'I'm paying him off, so I don't have to worry about him ever again. He may have stressed out Freddie, but he won't get me.'

It is warm and spring-like as we walk out of the station and Ruby shouts for a taxi, we are on the same mission as last time, hotel and refresh and then round to the jazz college. We walk there today, and I love the feel and smell of London, it is so grand and welcoming. Ruby sees me looking up higher and higher and says, 'Do you fancy living here?'

'I can see myself getting used to it.'

'Me too,' agrees Ruby. 'Me too.' Alphonso is waiting at reception, and he greets Ruby like a long lost lover, so many kisses and compliments. She still has her folder on her, and he whisks her away for a meeting, she waves to me and says, 'Good luck.'

Donna appears. 'Welcome back, Sonny, good to see you again.' She escorts me to the common room, and we grab a drink and chat, it's like meeting an old friend. She explains about the new haunts, the underground jazz bars and who the cool cats are. She invites me to a gig tomorrow and I say I'll check with Ruby who's come with me to London. 'I saw her with Alphonso. She is so glamorous. Is she your girlfriend?'

'No, more of a family friend.' Donna breaks the news to me that today is entirely different to last time, more informal, they just want to have a chat and then listen to me play as a trio. She sees the fear in my eyes. 'Seriously Sonny, you're the man who got noticed playing with Charlie Watts. What are you worried about?'

'Yes, but ... I ... I didn't know it was ...'

Donna stands up. 'Come on, that's the bad news. The good news is I am on bass, and Fi is on the kit, and we have an hour to practise.'

She drags me to the audition room. It's all set up. Fi is smashing the drums as we go in, she nods her shaved head but doesn't let up. Donna asks me about the pieces I've prepped, and I get my music out. The drums stop. 'Nice satchel,' says Fi as she introduces herself, and she insists I come to the gig tomorrow. Donna says, 'He's got his girlfriend in tow so we may not see him.'

'She's not my girlfriend,' I protest.

Donna winks at Fi and says, 'Yeah, right. Ok, these three are fine, perfect in fact for an audition. Three different composers, three different styles and great tunes. Good choices, Sonny.'

I tell them, 'I have the most amazing teacher, and she's helped me. Julia, who used to come here, and she knows Alphonso and ...'

Fi looks at me. 'I mean I'm not at all cynical, but you are the chosen one, aren't you?'

Donna takes charge. 'Come on, guys. We have one hour before they come in. She clicks her fingers. Ok, tune one, "I Fall in Love Too Easily" by Jule Styne. Four four and sixty beats per minute, nice and slow. Sonny, let's just play it through straight, no bells and whistles.' Fi counts us in, and it feels so relaxed, I have played this song hundreds of times with Julia and on my own, and it feels so much smoother with a rhythm section. I start smiling towards the end. Donna is in the middle. I am facing her, drums to my right. She nods at me. 'Good, that was fine. Let's run it again, enjoy it this time. Show us you are enjoying it, look up at us, let us know you know we're together on this, communicate.' And she emphasises, 'Communicate.' Fi sets us off, and I find the groove. Oh yes, I'm riding the wave, and I'm looking at the girls and taking them with me this time. 'Perfect,' says Donna. 'One last time. And this time, you take sixteen bars or thirty-two or whatever you need and go for it, just let us know what you are doing and when you want to go back to the top.' That's it. In fifteen minutes, we have run through three times and nailed it. I couldn't have done this without Julia.

'Tune two, "What a Difference a Day Makes" by Maria Grever. Ninety beats per minute, also in four four. Have you heard the Dinah Washington version, Sonny?'

I look up. 'I sure have, it's beautiful. That's the version Julia got me into.' Fi gets the brushes, and we go, the same format, three times through.

Donna shrieks at the last tune. '"Crocodile Rock", Elton John, four four and a hundred and sixty beats per minute. Wow, this will be fun. Sonny, all the bells and whistles first time, you must know this one.' I give her the thumbs-up, and Fi looks at me and waits. She wants me to lead. I close my eyes, the stadium erupts … 'One, two, three, four …'

An hour later and I have played all three to the panel, and they are making their way forward. Mrs Challinor looks me up and down, raises an eyebrow and shakes my hand, holding on to it. 'Do tell me, how is Julia?' I let her know that she is really well and that I have been seeing her twice a week. She smiles. 'Believe me, it shows. Well done.' And that's it. Two of them leave, and Alphonso remains. He's much more demonstrative, congratulating me enthusiastically and thanking the girls for their assistance.

Ruby runs in as they are packing up. 'Sonny, I just bumped into Eloise, she said it was perfect.' And she hugs me. I look at Donna, and she winks at me and nudges Fi. They both put their thumbs up and go boss-eyed on purpose.

'Ruby, this is Donna, who will be my buddy if I get in, and this is Fi. These guys saved my ass today.'

Alphonso grabs my hands. 'Sonny, let me put you out of your misery. I am very pleased to tell you we are delighted to accept you as a student, and we have awarded you the inaugural Smithson Scholarship for Jazz Pianists 1976. Your fees are covered, welcome on board.' My heart skips a beat, the girls jump on me, Ruby can't stop crying and Alphonso is air-kissing everyone. It takes a few minutes for us all to calm down, and I ask Ruby if we can take the girls for a drink to say thank you, and of course she says yes.

'Thanks, Ruby, you have been amazing since the day I played at ...' and for a split second I think of Freddie, and I glance at Ruby, and I know she's thinking of him too. I mouth, 'Thank you,' as she listens to Alphonso carrying on even if her mind is elsewhere. We walk out of college, heading for a pub and I ask Alphonso if I can make a phone call from reception. He tells the girls to go ahead. He'll walk me round in a minute. Ruby waves. She understands this has been a team effort.

I fetch a scrap of paper out of my pocket and dial the number. 'Julia, it's Sonny. We bloody did it.' I burst into tears and lose my ability to speak. Alphonso takes the phone from me, and he has tears in his eyes too. He thanks her over and over again and passes the phone back to me. 'Julia, thank you for everything. You've been amazing.'

I can tell she is crying. 'Thank you, Sonny, for keeping me going, for making me believe in music once again. You'll be in very safe hands with Alphonso. See you on Saturday night for the party.'

Alphonso puts the phone down and gets quite emotional. 'You are surrounded by exceptional women, Sonny. Ruby and Julia are two beautiful ladies and today Donna and Fi. These women are watching you grow into a fine young musician, but Ruby tells me you also have someone who is watching you grow into a fine young son, and that's even more important.'

He hands me the phone. 'Thank you, Alphonso. I am so excited, I'd completely forgotten.'

I need no scrap of paper this time. I spin that dial as fast as I can, and it connects immediately. 'Hello?'

'Hello, Mum, I did it.' I'm sure they can hear the scream in the pub.

Scattered Pictures

Saturday 6 March 1976

I'm lying in bed, I'm eighteen, I have just got my place at London Jazz College, and I am about to party. Does it get any better? I have about two hours of peace and quiet before the team descend to help prepare the music room. I run down the stairs in my scruffs ready to take Ringo out, but he's already been walked and is asleep in his basket. There's a note by the kettle saying, 'Dog walked, shopping with your mum'. And it says 'PS, Happy Birthday X.' Again. Ruby has been saying it all week. My birthday was actually on Monday. It was a little weird as we went round to Mum and Dad's. I was so nervous as I was thinking of my audition, and felt it was too early celebrate. Mum cooked my favourite meal from when I was twelve, bangers and mash with Heinz beans, and Dad asked me what I'd be playing on Thursday. When I told him about the Elton John track he almost lost it. I'm sure Mum kicked him under the table to stop one of his usual diatribes against the poofs and the pansies and pop music.

I add so much sugar to my cornflakes they are amazing, and the syrupy goo at the end wakes me up with a sugar rush. I have a steaming hot shower, and as I come down the stairs for the second time today, a team of people are streaming through the doors carrying tables, chairs, boxes and more. Ruby looks up and shouts, 'Kitchen,' at me and adds, 'you're not meant to see this bit.' She laughs as she follows me in. 'Right, birthday boy, you stay here until I say so. Ralf will be along in a while, you first and then me.' She pops some Champagne, and as we raise our glasses, she toasts, 'To London, for both of us.'

I am so happy. 'To London.'

Jack's head appears through the door singing, 'Hello young lovers, wherever you are.'

Ruby ticks him off, 'Jack, behave please,' and Karen gives him a playful slap. Ruby dishes out more bubbles, and then there is a strange man knocking on the French doors. Ruby swings them open. 'Ralfyyyyy, it's been too long,' she says, and air kisses London style. He drags a massive case behind him and as he finishes putting everything down Ruby thrusts a glass in his hand.

'Don't mind if I do, don't mind if I do.' He looks at me, disapproves of my long hair in one glance, beckons me to the stool and wraps a huge barber's cape around me. 'Happy birthday, happy birthday.' He repeats everything he says with a stronger emphasis the second time.

Jack and Karen make a hasty exit and Ruby gives a magazine photo to Ralf and says, 'The glamorous couple.'

He examines it. 'Ooooh, Robert Redford, Robert Redford.' He shows me the photo from *The Way We Were* with Barbra Streisand, who looks amazing, raises both eyebrows higher than I have ever seen, sniffs and says, 'I'll see what I can do.' I am just about to remind him when he grimaces, 'I said, I'll see what I can do.' Despite my fears, the next hour is hilarious as we trade stories about music, film and Hollywood gossip. After two more glasses of Champagne for both us, we are best mates and Ralfy Baby, as he will be forever known is coming to my party, happy days.

Ruby returns on the hour, looks at me and shouts, 'Oh yes, definitely Robert Redford,' and Ralfy Baby looks pleased. 'All the suppliers have left, the lounge is set so don't go in there.' It is nearly 2 pm, and Jack and Karen have secured the music room as I told them to and I tell Ruby she is barred. I nip out as the doorbell goes, shutting the door behind me. Ralfy Baby says I have two hours before he sets Ruby free.

I let Julia in. She is carrying a present for me and gives me the biggest hug and says congratulations. We head for the music room. It's time to practise. I burp loudly. 'Pardon me. I shouldn't have had the second or third glass.' The room is looking great, sofas have been squashed together, more chairs added, balloons everywhere and now Debs and Linda have stayed as well to do the bunting. We run through everything a few times and move the furniture again. This is a room for a party.

As soon as Ralfy Baby leaves I go into the kitchen for some water. Ruby closes the sliding doors and turns to me. 'Look at us, preened and ready to party. We are the glamorous couple.' I feel ready to sleep, let alone party. The London trip and the Champagne have caught up with me. 'Oh, oh, has someone peaked too soon?' Ruby takes charge, Alka-Seltzer appears, a cup of tea follows, then a cheese sandwich. Then more tea. 'Don't worry, we have three hours till the guests arrive. I'm going for a long soak, you have a sleep.' Ruby can be bossy, but she's also a mind reader. She stares at me. 'And don't you dare call me bossy.' We climb the stairs arm in arm, Ruby singing Streisand's 'The Way We Were'. She pushes me towards my room, 'I'll come and get you in a while – there's one final surprise.' I hit the bed hard and lose myself in dreams of Ruby. What have I done to deserve her?

I'm tossing and turning and aware that someone is in my room or my dreams or both. I'm sure I shut the curtains, but now the light is flooding in. 'Sonny, it's party time.' I rub my eyes and look up as Ruby bends down. 'Hello, pretty boy. You look ruffled, my little Robert Redford.' I strain to focus, but when I do, Ruby's breasts are in front of me, jiggling from side to side in her dressing gown. She reaches across to tousle my hair, and her left boob plays peek-a-boo with me. I'm wide awake and entranced. 'Come on, Sonny. Someone is having a party tonight.' I can't speak, my mind's racing as fast, my blood is pumping, I manage a cough as she stands up and adjusts her gown, tying the drawstring around her waist. She turns to the left. 'Ta-da.' There are three sets of clothes hanging on the cupboard doors. Ruby is very pleased with herself. 'I spoke to Johnny at Kendals, he had your sizes from the suit measuring. Take your pick. I'm off to get changed. You have thirty minutes.'

I'm trying things on when the doorbell goes, and Ruby shouts, 'You get it.'

I rush to put on my jacket and new shoes. It rings for a second time as I jump the last few stairs. 'I'm coming.' I am lost for words. I stare at Mum who looks like ... like I have never seen her before. She is so glamorous, she is wearing a gorgeous, sparkly dress, her hair is wavy, and she has makeup on. She's not like my mum at all.

She speaks first. 'Sonny, you look handsome, where did these come from?' And she feels my new corduroy jacket.

'Kendals.'

She mutters, 'You too.'

I realise where she was this morning. 'Ruby took you shopping, didn't she?'

Mum nods and does a twirl. 'I couldn't stop her. We were going to see the chef, but somehow ended up in Manchester having coffee and then she told me that Freddie had left loads on his account so I'd be doing her a favour.' She hates people spending money on her but adds, 'It's very difficult to say no to Ruby.' We agree on that, and she does look fabulous now that she's done it. When I ask her what Dad thinks of his new lady, she goes quiet and admits he doesn't know yet as United are playing, but he'll soon find out.

We head through to the kitchen, and I open the fridge. It has been topped up with a dozen bottles of Champagne. Mum looks at me. 'This isn't normal, Sonny.' I know what she's saying, and I've thought it too. She seems disappointed.

'Mum, what you go through every week with Dad, what you've been through, that's not normal either. What is normal for any of us?'

The doorbell saves me going on. Ruby shouts, 'Don't come out, it's the caterers.'

Mum tilts her head, and her eyes roll, and I ask her, 'Doesn't every eighteen year old have caterers?' We laugh about it as I pour us both a glass of fizz. 'Cheers.'

'You know I'm very proud of you, Sonny, and I love Ruby to bits. I just don't know where all this money comes from.' She feels the cut of the crystal glass. 'But wherever this ends up, I'll always be there for you.'

I'm in too deep. I'm loving this life too much, but I can't say it as it would break Mum's heart. 'That's why I am one very lucky boy.'

'You picked up the drums as a toddler on a plastic kit. Then there was the guitar when you were nine. Then the piano lessons, which Granddad paid for. You were always so musical.' She gives me a big Mum cuddle. 'Happy Birthday again and never forget we love you.'

Ruby comes in right in the middle of our cuddle. 'Put him down, Jess. He's a man now.' Mum laughs and lets me go, and we turn round and see Ruby in her new outfit. She has stolen my thunder.

Ruby is wearing a sleeveless top with wide flared pants, and nothing is left to the imagination – I can still see those breasts. She comes close and ruffles my hair. 'Don't you think your boy looks like Robert Redford?'

Mum dithers, agrees eventually and says, 'You look stunning, Ruby.'

'And so do you, Jess, just perfect. I hope Pete thinks so too.'

Ruby twirls and poses and cuddles and kisses everyone as they arrive, directing the catering staff to top up. We all end up in the lounge with staff serving canapes and dips. Dad arrives late. I'm sure he's had a few beers already. He says hi to Mum and doesn't even mention her new look. She looks at me, raises her arms and mouths, 'Why do I even bother?' He sits down with Jack's mum and dad, and I hear him saying he's never seen anything like it. My mates are having fun, mainly due to the free drink and we talk about the old days at school. Very late to arrive is Ralfy Baby who greets me like the brother or lover he's never met, just as we are finishing our air kisses Dad walks by, scans Ralfy and sneers. 'Who's this then?'

I say very loudly, 'Dad, this is my hairdresser, Ralfy Baby,' and Ralf takes my cue, camps it up and says, 'Pleased to meet you.' He offers his perfectly manicured hand. 'Very pleased to meet you.'

Dad refuses, mutters, 'Fucking hell,' under his breath and scuttles off. We burst out laughing. It's getting closer and closer to performance time, and I just want to get it over with. It's getting in the way of partying.

Julia looks nervous too, and we sneak off to the music room and have a quick playthrough. She has an amazing voice. I look at her. 'Stephen is going to be so surprised.'

'I know, he's never heard me sing in public before.' There is something about Julia; she's tiny and vulnerable, and I love her to bits. 'This is all a bit unreal, isn't it?' she says.

'You sound like my mum. She says it isn't normal.'

Julia looks teary. 'You know ...' A minute passes.

'Know what?'

'Freddie would have loved this, I'm sure. He loved positive people, and you've brought us all together.'

I wasn't expecting that. 'Have I?'

Julia becomes emotional. 'Yes, Sonny, I've spoken to Ruby about it. She adores you. You've kept her going through some very dark times. Even Jack said last week he never would have played again without you, and I am going to sing in public tonight. It's you, Sonny. It's you. You're the glue.' She begins to cry. I take her in my arms, just the two of us. This is a friendship that is going to last forever.

Ruby has hired a photographer for my party, and she's been sneaking around getting shots. Before we all move to the music room, she claps her hands and shouts, 'Time for some formal photos for the grandchildren.' First up is Mum and Dad, me in the middle.

'Smile.' Mum hangs on to me. Dad takes the mick out of my new jacket.

Ruby comes up with two full glasses of Champagne. 'We're next.'

The photographer jokes, 'Is this your girlfriend?' and I shout, 'I wish.' Before the bulb has even flashed I hear Dad's voice: 'Be careful what you wish for.'

I look over. The whole room turns around, and Dad is knocked backwards from a slap to the face. It sounds like a cymbal crashing. 'I was only joking,' he protests, but the atmosphere dies. Ruby walks out, the photographer follows, and Dad storms off too. Someone turns the music up, thank goodness, the desserts are served, and the hubbub returns slowly.

Mum tries to leave the room, but I catch her arm, and she apologises to me. 'Mum, you have nothing to apologise for.'

She looks devastated. 'I'm sorry. I shouldn't have hit him at your party.'

'I'm surprised you haven't done it before.' I lead her through to the kitchen, and Ruby is entertaining already. Mum goes to say sorry, but Ruby raises her hand and won't hear of it. 'Nothing stops the party,' she says, and she calls everybody through.

Mum and I are alone in the kitchen, Ringo in his bed.

'This is where it all started, Mum, at Freddie's wake.'

'God, that seems so long ago. I remember it so well. You surprised me that night.'

'I surprised myself. Dad missed that performance too.'

She looks at me. Her energy drains away. 'I don't know how to fix him, Sonny, I just can't do it anymore.'

'You don't have to, Mum, not tonight, not ever. It's his responsibility to change, not yours.'

She hugs me. 'You've grown up so fast.'

'I have got the best mum, and I'll look after you. Promise.'

'I don't know what I've done to deserve you.'

Julia coughs. 'Sorry to disturb you two, but everybody is ready in the music room.'

Mum wipes away a tear or two and Julia takes her hand. 'You are going to be so surprised tonight, Jess, you really are.'

Mum looks at me with pride.

'Again.'

A Nightingale Sang

Julia leads us in, and everybody is standing and cheering for me, and they all bellow happy birthday. Everyone is shouting, 'Speech, speech,' and for once I am at ease, not the usual bundle of nerves. Jack put in a small PA for us earlier, and he says he'll just test it for me, but in reality, he grabs the mic and commands the room. 'Ladies and Gentlemen,' the room takes ages to go quiet, and Jack is there 'Shushing' and 'Quiet please'. Jack is like the MC at a posh wedding, he is smart, funny and a natural at this game. He tells stories about our childhood, some of the scrapes we got into, some of the girls we kissed, and he reminds everyone that I have made it to London to study at music college. The room erupts. 'I am so proud to call this man my best mate.' He hands me the microphone.

The applause carries on for ages, and I remember reading in the prospectus there is a module called mic technique. I am going to have to get used to this. Then silence, just for a few seconds, and I am as surprised as anyone when this deep, confident voice emerges from the speakers. It's weird when you hear yourself: this voice in your head that stumbles and stutters, mumbles and mutters and rarely makes sense can sound so sonorous and capable. 'Hello and thank you for coming to my party. We are going to play some music,' I say, and the whole room cheers again. 'But before that, I have to thank a few people who have nurtured my dreams. Some for a very long time and some very recently.' I thank Jack and Karen, my musical buddies, I thank Mum for a lifetime of encouragement, my long lost granddad for paying for my first piano lessons. 'Now to two very special ladies who have had the most profound effect on my life. Without them, I would never have made it to London. Julia, who made the same move many years ago, and who is now the most amazing piano teacher and dear friend, and Ruby, whose house we are in tonight.' I can't stop the cheering. It just goes on and on, everyone is so grateful. I spot Jack and Karen either side of her, arms around her waist with Ruby beaming. 'To Ruby, who has taken me in, lent me this music room, encouraged me to reach for the stars, a million thank yous.' I look at everyone's faces, they are so happy for me, and I have said enough. Ruby walks up to me and gives me a hug, kisses me on the cheek. 'Start playing as soon as you're ready, I'll be one minute.'

I put the mic in its stand and look at Julia, 'Let's play.'

I begin 'What Kind Of Fool Am I' and again the room echoes with applause. I'll take this audience every night of the week for the rest of my life. I look at Stephen, and he nods back as he holds on to Julia. Little does he know. I finish the first verse, and Julia wriggles free and walks to the mic, and I am now the accompanist, not the birthday boy. She is about to show this room just what London is missing. From the first note, the room knows she is the real deal. She has gone up a few notches since practice. I turn to look at Stephen, and he's not there. In his place is Ruby and Alphonso, that's why she nipped out, and he's crying like a baby and Ruby is wiping away his tears. I spot Stephen stood up at the back. A shaky camera held up high. He is trying to focus through misty eyes. He spots me and gives me a thumbs-up. I have helped someone else achieve their dream, and it feels incredible. After a few minutes, Julia takes her bow, and the atmosphere is electric. I have an urge to let people know how that duet came about, it just feels right.

I stand up and take the mic. 'Thank you. That was a version that Julia originally heard in Manchester in 1966, and it changed her life. It made her want to study jazz.' Julia only has eyes for Stephen, so I get bolder. 'Julia,' she looks up, 'the man who taught Julia for three years is Alphonso, and he's here tonight.' I point to him on the sofa and Julia screams and runs to him. I love this role. Everyone is so happy. I play a couple of tunes solo and then get Jack up for some fun and surprise his mum and dad as we play a few tunes together. Jack announces the last song and calls Karen up to sing. Our little trio reunites for one final performance. 'Crocodile Rock' booms out, everyone sings along, and Julia takes over from me for the last few verses. I pull Mum up, and we dance like crazy with everyone else, whooping, kissing and hugging. What a birthday, something I will remember forever.

I snatch a beer as soon as the music stops and my closest buddies form a circle of love. Jack is pumped. 'It will never be better than this.' We are so high from the adrenaline of performing. It is something else. Debs and Linda break in congratulating us, then Jack's Mum and Dad come over and tell us we never played like that at their house. A few other mates remind us all when we ruined Mr Potter's lesson with 'Crocodile

Rock', and Karen said, 'That's what gave us the idea,' and we all burst out laughing.

I scan the room for Mum. I hope she's alright. I find her in the lounge sitting with Julia and Stephen, and Alphonso is holding Ruby's hands and speaking at a hundred miles an hour. I kneel next to Mum, and she puts her arm around me. Julia rubs my shoulder. 'I've told your mum how hard you have been working.'

Mum smiles. 'That was fantastic.'

'Thanks, Mum. I loved every minute, can't wait to get to London.'

My new friend and mentor has pushed me so hard. She is a cut above us all, and for one night only, she showed us. Stephen asks me if I want another beer, so I stand up and go to the kitchen with him, he gets very emotional as he says that was the best night of his life, he can't stop thanking me. He says Julia always told him about the performing and singing, but that was the first time he'd seen her. 'And the last,' says Julia, cuddling him from behind. He breaks down again, so I leave them alone to return to the lounge, saying goodbye to quite a few people as I mooch down the hall.

Alphonso is still hanging on to Julia, even though Mum has joined them, but breaks free as I walk in. He looks drunk already. 'My dear boy, you never told me how beautiful your mother was.' He admonishes me and tells Mum I will be in a very safe pair of hands from September. 'And what about Julia? She was my star pupil many moons ago, no?' We all rave about her singing tonight, and I am cocooned in a room full of love and beautiful people. Alphonso punctures the atmosphere. 'Where is your father, Sonny? I need to meet your father.'

Ruby escorts Mum out as fast as she can and leaves me to explain. I am about to tell the whole truth and nothing but the truth when Julia saves me. She gives Alphonso the biggest of cuddles and says Ruby has invited her round tomorrow for a good chat and she's going to bring Michael, and we can all have lunch. 'No problema, and Julia tonight was exquisite. I am so happy to be here for that concerto.' I kiss Julia and thank her over and over again. Stephen rescues her from my clutches, and they leave the party. Alphonso puts a record on and sits down, head back, and is soon snoring.

The numbers are dwindling. Jack's mum and dad leave and give Mum a lift home on the promise that I visit her tomorrow. She goes to say sorry on the way out but changes to, 'Happy birthday, Sonny, that was some party. All the best shows seem to happen here.' We kiss goodnight. Only Jack and Karen are left now, tidying up even when told not to. Ruby lets Ringo out the back, and we have our first catch up for hours with a mug of tea. 'That was some party, Sonny.'

'It was amazing. Thank you so much.' It feels natural to hold her hand. She is a little unsteady and says we are going to have so much fun in London together.

I may be right, or I may be wrong, but I'm perfectly willing to swear that at that very moment I heard … 'You know when you said you wish I were your girlfriend?' She squeezes my hand, and she looks vulnerable as I catch a glimpse of her. She's waiting for me to answer, and she comes closer, our lips are almost touching, and I know she's going to kiss me …

'Good night, you two,' shouts Jack from the kitchen and Ringo charges past us.

Inside, Jack pulls me to one side. 'Sonny, I saw that. You do know she was going to kiss you.'

I agree. 'I think you're right, but what do I do?'

Jack purses his lips. 'What do you do? What do you want to do?'

I tell him. 'I've never really thought it, but now I am thinking about it, it feels quite nice.'

Jack is my new relationship counsellor. 'Well bloody get on with it then.' He smiles. 'I knew it, I bloody knew it.'

I'm not so sure. 'Anyway, the moment's gone, it must be the drink.'

Alphonso wanders in and asks for an espresso. Ruby looks up from wiping the surfaces. 'At this time of night?' She pours him a glass of water and shows him to the guest room. She shouts bye to Jack and Karen. We have a little hug, and I tell them both that better not be the last time we play together. Karen changes her shoes to walk home, and I let them out and shut up shop. Ringo's asleep already. I lock the French doors. I check the music room and walk along the hall and turn the lights off in the lounge. Ruby is coming down the stairs. She still looks like a movie queen. She has the photo in her hand, the one she showed Ralfy Baby earlier.

I take a look at it. They look like a fantastic couple.

'Have you seen the film?'

I say, 'No, but I'd like to.'

'Maybe in London?'

She holds my hand as we climb the stairs. We've done this a hundred times, and yet it feels different, more measured and thoughtful. It's goodnight again. We get our cheeks hopelessly out of step, and we meet in the middle. And the kiss. This kiss.

This long, long kiss that lasts forever. This kiss that launches a thousand thoughts in under a second. Her arms, her breath, her little whimper as she pulls me in, and then her tension softens as she leans into me and I support her. 'Follow me, Sonny.'

Ruby leads me across the landing and I'm scared, so scared about ruining this moment. I sober up by the time we enter her bedroom, and Ruby sits on the bed and pats the sheets. Moonlight shimmers through the windows. She kisses me again and my chest tightens and the room spins a little.

'I...' She starts undoing my buttons and I forget to breathe. I don't say a word. Slowly, button by button, she's kissing me and undressing me and then I'm naked and thinking, 'This is it.' Ruby takes off her clothes, and I can't take my eyes off her. She straddles me. Her smile drops for a moment as she notices a bedside photo from her wedding day. She leans over and her breasts brush my face as she turns it over. I am smothered in kisses and hands and breasts and I submit willingly. Ruby kisses my cheek and whispers, 'Happy birthday.' She sits up, reaches down and caresses me. She raises her hips, hovers above me, teasing me for way too long. As she lowers herself I call out and I can't stop myself, and Ruby lifts my hands to her breasts and says, 'Ssssshh.' Her outline in the low light is beautiful and she continues to rise and fall and then she collapses on me, her breathing sounds so beautiful. We kiss for ages until she peels herself off and goes to the bathroom. I'm wide awake when Ruby returns, backs into me, and pulls my arms around her. 'Goodnight, Sonny.'

I'm lying in bed, I'm eighteen, I have just got my place at London Jazz College, and I have partied hard. Does it get any better? Well, yes, it does. I mean it did, it actually did, and I think of Jack who always says, 'I knew it. I bloody knew it.'

He really did, it's just that I didn't.

Ruby kissed me and lit a fire I can't put out.

NORTH, SOUTH, EAST, WEST

MONDAY 5 APRIL 1976

Stephen lets me in the house but can't look me in the eyes. Little Michael runs up and bear-hugs my legs, and I crouch down to play fight.

'Tea?' asks Stephen

'Yes, please.'

This aloofness has been going on for a few weeks now. I know Julia disapproves of my changing relationship with Ruby, and she must have told her husband. I haven't told anyone except Julia, not even Jack. I'm sitting at the piano dreaming of getting away to London as soon as I possibly can when he hands me the mug. Stephen studies me. I am fed up being treated like a naughty schoolboy. 'Stephen, I haven't done anything wrong.' We stare at each other.

'Look mate, I'm no good at this relationship stuff, but you are only eighteen and ...'

I'm frustrated and ready to fight. 'What has age got to do with anything?'

'Nothing really but ...' the front door opens and Julia calls 'Hello' to anyone listening. She appears in the room holding

Michael and looks at both of us and she knows what we were talking about.

'I'm sorry, Julia, I just can't go on like this. It feels like you are judging me for falling in love.'

'Give me five minutes.' Julia rushes out, and it feels even more awkward.

I look up at Stephen. 'Do you remember when I told you to tell your wife she looked gorgeous?'

'Yes.'

'I feel the same about Ruby. It is as simple as that.' I shrug my shoulders, he must understand.

'I know, I know, but ...'

'There are no buts. It's just Ruby and me against the world.'

He looks at me, and I can see he understands and breaks into a half-smile. 'I know where you're coming from. I'm a Catholic who married an English girl. I've been there with the disappointing comments and snide remarks.'

'Really?'

'Look, don't say anything to Julia, but good luck.' He shakes my hand as if we are sealing a deal. 'Just be careful.' He sounds like my dad. He smiles again and nods. 'Fucking hell, eighteen, you jammy bastard.'

'It's not like that,' I insist. 'It's so much deeper.' I mean it.

'Yeah, right.'

Julia shouts to him from upstairs, and Stephen winks at me as he leaves. It is so frustrating. I've been studying love for years, the language of love, the words, the dynamics and poetry but no one told me about the feelings. And now these two who are in 'in love' are telling me it's not right. I want to shout it from the rooftops, I want to tell Jack and even my mum, but Ruby says not yet.

Julia comes back in, puts her brew down and joins me on the double piano stool. She looks at the sheet music on the stand. 'What Are You Doing The Rest of Your Life?' Julia laughs. 'That's pretty apt, isn't it?' She makes me laugh. She takes my right hand, and we face each other. Julia is so sweet, and she says, 'Look, we all fall in love at different points in our lives.' She says there are no rules, no definitions of the correct age, colour or creed. There's just love, and it's as simple as that. 'If you are in love, then that's a beautiful thing.' She asks the question with her eyes. I pause. 'Are you sure?'

'I think I am.'

'If you are, and Ruby is too, then you have nothing to worry about.' She helps me understand what other people may think. What will my parents say? What will my friends say? 'Some of Ruby's friends may think it's too soon.'

'You sound like Ruby.'

'She's a bit older, Sonny, I presume she realises ...'

'It's wrong.'

'No. Not wrong, just different. Don't think of it as wrong.'

'I don't.'

'Sonny, this may take some time to work through. Just enjoy it while you can, without all the baggage of other people's opinions.'

I ask her what she means, and she explains that if our target is to get to London and be a couple, then it's not that far away, so fly under the radar for another few months and reach your destination together with no one any the wiser. 'And more importantly, no judgment from anyone up here.' I understand what she's saying, but I want to tell someone. I need to tell someone.

'Let's play,' she says, but my mind is elsewhere, and she knows it. We go through the motions, up and down and round and round. Julia calls it early and sends me packing. 'Do not let … being in love … affect your practice young man. Else you'll have me to answer to.' I smile. She smiles back. 'Are you worried?'

'A little bit.'

She understands me, I know she does, and I love having Julia as my confidante. 'See you Thursday. Chin up.'

I walk away, lost in my thoughts, not thinking where my footsteps are carrying me. In another world, far from here, Julia and I would make a great team. I daydream about how many times people fall in love in their lifetime, about how many potential partners we may meet and reject. How, like Ruby, we get second chances if partners die and how you feel if your partners change like Dad has on Mum. Why is it so hard?

I end up outside Jack's house.

A car window winds down. 'Hi, Sonny,' Mrs Hammond says. 'You after Jack? Watch this.' She beeps her horn, and he appears at the window as his mum gets out of her new Vauxhall Viva. The car looks smart. She's learned to drive since the accident, and Jack said something about an insurance payout, so things are getting better for his dad. He comes out, surprised to see me. We walk away from the house saying nothing at all, he knows me so well.

I point to bench. 'This is serious, Jack.'

'Ok, let me know then, and I'll see if I can help.'

'I don't know where to start, everything has gone so fast, but I just have to tell someone as my head is about to explode.'

I make Jack promise not to tell a soul. Once he agrees, I just blurt it out, 'I'm in love with Ruby,' and he looks at me like I'd be mad not to be.

He says, 'What's the problem. She's gorgeous.' He says she has a fantastic house, she lets me use the music room, and she's helped me get to London to study.

'It's more than that. It's way more than that. We are now a couple, we live together and we ... sleep in the same room.'

'Oh, I see.' Now he understands. 'Blimey, Sonny, when did this happen?'

'She kissed me at my party after you left.'

'So how did you ... you know.'

I look at Jack. I wouldn't have this chat with anyone else in the world. 'Have you and Karen?'

'Almost ... but we haven't got a nice space like you, so it's a bit hit and miss. You?'

I smile, laugh and then shout. 'Jack, it was bloody amazing. It was exactly like the movies, she took my clothes off, we couldn't stop kissing, and then ... Let's just say she took control.'

Jack was wide-eyed. 'That's beautiful, man.'

'The next day we pretended it didn't happen. It just wasn't spoken about as we had so many visitors and then as soon as I shut the front door, she pounced on me. We didn't even make it upstairs. Ruby dragged me to the sofa and ... we did it again.'

I tell Jack exactly how I remember the rest of the Sunday night. We chatted for a bit, we were both ok with what happened, and then she grabbed a bottle of Champagne, took me upstairs and ran the deepest bath. I was still so nervous. She undressed me, and we jumped in the tub together, it was heaven. Jack sat bolt upright.

'Bloody hell, Sonny, this is amazing.'

My recollection is perfect. I have relived those two nights for five weeks now, dreaming about them as I wrap my arms around Ruby and fall asleep. We stayed in the bath and talked for hours until we ran out of hot water.

'That's the night I moved in with her if you know what I mean. Now we have a bath every night. It feels so right.'

'And have you, you know ... Again?'

I remind Jack about his promise to keep quiet. 'Yes, of course we have. It's so weird how all these things we used to talk about, they become normal.' Jack asks me what I mean, and I remind him about schoolboy dreams, leaving home, not seeing your parents all the time, visiting pubs, and then I spice it up with seeing a naked Ruby every night as we get undressed, have a bath and then make love.

'This is too much,' says Jack. 'I'm overcome.' He acts all daft, mopping his brow and pretending to faint. I feel so relieved for finally telling someone, and we agree to meet on Wednesday evening as Ruby is going to London to look at some property. I tell him we're going to get a place in London so we can be together whilst I study and Ruby is probably going back to college too. Nothing can stop us.

He smacks me on my back. 'You are sorted, mate. It's brilliant news.' Then he says, 'Don't forget contraception. Remember the lesson at school.' And he mimes putting a condom on a cucumber.

As we walk back, Mrs Hammond is coming out of the house, and we see her lean over the bonnet.

Jack says, 'Wait till you see this, you'll be so jealous.'

We run like mad men as his mum steps back from the car. A bright new 'L' plate has pride of place.

'I'm learning to drive, Sonny. How about that?'

Mrs Hammond says, 'I must be mad teaching him, I've only just learned myself.'

Jack gets behind the wheel, pretending he's Stirling Moss and Mrs Hammond shakes her head.

'It seems like yesterday I was cheering you both on at sports day and now look at you. Growing up, eighteen, Jack has a girlfriend, college and cars.'

I give Mrs Hammond a hug, Mr Hammond waves at us from the lounge, everything feels great. Jack climbs out and locks it like it is his car. His Mum clicks her fingers for the keys and asks, 'Are you coming in, Sonny?'

'No, not tonight. Got to get back and walk the dog.'

Jack winks at me. 'Sonny said he needs a bath tonight, Mum.'

I run back home. I'm so much lighter now I've confided in Jack. I turn the key in the lock, and I hear Ringo barking, and Ruby runs out to meet me. Julia and my mum follow her. I look puzzled. 'Is everything ok?' Ruby bursts out crying, Julia says not to worry and leaves. Mum and me go into the kitchen.

'Have you seen the time, Sonny?' says Mum.

I look at the clock and realise it's nearly three hours since I furnished my piano lesson. 'Oops. Sorry.'

Ruby comes back in. 'No it's my fault, I'm sorry, I panicked. I called Julia when you were so late, and she said you might have been upset, then we rang your mum and ...'

Mum cuts her off. 'Where have you been, Sonny?'

'I was at Jack's house. Mrs Hammond's got a new car, Jack has got his L plates and we just ended up chatting.' I tell them I wasn't upset, just tired and the Easter break can't come soon enough as I have been working so hard.

Mum grimaces and sounds like Dad when she says, 'Julia thinks you have gone off the boil a bit since your birthday party.'

I walk her home and reassure her everything will be fine. I ask her about her studies to try and get her off the subject. She doesn't mention Ruby, so I assume our secret is safe. I was worried when I saw Julia there. 'Ruby panicked, that's all. And it's understandable after everything that happened to Freddie.' It all becomes clear. Julia told her I was upset, which set off a train of thoughts ... Oh God, what have I done? I shout hi to Dad and run back to Waverly for the second time tonight.

My heart is racing as fast as my thoughts are swirling and I get it now, she needs reassurance from me and not the other way round. I charge through the front door, up the stairs, undressing as I go and jump in the bath.

She looks at me with her watery eyes. And we kiss. And kiss again.

'I love you, Ruby.'

Autumn Leaves

The buzzer goes, and I drop the knife and rush over.

'Hi, it's Donna and Frank, can't wait to see you.'

'OK, come in. First floor.'

I let them in the building, open my front door and listen as they climb the stairs. I love this place. We live in Blenheim Street, Mayfair, in a beautiful period building with the highest ceilings imaginable. Ruby has rented it for three years. She goes off every day to Bayswater, and I walk to the jazz college. We have fallen into a daily pattern of studying, and at weekends we walk everywhere, museums, gigs, galleries. Everyone we meet assumes we are a couple, and there are no questions. These old familiar places become very dear to me. Ruby says they are like a well-worn pair of slippers, lovely to keep returning to. And we do. Autumn has been revealing in London, long walks through the parks, getting to know all of the landmarks and watching the world go by as we walk alongside the Thames.

I'm chopping the veg as they walk in and I shout, 'Won't be a minute, take a look around.' I can hear them in the lounge as

I finish drying my hands and go through. Frank is on the piano as Donna hugs me.

'Just your average student flat then,' she says.

I never get used to the money side: the scholarship, the ease with which we move. I know from my fellow students how hard some of them have it. I frown, feeling embarrassed.

'Look, Donna, it's …'

'I know, she's not your girlfriend but …'

I clear my throat. 'She is my girlfriend, actually. I haven't told anyone yet, but we are now an official item. You're the first to know, apart from my best mate.' When I let Jack in on my little secret, it was a massive thing for me, and I was so relieved, but in London this feels normal, and that's good.

Donna is delighted. 'You dark horse, keeping that under wraps.'

Frank comes over. 'Congratulations, Sonny, a girlfriend with a flat and a piano, wish I was that smart.'

Donna shoots him a look. 'I've got a flat and a keyboard.'

I'm intrigued. 'Are you guys together?'

And as we mix drinks and talk, Frank updates me on the past politics of girlfriends and boyfriends, the comings and goings of love amongst the pupils and staff. He teases Donna that she always fancied him really, but he was tied up.

She giggles and stops him rambling. 'And here we are. Together at last. They clink glasses. To love. Cheers.' And they have a snog just as Ruby walks in.

Ruby says hi. 'That sounds good.'

She kicks off her boots as I pour her a white wine, she looks at me, not quite understanding whether to kiss me as usual.

'Donna and Frank, this is Ruby, my gorgeous girlfriend.' I slide my arm around her waist and kiss her.

We enjoy a wonderful evening swapping stories of favourite gigs, places we visit, hopes for the future. The one difficulty we have is when they ask us how we met. We haven't agreed how to answer. We look at each other and mumble we're not sure where or when. I almost say, 'At her husband's funeral,' but manage to stop myself just in time. Ruby seems on the verge of telling the truth and then reins back. In the end, we move on and deflect. We'll need to sort this out later. The meal is great, my cooking is improving and we end up around the piano with a sing-song. Frank is Elton John, and Donna is Kiki Dee and these two lovers, who have only just got together, sing 'Don't Go Breaking My Heart' to each other. After too many drinks, we return to jazz and celebrate our love with a slow rendition of 'What a Difference a Day Made'. London is fantastic and being here with Ruby is bliss.

After we have said our goodbyes, Ruby leads me to the kitchen and we do the dishes together.

She looks sad. 'I miss Ringo.'

Jack's dad took Ringo on for us, as he is still recuperating after his accident, and the dog gets him out of the house every day.

'I know you do, but you'll see him at Christmas.'

'I know. I love our new life too. I always wanted to come to London ...'

Ruby starts crying, and I hold her tight. This has happened every night for weeks now, since Freddie's anniversary. She says she feels guilty about using his money. In the next breath she's spending a fortune. Sometimes I feel like an observer looking in. 'I'm going back up north for a few days this weekend, just a few things to tidy up. I need to see my counsellor too.'

'I didn't know you had a counsellor.'

'Yes you did, that's where I met your mum.' It's news to me.

I send her to bed and tell her that I'll finish off tidying the kitchen. Thirty minutes later, I sneak under the covers, and she surprises me.

'Sonny. You know when you introduced me as your girlfriend.'

'Yes.'

'I liked that. Thank You.'

'Well, it's true. You are my girlfriend.' I turn to face her, and I kiss her on the cheek. 'And you're gorgeous.'

She turns on her side. She strokes my hair. It feels good, and I rub circles in the small of her back. It's dark, but I know she is smiling at me.

'Ruby, we've never discussed contraception.'

She flips over. 'Fucking hell, Sonny, where did that come from?'

'I was just thinking ...'

'About having babies ...'

'About not having babies.'

Her heart is pounding, and I've ruined the moment.

'Sonny, I can't have children. I'm sorry. It's never going to happen.'

I'm ok with that, but I don't know what to say. Time passes. We're both wide awake, lost in our thoughts.

'Ruby?'

'Yes.'

'I love you.'

'I love you too.'

'Goodnight, girlfriend.'

'Goodnight.'

IPANEMA

FRIDAY 15 OCTOBER 1976

We hurry to Euston after breakfast, and we kiss on platform five before I head to college for an afternoon session on percussion. It's been a tough fortnight for Ruby, thinking of Freddie and then me being stupid and mentioning babies. I think a weekend's break might do us good. I walk into college, collecting a couple of letters from my pigeon hole, from Mum and Julia. Although we have a phone in the flat, Mum writes to me most weeks keeping me posted on her studies, how Dad is doing and any local gossip. It's great to hear from Julia, her first letter to me in London. She says Stephen's parents are coming over in December and they are thinking of catching the train to London for their first night away since Michael was born. She asks if we are free and to set up a gig and a meal. It's brilliant news, and I'm smiling when Donna walks in on me.

'Hello, lover boy, why are you looking so happy.'

I wave the letter. 'It's from Julia.' I fill her in on how she studied here years ago and how she helped me. Donna asks me how I met her, and without thinking, I say, 'She used to teach Ruby's husband.' Donna's eyebrows arch upwards. This is what is problematic about keeping secrets. They unravel when you least expect them to.

She is wide-eyed. 'You better tell me more.'

We head off to one of the practice rooms with a coffee. It takes about an hour to go through the whole story from when Ruby used to come around the house right up until we became lovers after my party. Donna is surprised that Ruby is thirty-four, and I find myself defending her age, her marriage, moving me into her house, right up to now when we are students in London. Donna gets my drift. 'Don't ever apologise for being in love. You have fallen hard, Sonny, haven't you?' She pinches my cheeks.

'I have to admit I have.'

'Good for you. She's one hell of a woman. Strong, determined and beautiful. You hang on to her.'

'I intend to. Forever.'

'You boys say the sweetest things.' She's up and pulling me along to our lecture. 'Wait till you meet this guy, he's done the lot. Rising star, fallen poster boy, drugs, scandals and tabloids.'

We're running late, and we enter the auditorium just as the room is settling down, everyone turns to face us. Donna mumbles, 'Sorry,' and we head for our seats. I don't recognise him at first, but he clocks me straightaway.

'Well, look who it is everybody,' Jimmy the Drums shouts, 'Sonny Boy Jackson. The darling of South Manchester transported to London by the money of Ruby Smithson.' He leers at us, and my fellow students eyeball me as I reach into my bag and keep my head down. Donna stays close, and the lecture and his playing are superb. All the time I'm thinking about why he called her 'Ruby Smithson'. Donna whispers: the rumour is he has been clean for a year ever since settling a court case. That sounds familiar. Lots of the drum students take part, and the Q&A goes on forever even though I'm desperate to leave. As the lecture draws to a close he announces he is playing a secret gig at an underground club tonight and as students, we are most welcome, a late session with special guests. The excitement in the room is palpable, and Donna squeezes my arm. 'We have got to go, Sonny. Sometimes he gets amazing drop-ins.' We file out, and I feel his eyes drilling into the back of my neck.

'Sonny,' he shouts, and Donna's excitement level reaches fever pitch. 'Come here.' Donna is shaking as we walk over.

He shakes my hand. 'And who's this?' I introduce Donna, and quite a crowd gather round. He is a lot kinder now. 'Last time we met you were playing with Charlie Watts.' The room fizzes.

I let him know about the anniversary. 'Just one year ago this Sunday.'

'Aye, twelve months already. Bloody hell.' It seems to throw him for a while. 'How's Ruby?'

I lie and say I don't know, as she is in Manchester, and again it was not what he'd heard. He looks confused.

'Will I see you two tonight?'

Donna is happy to get such a personal invite. 'Of course, who are the special guests?'

With a glint in his eye, Jimmy looks her up and down. 'Now that would be telling.'

We walk away, and Jimmy gives me the most street cred I'll ever get. 'Oi, Sonny, how's Ringo?'

The students gasp, I turn around and shout back. 'He's great thanks, he says hello.' Jimmy gives me the thumbs-up, revelling in the kudos of the in-joke and I bounce out of the room knowing we'll be seeing him later.

Donna hangs on to my arm as we leave college. 'You are frigging amazing, Sonny. Charlie Watts, Jimmy the Drums and now Ringo Starr.'

I smile at her. 'Things may not be what they seem.' I dodge the traffic and rush ahead. She soon catches up. This is so much fun, teasing Donna as we head home along London's streets. We link arms and dance through people two abreast past Wigmore Hall, across Oxford Street and right up to my front door. I fumble with the keys, Donna messing around, tripping and tickling me. She asks if we need to get any food in, but I'm well prepped. She flings the fridge open, and wine, Champagne, and food fill the space. 'Sonny Jackson, you are so not a student. This is insane.'

I cringe. 'If you saw my house in Manchester you'd know this is not normal.'

'You are so lucky to have met Ruby.'

'Maybe Ruby is lucky to have met me.'

'Well, that's true. But at her husband's funeral?'

'Ouch. Not strictly true, I had met her before.'

We raise our filled glasses. 'To ... love.'

Donna smiles. 'May we always be in love. Now tell me about your mate Ringo.'

I go back to a year ago when Ruby asked me to walk Ringo for the first time and it was the night I met Jimmy. I let her know all the intimate details, the music room, the photos on the wall with royalty, Dad missing my performance because he was drunk. Meeting Alphonso, of course, which brings us right up to date.

'So Ringo is a dog and Ruby has paid for you ever since.

Lessons, flat, food.'

Donna is brutal, but I have to agree. 'It does sound weird, doesn't it?'

'Kind of. It's full-on control freakery.' Donna softens. 'But she's so nice.'

'Listen, I'm loving life, and I'm not complaining. I've got you as my music buddy and wine in the fridge. What more do we need?'

She's intrigued by my situation and lets me know that if Ruby ever takes me hostage, she'll come and rescue me.

We drink too much, eat too little and hit the town. I love London at night, the hustle and bustle of people crisscrossing, diving underground and speed walking. We descend the slippery stairs into Basement One, an intimate little club that is already smoky and packed. We're not too late, the stage is set but no action yet. Donna drags me to the bar, and we say hello to a few students we know. It's all nods and winks across the floor as the place fills beyond capacity, and as I am looking for a place to stand, a cymbal crashes, the club turns as one to see Jimmy has kicked the evening off. He dazzles alone as the other musicians emerge from the mass of bodies to join him, carrying drinks and settling into position. The music is heady, loud and fast. We find a pillar, lean back and listen as the music drives everyone into hysteria. He is that good, way beyond my expectations, and the jazz's hypnotic power takes us to another world.

We emerge into the cold night air, and Jimmy insists that we go back to his. A ragtag group of musos and freeloaders make our way from Soho to Charing Cross, and we enter another underground world, Jimmy's emporium. It is a magnificent cosmos of tie-dyed hippy symbolism, rugs, Indian artefacts and hookah pipes. Jimmy is the lord of his domain, and half-dressed runners fetch and carry drinks and spliffs. Me and Donna are spellbound as we sit on a giant bean bag and drink whisky and soda. The music has Latin vibes, congas and bells, strings and the most haunting trumpet. We lie back and drift to distant shores. Donna clutches my hand, and says, 'Thank you, Sonny, this is amazing.' We shut our eyes and dance on golden sands, swim in aquamarine seas and watch the sun go down on Ipanema. Our dreams are interrupted by the flash of a camera as more drinks are delivered. Donna goes off to find the toilet and Jimmy pounces.

'Well, Sonny, how are you enjoying my boudoir?'

'Alright. The gig was awesome, Jimmy.'

'That's the easy bit, playing. Existing is so much harder don't you find?'

He drags me up, tugs my arm. 'Follow me.' We move along a narrow corridor. Donna comes out of the loo.

'You too, sweetie, follow me.'

We do as we are told, and we wind our way to a beautiful music room that looks out onto a basement garden. Jimmy switches some lamps on, and I see hundreds of photos on the walls. He leads me around the room. We stop at a 10' x 8' and a younger Jimmy is pictured with a beautiful young woman, long hair tied to one side in a ponytail, Mary Quant eyes, mini skirt. They both look like models.

Donna focuses. 'She is beautiful.'

He smiles. 'Sonny, you know her, don't you?'

I squint to focus. 'I don't think so.'

Donna points to a faded pencil mark. Jimmy and Julia.

I gasp. 'Julia?'

Jimmy looks very happy. 'Indeed it is.'

Next is an even younger Jimmy with his arms wrapped around another man. They are on a speedboat with the famous Carlton Hotel in Cannes behind them.

'Freddie?'

'It is,' says Jimmy. 'Before he met Ruby Smithson.'

'Is that her maiden name?' asks Donna.

'It was, and now she is the proud sponsor of the Smithson Scholarship at the London Jazz College.' He turns to me. 'You've been bought, Sonny, just like Freddie.'

I look at the photo again, then back to Julia, and I try to take in another hundred faces. The room is starting to spin.

'Were you and Freddie ... I mean ... Were you?'

'It doesn't matter what we were, Sonny, he's gone now.' Jimmy begins to cry.

Donna's hand finds mine. She squeezes me.

He repeats. 'You've been bought, Sonny, you just didn't know it. Until now.' He's smug and triumphant. 'I can make and break careers, you know.'

I look at him with contempt. 'Julia. Make or break?'

'Break.'

'Freddie?'

'Make. That music you were listening to?' He picks up a vinyl album and shows me the cover with the same photo in Cannes on the front. 'That's what Freddie and I did when he was in town. We made music.'

'He's dead, wouldn't you agree you broke him?'

'I think you may need to look closer to home for the answer on that one.'

He flounces out. I'm so angry and start cursing and pacing the room. I remove the frame from the wall, and Julia slips out, I ask Donna to hide it in her handbag. I do the same with Freddie. I may need this as evidence. I half-inch the LP too.

Donna looks at me. 'Shall we get out of here?'

'There's one more thing I want to try.' I pick up a glass pestle, steel mesh and gold razor blade from one of the shelves. I place them on the piano and I catch Donna looking at me as I line up the white powder.

She's not frightened. 'Are you sure?'

'Julia told me once of these amazing highs.' I pick up a stainless steel straw and I snort my first line of coke. Donna follows, and we hold hands, sit down, and all of my anger subsides. We look at each other, and in that moment I decide my revenge is to steal all of Jimmy's coke and paraphernalia.

We wake up on Monday lunchtime in my apartment, still wearing the same clothes. The curtains are drawn, it is dark and cold, and we have burned through all the coke. There are two photos on the table and an album. I swear, on my mother's life, that I will never do this again.

I try to focus. Donna is on the sofa. I'm in an armchair. I hear things, noises in my head, someone tap tap tapping, keys jangling, trumpets blaring and wood creaking.

The door opens in slow motion. Light floods in.

'I can explain everything.'

AIN'T NO SUNSHINE

SATURDAY 23 OCTOBER 1976

I knock on, and Stephen opens the door, he looks pleased to see me and Michael is hiding behind him acting shy. Julia comes down the stairs as we chat. It feels great to be back. I can relax here, this neat little family unit, a house filled with love and music. The boys go off for a Saturday treat, swimming and then the park, leaving Julia and me to talk. She doesn't know why I am here. Maybe she thinks I have half term or a study break, but I need some answers, some help to fix the monumental mistake of last weekend. We do the usual catchups, family, friends, gigs and music.

She sees right through me. 'Now tell me, Sonny, why are you really here?'

Where do I start? 'I've made some mistakes.'

'Haven't we all?'

'I don't think I can put it right.'

She holds my hand. 'Impossible. I'm living proof of that.'

'It involves Jimmy.' I open my rucksack and take out the photo.

She winces. 'There's my biggest regret, right there.' She stares at the photo for ages, lets out a guttural scream and shreds it. 'That feels better. How did you get it?'

I tell Julia about last weekend, the gig, the drink, Jimmy's lair and the drugs and how I removed it from his wall. She shakes her head.

'Ahh yes, Jimmy's wall of fame. I remember it.' She confesses this is what he does. He sucks you in, and he needs to feel in control to play his games. 'If you let him control you, you lose.'

'He said he makes or breaks people's careers, is that true?'

Julia explains that's not true, not in the conventional sense. He doesn't invest, or put on gigs or run festivals. He just has the desire to control. And hurt people. She asks me if I have seen him again and I tell her I haven't. Ruby sent me packing on the Monday, and I have been hiding ever since at Mum and Dads.

'What does your mum think?'

'I haven't told her everything, not the drugs anyway and not about Ruby. She thinks I am having a breakdown due to college work.'

'And are you?'

'No, it's not that. I love college. It's just the aspect of Ruby controlling me. Jimmy said ...'

'Stop right there. Rule number one. Ignore what he said.'

'But he said Ruby bought me ...'

'What do you think? Do you think she planned it all? Freddie dying, you meeting Charlie Watts, Alphonso happening to be there.'

'No, of course not. That's impossible.'

'Well, you have your answer. Of course not, it may be what Jimmy wants you to hear, but you know the truth.'

The phone rings. Julia points me to the music room. 'Play a little. There's some music on the piano.' I step into the music room. 'Ain't No Sunshine'. Julia sure knows how to pick a tune when a man's down, and I wallow on my own for a few minutes. It's the first time I have played in a week, and it feels good. Julia apologises for the call as she hands me a mug of tea. She digs me for more information, and I tell her I have a week off as Mum rang in and said I was ill.

'What are you going to do?' is such an easy question for her to ask, but I'm stuck.

'What did you do?'

Julia thinks back to her early twenties, and lets me know it was Alphonso who saved her. He knew Jimmy was no good, so he intervened and escorted her back home. He covered for her at college whilst her mum nursed her back to health. She admits that without his help, she would never have escaped.

'I'm not as strong as you, Sonny. I would have drowned. Jimmy would have enjoyed watching me.'

'How about Freddie, where does he fit in?'

'It's bizarre, but I never saw Freddie in London, even though I heard later that he was at Jimmy's quite a lot. I only got to know him in the last few years. He was so sentimental and worshipped Ruby.'

'I can understand that bit.' We laugh.

'Did you know he made a record with Jimmy?'

I fetch the vinyl out of my bag, and we go to the front room to listen. Julia is amazed by the trumpet. Freddie always said he didn't play very well. It's beautiful music. Julia stares at the cover, 'They look like two young boys.'

'Lovers?'

'Probably. Jimmy always had a thing about clean-shaven, smart young men. He wasn't shy about telling me.'

'I think I'll grow a beard. Just in case.'

She laughs out loud. 'You are so young. You need to talk this through with Ruby.'

'If I ever see her again.'

'If I know anything about love, you will be seeing her very soon. Now listen, if you had the choice between Ruby and a music career, what would you choose today?'

'Ruby.'

'Once again, Sonny, you have answered the question.' She strokes my hand. 'Forget Jimmy, choose Ruby. Choose love. Every single time, choose love. Please.'

'Is that what Alphonso told you all those years ago?'

'Yes, even though I couldn't see it at the time. He sent me back to my roots for love.'

We talk for ages. Julia is my voice of reason, reminding me about the essential things in life. The doorbell rings and Julia jumps up, but she looks back as she leaves the room. 'Sonny, you were right to choose love.' She goes to open the door for what I assume is her next student. I remove the vinyl from the turntable and place it back in the sleeve.

I am looking at the young boys on the cover when she walks in.

'Hello, Sonny, I've missed you.' I look up as my lover walks in.

I rush into Ruby's arms. We hug each other, and I don't want to break away. She eases me back.

'So you know about Freddie and Jimmy then?'

'Not really. I stole this. I suppose I can guess.'

'Just remember, he always came home to me. Let's go. I've arranged for Ringo to be at home this afternoon and we need to talk.'

We let ourselves out, and I take her hand as we walk home. I don't care who sees me. Today I have chosen love. We're nearly home when June pops out of her shop and does a double-take.

'How's the music going in that there London?'

I tell her. 'Just fine, thank you. Just fine.'

'And how are you, Mrs Wilson?'

'I'm fine too, thank you, June, and please, call me Ruby.'

'It was tragic what happened to your husband. He was such a lovely man …'

We continue to hold hands, and I'm not sure June knows what to say next. Ruby puts her out of her misery. 'Goodbye, June, lovely to see you as always.'

She waves us off, pleased she'll have some juicy gossip to share. I whisper, 'What about Mum? I haven't told her yet.'

Ruby squeezes my hand. 'Don't worry about that, she's coming for tea.'

'Really?'

'She already knows.'

Many Rivers to Cross

Ruby opens the door. It's good to be back at Waverly. Some houses have familiar smells that comfort you. We go straight to the kitchen and put the kettle on.

'I saw my therapist last week.'

'And ...?'

'She cleared a lot of things up for me, a lot of baggage that I've been carrying that has been weighing me down for so long.'

'I'm sorry.'

'Thank you, but ... It's not your fault, it's from way back.' She looks nervous as she makes the teas. A minute passes. It's as though Ruby has a speech ready. She shakes her head. 'I don't know where to start.'

'Ruby?'

'I saw her because of something you said. It triggered something in me, it's not what you said, that was harmless enough, but ...'

'What was it? I'm sorry.'

'No,' She faces me. She's upset. 'Don't keep saying sorry. This is between me and Freddie and me and ... my body.'

Ruby sips her tea. I have not got a clue what she's on about.

She slips her hand in mine. 'We spoke about honesty, we

spoke about truth and how certain things were holding me back. I haven't told you or many people what happened.'

She leads me up the stairs, and we turn right towards Ruby's bedroom, but we stop outside the locked door. 'Wait here.' She returns with the key, and her hand is shaking as she turns the lock. My mind races, I've watched horror films with Jack where we have been scared out of our minds, and these images flash before me. She seems reluctant to move as we enter a tidy, light green nursery. It's perfect, not a speck of dust or an item out of place. A wooden crib rocks as Ruby touches it, and framed photos of a tiny girl, wrapped in pink, and footprints and handprints are on the walls. Ruby winds up a mobile, and it begins its soft lullaby. There is a photo of Freddie and Ruby together, holding her tightly, looking so proud. Ruby sits on the floor, her back to the wall, and she is heaving as she did at her husband's funeral. I sit alongside her, and we squash together. I want to touch as much of her as possible. She has to feel my love for her, my physical support.

'It was when I mentioned contraception, wasn't it?'

Her head dips. 'I can't have any more babies, Sonny. I couldn't even have one properly.' It's been right under my nose. This is why she is best friends with Mum, they met at counselling and Mum still has Maisie's room. Just like Mum, Ruby is not ready to let go. I'm sitting in a shrine.

'What is your daughter's name?'

'Matilda.' The floodgates open. 'Tilly.'

'Tilly. That's a beautiful name.'

We spend an hour or two just sitting together as Ruby opens her heart about her marriage, pregnancy and stillbirth. Matilda's death broke Freddie. Ruby is certain his accident would not have happened if she had been healthy. Yes, he had his demons and yes he was drawn to London and Jimmy, but he always came home. 'Funnily enough, the more successful he became, the more he lost his grip on reality.' She says he was convinced he was a failure because of Matilda. When he saw what childbirth did to Ruby, robbing her of the chance to conceive again, he felt responsible. 'It tipped Freddie over the edge.'

'Where does Jimmy fit in?'

'He was certain he was owed money for songwriting and they fell out, but Freddie still went to London, still took drugs and still saw him.'

Ruby says she tried to convince him to pay Jimmy off, as she had done, but he was too proud. 'In the end, he put all his papers in order and quit on me – and it still hurts.'

I leave the room to fetch wine. I need some courage to say my piece after what Ruby has just told me. There's no point in putting it off. Honesty is the best policy now. I hand Ruby her glass, she looks up.

'You ok?'

'I am, but I've got a few things to ask.'

'I owe you some answers. Donna said you were upset by what Jimmy had said.'

I discover that far from this being a random meeting, Ruby searched out Donna in London, knows all about our weekend in detail, rang Julia and got her to invite me to her house and caught the train up to meet me.

She looks at me. 'I know you are worried because Jimmy said I planned and executed all of this, and paid for it. Donna told me how hateful Jimmy was.' She is gripping Matilda's blanket, tightening her fist into a ball and screams at me. 'But I didn't want Freddie to die, I didn't. I am not controlling this story.'

'I can see that, but the scholarship and the flat ...'

She apologises over and over again and says, 'I feel like I am on a beautiful roller coaster and I don't want to get off.' Ruby says she dreams about Matilda all the time and thinks she may have been the one to calm Freddie down. We hold hands and talk about how we are going to move on from this. We agree that Jimmy is a no no. Let's just avoid the subject. We agree that drugs shouldn't feature in our relationship, except alcohol. In the end we plan to go back to London tomorrow and start again, just the two of us.

'One last thing,' I ask, 'how come Freddie ended up having lessons from Julia when Jimmy almost destroyed them both?'

Ruby is evasive. 'Ask Julia for her version, but Freddie said that he walked in on the aftermath of an attack where Jimmy almost killed her.' Julia didn't know him then, but when he heard she was back in Manchester, he called her to make sure she was alright. At first, Julia assumed Freddie was trying to lure her back to London, but when she knew he was genuine they became good friends through music. They just didn't talk about Jimmy. 'I think if I'd trusted her a little bit more, she could have helped me with Freddie.'

'I showed her a photo earlier that I stole from his wall. She was so angry she ripped it up.'

'I saw the photos and the LP in London when I came back to the flat.'

'I'd forgotten that.'

'Donna's nice, isn't she?'

'Do I need to say sorry to her too?'

'I don't think so. She said she had a fabulous time. And she's missing you.'

The bell rings, breaking our spell. Ruby says she'll go and fetch Ringo and let Mum in. I've been home all week, and we haven't really spoken. I think she's been leaving me alone, assuming I'm stressed out. Mum tiptoes around the room and does precisely the same as Ruby. She rocks the crib and lets the mobile sing its sad elegy.

'Do you want to talk?'

'You know about Ruby and me?'

'Yes.'

'You ok with it?'

'It was a shock.' She sucks in a breath. 'But one thing I've learned over the years is perspective. It's not as big a shock as losing Maisie or Ruby losing Matilda.' She sits down and holds out her hand.

I place my right hand in her left. 'Mum, you're amazing, I don't know how you do it.'

'Sonny, you know I think the world of Ruby.' She deliberates. 'I didn't see this coming, but if you're happy, I'm happy for you.'

'You always know exactly what to say.'

'That's what my tutor said.'

'You'll make an amazing social worker.'

'She said that too.' We both laugh. I see Mum's confidence shining through.

'Do you think about Maisie?'

'Every single day.'

'Things must be so hard for you and Ruby. I didn't understand it until I came in here.'

'In counselling, they say not to think of it as a cross to bear. Better to remember the joy and happiness they brought.'

'And can you?'

'Yes, most days.'

'What about Dad?'

She frowns. 'Work in progress. He's got many rivers to cross and finds it hard to let go, even after all these years.'

We chat about her first boyfriend, Granddad, Dad, all the relationships in her life. She pushes and pulls me and cajoles me into thinking about the last week as a little bump in the road. She makes me feel so much better as she always does.

'You going back to London?'

'Yes, tomorrow. Back to college on Monday.'

'Sonny, you'll be fine. I promise.' She pauses again. 'I taught you well.'

The three of us have a huge portion of fish and chips and end up walking Ringo for a couple of miles. Sometimes I hold Mum's hand, and sometimes I hold Ruby's. I am a fortunate boy.

Later, I smuggle the album into the lounge. Ruby sits back, relaxes on the sofa and listens. 'Who's this?'

'It's Freddie, and it's beautiful.'

'He was such a lost soul.'

'I don't want us to have a relationship and not talk about him.'

'You're right. You are so young and yet so old, Sonny Jackson.' She kisses me.

'Sorry about last weekend.'

'It's okay.' She reaches for my hand. We listen to the music.

'Ruby, thanks for teaching me how to love.'

She turns and smiles. 'And thank you. For teaching me how to love again.'

We kiss and head for the bath. Traditions are important.

Search for Peace

Friday 17 December 1976

It's my final day in college this term, and we're demob happy, messing about and wishing everybody a happy Christmas. Last night was our end of term concert when all first years had to 'Show up and show off,' as Alphonso dictated. I was a little thick-headed this morning, but after breakfast and coffee, I'm feeling better. Donna meets me in the common room for lunch, and we have a review of my first term. We have become good mates. She takes the mick mercilessly, but I don't mind.

I ask about her love life. 'Are you and Frank on or off at the moment?'

'On. I think he just wants Christmas with me. Then he'll dump me again. What about you, lover boy?'

'More than on, thank you for asking.'

She sniggers. 'You've done well, Sonny. It's been a great term, hasn't it? Apart from the "lost weekend".'

That's our name for the incident in October. I still can't believe what happened, it was way out of my comfort zone, but Donna's more relaxed about it. She smirks. I know what she's thinking.

'Go on, Sonny, just once more, it was such fun.' Her eyes

implore me. 'It can be your reward for such a good term.'

I want to say yes, to try it with just her, not with all the anger I had last time, but Julia and Stephen are arriving tonight, and we are cooking a meal. I need to leave now as I promised Ruby I'd get some shopping on the way home. Donna pleads with me to spend the afternoon with her. 'Sorry, I can't,' I say, and I stand to leave and wish her a happy Christmas. We kiss each other goodbye, and I tell her to call me if she needs anything. I give her the London number and for Waverly too. 'There's an answerphone if you need it.'

I walk out wishing I was brave enough to try coke again. The high was terrific but, I argue with myself, it's not called the 'lost weekend' for nothing. I flip and flop, punch and counter all the way to the market. My heart says go for it. My head says don't. I look up as I approach the fish stall and I recognise the guy in the apron.

'Hello Stevie, what are you doing here?'

Stevie is a drummer in year two and he works here at weekends, but seeing as it's the holidays he's working every day till Christmas Eve as he needs the money. He asks me what I'm doing till January, and I'm embarrassed to say nothing. I tell him I'll be going home at some point to see Mum and Dad but not much more.

'You're lucky, mate, I've got to earn some dosh as my grant is rubbish. I've only got me mam, and she earns crumbs.'

'You gigging at all?'

'Nah, just some bits and bobs for fun, no earnings.'

'Have you heard of Bobby Durham?'

'Of course, he's Ella's drummer.'

I love helping people out. Ruby's influence is rubbing off on me. I tell Stevie we're off to see Tommy Flanagan at Ronnie Scott's tomorrow and Bobby is on the kit, and he can have a ticket on me if he wishes. Stevie's face lights up, and we agree to meet in the pub next door before the gig. He is delighted as he serves me. I'm sure he knocks a few quid off.

'Do you know Bobby then?

'I met him last year at Ella's gig, but it's Tommy Flanagan who has invited us tomorrow.'

He looks amazed. 'How do you know all these people?'

'It's my girlfriend. She knows everybody. I'll introduce you tomorrow.'

I walk through the stalls to get some veg, and Stevie's voice is louder than all the other traders. I've left him on a high.

It's cold and damp, and the bags get heavier the further I walk. My arms have stretched by the time I open the door and fling the shopping onto the counter. 'Surprise.' I turn round, and Julia is looking at me with a drink in her hand already. She gives me the biggest squeeze. 'We got the earlier train as Stephen blagged the day off.' Stephen and Ruby come in as I am putting the fish in the fridge.

'Look at the wee boy. He's gone all domestic on us.' He gives me a big hug as he laughs at me.

Ruby looks on, smiling. 'He's well trained, Stephen.'

Stephen is not one to mince his words. 'I still can't believe you two have got it together.' Ruby looks daggers at him. 'Well, I'm just saying,' is his defence. 'I'm only codding ya all.'

I put my arm around Ruby. 'Well ain't I the lucky one?' She has a drink ready for me, and we toast friendship. We go through to the lounge and talk for ages. It's so good to see Julia again. Ruby gives Julia a tour of the flat, and Stephen tries to talk football with me. Man United are in town tomorrow playing Arsenal and Stephen has got a ticket for the match. I've heard Dad over the years, and I join in with the banter, and I fool him into thinking I know what I am talking about. The conversation flows as we compare players and stats. Stephen convinces himself Tommy Docherty is the manager to lead United to glory and I just repeat what I've heard Dad saying that he'll be gone soon if he doesn't win the league. Stephen is getting going. 'You'll see, we'll have won the league by the time we play Bristol City on the seventh of May next year. You don't want to go to Ashton Gate needing points.' I laugh with him. I haven't got a clue, but we talk Best, Charlton and Law for what seems like hours. When the girls return, I spot that Julia has been crying as she sits next to Stephen and snuggles in. Ruby tops us up, and we discuss my culinary skills. I shouldn't be drinking this much before being in charge of sharp knives.

I shower and change and have a strong coffee before I get down to work in the kitchen. Ruby wanders in and helps me. We send Stephen and Julia out to have a walk in the cold air whilst we prep. As soon as the door closes, I say to Ruby, 'All ok? Julia looked upset.'

'She'll be fine. We just started talking about Freddie, which led to Jimmy and what happened to her in London.'

'I hope she'll be ok. She deserves to be.'

'The weird thing is she said she wouldn't mind seeing Jimmy in person to tell him to fuck off and show him she's survived.'

'Now I know you are telling tales. Julia doesn't swear.'

'Oh, she swore, Sonny, believe me.' Ruby bangs her knife on the chopping board. 'She was so angry. She said the last time she saw him, she was being taken into the back of an ambulance, bruised and battered.'

'Bloody hell, I didn't know it was that bad.'

Ruby looks at me. 'I've never told anyone before. It was Freddie that called it. He was in London that night, and he saved her life.'

I stop what I'm doing. 'Did you tell her?'

'No, I couldn't, I'm not sure I should. It doesn't change anything, does it?'

We grab another glass of wine, and we think and talk it through. There is no resolution, no easy answer. The buzzer goes, Ruby says, 'Say nothing,' and they're back, glowing from the fresh night air.

I shout, 'Ready in fifteen,' and they go to their room to get ready.

The atmosphere has changed. Ruby cuddles me from behind, but I turn away, and she follows me. 'Sonny, are you ok?'

'I just wish you'd told me. It feels like we are keeping secrets all over again.'

We're whispering whilst busy. 'I know, I know,' says Ruby, 'I didn't want to tarnish Julia's love for Freddie – that was made in Manchester, not in some sordid orgy in Charing Cross.'

'Orgy? No one has mentioned orgies before.'

Ruby comes close. 'What do you think they were all doing? Jimmy is addicted to sex and drugs. Always has been.'

'And Freddie?'

She doesn't answer, and it all makes sense, the rumours and

innuendo, the photos and incense and drugs, the bean bags and low lights. My eyes are open. 'Bloody hell. I think Donna and I got off lightly.'

Ruby scowls. 'Now you know why I was worried. For you and Freddie.'

Julia appears at the door. 'What are you two whispering about?'

I look up. 'Julia, you look ravishing.'

'Someone's got a new vocabulary since they've moved south. No one has called me ravishing before.'

Stephen puts his arms around her and in his poshest English accent adds, 'Darling, you look ravishing tonight.'

We laugh as Ruby takes them through and sets the dishes on the table, and I assume the role of chef and serve up. I do a pretty good job, only missing the tartare sauce off my shopping list. Ruby gives me eight out of ten for presentation, Stephen gives me ten for effort. A year ago I was being called down for meat and veg from my tiny bedroom, and now I'm eighteen, living in a beautiful flat in Mayfair, playing music every day and having fun nights like these. I look across at Ruby. My girlfriend does look ravishing tonight in her brand new striped Biba trouser suit and platform boots. Julia suggests some music, and we jump on the piano for fun, nothing too serious. Julia takes the left seat on the piano stool, and we run through some old favourites. I see Ruby jump up as she heads for the phone. It'll be Alphonso; he usually rings on the weekend, and they can chat for hours sometimes. Julia begins to sing 'It Don't Mean a Thing If It Ain't Got That Swing' and even Stephen is dancing around and scatting. We are cut short as Ruby charges in and shouts, 'Sonny, it's Donna, she's in trouble.' I get to the phone in seconds, and Donna is breathless and slurring. She apologises for calling me, but the numbers I gave her earlier were still in her purse. She's at Jimmy's and worried she's gone too far. I tell her to calm down, I can't understand her, but she gets more hysterical, says she's told them she needs the loo, but she's found the phone and needs help now. She thinks they've drugged her. Most of her clothes are missing, but she'd found her handbag and grabbed the purse. I hear men shouting, getting nearer, and then she screams, and the line goes dead. I put the phone down, and all eyes are on me.

'I think Donna's about to get raped. She's at Jimmy's.'

We freeze. My mind is racing, but I can't speak. I look at Julia, I now know what she's been through, and we are all rooted to the spot. Julia is the first to react.

'Come on, Ruby. We have to save her now. I've wanted to do this for over ten years.' We're like statues. Julia screams at us, 'NOW, all of you. This is not happening again.' She shocks us into action, we charge down the stairs and out into the street, Julia hails a cab and shouts, 'Buckingham Street, Charing Cross. As fast as you can, please.'

Stephen looks stunned. 'How do you know where we are going?'

Julia says, 'Later Stephen, I promise. But right now, Donna's in danger.' She is the calmest out of all of us. She instructs me to ring the buzzer when we arrive and say I am joining the party. She says Jimmy has cameras so they will wait around the corner until the door is open. And then we march in and save Donna. She looks at her husband. 'There is a secret room where all the … Where all the orgies takes place. We will need to get in there as soon as we can.' Stephen looks shaken. Ruby has her head in her hands.

I ring the bell, and a small screen lights up, 'Yes?'

'It's Sonny. Jimmy said to call by anytime.'

'Hang on.'

A minute passes. I say nothing.

'You on your own?'

'Yes.'

'OK, come in and shut the door behind you.'

I hear the buzz and pull the heavy door open. I jam my foot in it and signal to the others. Julia leads from the front, straight in and turns left down the corridor. We pass the bean bags, the semi-naked hostesses and so many people spaced out on the hookah pipes. And then she pulls back a kaftan rug on the wall to reveal a hidden door. She looks at us. 'All in at the same time, no messing. Stephen, if you need to punch anyone, punch hard, punch fucking hard, these guys nearly killed me.' He looks shocked.

I hold Ruby's hand 'You alright?'

She nods. 'Payback time for Freddie, I think.'

Julia checks we are ready. 'Let's see if they have changed the code?' And she does a series of knocks on the door, like a rat-a-tat-tat and a couple of seconds later it eases open. Julia yanks it back so fast that a hand comes with it followed by a body, which stumbles onto the floor. She knows him. 'Marco?' He looks up and recognises her as she smashes her boot into his ribs. We follow her in. It takes about ten seconds to adjust to the light and the music. I see Donna on a low bed, just her panties on. I hope we are not too late.

Ruby pushes me back. 'I'll get her dressed, you two boys shut the door.'

Julia turns the music off and tells Stephen to reach up and move the cameras so they can't see what we are doing. I can hear Donna moaning. She's coming round. The door begins to open.

Jimmy is high, but he looks at me, he's got a bruiser behind him. 'Sonny, how very nice to see you. Rescuing your friend, are we? Or returning stolen goods?'

A size six platform boot flies through the air and smashes his head open, and I see Julia standing over him holding Donna's other boot. He is on his knees. She looks at her husband, 'Stephen, this is the piece of shit who drugged and raped me.'

He looks at her. Then at me. He can't make his mind up. Jimmy falls over, looking up, blood pouring from his wound. Ruby comes into view, holding Donna. She looks down at him. Through the blood, he gurgles, 'Ruby, I'm so sorry about Freddie.' She drop-kicks him in the bollocks, and he screams like a baby.

'Don't ever let me hear you say his name again.' She squares up to Marco, 'Give us ten minutes. If you dare come out of this room I'm calling the police.' She takes us out and slams the door behind.

Stephen is still in shock. He doesn't move until Jimmy gurgles, 'Julia, I always …' The voice fades as Stephen smashes his fist into Jimmy's face, and Julia rubs his back and smiles at her hero.

Ruby says, 'Wall of fame,' to Julia, and she spends the next five minutes searching for any sign of Freddie and destroys all the photos. 'Let's go.' Stephen puts Donna on his shoulders, and we rush out. As we pass the entrance, Marco reappears and tries to regain control, 'If you cause any trouble, I'm calling the police.'

Julia looks at him with contempt for his empty threats. She knows what is on the premises. Her final words before leaving this hellhole put the fear of God into him. 'Don't bother. We've already called them. You have five minutes.' As we leave the building, we hear the shouts of panic as they start to dismantle a decade of abuse. Girls and boys are getting dressed, drugs are being flushed and tapes destroyed. We make it to the Strand and jump in a taxi.

At home, the ladies shower Donna, and she starts to recover. We laugh and we cry. And we laugh again. Donna comes over to me and says 'Sorry' a hundred times. She latches on to Ruby and says 'Thank you' a thousand times. Stephen is even more proud of his wife than before. Ruby and Julia talk about Freddie. They know that he was not involved in the abuse. We listen in silence.

Julia says, 'When I saw the album cover I knew it was Freddie who saved my life.'

Ruby looks shocked she has remembered after all this time. 'I'm so sorry.'

'It was a surprise to me, but I remember those eyes, his beautiful eyes. He was the last person I saw before I lost consciousness.'

'He called the ambulance for you.'

'Have you always known?'

'No, he told me years later. I never knew about the album though.'

Julia and Ruby reach out to each other, joined by their love for one man and their hatred of another. Stephen looks at his sore knuckles, smiling.

The events of tonight bind us together. It takes ages to succumb to tiredness, the adrenaline wearing off. Donna stays. I hold Ruby so tight, and she kisses me goodnight.

As I'm drifting off she whispers, 'Tonight was for Freddie. Thank you.'

On a Clear Day

Saturday 18 December 1976

Breakfast is quiet. No one mentions last night. It does not feel like the last Saturday before Christmas. Stephen pipes up, 'I think I'll still go to the match if that's ok?' I make another pot of coffee as Ruby clears the table.

Julia breaks her silence. 'Ruby, have you got Alphonso's number?' Ruby gets her Letts diary out, and they go off together to call him.

Donna looks at me. 'You ok?'

'Yeah, you?'

'I was pretty stupid wasn't I? I'd only met him once, but with Frank pissing me off every other day I just got so low and thought I'd have some fun.'

Part of me thinks I should have gone with her. 'At least you're back now safe and sound.'

Stephen helps me out. 'Just think of it as a wee bump in a very long road.'

Donna smiles for the first time today. 'Just a wee bump.'

Julia tells Stephen she is off to meet Alphonso whilst he goes to the football.

'I'll miss the match if you need me to.'

'No, I need to close this chapter and move on. Ruby's going to come with me.'

And just like that, we have some plans for the day, life restarts, and the show goes on. I ask Ruby if she minds Donna staying for another night and she says of course not, but 'Don't forget the gig tonight.'

'Ahhh, forgot to say, I've invited Stevie too. I said we'd meet him next door.'

'The more the merrier. No problem, it will be fine.' Ruby sits on the bed, brushing her hair.

'Do you think Julia's going to be ok?'

'She's one of the strongest women I know.'

I agree. 'She was incredible last night.'

We're in the pub, Stevie has joined us, and we look like three couples out on the town before the Christmas rush begins. No one would have any idea about what happened last night. I make sure Donna is ok and have told Stevie to look after her. She's bonding with him over drum and bass combinations. Ruby says, 'Alphonso was superb.' He'd heard some rumours but never anything definite. Now that Julia has revealed the truth, he will see that Jimmy never teaches again. I circulate, feeling responsible for everyone. Julia is looking forward to the gig. She seems happy tonight, and she confides in me, 'I can't tell you how much I enjoyed smashing that eejit over the head.' She bursts out laughing, her whole body shivers and she squeezes me tight. 'Thank you, Sonny, I don't think I'd ever have done that if I hadn't met you.' She winks at me. 'And watch out for Alphonso, he's got a twinkle in his eye for Ruby.'

The gig is incredible, and Stevie is delighted at half time to meet one of his heroes. Tommy takes me to one side. 'Fancy sitting in?

'I've got a better idea.' I let him know it's my good friends Donna and Julia that need a lift. He takes them backstage and introduces them to Keter Betts.

Donna comes bouncing back and jumps into my arms. 'Sonny, I love you. I've just met him, and he's so humble.' She tells Stevie all about him as Ruby catches my arm.

'What are you planning? You've got that look?'

'You'll see.'

We settle down for set two at Ronnie Scott's. As usual, I daydream how different this is to last night and once again, how lucky I am to be surrounded by such good people. I look across at Donna. She's smiling and holding hands with Stevie. Tommy Flanagan takes the mic. 'Ladies and Gentlemen, we have some exceptional guests in the house tonight.' He introduces Donna, and she takes Keter's double bass and works her way into a groove with Billy Durham. Alphonso nips into her seat. He must have been watching from behind us. Stevie is in awe. Tommy leans in once more. 'One more special guest for you. Please welcome Julia Betteson to the stage.'

She flies down those stairs, takes the mic, and the spotlight finds her. Stephen is close to tears.

Ruby whispers in my ear. 'I love you, Sonny Jackson'

'You taught me everything.'

We walk home, wrapped up and singing songs. It seems Christmas has arrived for all of London but especially for us. Ruby promises hot chocolate when we get in, Stevie is staying now, Donna feels safe tonight and Julia has fulfilled a dream she held long ago.

I notice Stephen shaking his head. 'Alright Stephen?'

'Not really. United lost three to one.'

Julia catches my eye. She smiles and blows me a kiss.

Ruby brings in the hot chocolate. 'To friends.'

'To friends.'

Looking at the Peaches

Monday 4 July 1977

Jack screams into the drive and beeps his horn. It's 7.30 am, and I bend down and kiss Ruby goodbye. 'Don't forget I'm going to Mum's for tea.'

It's great to be back in Manchester, and Jack's got me a summer job at the factory, making batteries. Ruby and I are back at Waverly. Even Ringo has the odd day with us.

Jack's on the drive waiting for me. 'Eh up, lazy student, how are you doing?'

I'm still tying my laces. 'This is early Jack, a shock to my system.'

Jack squeals the tires of his Fiesta, the Stranglers are on the radio, and I'm off to see how the other half live, I thought it would be good to earn some money for a change, plus Ruby never lets me off the leash since the lost weekend, I think she sees me going off the rails. Jack says an early start equals an early finish so it's best to crack on and then we can have a beer on Friday. I've never been in a factory. The induction lasts thirty minutes, that's it. Gloves, goggles for certain parts, and they send me to 'Packing'. There's a whiff of rotten eggs across the site, and the foreman says I'll get used to it. And then it's down to work, seven hours a day for two months. Tea break in the morning, lunch at midday, finish at four. Some people have been here for thirty years or more. I watch them work. It's humdrum and repetitive. Lunchtime becomes a frenzy, a rush from the floor to outside. Sandwiches appear, a football is retrieved from a locker, and there is a huge kickabout, and these quiet workers become animated friends. The rivalry between reds and blues, bonds across families, arguments from the weekend pub visits all rise to the surface in a show of love. I soak it up, and it is beautiful to watch. Jack finds me, and we sit together on a wall overlooking the match. We compare packed lunches, swap one or two items. It's like being back at school.

'Can you do this for the rest of your life, Jack?'

'No way. Karen and me, we're going to emigrate after a few years.'

Jack spends twenty minutes telling me about their dreams. Karen wants to train as a midwife, he is thinking of going to night school and learning carpentry, and after that, they may travel and try to settle in Australia.

'Bloody hell, mate, where did all this come from?'

'I dunno. Karen's got an auntie out there and Dad's talking about his pension so we may all go.'

'It sounds fabulous, put me on the list for visiting.'

Jack says he'd wished he'd paid more attention in geography now. He asks me how my first year has gone, and I tell him pretty well. I own up to the lost weekend, and he looks at me like I am a complete idiot. We had the odd puff together at school but nothing so dangerous. I tell him about Donna, my official buddy, who has become such a good friend.

'Is she a good friend or a really good friend?' He still loves teasing me.

'Don't be stupid, Jack, I've just got her together with Stevie, her new boyfriend.'

'And how are you and Ruby doing?'

The hooter goes, the games stop, lunch boxes get snapped shut. It's a three-minute warning to get back to your stations. I shout at Jack, 'Tell you later.' I spend the afternoon shift reflecting on my thoughts. Jack has changed. It seems he's had a late growth spurt, lost weight and he's nothing like Billy Bunter now. He and Karen are settled. It has been a good year for me too. Superb flat, nights outs, theatre, gigs and West End shows. But, and there is one huge but, everything is paid for by Ruby. It's wearing me down. I know she says she doesn't mind, but it matters to me in hundreds of small ways. These thoughts build up until I need a bit of space and we have a blow-up, then we make up and carry on as though nothing has happened. There's only one person who can help me with my strange thoughts, and I'm seeing her for tea after work. We jump in the car at the end of the shift, and Jack runs me back to Mum and Dads. He's forgotten about our unfinished chat at lunchtime.

Mum greets me, 'The prodigal returns,' and the hugs and kisses feel great. Dad comes out and shakes my hand but he gravitates to Jack to discuss the car. Some things never change. The three of us eat together and talk about my studies and London, and Dad asks me about my accommodation. I flash a look at Mum, she shakes her head, and I lie to Dad about the college having sorted me something out. I think he knows I am lying but says nothing and we finish up chatting about his work and United.

Dad is impressed that I have a job, even if it's only temporary, and invites me for a beer sometime. 'You can come to the Working Men's Club now,' and he laughs at his own joke. Mum doesn't appreciate it. She says she'll walk me round to Ruby's as she has something to return.

As we're leaving Dad comes to the front door. 'I saw Jack's dad last week walking that stupid poncey dog. Apparently, Ruby has moved to London as well. Say hi from me.' We can't leave quickly enough. We scoot up the road, both knowing the cat is out of the bag. Because of the dog. I try to remain philosophical, but it's hard when you think of Dad. He isn't like Mum. He's two dimensional. We are both searching for solutions but coming up with none. I delay going to Ruby's, and drag Mum towards the church. We need time to think this through. We stare at Maisie's grave, and Mum flicks seeds and grass away and tidies up.

She looks up. 'Any ideas?'

'He obviously knows.'

'Well, we agree on that.' Mum's sarcasm bites as it is so unusual. 'I suppose I'll have to tell him formally.' Mum says it's always about choosing the right time with Dad, if he's too on edge he blows up. She says she'll think about it. I tell Mum I need to talk, and we sit at our bench. 'What's on your mind?'

I let it all out and tell Mum that Jack asked me a question earlier and I've been mulling it over all afternoon. 'Sometimes, I think Ruby is controlling my every waking moment.' It's the audition, it's the flat, scholarship, shopping, Champagne and I let out a long cry for help. 'It's everything.'

'Oh, Sonny, you have got it bad, haven't you? You're only nineteen, and you have your whole life ahead of you.' She goes into fix mode. She is brilliant as she brings me back down to earth. My perspective is wrong. Ruby's offerings are generous, even if they seem over the top. I am safe and secure and pursuing my dream. If, after considering everything, I think the relationship isn't working, I still have a music course, a roof over my head and plenty of friends. She challenges me. 'Have you and Ruby run your course?'

'No, I don't think so.'

She sends me on my way. 'Just talk to Ruby, and see if a summer working will make a difference.' She said all relationships improve with a little space. 'You are only on day one at the factory.'

I walk home feeling a little better, and as I get to the drive, the door flies open, and Ringo charges out, followed by Ruby. She bends down to put the lead on and says we are going for a walk. 'I've got something to tell you.' She stands up and gives me a huge kiss. 'Hello, my little worker, have you had a nice day?'

'It's been … how can I say it … boring.'

'Well, it's about to get a little more… interesting.'

'Oh no, what have you done?'

Ruby is teasing me. 'Let's say Ringo has given away our little London secret.'

'Jack's dad meeting my dad?'

'How did you know?'

'Dad said he found out you had moved to London.'

We discuss tactics, and in the end, Ruby says to leave it to her, she'll sort it, as I'm the worker now. Mum's right again. Absence has made my heart grow fonder, even on day one. We race home. She says she's enjoyed pottering around the house all day and the summer will be great for us. Tomorrow she's going to attack the garden.

Ruby says she loves London but, 'Do you know the best thing about being home?'

I look up from undoing my safety boots, she's already stripping off.

She turns to face me from halfway up the stairs, 'Having a big bath instead of a shower. Count to ten, lover boy and come upstairs.'

As I start counting, trousers fly over the banister, then t-shirt, bra and knickers.

It's going to be a good summer. 'Coming, ready or not.'

Wonderful World

Saturday 16 July 1977

It's barbecue night. A midsummer treat from Ruby to all of my friends and family. Although, because it's Ruby, this is not your average burgers and burned sausage fare. She has ordered a hog roast company and staff too, so we just have to concentrate on drinks. Ruby is loving having space again. She says a hot summer in London with no garden wouldn't have been fun. Mum has been to visit loads, usually when I am at work, and it's great to see Ruby and her together. I stare up at the ceiling. I've done three weeks at the factory, and my body has almost got used to the workload. The banter in the packing bay is fun, and I get to see Jack every lunchtime, which is nice. I turn over to look at the clock. It's 11 am. I need this lie in, even though my bedtime has been getting earlier every night. I am so tired. Today I have promised to help around the garden and fetch a load of ice with Jack. It would be so much easier if I could drive. I haul my aching body to the shower and dive in and can't stop singing "Watermelon Man." I'll need to get back into my piano soon. It seems like all the eighteenth birthday crew are coming and I'm looking forward to seeing everyone.

My cup of tea has arrived, and I take my first noisy slurp and say, 'Just gorgeous' out loud as I look out over the garden.

'Thank you, darling.' Ruby jerks my towel off and I spin round. 'Someone was a sleepy head this morning,' she says, and gives me a long tea flavoured smooch.

'Work or play?'

'Down boy.' She throws the towel back at me. 'Work, of course, we have so much to do.' She runs out of the room before I can change her mind. 'See you downstairs, breakfast is almost ready.'

I jump the last few steps and bound into the kitchen. I'm starving. I'm surprised when Mum looks up, and Dad is knocking back a coffee. Ruby smiles at me. 'Told you it was work.'

I know what she means now. 'Morning all.' I grab my porridge and coffee.

'Good week at work?' says Dad.

'Boring and normal,'

'That sums up my career.'

Mum chips in. 'Blimey, you two sound fun today.'

They have come round to drop off the salads, all home-made. Dad has bought some Watney Party Sevens as a present and some cans as well, he asks me for some help getting them in. Ruby throws him the key to the garage and says, 'Mind the Jag.' She adds, 'In fact, can you give it a start as we agreed?'

I look at Mum, am I seeing things? She smiles and shrugs her shoulders. I'm sitting on the hall floor putting on my shoes, and I hear this throaty roar. It sounds beautiful. Dad's on the drive already, waving at me to get in. It smells like a lovely old leather sofa and rumbles like an aeroplane getting ready for take-off.

Dad looks at me. 'Ice for the party?' We pull out into the road.

I scream at Dad. 'Is it insured?' He floors it, changes gear and pulls away again. I've never seen him so excited. He pulls up at the pub where Ruby has ordered buckets of ice, and we get out and admire the car. Quite a crowd gather round. Dad says he has come to a deal with Ruby, she has had it serviced and set up and he is to keep it ticking over whilst we are in London.

He goes to the cavernous boot. 'And do you want to know the best thing about it?' He opens up and shows me two sticky L plates. 'It's your turn next week.' We drive back a little more sedately. 'Did you know I've always wanted to drive a Jaguar? This is a dream come true.' I'm not sure how this has happened, but Dad is happy, and I'm going to learn to drive. He caresses the car onto the drive, and I unload the ice as Dad moves the beer into the garage. Ruby and Mum are in the garden setting out the tables and chairs, and the hog team are firing up a gas cooker with a suckling pig on the spit. I give Ruby a kiss and say thanks for the L plates, and she says she'll tell me all later on. She commandeers Dad and instructs him to drive her to the florist, and as they are leaving the garden, I hear him joke, 'Shall I wear my cap, madam?' Ruby is laughing loudly.

I move a couple of the chairs to a quiet spot and make Mum sit down. 'What on earth is going on?'

'I can't believe it either. It's just your old Dad starting to come back. Ruby visited two weeks ago and asked to speak to him.' Mum says they went into the front room and didn't come out for over an hour. She has been back twice since. 'Has she not said anything?'

'No, I had absolutely no idea.'

'Well, do you know what your dad's first words were after the meeting? He said he's sorry.'

'What did she say to him?'

Mum told me Dad said that Ruby was brutally honest and to the point. She said Freddie had died because he was stubborn and unable to talk about his feelings and that she wasn't going to see another life lost. She told him he was wasting his time being angry about things he couldn't change and missing out on relationships that he could be part of.

'Is that all?'

'She actually got him to join a bereavement group. She knew she couldn't do it on her own, but ...'

Mum leaves the conversation hanging.

'Mum? You said but?'

'But, that was only the beginning.' Mum told me that on the second visit Ruby walked him to the graveyard to talk to Maisie and then round to the garage to speak with Freddie, and she told him to enjoy the love that is here today and remember the love that is in the past. Apparently, that's where the idea of Dad looking after the car came from. 'She told Dad that if he burned his bridges, he wouldn't end up enjoying retirement or his grandchildren.'

I stare at Mum, searching for the right words as my mind races.

'She can't have any more children, Mum. You know that.'

Mum knows what I am thinking. 'Maybe she was just giving him a jolt.'

'It certainly worked.'

'It sure has. He's like a new man. In September, we are going abroad for the first time, and he's agreed to start couples therapy when we get back.'

'And is Dad happy with me being with Ruby?'

'I think he's getting used to it.'

Mum looks so happy, back in a fifty-fifty partnership. And we talk about her first year's study. She is up to speed now and begins her full degree after she gets home from Spain. The roar of the Jaguar gets louder, and Ruby and Dad find us in the garden.

'That car is amazing; no wonder Freddie loved it.'

Ruby beams. 'It was his pride and joy.' The hog revolves, spitting and fizzing now and again. We tidy up, fill the vases with flowers and declare ourselves ready for tonight. Dad puts the car back in the garage and leaves with Mum, and we take Ringo for a walk.

I ask Ruby about the Jag and visiting Dad, and she sets me straight on so many things. She says she 'Just does' in life. 'I was so frustrated with Freddie at times.' He could never decide what to do. And when he'd made a decision, he then worried he'd chosen the wrong route. 'It's so tiring, constantly being in a state of flux. It was worse for him of course.'

'So what did you say to Dad?'

'Do you want the full-on Ruby Wilson version?'

'Go on then.'

'Ok, but don't tell him I told you this.' Ruby winds up her thoughts, and they all come spilling out after she fires the starting gun. I can't believe she told him what she did. She said Maisie has gone, and she's not coming back. It wasn't his fault, get over it. Mum is a beautiful woman, that's why he married her, so he has to re-visit those thoughts. And finally, 'I told him his son is in love with his first proper girlfriend. Congratulate him for God's sake.'

'You said that?'

'Then he started to talk. And cry, and he kept on talking.'

'It sounds too easy.'

'It's not easy, you just need to find someone to have the conversation with, and that's not your partner. We all have doubts, Sonny, every day.'

'And?'

'And if we never overcame them or even wanted to overcome them, we wouldn't live, we'd exist. That's boring.'

I walk along, holding hands, and think that I am getting more and more from Ruby every day. She is a giver, not a taker. Look what she's done for me since Freddie died. I ask her how come Dad is looking after the car. It's simple, she says, they went into the garage to talk about Freddie, Dad admired the car, and she thought what's the point of it sitting idle. She could see how happy he would be driving it, so she sorted it. 'His little face lit up. How could I say no?'

'Do you still want children? Mum mentioned something about grand ...'

'I can't, Sonny. You know that, let's not mention it again.'

The party kicks off, and we all play catch up on our news. You know when you are young, and all the oldies say life gets faster, it really does. Jack and Karen are still such a good team. We talk for ages about their plans. Jack's mum and dad are so excited for their future too, and Ringo sits at Fred's feet, and Vera dotes on him. It's weird calling your friend's mum and dad by their first names, but I get used to it. Everyone knows about Ruby and me, so the pressure is off. Just as food is about to be called, I hear a black cab pull up at the front, I look across at Ruby, and she raises her eyebrows and says, 'It wasn't my idea.' I look at Julia, and she takes my hand and walks me through the house. Why do these women always surprise me? I open the front door as Julia shouts, 'The London contingent.' Donna and Stevie, along with Alphonso, join us.

Donna looks at the house. 'Bloody hell, Sonny, this is amazing.'

Julia says, 'It is so good to see you guys again,' and Alphonso takes her through.

We enter the garden to whoops and cheers, bubbles and food. Ruby gets hold of me. 'I told you, Sonny, life is for living. And surprises.'

I give her a big kiss, which gets even more cheers, even from Dad, who I'm sure was the one who shouted, 'Put her down.' I feel like I've learned more today than in a whole year and as I look at Mum and Dad, I'm happy that we're getting back on track. Ruby clinks her glass, and we all turn to face her.

She glances at all of us but focuses on Dad. 'To absent friends.'

We all toast, Mum and Dad hug.

'And to friends, old and new.' She looks at Donna and Stevie. They make such a good couple. Julia bursts into tears and Stephen pulls her in close.

We drink and eat and chat about our lives, and of course we end up around the piano later on, and Dad gets to listen to me properly. Having Donna and Stevie turn up means I have a ready-made trio, and we play for far too long. I can't persuade Jack or Karen to play tonight, and I try my hardest to get Julia to sing, but she point blank refuses, it's not like her. I end up playing 'Wonderful World', and even Dad joins in. It's been such a great summer. We flop around midnight and end up in the kitchen as you do. We are talking and making teas as we say our goodbyes. I climb the stairs weary and wobbly. Thank goodness I don't have to get up tomorrow. Ruby has already jumped into bed.

I snuggle in. 'Thank you for continuing to surprise me.' She turns to face me. 'And for rescuing Dad, he loved tonight.' Ruby can't speak, tears are running down her face. I ask her what's wrong, but she keeps crying.

'Ruby, you're frightening me, what's wrong?' Her cries get louder, and she soaks her pillow in sadness. 'It's Julia. She's found another lump.'

Higher and Higher

We're going back to London today. Year two beckons and I'm itching to get going. I'm up and packing and tidying away our summer mess, gathering my thoughts and possessions. The great thing about London is you don't need a car; the downside is we have to haul all our stuff back by train. I had a few lessons in the Jaguar but not enough time to pass my test – maybe next summer if Dad still has the patience. He lost it when I went around a roundabout the wrong way. When he'd finished shouting at me, we laughed for ages. 'Turn right does not mean turn right.' It became our little joke. The kettle boils, and I make a tea for Ruby and take the stairs two at a time. I kiss her goodbye and promise, 'Give me two hours max.'

She opens one eye. 'Your mum and dad are here at midday, don't be late.'

I charge out of the house, remembering the present that arrived in the post and the one I bought yesterday. It's going to be a beautiful day. We just need the clouds to clear. Plenty of people are out already, taking advantage of the weekend to do jobs and run errands. I spy June putting out her flowers, and she waves at me. I pick up my pace. I want to spend as much time as I can with my new buddy. I ring the bell and see the curtains twitching, and then his little face appears with a huge grin.

Julia opens the door. 'Hello, Sonny, thanks for coming on your last day.'

'I couldn't miss saying bye now, could I?'

I tumble into the front room amongst toys and books and Michael piles on despite his mum telling him to be gentle with me. After Julia went back into hospital, I gave up the factory and so for the last two weeks I've been here every day looking after Michael and making sure Julia got plenty of rest when she came home. It has been more challenging than the packing bay, but Julia's Mum has been helping with a few overnight stays, and my mum came and helped me out too. Michael jumps on me and shouts, 'Piano,' so we go through and jump on the stool. I take the left side now, and he jumps up onto a cushion, and we mess about as usual. He is getting used to the keys and loves the sounds he can make. His mum slumps in the chair, she looks so tired sitting there. Stephen arrives home with more shopping than I have ever bought; he's going to cook this weekend and freeze the meals, so Julia doesn't have to do any lifting. He takes Michael into the kitchen to help him, knowing we have to say our goodbyes.

Julia smiles. 'Thanks for helping out, Sonny.'

'Don't be stupid, that's what friends are for.'

'You know when we were in London, that was one of the happiest nights of my life.'

I take her hand, light as a feather and tell her that there will be so many more nights like that one, as soon as she has regained strength and the chemo is finished. I promise to come back and give Michael more lessons and to help lighten the load. Julia begs me to study hard, enjoy London and no more drugs, and I tell her again that I'll stick to the rules. She looks beaten, and I hate leaving her like this.

She senses my fears. 'Mum's coming over tonight. She's going to see me through the next week.' Michael rushes back in eating a gingerbread man, followed by his dad. I stand up and shake Stephen's hand, we look at each other, both afraid to say what we are thinking.

'Thanks for the last fortnight. I just couldn't have done it without you.'

'Take care, and look after that wife of yours.' I reach into my bag and get the presents out. A toy train for Michael – he gets on all fours and starts pulling the engine behind him. I hand Stephen a wrapped frame. He looks puzzled as he begins to undo it, and starts to weep as he peels back the tissue paper. Julia looks at me, and I barely manage to speak. 'It was that night you were talking about.' Stephen turns the frame around. There she is, Julia on stage at Ronnie Scott's, spotlight on her as she sings out loud. She bursts into tears and holds the photo to her chest, then sneaks one more look. Alphonso had to call in so many favours to get this to me in time, but it is worth it. Michael looks up from the floor.

'Sad Mummy?'

'No darling, happy tears. Look at this.' She proudly shows him the photo. He points and says, 'Mummy,' and goes straight back to his train.

Stephen opens the door. Saying bye is the hardest thing to do. He pats me on the shoulder, no words. He leaves to go and play trains. Julia kisses my cheek. 'I love you, Sonny. Thank you.' She is sobbing.

'Hey, I love you too.'

She wipes her nose, clears her throat and looks me straight in the eyes. She's serious. 'Sonny, if I don't make it this time, check up on the boys for me and tell Michael all about the night I sang at Ronnie's. And make sure he keeps up his piano lessons.'

All the air leaves my body, I don't want this conversation. 'Julia ...'

'No more, shhhhh, shhhhh, just promise me.'

I nod, and we have one more gentle embrace, she is so fragile. I try to give her hope. 'See you at Christmas.' I cry all the way home.

Ruby is putting the bins out as I turn into the drive, as soon as she looks at me, my tears run like a waterfall. She takes me inside, and I tell her I think Julia was saying her final goodbyes, and we won't see her again. She calms me down and explains that Julia is more scared than any of us, that she has beaten cancer once and she will do again. 'She is covering her negative thoughts with positive ones that involve you and Michael, that's natural.' Ruby insists we will call her every week and ask Mum to pop round too. She says, 'I was going to come back up for Freddie's anniversary on the first of October, God bless him, so you can come with me.'

That's what we agree on. We'll come back in a month, and I can check on Julia. That makes me feel much better. Ruby kisses me. 'You are such a nice young man, Sonny Jackson.'

'And you are Mrs Fixit. Any little problem, you deal with it.'

'That's why we are such a good team. Now get your skates on, lunch in thirty minutes and our train leaves at four-thirty.'

Mum and Dad arrive bang on time, and we have lunch in the garden. Ruby is giving Dad keys and making sure he understands the doors and garage. Mum and me sit back in our Habitat chairs.

Mum says, 'You ready for your second year?'

'Are you ready for your first?'

'Raring to go, although holiday first of course.'

I'd forgotten that, Dad's surprise booking of a week on the Costa Brava. They'd had to rush around for passports and clothes; not many people in our street have been abroad.

'Is Dad ok?'

Mum nods. 'He's better than ever. I've got a lot to thank Ruby for. Years of counselling has helped Ruby develop all the skills required to help others. It's not just your dad, down at the centre they often used to call Ruby in to help newly bereaved parents. She's amazing.' Mum looks at me, leans over and pats me on the knee, 'But you already know that.' I tell Mum about Julia, and she promises to visit next week and let me know how she's doing. Mum surprises me by asking about Ruby's friends and family and how many I had met over the last two years. When I tell her none, she says it's the same for her – anytime she asks Ruby always moves on.

'I know she went to visit an uncle, her mum's brother, and she told me about Trish, who she used to go dancing with before she met Freddie, that's it.'

'It's weird, no friends from before.'

'She's brilliant with my friends though, here and in London.'

'I know.'

'She's got you.'

'Yes, and now she's put your dad on the payroll too. Driver and handyman.'

Mum looks pensive trying to work it out, and Ruby calls us in. The final surprise of our summer in Manchester is getting driven to Piccadilly Station by Dad in the Jag. Mum sits up front, me and Ruby in the back. We park up, fetch our bags and prepare to return to the flat.

I give Mum a massive hug and remind her to visit Julia. Dad shakes my hand. 'Enjoy your second year,' he says, and then Mum and I are astonished when he leans in and kisses Ruby goodbye. She confuses him by insisting on both cheeks. 'Continental.' Dad never kisses or hugs. Ruby surprises them. 'Why don't you come and visit us in London? We could see a show and go out on the town.'

Mum looks excited. Dad says, 'Why not?' The deal is done. We wave as the Jag disappears. I follow Ruby into the station. That was one crazy summer, I think, I'm more in love than ever. She makes people happy, even my dad. I giggle to myself, and she catches me and asks me what's on my mind.

'You. You're on my mind.'

She smiles. 'I hope that's a good thing.'

We bash cases and bump into each other for a kiss.

'It's a very good thing indeed.'

School Days

FRIDAY 9 DECEMBER 1977

As the train pulls in, there is only one question I need to ask. Mum sees me first and waves, and I can see Dad struggling with the cases. Their pace quickens the nearer they get and then we're together amongst thousands of visitors to London. 'How's Julia?' I relax when I hear she has finished treatment and has put on weight. There are two weeks until I return home for Christmas and this weekend is all about fun. We jump onto the Victoria line and head towards Green Park. Dad is fascinated to see me whizzing around.

'How do you know all these routes?' I tell him it's easy, but I don't use the tube too much, more walking and buses, which are quicker for short distances. He studies the map, shaking his head and muttering at Mum.

I settle them into the flat, and we sit in the front room with our cups of tea, Dad telling me about the few times he has visited London. Mum asks me how music college is going, and I tell her, 'This term has been great, loads of in-depth workshops and visitors pulling us along.'

Mum has hundreds of questions. 'How's that young couple

that came up in the summer?'

'Donna and Stevie?' They're good, still together. We may see them tomorrow at a gig.

'And how's Ruby's new course?'

I hear the key in the door. 'You can ask her yourself?' I jump up and shout, 'In here,' and she wanders in after a week of studying. We do the meet and greets, and Dad gets double kisses. Ruby explains all about her new counselling course to Mum.

'It's like being back at school.'

Her change of direction was Mum's idea in the summer, and they talk about being mature students in with the youngsters. Dad and I hot foot it out of the flat for a beer. We drop into a tiny backstreet pub and Dad says, 'This is how I imagined our adult relationship.' He buys a round, and he chooses a table in the darkest corner. There's a speech coming.

He clears his throat. 'Sonny, you know I'm doing therapy, don't you?' I nod whilst sipping my beer. Dad tries a few times to start, going back to his beer for comfort, gripping his glass so tight it might shatter. He can't say anything. He just can't speak. I lean in and peel one of his hands from the pint jug. He looks at me, his eyes moist.

'I'm sorry. I'm so sorry.' We sit there for five minutes, which feels like hours before he wipes his eyes and begins. He talks about Maisie and how she destroyed his dreams and how it broke his heart.

'I always wanted a daughter, and then she was ... And then we lost her ... And ...'

'Dad, you don't need to explain everything to me ...'

'I need to say sorry. For how I've acted, for my anger, for hundreds of little things. I'm so lucky that your mum has stuck by me …' I fetch another round and Dad is composed when I return. He tiptoes around twenty years of anguish. It is so hard for me to listen to him, but even harder for him to talk. We finish our pints, rise together and shake hands.

'Thank you, Sonny, it's been good to talk.' We get back to the flat. I see Mum cuddle him and ask him if he's alright. They must have spoken about it in advance. As we're getting changed, Ruby asks me how it feels to have Mum and Dad visiting us.

'Surprisingly normal.'

'That's good. It's lovely to have Jess here. We go back so many years.'

'Err, that's not so normal for me.' I pull a face. 'Living with Mum's best friend.'

Ruby laughs. 'Thought you'd have got used to it by now.'

I let that one slide, and we take Mum and Dad out to one of our very favourite places, Mirabelle on Curzon Street and Ruby loves the attention as we are shown to our seats. A year ago, this fuss would have annoyed Dad, but he seems to enjoy it now. He says he's taking Mum shopping tomorrow, and Ruby gives her a list of must-visit shops. After dinner we take a late stroll through Green Park up to Buckingham Palace, I feel like a guide showing the tourists around town, but it's fun. Mum and Ruby walk arm in arm ahead of us and Dad starts reminiscing about Granddad buying me my first drum kit. 'Who'd have thought you'd end up in London studying music?' He goes through his gig life and is passionate when discussing music. It's great to see that side of him coming back. He lowers his voice and asks me if I mind everything being paid for by Ruby. I tell him about Freddie's hit record and that she still collects royalties every six months and that she just loves spreading it around. 'Did you see the prices in the restaurant? I've never seen anything so expensive.'

Dad can't understand that Ruby takes me to all the places she used to go to with Freddie, but she likes the familiarity. I used to think it was funny, but I tell him, 'She says it makes her feel safe. And that's important after what she's been through.'

'Listen,' Dad says, 'if you ever need a pot of money for anything, just let me know. It can't be good to be a kept man.' He laughs and adds, 'But you seem to be doing ok.'

We taxi back to the flat. Mum finds me in the kitchen, and thanks me for listening to Dad. She says, 'It hasn't been easy for him, you know, but he is getting there.'

'Are you happy?'

Mum holds me close, and I hear a sniffle or two. 'Of course we are.'

She looks happier than I have seen her for ages.

LOVE AND AFFECTION

SATURDAY 7 JANUARY 1978

I sit at the piano playing old show tunes and I spy her mouthing the words. Julia is lying on her day bed, blankets up around her chin, keeping warm. She smiles as I finish 'It Had To Be You'. I move to the chair, and we just sit together chatting about music and composers and London and life as we have done every day for the last few weeks. Christmas and New Year were complicated, Michael wanting to celebrate and charge around and Julia still so low. Even though I visit every day to see Julia, it's been a sanctuary for me too, a chance to play and talk. It's a habit that I can't escape from. She's the first person I think of when I wake in the morning. We haven't been sad, far from it, but we both know that our time together is a form of escapism, Julia from treatment and me from Waverly. Our unwritten rule is to carry on through the day, with Stephen bringing in drinks and Michael entering with toys. We just carry on. Until today.

Julia clears her throat. 'Sonny, I want you to play that song at my funeral.'

At night, lying awake with just my thoughts keeping me company I thought this day might come, but it hits me right in the gut, it draws the breath from my body and the words from my mouth. I reach for Julia's hand underneath the blanket, and I imagine being in her position, having to think about her own mortality. Time stands still.

'Are you frightened?'

'Yes, but not for myself, more for Michael and Stephen.'

Minutes pass, and every time I think Julia is sleeping, she opens her eyes and smiles at me. Her dark hair frames her face, and she is still so beautiful. I think back to when we first met in Freddie's music room, I was so young then with no experience, and she just said, 'Let's play,' and we bonded and we've become the best of friends. That meeting was down to Ruby, as was the audition, and the scholarship and the flat. This Christmas break has been stifling, and here I am with the 'other woman', as Ruby screamed at me last night when I told her I was not returning to London with her. Julia fidgets, and I hold her drink as she sips through a straw, 'Shall I play some more?'

She squeezes my hand. 'No, you've done more than enough.' Her other hand makes its way under the covers and hangs on to me for dear life.

'I love you, Sonny.'

'Hey, I love you too.'

She raises her eyebrows. 'You know, in another life, you and me ...?'

We both laugh out loud, 'Sure, we would have been the best.'

'Wouldn't we just?'

We would, we surely would.

Stephen pops his head around the door. 'What are you two laughing at?'

Julia shoots straight back, 'Wouldn't you like to know?' He smiles.

Stephen brings fresh tea and some crackers for Julia, and she sits up a little. I tell them that I have changed my mind about going back to London today, college doesn't start for two more weeks, so they are stuck with me visiting for now. Stephen can't thank me enough. He told me last week he's under pressure with bills and needs to keep working. As Julia drifts off to sleep, I sneak out, promising Michael another visit tomorrow.

I know Ruby is leaving later this afternoon, so I aim for Jack's house, anywhere to delay the inevitable. Vera opens the door and welcomes me with one of her legendary hugs. She shouts upstairs to Jack and offers me her biscuit tin. I'm starving, and several digestives disappear. She picks up on my sadness but doesn't say anything. She strokes my arm as I nab another biccy, and she knows about my daily visits. 'You going back to London soon?' I tell her I have delayed my ticket for a fortnight to help Julia get stronger again after her infection. 'Let's hope she's back on her feet soon then,' she says, and Jack arrives to save this excruciating conversation going on any longer. We head off as usual, away from the bat-like ears of parents.

'What's up?' says Jack as we head to the Rising Sun.

'Where do I even start?' We grab two beers and try to put my world to rights. I fill Jack in on the blazing row we had last night when I told Ruby I was staying for two more weeks in Manchester so I could help Julia get back on her feet.

'What's wrong with that?'

'She said I care more for Julia than I do her.'

'Bloody hell, that's harsh.'

'I know, but I think she knows it's true.'

'Sonny?'

'I have fallen in love with Julia. There, I've said it.'

'But you can't take it ...'

'I know that, it's not going anywhere.'

'And Ruby?'

'It just got out of hand, and we ended up saying some stupid things to each other.'

'Lovers' tiff?'

'Maybe. Maybe not, probably a bit more than that.' I tell Jack about the same old arguments about money and how difficult it is for me sometimes to be the 'kept man', as Dad says and that she can't possibly understand real life. She hit back with tales of her parents dying young, Freddie dying too soon and far from having it easy that's what real life is all about: getting knocked down and bouncing back. We fetch a second round, and Jack lets me know that he's starting college every Tuesday night and Wednesday all day. The factory understands he wants to get a trade, so they are supporting him. It's brilliant news, but I'm just finding it hard to be optimistic after my conversation with Julia. I knock it on the head after a couple and tell Jack that I'll call round in a week or so before I head off.

I stroll home, thinking about what to say and how to put it right. We drank far too much last night, and now I've hit the booze again in the early afternoon. Is my drinking getting out of hand? I call into a shop for a packet of extra strong mints. I turn the key in the lock and see Ruby's cases lined up in the hall and hear her in the kitchen.

She doesn't mince her words. 'Welcome back, Sonny, to my house.'

It catches me off guard, but I don't want to fight today. 'Sorry I said those things, I was out of order.'

Ruby looks hungover. 'I'm sorry too. Sometimes I am not quite as together as you think.'

'I didn't mean to ...'

'Sonny, I do get jealous you know, every day you leave me to ...'

'Ruby,' I shout, 'do you know what I've been doing today? Do you? It's not all about you.'

She is visibly shocked by my volume. 'No. I don't.'

'I've been planning funeral songs with Julia.'

She chokes. 'I didn't know, I'm sorry. Has it got that bad?'

'She is scared for Stephen and Michael. I don't think she's going to make it.'

Ruby comes and hugs me and apologises for being so stupid. 'I thought it was the beginning of the end for us. I didn't realise.'

'I just need to help a friend in need. As soon as Julia is strong enough, I'll be back to my studies.'

'And back to me in our flat? I can't live there alone.'

'Of course.' We kiss.

Something changes in that moment. For the first time, I know that she needs me, not wants me. She needs a man in her life to exist, and her sympathies for Julia evaporated last night when she knew I'd chosen to stay a little longer. We make some small talk, and I say the right things so she can travel to London without worrying about us. There's only one way to make her see sense, but I daren't say it yet. Dad pops round, pulls the Jag out of the garage, and we head into Manchester. We hold hands all the way. I put the cases onto the train, and we say our goodbyes. I leave it until the whistle goes. 'What would Freddie have done if Julia had been this ill when he was alive?'

She winces, I know I have hit the target. Ruby will think of this all the way to London, and she will remember Freddie as the most generous man and loving husband, and I know she will regain her respect for Julia. I watch as Ruby takes her seat, wiping her eyes already. We stare at each other for as long as we can. The train inches forward. I feel this is the beginning of the end but I don't know how long these things take. We blow each other a half-hearted kiss.

I jump in the front seat. Dad turns his head. 'How you doing, Sonny? That was a quiet journey.'

I confide in him for the first time. My thoughts about Ruby needing someone, anyone to live with. 'She chose me because I was there.'

'Listen, Sonny, she happened to be in a club when she met Freddie, that's chance. Freddie happened to have a hit song, that's chance. She didn't choose to become a widow so young. You happened to be in a room with pro musicians when Alphonso was present. That was chance.'

'I know, I know but…'

'What I'm saying is, this whole episode was not pre-ordained, it can't be.'

'I know, but sometimes it feels like it. She needed someone, and I happened to be there.'

'Thirty years from now, you'll look back on these times with love and affection.'

'Really?'

'Sonny, I've seen you grow up, change, mature, whatever you like to call it in the last two years. You've transformed into this young man who is almost twenty, self-assured and positive.'

'It doesn't feel like it.' He puts his foot down, and we pull away from the other cars.

He whoops. 'She chose me to drive Freddie's car.' He's laughing at all the power under his feet.

'Brilliant. Thanks, Dad.'

We pull up at the house and put the car away. Dad insists, 'Come to dinner tonight. Mum's doing a roast.' It's music to my ears, and I am delighted to accept.

The Meaning of the Blues

Saturday 21 January 1978

I leave Manchester Piccadilly at ten past two. The train creaks towards London. It's a nice crisp day, and I enjoyed my last northern winter walk for a while this morning. Julia was in good spirits, sitting up and eating and looking stronger. I hope these experimental drugs do the trick. We finished our plan for her funeral songs in that first week, and the subject hasn't been revisited. I dropped in at Jack's house on my way home to pack, he's loving carpentry and says it feels right. Karen is going to study from September onwards, and Fred is still walking Ringo every day. Mum and Dad dropped me off and told me they have plans for the builders to visit, so I'm to expect a new house on my return.

I put my head back, shut my eyes and realise my world is changing around me. I am looking forward to getting back to London, and I play through my conversations with Ruby over the last two weeks. We have spoken every night on the phone, sometimes twice. Dad is right of course, so much of our lives are chance, who we are with, where we are at a particular time of day, what we are doing at that exact moment someone enters the room and changes the direction of our lives. We pick up speed, my head is swimming with thoughts, and as we rattle south, my love for Ruby grows. She has overcome so much, and she is the most generous person I know. She loves the gigs and shopping and fancy restaurants, and she always picks up the bill. After our bust-up two weeks ago, Ruby rang Michael and Julia and said Freddie had left some pots of money for family and friends in crisis and she got her bank to transfer a large sum of money. She uses Freddie as an excuse. I suspect it makes giving more comfortable for her. The journey is airless and oppressive, so I walk the thirty minutes to the flat, time to wake up. I get some flowers on the way and write out a little love note on the card. Mum's right too, absence does make the heart grow fonder. I take the stairs two at a time. I'm thrilled to be back.

I ease the door open, there are bin bags and wine bottles ready to go out, the hallway smells of food, and Chet Baker is singing 'You Don't Know What Love Is'. Alphonso greets me in silk pyjamas and a towel on his head. I'm stunned. It's nearly five pm.

'Hello, Sonny, how's Julia?' He doesn't explain what he's doing here.

Ruby appears, straight from the shower by the look of her, her dressing gown on and also with a towel on her head. I'm staring at a convention of Hussars. Ruby kisses me on both cheeks and says Alphonso stayed overnight because they ended up talking till gone two and drank far too much. 'We're going out soon to eat, but we won't be late.' She turns towards the bedroom and waves her hand at me. 'There's plenty in the fridge.' Alphonso ambles to the spare room. I'm not sure who is more embarrassed.

I have been in the flat one minute, and my dreams vanish. I leave my bags on the floor, turn off the music, grab a water and take a seat on the sofa. On the train I was thinking of a return to normality, now it appears the writing is on the wall. Ruby appears and startles me. 'We're going out. We'll talk later.'

Alphonso waves from across the room, 'Buona notte, see you on Monday in college.'

I wave back, is this happening? My college lecturer is going out with my girlfriend, and I am being left alone. I unpack, check the spare room and bathroom have been used, and then I tidy up the mess in the kitchen and put the bins out. I do the only thing I can think of doing and call Donna. 'I'm back.'

I tell her what just happened, and she says, 'I'll pop round in an hour,' and then gives me the best advice of the day, 'Call your mum. Mums know best.'

I reveal to Mum what's happened since I said bye to her about four hours ago. 'Alphonso. Are you sure?' is her first response. 'He's about twenty years older than she is.' I remind Mum that I am sixteen years younger than Ruby, so it's feasible, and she gives up on that argument. She defends her friend and asks me to give her the benefit of the doubt. 'Make sure you speak with her.' I ask Mum if Ruby has said anything about us not lasting as a couple and the pause says everything I need to know. Of course they have spoken about me, they've been best mates for over ten years.

'Mum, I don't know what to do.'

She listens to my fears, calms me down and says to take it one day at a time. I sense her using her social work mantras on me. 'Don't over think, or plan too far ahead.' I have to keep in mind all the positives in my life. Even if the worst happens I still have college. 'You have a home in Manchester and a bright future.' She cuddles and massages me from a distance and makes me feel a whole lot better, and finishes the call by saying, 'We love you, you know that.' I do know it, and I tell her. 'And so does Ruby. Let me know how you get on.'

I open a bottle of white wine and that first mouthful is cold and minerally and lasts all of ten seconds. I look at the label. It's a Gavi, Alphonso must have brought it round. The buzzer startles me and Donna is inside and hugging me as I pour a second glass. It's so good to see her. 'How's Stevie?'

'He's fabulous.'

'Where is he?'

'He worked today. We're meeting for brunch tomorrow and going out for the day.'

'Listen to you, brunch and Sundays out, so middle class.'

'Says the posh boy drinking wine in his sumptuous flat.'

It's great to have my buddy back. We bounce off each other in the best way. She asks about Julia, and I tell her about the dark moments and the good times and then she dives right in. 'So, Ruby and Alphonso? Tell me more.'

I'm more relaxed than when I phoned her. 'Maybe I overreacted. I know he used the spare room because I checked.'

'Nothing to talk about then?'

I go through Christmas and the big argument and Ruby getting jealous because I was visiting Julia every day. I sound like I am moaning and whining on about nothing.

Donna cuts in. 'Any good news?'

'Well, she chucked five thousand quid at Stephen and Julia last week.'

'Bloody hell. What for?'

'Because she can.' My anger starts to subside. 'And she really is a lovely woman.' This brings me to my senses, and I apologise to Donna for calling her.

'Hey, don't worry, that's what mates are for.'

She lets me in on her plans for when she graduates. Donna and Stevie want to go to New York, her to study and he's thinking about working there. They are visiting at Easter and I should book in and come with them. 'You could use a break.' She says that Skytrain is cheap if you book now and they are going for two weeks including an audition for her at Juilliard. Donna gives me the run down, and I promise her I'll think about it. We say good night.

I shower and jump into bed even though it's only nine, and I lay there thinking about a trip to America, how good would that be. Jazz and hotels and river trips with two friends. I think of looking up Tommy Flanagan, that would make the trip special. I could visit Blue Note Jazz club, maybe play a little. I drift in and out of sleep, thinking of Maisie for a while; she never had these chances. I think of Julia, who may never get these chances again, and I think of Freddie, who had the whole world to play in but couldn't see the wood for the trees. I think of Dad, who is pulling back from self-destruction because Ruby was brave enough to challenge him. And only two weeks ago he told me I would look back at these times with affection. I believe him, but it's difficult in the present. I should be more grateful. I know I should.

I turn on my side and Ruby is looking at me. 'Hello.'

'Hello.' She kisses me and guesses my thoughts.

'You know I would never cheat on you, don't you?' She snuggles in.

'I'm sorry.'

'I'm sorry too. We've all had a lot on our plate.' She warms her cold body on mine, and we kiss each other more than we have for the last month and make love like we did the first time. We lie on our backs panting, thinking, hoping.

'Sonny.'

'Yes.'

'Whatever happens to us, I'll always love you.'

'Goodnight, Ruby.' She turns over, and I cuddle her from behind. I kiss her neck and reach down to hold her hand. She is a remarkable woman. 'Ruby, I'll always love you too.'

Bye Bye Love

Thursday 23 March 1978

I'm sitting on the train hoping I make it in time – Gatwick is so far out of London. I keep checking my watch, but the hands are static, and I am cursing myself for being goaded into arguing with Ruby. She knew for three weeks I was going today, yet we saved the big argument for this morning. She demanded to come, said she knew people in New York, said she could make things easier for me. All the things I want to escape from. When I said I was seeing Tommy and some of Ella's crew, she let me have it big time.

'Who do you think introduced you to all these fucking musicians?'

That hit home. It's true. Of course it's true, but people don't own people; she can't control the rest of my life based on who she introduced me to. I wouldn't be able to move. I sit here going round and round, re-living the hurtful things we said to each other in her flat, not 'our' flat as she screamed at me. When she asked, 'Why do you say you need to escape? Who are you escaping from?'

I said it, out loud, with tears in my eyes. 'You, Ruby, I need a rest from being stage-managed.' She looked at me as though her world had ended. There was no way back.

She burst into tears. 'You're just like Jimmy, always on the take.' She ran from the room. I didn't follow. Her questions had worn me down over the last few weeks about why I was going, how had I got the money, who was I meeting? All questions that reminded me of Ruby when I was seventeen, but I'm twenty now and ready to face what the world has to throw at me.

'This is the end of the line.' A disembodied voice on the train inserts itself into my thoughts. I wipe my eyes, look up, and the mass of people are moving like ants returning to the nest. It's Gatwick, I'm here, and I'm stepping from one world into another.

'Where have you been?' shouts Donna as I get to the gate.

'Don't ask.'

'Not a smooth exit then?'

I tell Donna all about the big bust-up. She's heard about the arguments over the last few weeks as tensions rose. She also had to get involved with me officially as my student buddy. I got hauled in about my attitude and progress. It was weird being lectured by Alphonso, someone who I saw more and more as he continued to visit the flat. He appealed to me to work hard 'in difficult circumstances', to put the practice in and get the rewards. Donna had been present, and she was asked to keep an eye on me. It's true. I had slipped behind, first Julia, then Ruby, any time my head wasn't in the zone I avoided the work. That was most days. I remember when Dad used to bawl at me for being lazy, for staying in bed and 'For having ideas above your station like Walter Mitty.' That's how I've been and as Alphonso said last week, 'You're not a teenager anymore, Sonny,' which was a touch ironic, as he was at my twentieth birthday dinner three weeks before when we all went out on the town.

'Alright, Stevie?'

He's walking towards us with snacks for the plane. He's been double shifting at the fish market to raise money for this trip whereas I rang Dad and told him of my predicament. He sorted it out for me. He went to the Midland Bank, where he knows the manager, and they set me up with my first account. Dad then deposited five hundred pounds in it for me. He used our home address to keep it simple and posted me my cheque book, which I have kept hidden from Ruby. I went straight to the travel agents with Donna and Stevie, and we booked our flights. I also withdrew some cash and took us all out for a Wimpy. It felt so good buying my friends a meal with my own money. Well, Dad's money. He rang me up and told me all about traveller's cheques, dollars and how to stay safe abroad. I left him the hotel details in case of emergencies, and I pleaded with him not to tell Mum as I didn't want Ruby to get to know and he joked down the phone, 'Mum's the word. Or not in this case.'

My God it's noisy. The take-off is exhilarating, and we scream like we are on a roller coaster. The constant hum of the jet engines and the passenger noise keeps me awake the whole flight. I have plenty of time to think about Ruby and me, and I'm sad we parted on such bad terms. Donna chips in with advice, and listens as I go over and over and around and around my three years with Ruby.

She takes my hand. 'The thing I love about you, Sonny, is that you always end up saying you love her and you always end up saying she's an amazing woman.' I smile as I think of all the

good times. 'So, write her a postcard when we land and tell her.'
I promise myself I will.

I drift off to sleep trying to be positive, but all I can hear is
Ray Charles singing 'Bye Bye Love'.

'Ladies and gentlemen, welcome to John F Kennedy airport.
The time in New York City is five pm.'

BUT BEAUTIFUL

SATURDAY 1 APRIL 1978

New York is the best, and we are having so much fun. Donna had her audition last Monday, and because she said we were staying in town, a couple of students latch on to us and show us the ropes. Martha and Vincent are at Juilliard, and they book some practice rooms for us and introduce us to loads of young players. People seem to assume we are already a trio and we're cool with that. Over the last week I have re-discovered my love for jazz, just out and out playing, swinging hard. The NYC guys are lamenting that funk and disco are in vogue, but we are taken to so many bars late at night playing the music we love. 55 Bar, Brooklyn Academy and the Village Vanguard. Sonny Rollins playing live was a treat, and Stevie got to meet Elvin Jones. Tommy Flanagan dropped into college and found us in the basement. He'd got my letter, and he talked to me like a long lost friend, we had a little play together, and Stevie and Donna were on fire. Tommy called a few of the teachers during a break, and we played a set in the afternoon with so many people dropping in on saxes, trumpets, vibes and percussion. They talked to Stevie about studying here. The impromptu session has led to a support slot at Blue Note tonight as a warm-up for Donald Byrd. Vincent is on trumpet and Martha on synths and a few vocals. I have never practised so hard. I'm twenty and about to play live in New York.

We sit in Tom's Restaurant on Broadway talking about tonight's show. Lots of paper and scribbles, we have just thirty minutes of playtime and all on house instruments. Our practice slot is after the main band have set up, so time is tight. We decide on four tunes from the seven we have been rehearsing. Donna looks across the table as the burgers arrive. 'What do you think, partner?' I'm so happy, this life feels a million miles from London. If you can play, you play. In London, it's more if you know someone who knows someone, you can play.

I change seats and squeeze in between Donna and Stevie. 'No one knows us here and yet ...'

'They love us,' shouts Stevie, he puts on his best New York accent. 'They sure do.'

'But they do,' I whisper.

'Sonny, we are all good players, you know,' says Donna, 'Don't be too surprised.'

It's funny how sometimes our progress in our minds is not measured correctly. Julia used to tell me about how those daily practices add up to something tangible, and I am nearly two years in. I have played music full time for almost three years when you consider how much I did up to my audition.

'I suppose sometimes I forget that, but coming here and meeting these new players, well ...'

'You've upped your game, mate,' says Stevie.

'Et tu, Brutus.' Stevie looks perplexed.

Donna laughs and shakes her head. 'Ignore him. He loves his Shakespeare.'

We finish our food, agree to meet the guys later and head back to our little hotel to get our heads down before tonight.

I hear them chatting next door. This sleepy backstreet hotel has paper-thin walls and original wallpaper from the 1930s. The spring-like day becomes a chilly late afternoon, and I lie back and dream of a globe-trotting career as a professional musician. It would be good moving across continents, rhythms and cultures and soaking up the people and places. I've loved New York this past week, even more exciting than when I first went to London with Ruby. My head spins with questions. Is it because I'm older or less shy? Is it because I am with friends and not a new lover? I think I am just in a different place mentally, and happy to accept the gifts of friendship and collaboration which are here in abundance. I can't sleep, I don't need sleep, I'm alive and buzzing. The whoops coming through the walls tell me that Donna and Stevie are also wide awake. I stretch behind me and rap hard. The noise stops, and Donna bellows, 'Come round.' Then she adds, 'Bring cawfeee,' in her best NYC drawl. I jump up and grab some sachets.

'Hello,' shouts Donna. 'Welcome to our boudoir.'

I throw the packets at Stevie, who has filled the maker and is desperate to brew. We sit on the bed and drink hot steaming coffee and talk about how lucky we are. Stevie says he would be finishing a gruelling ten-hour shift on the market now and he's had enough. He talks himself up and says he wants to come back here with Donna in September. I say I might apply next year and Donna says, 'I've got to get my scholarship first.'

We stop, backtrack, and then we crash like Icarus. We've got ahead of ourselves, we've flown too high too soon. Donna is going into Juilliard on Monday morning before we head home through the night. She can't afford the fees unless they say yes to a scholarship. Stevie gets up for more sugar, Donna is restless and our passion for New York has cooled a little. For once Donna looks worried, and I reach out and tell her she will be fine. 'I know, I know.' I break the deadlock and get the setlist from out of my pocket, but it doesn't do the trick. We've gone from rejoicing to praying for Donna. Just two more days.

As we walk into the club, Donald Byrd is on stage with his six-piece band the Blackbyrds. Martha and Vincent are already there, and our jaws hit the floor, they are playing a tune called 'Funky Junkie', it is like nothing we've heard before. One huge melting pot of ideas, electric bass, synths, vocals and of course screaming trumpet from the man himself. Our mood swings back to the top, and we catch a couple of tunes. He walks over after they have finished and says hi and mentions he has heard great things about us. 'Really, from who?'

'I'm a Manhattan music man,' he taps his nose, 'but I still have my contacts at Juilliard.' He promises to watch our set and shoots off. We look at each other.

Stevie speaks first. 'That was like meeting the pope.'

Vincent is hopping from foot to foot. 'Donald Byrd, Donald Byrd. He's coming to see me play.'

'And who was that on the keys?' says Martha

'That was Kevin Toney,' booms a voice from the speakers. 'Right guys, on stage please, we've got under one hour until doors open.'

No more times for nerves. We move through an empty club and onto the stage. I have a grand piano, and Donna is given a double bass, Martha jumps on the Odyssey synth and is baffled. Jake the sound man dives backstage, and the Kevin Toney joins us and sets Martha straight on the bells and whistles, this is what is beautiful about jazz: there are no egos. In five minutes we are set and ready to play. Jake sorts our sound out, and Kevin stays and watches the warm-up. I'm in heaven.

When we peek at the club just before show-time, it's buzzing. Jake puts water on stage for us. We have ten minutes to go. Stevie is tap, tap, tapping, Vincent is whooshing and blowing air through his lips, Martha is humming and aaahing, and Donna is gluing over her blistered fingers. This is my landscape pre-gig. We all have our rituals to perform. I have the setlist ready for my stand, and I've asked Vincent to do the intros; he has this mellifluous voice like Harry Belafonte. Jake calls us to the stage. We eyeball each other, nodding in staccato, repetitively, silently wishing each other well. We begin our walk to the stage, ladies first. The applause grows, and I'm taken back to my eighteenth birthday party when Jack and Karen joined me in the music room. I look at the lights, hazy in the smoke and wonder what Ruby is doing right now. I take my seat, glance at the audience and listen as Vincent introduces us as the London Jazz Trio and friends. I play my way in to 'But Beautiful', and we settle down. Donna looks across and smiles at me just like she did at my audition, she calms me. It seems like only a few minutes have passed when Vincent announces we are on our last song. I check my watch. How did twenty minutes go so fast?

'Ladies and gentlemen,' he elongates his words and goes

around the band and introduces us all to huge applause. We each take a bow. 'One last thing. I chose this song because I love the Jazz Messengers,' and the place goes crazy. 'And on this, our last tune, I am pleased to tell you we have a very special guest,' he pauses for maximum effect, 'Mr Donald Byrd.' Vincent looks at me, and he's got a grin wider than the Hudson River. He gets to play with his hero. I count us in, and we take the roof off. I turn around at the end of the tune and notice the Juilliard gang at the bar, cheering their own, and I spy Tommy applauding. This is the life. We all stand up and take a bow together with Donald Byrd. He thanks us and goes backstage and we walk to the bar.

Tommy showers me in congratulations as Donna and Stevie get dragged away. He says he is sure to update Alphonso on the gig. He asks me if I am going to come back here and study one day like my pals. I look surprised, and he says, 'Whoops, guess I've let the cat out of the bag.'

'Are you sure?'

He takes a moment. 'From what I've heard, you guys have had a first-class week, and Juilliard are offering both your friends international scholarships right now.'

I see them creep around the corner. They are trying to keep it quiet from me. Donna and Stevie are holding hands, and I know they are thinking about the rest of their lives. The nearer they get, the more they smile.

'Guess what?' says Donna.

'Congratulations,' I scream. 'I've just heard.' We dance and jump, and we holler and whoop with delight. Vincent and Martha join us in celebrating.

Donna looks at me. 'You next, buddy.' It wasn't a question.

Stevie looks elated. 'I only came for the ride. Now I'm coming here to study. Blimey, wait until I tell me old ma.' We laugh some more and cry, and a round of beers appear and as our performance adrenaline leaves us as we collapse into seats. All through the music, I can see them whispering to each other. I think they will be thrilled to be in New York. At half time, I chat with Tommy, and he asks me how my young lady is.

'Ruby?'

'No, the other one. The lady who sang when Donna sat in on bass.'

The blood drains from me. All this week whilst I have been here I haven't given her a single thought. 'You mean Julia?'

'That's the one.' He smiles. 'She was so charismatic, so beautiful. Her voice reminded me of Blossom Dearie.'

'I'll tell her. She will be happy to hear that.'

We hit the town later, our newfound friends and friends of friends too, spreading the love all over West Village. I even see Waverly Place which is where Freddie got the name for his house. These old familiar places keep cropping up wherever I go, and of course, I think of Ruby. We toast Donna and Stevie a hundred times, and they talk accommodation with Martha, and they still have to visit the college on Monday to sign up. We end up in some bar, and the first photo I see on the wall in the gents is Blossom Dearie singing on stage at the Blue Note. I squint to read the writing; it's dark, and I'm drunk. I've never done anything like this before but I twist the frame and slide the photo out and tuck it inside my shirt. At three am we stagger home, arm in arm. This has been the best night of our lives.

Stevie mumbles. 'We get to live here in six months.'

Donna smiles at him. And then she cuddles me. 'Sonny, thanks again for the intro. You can be the best man when Stevie asks me to marry him.'

He laughs. 'In your dreams.'

The night porter looks weary as we ask for our keys. He must see a hundred drunks a week.

'Your room number?'

'202.'

'Here you are sir, and there's a message for you.' He hands me a folded note.

'To Sonny.

Urgent. Call home. It's Julia.

Dad.'

I sober up instantly. The best night of my life has just become my worst nightmare.

Trying to Get Home

Monday 3 April 1978

I'm in the diner with all the bags. I'm shaking and cursing and checking my watch over and over again. I've had too much 'cawfee' and they keep refilling. I can't do anything but sit and wait. The plane is at five, and it's only midday. We've packed and checked out, and they've gone to college, leaving me all alone. I called Mum this morning. Julia's at home with nursing support. I cried for so long I ran out of coins. I went out and changed a twenty and called Ruby in London. She was surprised to hear from me and started asking me questions about who I'd met, which clubs I'd been to. I cut her off, I just couldn't handle the enthusiasm and asked her if Dad could drive the Jag to London to pick me up as Julia was spending her last few days at home. Her attitude changed in an instant, and as usual, she was magnificent.

She told me not to worry Dad. 'Tell me your flight details, and I'll have a driver ready for you.' Freddie used to have a chauffeur for artists flying in, and she said she would call him. 'Do you want me to come with you?'

I paused for just a few seconds and said, 'No, not at the

moment.' I knew that sounded cruel.

'It's not a problem, Sonny, update me when you can.' She sounded frustrated.

'I'm going to stay at Mum's.'

'I thought you might.'

We left it like that, and I'm now sitting here with a Sprite thinking I didn't mention Waverly Place, or Blue Note or Tommy, I just asked about her using her car. When I get home, I need to put that right, or maybe I should call her from the airport. Why didn't I think it was alright for Ruby to come north with me? I replay the conversation, and it still doesn't seem right. I just knew I couldn't handle Ruby being there.

Donna massages my neck. 'Hey, Sonny, you ok?'

'Not really, how did you get on?'

'We're in. We're signed up. Just got to do visas and stuff in London.'

I manage 'Congratulations' to both of them and settle the bill. I check my watch for the hundredth time as the cool air helps with my sugar rush. A big yellow taxi is outside, opposite a pink hotel. We jump in, and I shout, 'JFK please.' It's a twenty-five minute ride, and as we cross the river and head out, I am not thinking about what we are leaving behind, only what awaits me.

I take the window seat and wallow in my thoughts. We're above the North Atlantic. All I can see is water and clouds as we climb higher and I think of where Julia is going, and tears flow. Donna holds my hand, and I drift in and out, but the same thoughts keep knocking me awake. The unfairness, the beauty, poor Stephen and Michael; how will they cope? Donna forces me to eat and drink. She says I will need my energy to support Julia, and as we begin to descend, she pays her own tribute. 'You know that time we were at Jimmy's. She was fierce, a strong woman who took control. I loved her that night.' I'll take that. 'Fierce.' It takes me back to my English studies and what was said about Hermia, 'Though she be but little she is fierce.' That's my Julia.

Ruby Tuesday

Tuesday 4 April 1978

As I exit 'Departures' I see my name on the board, and we hug and kiss our goodbyes.

Donna is weepy. 'Call me.'

'I will, I promise and … Congratulations you two. That was a great week.'

They leave hand in hand and Phil the driver carries my bag and says it's just five minutes to the car. I can't get there fast enough, I'm pushing him along, and now there's a bloody queue for payment. My heart is racing, and my thoughts are spinning out of control. Phil points me to a green Jaguar, opens the door, and we are off. He puts some jazz on, and I drift off to some big band music. At the services in Birmingham I make a quick call to Stephen, telling him I'm a couple of hours away and ask him how she is. 'Comfortable,' is the answer. What a bloody word that is, a cover-all that means drugged up to the eyeballs. I'm calmer now that I have spoken to him. Phil offers me a coffee, and I admit I'm all out, America has done me in for caffeine. Water is good.

'You a musician then?'

'Yes, I suppose so, just been playing in New York.' I might as well as enjoy the second half of this trip.

'You know Freddie?'

'Yep, he used to come to my house and play trumpet.'

Phil glanced over his shoulder. 'Trumpet. You should have seen him on the piano. What about Jimmy?'

'Yes, I knew Jimmy too.'

'You know Charlie Watts?'

'Yes, I played with him once.'

'You're kidding me. He's fun. Told me once that Ruby Tuesday was written about Freddie's wife?'

'Seriously?'

'You know Ruby?'

'Yes, I see her from time to time.'

'Bloody shame what happened to him like, but she's a diamond. I always loved having Ruby in my car, so polite and one of us.'

'What do you mean, one of us?'

'You know, working class, nothing pompous, salt of the earth like. She wasn't even called Ruby when he met her.'

The fun stops. I turn towards him, speeding along in this magnificent beast. I can't believe what I've just heard.

'What was she called?'

'Susan. She was a singer and had a mate called Trish on guitar.'

The story unfolds, and for a moment I forget why we're bound together in this car hurtling towards Manchester. They used to busk in Manchester and Freddie would see them on the way out of the office. Susan had a great voice, and she badgered Freddie for help when she found out what he did. The girls made sure they were at a dance when they knew he would be there and 'The rest, as they say, is history.' Freddie changed her name to Ruby so she could make her first record and when that failed, she agreed to marry him. He told her he would look after her forever if she dropped the singing and became his wife.

'What about Trish?'

'I never heard of her again. You'd have to ask Ruby.'

'Was she happy giving up the singing?'

'She told me once it was the best decision she ever made. She loved Freddie. She loved Waverly, the house where they lived, and she got to meet all the famous stars and dine in the best restaurants. All that after being brought up in a children's home like me. I think that's why we got on so well.'

Today of all days, I thought I'd be thinking about Julia, and now all I can do is worry about Ruby. 'That's why she doesn't have many friends. They kept moving her around.' And then as a young girl, she was adopted, but her parents weren't nice to her. He says he judges people on how they are and 'I have always found her to be honourable and loyal.' I have to agree. Those are traits I recognise. In no time at all, I am directing him through the back streets towards Julia's house. We jump out of the car, and Phil fetches my bags.

'I'm sorry I can't invite you in for a cuppa, it's not my house.'

He shakes my hand. 'Don't you worry about me, I'm rushing back for a dinner date.'

He's smiling in anticipation, and I wish him good luck. 'I hope she's worth it.'

He backtracks, it's not a date as such, he's taking Ruby out to dinner. 'She said she hates being on her own in the flat, just a fear of being alone since childhood, I guess.' He pauses, perhaps remembering his own problems from way back. 'It will be lovely to catch up with her, and it's a real treat as it's her birthday today.'

'I'd forgotten.'

He looks perplexed. 'We're going posh tonight?'

'The Mirabelle?'

'How the f …?' He looks stunned, calls me a 'Bloody mind reader' and heads back to London. He's told me more in two hours than Ruby has in three years. I can't believe I've forgotten her birthday.

Someone to Watch Over Me

I haul my luggage up to the front door and knock on. Julia's mum Marj answers and ushers me, in saying she's asleep at the moment. She directs me to the kitchen, and Stephen sits at the table head in hands. Michael looks up from his Lego, smiles at me, gets up and jumps into my arms. 'Hey, little man.' It's good to see him, and he holds me tight.

Stephen stirs, he looks so tired and I apologise.

'Sorry, I must have nodded off.' He looks beaten.

We shake hands over the table. 'How's she doing?'

My eyes search for good news, but there is none. He can't bring himself to say the words and then shakes his head as the tears flow, and I make out, 'Not long now.' I grip Michael even harder.

I don't want him to see my tears, but Michael breaks the silence with, 'It's raining,' as they splash onto his neck and we somehow laugh together, wiping our faces. 'Mummy said not to be sad,' and we look at this four-year-old dishing out advice as he returns to his toys. The kettle clicks, Marj delivers the tea, takes a seat. 'The nurse is with Julia, so don't worry.' Stephen asks me about New York, and I lie and say it was okay. He remembers Donna and is pleased she got in. Marj thanks me for giving Julia the night at Ronnie Scott's, 'She won't stop talking about it.' Amongst all the small talk we avoid mentioning what's really happening in case that sets us off again. Tea and cake sustain us for some time until the nurse enters the room.

She startles us, and we look up, desperately wishing for hope, even a miracle. 'Are you Sonny?' I nod. 'She remembered you were coming today. She's quite lucid at the moment, so why don't you come through?' We stand and march behind her like tourists at an attraction. Michael runs ahead, the least fearful. No one has prepared me. I try not to show my horror. Julia lies in a hospital bed in the music room, drip in her arm, blankets up to her neck. She is tiny. This is not the vibrant singer etched in my mind. Michael climbs onto the foot of the bed and strokes her legs through the blankets. I take a deep breath, bite my cheeks and clench my fists, anything to prevent me sobbing.

'Hello, Sonny. How was New York?' Julia's voice has changed. Breathy and higher pitched.

Nurse Freda pushes a dining chair up to the bed and directs me to sit down. I'm now so close to Julia I could kiss her. We brush cheek to cheek and I stroke her hair and try to give her some of my warmth. She's still my Julia.

'New York was fantastic. You'd have loved it.'

She smiles as I take her hand and regale her with all the tales of fun, practice and performance. She 'oohs' and 'aahs' and at times seems pleased to be involved in the story. Julia nods off every few minutes, then wakes and smiles as I keep up the stream of jazz songs that we had to learn on the fly. I finish up at Blue

Note with Donald Byrd joining us on stage, and she murmurs, 'Just like old times.' I'm not aware of anything else, just me and Julia, eye to eye, breath for breath, talking about what we love. I tell her about Blossom Dearie and how I've got a signed photo for her, and she manages, 'Really?' She looks delighted, and I promise I'll bring it with me tomorrow. I think back to when I told her about that one song when I first got hooked. She understood; she got me, and I got her. The bond can never be broken. 'You're here to watch over me.'

'I am.'

I talk and talk until Freda touches my arm and whispers, 'Rest time now,' and I kiss Julia goodbye. She squeezes my hand and whispers, 'Make sure Michael continues the piano won't you?' and I promise with all of my heart. No one else is in the room, she falls asleep, and I slip away.

I return to the kitchen table. Marj pushes a tea under my nose, followed by cheese on toast. I am so hungry. Stephen slurps his tea. 'Thank you, Sonny.'

'What for?'

'For being here, for talking to Julia, for being so ...'

Marj finishes the sentence, 'Normal. She lit up when you talked about music.'

I ring Dad for a pickup and promise them I'll be back tomorrow morning.

Dad throws the bags in the boot, and we sit in silence for a while.

'Alright, Sonny?'

'I will be.' He pats me on my thigh, and I realise he's been through this before with his parents and Maisie. The thigh rub is his way of showing me he understands what I have been through today.

'I thought I wouldn't be able to do it.' I was scared before talking to Julia, but, 'It ended up being the most natural thing in the world.'

'I'm so glad you made it back in time. It will mean a lot to the family.'

'So am I, Dad. So am I.'

As we near home, I remember there is one more thing I have to do. I run in, say, 'Hello,' to Mum and dash through to the front room, shutting the door behind me. I lift the receiver and dial.

'Happy birthday, Ruby.'

'Hello, Sonny. How's Julia?' I break down.

We talk about London, and I tell her all about New York and Tommy and how we ended up at Blue Note on stage. I can hear how happy she is for me, genuinely happy. She thanks me for the postcard I sent.

I wander back to the kitchen. Mum knows me best. 'How's Ruby?'

I hug her and say, 'Fine.'

She twitches her nose. 'Sonny, you smell. Take a shower.' That's twenty-four hours of travelling for you.

'And how is Julia?' I smile, not for me but for Julia.

'She is surrounded by love.'

THESE FOOLISH THINGS

FRIDAY 7 APRIL 1978

Stephen answers the door, Michael rushes out and shouts, 'Piano.'

'Of course, little man, if that's what Mummy wants.'

He puts his arms out to me, and I scoop him up, and we head to the music room. The piano is squeezed into the corner now as the hospital bed has taken over. Nurse Freda is finishing her bedside duties but beckons us in. We see her every morning. She looks at Michael. 'Are you playing today for Mammy?' she says, and he is excited. He jumps on the stool and starts bashing away. I see Julia's eyelids flicker and maybe the merest hint of a smile. Freda leaves the room as we begin our rituals. I have done this every day this week. He loves playing, and he gets stronger as Julia gets weaker. Since we said our goodbyes on Tuesday Julia hasn't uttered another word. The drugs dull the pain, she looks very peaceful, and Michael still chats to her and kisses her every time he leaves the room.

Freda comes back and checks the pump, but we carry on up and down the scales and three blind mice. We sit in the kitchen at lunchtime, and Freda updates us. Weeks have turned into days and now 'Just a few hours I think.' Silence. We don't discuss how or why, we just feel our way into an afternoon that comes naturally. Marj dusts the room, Freda washes Julia and puts on new sheets, Stephen makes some calls and Michael and I go to our sanctuary, the double piano stool. I have sat here so many times with his mum, and now she is passing the baton of teacher to me, and my first and only pupil is the most precious.

I just play whatever comes into my head. Michael leans in and cuddles me and then falls asleep. Marj moves him to the foot of the bed where there is his little indent from days of love. I'm aware of people coming and going to say their 'goodbyes'. I simply carry on. And over a few hours, Julia fades away. No tears today. Michael wakes and says, 'Is Mummy gone?' and we say yes and he says, 'Goodbye, Mummy,' and goes with Marj to get his milk. Freda leaves the room. I stand up and hug Stephen.

He feels strong. 'Thank you.'

'It was a privilege.'

'Will you play at the funeral?'

He knows the answer, Julia has organised everything. I place Julia's hand in mine and think about a friendship that I thought would last forever.

'Wasn't I a lucky wee boy to have married such a fine woman?'

We gaze at Julia lost in our memories. We hug each other once more and I take my last look at his beautiful wife.

I say bye to Marj and give Michael one last cuddle. 'Piano,' he shouts at me. I look at Marj for help, and she peels him off.

'Maybe tomorrow, young man.' I open the door to leave and Marj shouts at me. 'Don't forget to sign the book.' It's an old Irish custom, all visitors to the house and at the funeral check-in so the family knows who's visited. She points to the hall table, and I sign my name at the bottom of the page. I have a glance. Quite a few I recognise: Mum and Dad, Fred and Vera, Miss Wolstenholme. Stephen has rung so many people. I missed them all, lost in my own thoughts whilst playing. I flick the page over and there she is halfway down, that familiar handwriting. Ruby Wilson.

FIRE AND RAIN

SATURDAY 8 APRIL 1978

I need fresh air. I need some space to think, I've been in my own little bubble for the last few days. I don't want to speak to anyone except Julia. She'd understand. I'm lost, so lost without her. Mum tried to talk to me this morning, but I just put my hand up and she understood, and said, 'Tell me when you're ready. I'll be here.'

As I walk along these familiar Manchester roads, I think about New York. The tall buildings, long straight blocks, the buzz of the city, the diners we visited, too much cawfee. And fun. And now I'm miserable and sad, and I feel for Stephen. I knew I'd end up back at the house, it feels the right place to be. Marj lets me in, and Michael leaps at me for a cuddle. It is so heart-warming, feeling the love of a child. 'Piano,' he shouts and takes me through, the curtains and window are open, blowing through some spring air. The hospital look and feel has vanished, and it's back to being a music room, with pride of place going to Julia at Ronnie Scott's. I lift Michael up, and we look at the photo together. 'Isn't your mummy beautiful?' He repeats, 'Mummy gone,' and my heart breaks. I breathe in through my nose and bite my lip, stemming the tears I'm desperate to cry, and we have half an hour together on the piano. Stephen pops his head around the door and smiles at us. Michael jumps down to play with his toys. 'You don't have to keep coming if you don't want to.'

'I do want to, I really do.'

'Are you sure?'

'It's helping me.'

We sit and chat and plan, next week is going to be busy with Michael and the arrangements. 'You must call me if I can do anything.'

I walk for miles and end up at the church, as I knew I would. It has become a safe space for me, and I wander around the graves and have a chat with Maisie. What would she think of her younger brother? What wisdom would she impart? I walk to 'our bench' as Mum calls it, head down, morose. Through the branches, I can see a couple sat on it already, and they look at me as I turn the corner. Mum pats the bench, and I sit between them. Mum puts her arm around me, and Dad places his hand on my thigh. Silent support flows through me.

Mum squeezes me tightly. 'We thought you'd end up here.'

I break the news. 'Ruby's back.'

'I know, we saw her at Julia's yesterday.'

'Stephen did an amazing job of contacting everyone.'

'It was lovely to be able to say goodbye.'

Dad coughs. 'Well done, Sonny. Beautiful playing yesterday.'

'The least I could do.'

'It was,' he's lost for words. 'It was …'

'Appropriate,' says Mum.

I ask Mum, 'How did Ruby make it in time?'

'She's been phoning me every day to see how you were, and

she decided to come up on Wednesday. She's been waiting for you to call.'

She could have chased me, but she didn't, she waited. Dad heads off, leaving Mum and me, and I tell her about my car trip with Phil. Mum doesn't know any of the details. 'If Ruby wants you to know her history she'll tell you herself.' She's right. It changes nothing for me. I just have a greater understanding of her. I walk Mum home, pack a few things and head off to Waverly. Mum knows I have to go. 'Be kind won't you, to Ruby and especially to yourself. You've been through a lot this week.'

'Mum. I don't think I'll be going back to college.'

'You don't have to decide today. Do what you have to do and take your time.'

I visit June on the way and buy a huge bouquet. I need to make amends. She teases me about being back in town, and I play along. 'That's me. London, New York, Manchester.' Ruby's car is in the drive, and for a moment I have second thoughts. I look at the flowers and remember what Mum said about being kind. I talk myself into seeing her, but I don't feel it's right to use my key, so I knock and hold the flowers high. The door opens, and I jump out from behind, 'Surprise.'

Alphonso looks at me, 'Hello, Sonny. We've been expecting you.'

Ruby puts the flowers in a vase, Alphonso makes some fresh coffee, he appears at home in the kitchen. We talk about Julia, we all have so much affection for her. Alphonso says she had it all. I tell them I've been teaching Michael to play and he's a great student, and Alphonso asks me, 'One for the future perhaps?' We keep bringing the conversation back to Julia, and she makes us smile as we recall the effect she had on everybody, how people always felt better after being in her company. I see Alphonso look at Ruby and I know what he is thinking, she always makes him feel better too, and I get that. After a strange week, I can't stomach staying here.

'I'm off.' Ruby walks me to the door. I pick up my bag.

'You were going to stay, weren't you?'

'I thought so.'

She holds my hand. 'You still can if you wish.'

'No, it wouldn't be right.' I'm thinking of Julia.

Ruby stares at me, brushes my cheek with her hand, 'You were brilliant yesterday, and Julia looked beautiful, very peaceful.'

My eyes are watery, my heart is stuttering, maybe the caffeine again, or the realisation of who I lost yesterday, or possibly who I am losing today.

'Thanks for the flowers.'

There's so much I want to say, so much I need to tell Ruby, but today, the day after Julia died, is not the day.

'You're very welcome. And …'

'Sonny?'

'Thanks for coming yesterday. You and Freddie were good friends to Julia, I know that …'

We hug on the doorstep at Waverly, just like we did in October '75 at Freddie's wake when I first called her Ruby. She's been through so much in such a short time, and I am beginning to understand the weight of losing someone you love. It plays on your mind.

Ruby lets me go. She's crying too. 'I'll always love you, Sonny.'

We part with a kiss on both cheeks. 'Continental.'

I think about her words as I walk back to Mum and Dad's.

She said, 'I'll always love you.' I know what she means, I get it, she means she'll always love me 'Because', and then there is a long list of reasons left unsaid:

'Because you were there.'

'Because I was lonely.'

'Because I missed Freddie.'

'Because I needed company in this big house.'

If I'm honest with myself, I have the same feelings. I'll always love Ruby because she helped me escape Dad, because she took me into this fantasy world, because of the music room, because of London, because she introduced me to Julia. Oh my God, Julia. I've lived a lifetime this week; a husband has lost his wife, a son his mother, and I've lost a friend. A true friend. I can't see me ever going back to London, not now.

The front door opens as I approach, and I collapse into Mum's arms. I'm a wreck.

'Ruby called, she said you were on your way back.' She puts me to bed like a five-year-old, and even tries tucking me in. I look around the room, it's different. I'm in a double bed, cream walls, new wardrobes. Mum says, 'We told you we were getting the builders in. You haven't noticed a thing, you've been in such a state, coming back late, leaving early, looking after Julia and her family.' She says, 'You're exhausted, maybe I'll call the doctor tomorrow.'

'I'll be fine, Mum.'

'You need to rest now.'

I pull a bottle of whisky from under my pillow. My mind is off again, analysing words, what does the 'Now' mean? I understand what it means: 'Now Julia has gone.'

I go to sleep dreaming of Julia and Michael.

THREE LITTLE BIRDS

MONDAY 10 APRIL 1978

I didn't get up at all yesterday. Apart from nipping to the offy. I felt numb and was happy to stay in bed all day, sustained by tea and toast, which arrived regularly. Sleep brings no peace, just a headache and problems with my mind whirling faster than a helicopter. I can't stop fidgeting, willing myself to shower and go downstairs. It's just over a week until the funeral.

I sit at the kitchen table. It's new. I look up, and I'm in a different world, a place where I am meant to feel safe, and yet it suddenly seems so strange, a kaleidoscope of colours and smells I don't recognise. I want to make some toast, but the toaster isn't there anymore. I try to look out the window, but the curtains have gone, my life is unravelling, and I feel lost. I'm staring at the window when Mum comes in.

'You ok, Sonny?'

'I've lost the curtains.'

She laughs a little, leans past me and pulls a cord. Light floods in, stinging my eyes, and I sit back down. 'We've upgraded to a Venetian blind,' says Mum. 'Fancy some toast?'

'I've lost the toaster as well.'

She smiles and says she'll give me the grand tour later. 'But for now, just sit there, and I'll butter it for you.' She pulls back a fancy corner cupboard with a revolving shelf, spins it and retrieves a new toaster. 'Lazy Susan.'

'Who's Susan?'

She ruffles my hair. 'Don't you worry about a thing, Mum knows best.' Bread emerges from a new bread bin, and within two minutes I'm tucking in to some posh brown bread with Mum, butter dripping down my chin. A mug of steaming tea sits in front of me. Mum looks at me. 'What are you thinking about, Sonny?'

'I'm thinking where is the white bread? This loaf has got lumps in it.'

'Seeds,' she says seriously. 'They're seeds, and they're good for you.'

I smile and she realises I am winding her up. 'We do have brown bread in London, you know.'

'Do you like the new kitchen then?'

I take a look around for the first time. 'It's pretty good really. Why did you change?'

Mum took me through all the heartache of living in a house built in the 1950s and hadn't been modernised. Dad had vetoed everything over the years, mainly for financial reasons but really because he didn't like change. Since he started getting some help, he's a new man. 'I know you don't quite believe it but ...'

It seems so superficial. 'As long as you're happy, Mum.'

She takes my hand. 'Sonny, I do know what you're going through. We both do. You will get through it.' I know I will, deep down I know it, but everything just feels so heavy at the moment, and I can't face Ruby after what happened yesterday.

The stairs creak above us. Mum shouts, 'Speak of the devil.'

Dad plonks himself down and winks at me. 'Any Sunblest, love?'

Mum turns from the sink and sees us both smirking. 'Make your own bloody toast, Pete, taking the mick out of me.' She still makes him a mug of tea and puts his bread in. Some things never change.

'What you doing today, Sonny?'

'Think I'll take a walk somewhere.'

'To Ruby's?' asks Mum. She knows how we parted yesterday.

'I'm not so sure, maybe later in the week.' Dad offers me a lift, but I hit the streets alone and lose myself in my thoughts.

I end up in Manchester leafing through vinyl records and thinking what Julia would say as I examine every work of art and read the liner notes. The eldest member of staff comes my way. She's about forty, still a hippie and she sidles up to me. 'Looking for something?'

I hold up Electric Warrior by T-REX, and she smiles approval. I want to speak, to utter the truth but I'm stuck. I pick up the album behind, Dandy in the Underworld. We look at Marc Bolan's beautiful face, and she whispers, 'So sad that he's left us.'

'One of my best friends died last Friday. I just can't see the point anymore.'

She holds me and smothers me in a mountain of tie-dyed cuddles. 'I'm Cindy.' Her long dreads and beads bounce around my ears. 'You poor thing, I wondered why you looked so down.'

'It's just …'

'Come out the back.' She leads me behind the counter and

along a corridor, makes me a coffee, and we talk for ages. I let everything out. All my hopes and fears pour out of me in front of this stranger. It's easier talking to a stranger. I tell her about Maisie, about Ruby and my music and Dad. But most of all, about Julia.

'I understand, I really do.'

'She was the most amazing lady.'

'Listen, if you believe in anything, if you have some faith, then I know that everything you do in the future will have a little bit of Julia in it.' That sounds nice. Cindy asks me why I ended up here.

'Because this is where I always imagined coming with my sister.'

She cuddles me again and says, 'You'll be fine. I know you will. I can feel it.' I tell her about the music and what I am playing at the funeral. 'Maybe I'll come and pay my respects.'

'You'd do that?'

'If you want me to. If it helps you.'

This expression of love lifts me and Cindy knows she can let me go.

ASCENSION

FRIDAY 14 APRIL 1978

Yesterday was the saddest day of my life. My dreams of the coffin turned into reality, and I sat there staring so bloody hard my eyes were drilling holes in the wood imploring Julia to return from her sleep, like Romeo's Juliet. I spoke at the funeral, and I played the songs chosen by Julia. Michael came up and sat on the piano stool with me. We whispered our tear-stained goodbyes throughout the service. I was in a trance. Cindy from the record shop did turn up. She was a symbol of hope; we had said so little, but she understood me.

I looked at Ruby and thought of how she must have felt walking down the aisle before sending Freddie on his final journey. I remembered her heaving with sorrow, and now I know I understood nothing. I didn't take a swig until after the service, and then crashed and burned.

Losing Julia has left me numb and although we spoke about my future, and Michael's, I didn't give those conversations respect. I was afraid of having them because they somehow signalled the end. I am lying here alone wishing I had been more open. Julia always told me to take on the world, to study and travel and collaborate. I can't see past my tiny little bedroom right now. I was so in love with Julia, and in love with music and learning, and I have lost the lot. I pull up the sheets and ignore the knock at the door.

I squint through one eyelid and the clock says midday. They'll be gone by now. I come round at quarter past, take a leak and rush through some cornflakes. 'Fuck it,' I scream at nobody and nobody replies, 'You know you want to.'

'Do I? Do I really want to?' I smile at the thoughts running around my head, the conversations with 'Nobody' which leads me to the drinks cabinet and I knock back some of Dad's Scotch, lace up my boots and rush out. I suck in the air, my lungs need fresh air, but my head needs something else. I take the bottle out of my back pocket and take another hit. I sit on a swing in the park and drink the rest. The internal battle inside my head continues. I win the argument and decide to go to town for some drugs. I want to lose time again like I did in London with Donna.

I head for the bus, buy some more Scotch on the way, and look forward to a solitary session, although someone in my head keeps interrupting saying, 'Stop, you promised.' I apologise a thousand times but I can't stop now. I'm swigging away on the top deck when some lardy wino demands I share it with him. I wave him away, but he comes right back at me. I can see other people starting to move, but I'm in no mood to back down. His bark is probably louder than his bite, and he presses the buzzer to get off. Out of the corner of my eye I see his fist flying towards me and it cracks me in the face, I hear the bones splintering in my head. That's it, I lose it, and for the first time in my life, I launch into a flurry of punches, and he's on the floor, and out of my good eye I continue to rain blows. This is for you, Julia, for all the pain you had to put up with, the years of treatment and worry. My fists collide with his face again and again, blood spurts out of his busted nose. I'm aware someone is trying to pull me back but I'm not having any of it. This is for you, Julia, for the misery and for the suffering you endured, and I am sorry I never told you I fell in love with you. The tears and blood cloud my vision, and I can't see straight but I attempt one last punch as a policeman hauls me off. My fist cracks against the side of the seat as he jerks me back and I collapse on the floor. That felt so good, but I am exhausted.

In the back of an ambulance, they clean me up as best they can. I listen to them arguing outside.

'We're going to have to arrest him, he committed a serious assault.'

'He's too injured, we're going straight to hospital. He needs X-rays. Have you seen his face?'

This goes on for minutes, neither side giving in, and then the morphine kicks in; it's gorgeous and I float away. This is the feeling I wanted when I left the house. I want to be on my own rising above all this shit. They make me wait six hours to sober up, then they wheel me to theatre.

The policeman is there when I wake up on a ward. He gets permission from the doctor to talk to me and the game begins.

'Why did you beat him up?'

'He hit me first.'

'We know that from the witness statements.'

'That's it. He deserved it.'

'Who's Julia?'

'None of your business.'

'The witnesses kept saying that you were shouting, "This one's for Julia".'

I smirk and it's painful, my sunken cheek has been repaired and my eye is still closed. My right hand is killing me and looks twice the size it should be. Mum would say I have to stop lashing out but I'm glad I did this time.

'Who's Julia? We're worried about her.'

'You should be. She's dead.'

His face changes, and he reaches for his radio. I press the button and tell the nurse I am going to be sick and ask for privacy. The curtains close around my bed and don't get pulled again until Jack appears.

'Fucking hell, Sonny. What happened to you?'

'Where do you want me to start?'

'What were you doing to get in this state?'

'Some idiot tried to steal my drink, and when I said no, he punched me.'

'Sonny, you were never a fighter.'

'I know, but … He hit me first.'

'When can you come out?'

'Tomorrow, I think. It depends on the police. Can you do me a favour, tell Mum and Dad not to worry.'

'Are they ok?'

'They're driving me mad. Over-protective and fussy.'

'Listen, I'll think of something, get some sleep.'

Jack promises to let everybody know I'm okay and I sleep like a log. It must be the drugs.

In Dreams

Monday 17 April 1978

The weekend in hospital is so lonely, hardly any staff, and I banned Mum and Ruby. They can't see me like this. The police visited and I told them the truth about Julia, and they said they'll be in touch. The wino is recovering with a broken nose.

Jack and Karen bounce in. 'I phoned Debs, we cooked up a plan last night. We're worried about you.'

'Tell me more.'

Karen says, 'We've decided you are surrounded by oldies, and you need some space, so you're coming with us. The top team from college is born again.'

'Is Debs coming home?'

'Other way round, we are going to Debs. Me and Karen have got the week off, I've told your mum and I've told Ruby you are having a rest.'

He's brought a bag in from home packed by Mum and we sit and wait for the discharge notice, and we walk to the station.

The motion of the train sends me to sleep.

I wake up as the train pulls into Edinburgh station. Jack carries my bag, Karen walks ahead, and there she is.

'Hello, Debs.'

'Sonny, what the … You look terrible.'

'I'm sorry.' I burst into tears.

'Come on, let's get you back to mine.'

I have been asleep for over three hours with no benefit. My head still hurts, my mouth is dry and I can't see a future. We meander along the busy streets, past the library and up past the uni. My head throbs and my hand is not my own.

Deb's house is huge. 'Not everyone's back for the new term, so I'm giving you a couple of their rooms. No fighting.' That's it, my mates take control, take me to my room and send me for a bath.

I hate baths at home, I think it's a fear of Dad shouting that he's coming in because he needs the loo, but here, in a separate bathroom, I drift and dream for hours, topping up the hot. I don't want to go home, I don't want Ruby and I don't want to go back to London. I'm ruled by negatives. I'm not sure anymore, I'm just not sure. I can't see a way out. My mood sinks and I close my eyes and slip under the water and all the noises stop.

Freddie is in front of me, in his shirt and tie. 'It's not that bad is it?'

I say hello to Julia, and she smiles and says, 'Don't worry.'

Maisie appears as a grown up and we dance. I see green hills and sunshine. I smile as Julia waves and then … The water rushes in, suffocating me, threatening to overpower me. I suck in water, I can't catch my breath as my dream ends.

Debs crashes through the door, a mug of tea splashes across the floor. 'Noooo.'

I haul myself up, coughing and spluttering. She hurls a towel at me and pulls me out and clings on to me. She rubs my back and whispers, 'Sonny, I'm sorry, I am so sorry. I didn't know it was this bad.'

I know what she's thinking, but it takes me a while to talk.

'I wasn't trying to … You know.'

'That's what it looked like.'

'I wasn't, I promise. I just lay back and all the voices stopped. It was so peaceful.'

'Sonny, you need some help. Please let me help?'

'If you can.'

'Tomorrow, I promise. Now get changed and come down, you need to eat.'

We sit around the kitchen table.

'This reminds me of the canteen in college.' We used to rush there at lunch times.

'Good times,' says Debs.

Jack and Karen smile at each other.

Debs takes my left hand. 'You are allowed to smile.'

'I can't, not yet. I feel so guilty. I think my face might break.'

Jack says we are going for a walk, just the boys, and he forces me up and out. He has a handwritten map from Debs. 'We're going to see Arthur.'

An hour later, we are at the top of Arthur's Seat, a huge hill overlooking the city. The lights sparkle below us as people drive home and the tourists drive in. It's a nice evening, we sit on some rocks facing the castle.

'So,' says Jack

'So what?'

'Debs told me about the bath.'

'It was nothing, honest.'

'Why do you feel guilty, Sonny? It's not your fault that Julia died.'

'I know, but I keep thinking …'

I go back to that night in Ronnie Scott's, when she mesmerised the whole room, that's the night it first crossed my mind. Just a fleeting thought as she sang on stage, a moment of madness but a seed was sown.

'I'm in love with Julia.' Tears come easily.

Jack puts his arm over my shoulder. 'Bloody hell, Sonny.'

'I know, it sounds so stupid. I can't believe I said it.'

'Did you tell her?'

'I think she knew, but no. I didn't tell her.'

'What about Ruby?'

'She knew. Well, she guessed.'

'Did you speak about it?

'No, of course not. And you mustn't tell anyone.'

'I won't. What are you going to do?'

'What can I do? Julia's dead.' I wipe my eyes.

We sit and talk for ages, going over the last few years. I mention Germany but Jack says he can't, not now. He has plans. He's grown up whilst I've been in London and they are looking forwards not backwards. We laugh about Mr Potter, the day we got our new suits and the night of the storm. It's nice to be with someone my own age. I've missed hanging out. It's going dark as we descend into the city. We wind our way along Queen's Drive and head for the house.

Jack puts his arm around me. 'When all this is over, you've got to go back to London and finish your degree.'

'I don't think so. One, I don't want to and two, look at this hand.' It's still swollen and painful.

'Listen, I'm your mate. No messing.'

Jack knocks on the front door, he really is getting too sensible.

I nudge him. 'Jack, you've got something on your trousers.'

'I'm not falling for that again, Sonny.'

'No seriously, it must have been from when we were sitting on the rocks.'

He turns to look.

'Pooh bum.' And for the first time since the funeral, I'm in stitches.

'Someone's looking better.' Debs pulls me in for a cuddle.

'Thanks for telling Jack to bring me here, I needed this change of scenery.'

'We're your oldest pals, and we'll always be here for you. And no more drinking.'

'That's what got me into this mess. I just wanted to forget everything.'

They send me to bed, and Debs promises we will go out tomorrow, just the two of us.

I lie awake in bed thinking about the first girl who understood me, Debs. The innocence, the poetry, the intensity and thirst for knowledge.

But when I sleep, I dream of Julia. All of the time.

New York State of Mind

Tuesday 18 April 1978

After breakfast Debs takes me to the park below the castle.

She opens her rucksack. She has brought her A Level English files and we spend hours looking at the silly notes we used to send each other. It feels a world away. 'I can't believe you've kept them all.'

'You know when we were studying all the lovey dovey stuff?'

I guess, 'The Romantics?'

'Yes, I thought these notes were our way of saying we loved each other. I kept them in case …'

'In case we ever got together..'

'Now I am bit older, I realise that sometimes we are in love with different people at different times.'

I remember laying on the footy pitch at school with Debs, staring at the clouds. 'The wrong times?'

'No, not wrong, just different.'

They were happy days, daydreaming. 'Do you remember "Ships that pass in the night?"'

Debs guesses, 'Longfellow?'

'Yes, Tales of a Wayside Inn.'

'You know what I mean, don't you, Sonny?'

'Yes, I do. That was me and …' It's all I ever dream about this last week. She's right, we love different people at different times in our lives, and Julia and I were …

'Sonny.' She breaks into my thoughts.

I glance at Debs. 'I did fancy you though.'

She waves a paper. 'I know and I've got the poem to prove it.' She snaps the file shut.

'I don't write any more. Do you?'

'Every day. Listen, I'm sorry about Julia.' We talk about my eighteenth birthday party and how Julia got up and sang and stunned everyone with her voice. They are lovely memories of good times.

'She did it again, you know, at Ronnie Scott's, she was amazing.'

'I can believe it.'

'And how is your course?'

'You'd love it, Sonny, the department is so cool, the degree totally suits me.'

'That's because you're such a square,' and she agrees, but only when it comes to English.

'Do you ever wished you'd have come with me?'

I think about it, I mean I did love English, I still love it, but music is something else. 'New York was amazing, the fun we had playing every day and sometimes all night too.'

'What was Blue Note like?'

'I've never seen anything like it. Being in the lights, hearing the audience giving immediate feedback, playing with your mates. Nothing beats it.'

'Sonny, you were right to choose music. When are you going back to London?'

She catches me out. 'I'm not sure I can.'

'After everything you've just said, you'd be mad not to.'

'I think I'm splitting up with Ruby.'

'Bloody hell, Sonny, talk about all your buses coming along at the same time.'

'I know, I know, it's just ...'

'Sonny, take it easy, you've been hit by a cannonball.'

'That's how I feel. And by the way, you're mixing your metaphors.'

'What?'

'Buses are modern, cannonballs are ancient. Not good together.'

She screams, and we laugh out loud as we roll back the years and talk for ever about our teachers, mates, novels, poems and Shakespeare. They were the good old days, nothing to think about except words. Debs surprises me again by saying at one point she was sure we'd get together and I ask her about Linda from Outward Bound. 'That didn't work out, and ... I'm not gay anymore.' We laugh together. 'I just love whoever I love.'

She kisses me on the cheek.

I tease her. 'So I've got a chance then?'

'Err no.'

'Why not.'

'Because I live with Hamish now and we are an item.'

'Where is he?'

'He's away with his family, back next week for the new term.'

We descend into tears as I tease her about becoming

the archetypal English girl who goes to Scotland and bags a Scotsman.

'I know it doesn't look good for my feminist credentials, but he's gorgeous, you must come and stay again, you'd love him.' We spend another hour winding each other up and talking about everything and anything. Debs is ace company, and I really want to come back at some point.

She walks me through town, into uni and the gardens, across the bridge and for a couple of hours I forget about Julia. It's not until Debs is queuing to get a coffee that the guilt descends. How can I be out? How can I be laughing and joking with friends and talking about the future? The deceit floors me.

I sit outside, all alone, and the tears start again.

'Sonny. Sonny. What's wrong?'

Debs splatters the coffees on the table as she cradles my face, and hugs me. 'After last night, we need to get you sorted.'

'I think I'm done. I can't believe I beat that guy up, I feel so angry.'

'Come on, drink up and follow me.'

She leads me to the medical centre and I pour my heart out to a doctor I have never met who listens to my story.

'Listen, Sonny, you've been hit hard, you recognise this, you're a smart kid. Sometimes our minds play tricks on us, and we overthink. You just need to rest for a while. No distractions.'

Dr Brangan prescribes Valium for three days. She says it's a time-out for my mind. She asks if I am okay staying in Edinburgh.

'I guess so.'

'Come back here on Friday, we'll see how you are. How does that sound?'

'It sounds too simple.'

'Just take it one day at a time, I'm glad Deborah called.' She calls Debs back in, and updates her on the prescription. 'You're in good hands.'

LET IT BE

FRIDAY 21 APRIL 1978

Debs and I walk to the medical centre, we've meandered all over Edinburgh for three days like tourists. Even though the drugs made things hazy, my friends have looked after me from morning until bedtime, and my anxiety and anger has started to subside.

I knock on the door and hear, 'Come in.'

I push with my left hand. Dr Brangan smiles, 'How are you Sonny?'

'Much better, I've got the best of friends.'

Take a seat, please. 'Tell me about your friend who died.'

'Julia.' I smile, and the doctor relaxes into her seat.

'Good memories?'

'Yes. Very good, there was this one time …'

I go on and on about the time we rehearsed like mad for my eighteenth birthday party and how she stunned the room, and then I mention the time when we went to Ronnie's, and it seems to me that I go through our whole lives together. I can't stop smiling.

'She sounds like a very special lady.'

'She really was very special.'

'Hang on to those thoughts, not the anger. Don't be afraid to talk about her, it helps.'

'Thank you.'

She takes the bandage off my right hand, extends my fingers, makes me clench my fist.

'You're very lucky. All sorts of ligament damage but no broken bones. Let's hope the nerves are ok. Start moving it now, a little bit more every day.'

She walks me to the door, and calls Debs over.

'He's free to go back to Manchester anytime now. You guys really helped.'

'It's been lovely having him stay, thanks, Dr Brangan.'

'And Deborah, is he a really good pianist? The way he talks about the music, it sounds exhilarating.'

'He is.' We walk away slowly, Debs put her arm around me, and I can't stop smiling.

'You ok?'

'I was thinking about Julia.'

'That's a good thing, right?'

'I guess it is. I just need to learn to live with it.'

Jack and Karen have made sandwiches and we gather round the table like we always did. Jack confesses he's been calling Mum everyday as she has been worried, and I'm good with that. Karen says she needs to get back, so we plan our train journey for tomorrow and head into town to get our tickets. I dive into a phone box and call home. Mum is happy to chat but my money starts to run out and as the line beeps I hear one last shout, 'I've got a surprise for you …' and she's gone.

We end up climbing the hill again, and we look out over Edinburgh. Karen gets excited about Australia, she and Jack seem sorted on their plans for studying, emigrating, kids in the future. They have it mapped out.

Debs gets serious with me. 'Sonny, on Monday you spoke about New York and music with so much passion, don't forget that will you?'

'It's not at the front my mind.'

'Well it should be. We need to keep talking about Julia like Dr Brangan said, and you know Julia would have wanted you to carry on.'

Jack and Karen take a walk, and Debs makes me stand up and she takes my hand and we gaze into the distance.

'I want you to come back here, Sonny Jackson. Come back as a pianist, a professional musician. And tell me you did it because you wanted to.'

I grip her hand so tight, she gives me a little shove and wriggles free. I look up and will my tears not to fall.

'I'll be watching you, and so will Julia.'

WISH YOU WERE HERE

SATURDAY 22 APRIL 1978

We leave Manchester Piccadilly and head for home on the bus.
I tell Jack and Karen I need some air before facing the parents
and now I am all alone sitting on a swing in my childhood park,
ebbing back and forth. I used to love coming here with my mates,
messing about on our Raleigh Choppers trying to impress the
girls by pulling wheelies. Jack and I were pretty quiet compared
to some, but we had our moments. As we got older, we used it as
the meeting point, the place to start the fun for our little gang.
I'm twenty now, and the fun left me last week.

A little old lady winds her way towards me with her dog
pulling her along. Bent double, stick supporting her, she inches
forward. 'Hello, Sonny, will you walk with me?'

She surprises me, breaks my train of thought. I look up. It's
Miss Wolstenholme. She offers me her arm, and I am proud to
take it.

'What happened to your face?'

'It's a long story.'

We stroll around the path. She begins a tale about a young girl, a pianist who dreamed of being different from her mother. She was an obedient child who studied hard, went to Sunday school and learned to dance. She never got into trouble, never drank and never cursed. She fell in love, and she danced every weekend. She met her boyfriend, who became her fiancé within weeks. They made plans to get married, for her to move out and to have a family. He was called away to fight for his country. We sit on a bench, and she leans on me for support.

'We loved each other, but he never came back.'

'I'm so sorry.'

'I was that girl, in 1916, and I lost my Bert, but that love has lasted me a lifetime. It sustains me still.'

Miss Wolstenholme weeps, and she digs deep for her handkerchief. 'When I looked at Julia's coffin, I recalled my dancing days and the love we shared. We all go on somehow, we're changed, but we carry on.' She sits and smiles, her back straightens a little and her cheeks become rosier as she thinks about Bert. She raises her watery eyes to mine.

I pick at the scabs on my right hand.

'Sonny, your hand, same story as your face?'

'It's my own fault. I was so angry about Julia, I lashed out.'

'Listen, you and Julia were my outstanding pupils. Don't give up now. She wouldn't have wanted you to.'

I haven't told her anything, but she senses my doubts. She places her tiny hand, wrapped in its old leather glove, on my thigh. Now and again, she taps me as we sit in thought.

I silently promise her I won't give up, and she continues her walk alone, waving her stick at me from afar. All these years I had thought of this little old lady as a spinster who chose to live in her parent's house, I was so wrong.

I sit on the bench for ages, crying and smiling and laughing and joking, rewinding and then playing scenes over and over. I can't go back and change anything. I can't change Dad as the angry young man. I can't change Ruby as my fairy godmother who pushed me to London. I can't bring Julia back to life. I can only change the future, my future. I am going to finish my degree, work hard and make Julia proud. I know what I want to do. I just have to figure out how to do it.

Take Five

Sunday 23 April 1978

Donna wakes me with a cup of tea. It's so good having her to stay. Mum had called her when she knew I was coming home. She told Donna she thought I was having a breakdown, and she rushed up. That was my surprise. It's been a weird week, but I am back from Scotland and feeling better. This house has changed so much, the dreariness of my teenage years has given way to this beautiful home for Mum and Dad. We sit on the bed discussing it, and Donna says it feels comfy and friendly. I look at her. 'It's not me, I don't feel I belong here anymore.'

'You have to decide what to do, what is best for you, not everybody else.'

'I know but …' I can't say it.

'Is Ruby a problem?'

I think about it. 'She's not a problem. I just can't see me going back to the flat.'

'Have you told her?'

'I can't, can I? How do you tell the woman who has given you everything …'

'That you want nothing.'

'I'm very grateful, but I want …'

Donna gets me to say it, over a week after Julia passed away, I admit it. 'I think I want to finish my studies, I just …'

'Don't know how to work it out?'

'I'm stuck, aren't I? I don't know how to …'

'Just take five minutes to think about it, we'll find a way.'

Donna finishes her tea. 'Julia would have wanted you to finish too.'

She leaves the room, and I lie back on the bed and think where all this is going, and I have imaginary conversations with Julia and Ruby and Mum and Dad, and they all end the same way with me saying, 'I don't know.' I'm twenty, I'm lying in bed at my parents' house and I can't make a decision.

Mum knocks on the door. 'Breakfast time, we've got a visitor.' I drag my body from under the covers into the bathroom. Mum has this theory about sticking to a routine and repeats her mantra every morning, 'Breakfast is the most important meal of the day.' I look into the mirror. No wonder they are worried about me, I look a mess. I rub stubble, stretch my eyes wide and resolve to do something about it. I stumble downstairs and into Mum's new kitchen, and I have three faces staring at me, Ruby has joined Mum and Donna for a brew. They stop talking as soon as I enter.

'Double, double, toil and trouble.'

Ruby looks at me, checking out my face and hand. 'Don't say it.'

I smirk. 'Weird sisters, otherwise known as the three …'

Mum cuts me off. 'Sonny, don't you dare …'

Donna says, 'Nice to have you back on form, Sonny the bard.'

Mum brings the porridge to the table. Something else she insists on every day.

I remove the lid, the steam rises. 'Ah, the cauldron bubbles.'
We laugh together.

Ruby stands up, so does Mum and they announce they are
going out for the day. Ruby says, 'Donna wants to practise, so
take her to Waverly and use the music room.' She adds, 'You've
got your key. Enjoy.' I fear am being hijacked, but Donna insists
it was her idea and she's not letting me off. I guess it's a little
easier when others make decisions for you.

Playing again is fun, one handed most of the time, not
thinking too deeply, just messing around together. Donna
makes it easy for me, suggesting tunes, pushing me on, I lose
myself in the music and time flies by. I decide to introduce her
to my most precious student, and we shoot off to Stephen's for a
cup of tea. We show Donna the music room and Michael points
to the wall and says, 'Mummy.' Donna lifts him up, and tells him
how she was also there that night. She tells him a story, 'Once
upon a time, there was a brave lady and a young prince who
saved my life.' Stephen and me sit on the sofa, and we hear that
night retold as a fairy tale, and the derring-do of the protagonists
entrances Michael. 'And the prince returned to London, finished
his studies and became a world-class pianist in New York City.
The end.'

Michael claps and shouts, 'Again.'

Stephen cheers. 'I liked that ending.'

I look at Stephen. 'Are you sure I can do it?'

He says, 'Are you for real? Julia told you to finish your studies,
you eejit.'

They all look at me. 'I liked that ending too.'

We walk back to Mum's, and on the way, Donna offers me her

flat. It's gorgeous, and it would suit me. She says I'd be mad not to finish my studies. She's sure she can move in with Stevie for two months before she moves to New York so I can have it for my last year of study.

'It sounds great but …'

'But what?'

'How do I tell Ruby?'

Donna hits me with the truth. 'Perhaps Ruby knows already. She will be having the same thoughts. It's obvious you two love each other, but you can't live with each other anymore.'

'Really?'

'Sonny, trust me on this one. A woman knows, ask your mother.'

After dinner, I do ask her, and Mum doesn't say much, yet she says everything. 'Ruby is desperate to talk to you, but she knows she has to wait until you are ready.

'Why?'

'Sonny, she understands what grief does to you.'

'What do you think, Mum?'

'You're strong enough now, go and see Ruby tomorrow.' I head off to bed, lost in my thoughts, leaving Mum and Donna chatting. As I hit the bottom stair, Dad calls me. I take a seat on the new sofa.

He talks to me about life and ambition and says, 'I guess you can't see the wood for the trees at the moment.' He surprises me. 'Stick with your passion, don't get stuck with something mundane, and do something to honour Julia.' He says Mum has told him I've been struggling for the last week and I agree. He jokes, 'I've been struggling for twenty years.'

'Thanks, Dad.'

'What I am trying to say is that I will be there for you, Sonny,' he looks at me. 'I love you, Sonny.'

We look at each other, I know he's struggled all these years, and he's reaching out to me.

'That means a lot.' I tell him about Donna's offer and I may need some help and that I'm going to see Ruby tomorrow to clear the air and it is becoming more obvious what I need to do.

'Well, good luck tomorrow.' We stand and hug, no more handshakes.

I head towards the stairs again, I can hear the girls still chatting away in the kitchen. I decide I haven't been entirely honest and open the door.

He looks up.

'I love you too, Dad.'

ONCE I LOVED

I had the best night's sleep since I've been home, from about 10 pm until eight this morning. After chatting with Dad, the fog lifted, and I sat in bed working out what I had to do. He was right, I do have to honour Julia, but today I have to thank the woman who inspired me. I wolf down some cornflakes, push a note under Donna's door and head out into the cool morning air. My pace is quicker. My head is clear.

It's nine when I knock on the door, and I hear soft footsteps padding across the hall. She opens the door, the woman I fell in love with many years ago, still in her pyjamas, hair tied back, holding a mug and looking beautiful.

'You're early.'

'I'm sorry.'

'Hey, don't be sorry, come in.'

The words I have ready, the words I practised in the mirror this morning and repeated on the walk here, aren't the right words any more. How could I have got this so wrong? They are words for the page, not face to face. I haven't broken up with anybody before, and it's difficult with someone who has given me so much. We sit on the kitchen stools facing each other. I can't start.

Ruby helps out. 'Listen, Sonny, I get it. Two years ago, I was mired in grief. I thought I was going to drown in my own tears.' And on and on she goes, telling me how she felt after Matilda was stillborn, how she felt after Freddie killed himself. 'I was so caught up in my sadness, I thought about ... Well, you can guess.' She holds my hand and says, 'You saved me, Sonny. You saved me.'

'I never knew.'

'You didn't have to, but you did.' She knew people were saying it was wrong, we were wrong, it was too soon and it wouldn't last. None of that mattered at the time. 'I just needed company because ...'

'You were lonely.' I remember what Phil the driver had told me.

'Yes, I was so lonely but ... But more than that, I knew I had so much more to give.'

'Thank you. Thank you for giving your love to me.'

'You are so bloody polite!' she screams and smiles at the same time.

'Ruby, I have made a decision. I am going back to study. I owe it to Julia, to Mum and Dad, to myself but most of all, to you and Freddie.'

I get some of my words out, the ones I had rehearsed.

Ruby is in tears. 'Thank you for talking about Freddie.' She says when she meets people, they never mention the ones who have passed away. She recovers her composure and surprises me by asking, 'Where are you going to stay?'

'Dad said he would help me rent Donna's flat for this term, and my final year.'

'That would be nice. Can I come and visit?'

I breathe normally, it's going to be all right. 'You better had.'

We sit here like two old friends reunited after a fifty-year absence, and we hold hands and laugh and cry. 'I loved taking you to all the old familiar places which I used to visit with Freddie.' They became our places for a brief passage in time. She says, 'Follow me,' and leads me upstairs, and I know where we are going. She pushes open the unlocked nursery door, and it is how I remembered it.

'Last time we were here, I was saying sorry to you for lying and hiding things.'

'I know, but ...'

'This time ...' Ruby traces the tiny feet and hands on the photo on the wall. 'This time, this time I can honestly say I have come to terms with my grief for Freddie. It has taken me so long, and I'm sorry if you got caught up in it all.' Ruby begins to cry again.

'Don't say sorry, don't ever say sorry. I didn't feel caught up.'

'I think I was trying to save you, you know I had such an unhappy childhood and ...'

'I'll always love you, Ruby.'

'I understand that. I'm going to change this room when I come back in the summer. I'm ready to move on now.'

'You sound like Mum.'

'She had to wait a bit longer than me.'

'Please don't change the music room, it's perfect.'

She laughs. 'I won't.'

All of my thoughts from last night and this morning were wrong. The pain and anguish I thought I was inflicting today turn out to be a celebration of our love without jealously or rancour. Ruby leans in. I can hear her breathing as she smells me like she used to. I feel her heart beating against my chest, and my fear for the future melts away. We are going to be ok, in different flats, living separate lives. But she'll always be my first love.

She looks up and kisses me, ruffles my hair. 'I'll always love you, Sonny Jackson.'

'And I will always love you, Ruby Wilson.' We hold each other tight.

This is not how I expected the morning to go. After lunch, I leave Ruby, happy and sad at the same time. I stop at Stephen's first and then Jack's. I am telling everybody I am going back to London. I have to do this. I need to shout it out loud to believe it myself. I know I have been lazy in the past and had things handed to me on a plate, but I am going to go back to college and make everyone proud. Stephen and Michael cheer for me, Jack says, 'I never doubted you had the ability,' and I knew what he meant. I had drifted.

I pick some flowers from June the florist. 'For Mrs Wilson?'

'No, not this time.' Buying the flowers makes me feel better.

The doorbell is formal, and it rings loud and clear. After a couple of minutes, Miss Wolstenholme arrives and looks delighted to see me. She invites me in, and I give her the flowers and tell her I am going back to London to finish my studies. She looks relieved. She points to the music room and goes to fetch a vase. I have a little play for old times' sake and she wanders back in smiling.

'I always assumed the photo above the fire was your dad, but it's not, is it?'

She gazes at the portrait of a young soldier with his uniform on and slicked-back hair. She can't disguise her feelings. 'That's my Bert. Wasn't he a handsome young man?' I have to agree he was. She wishes me well. 'You've made the right decision.'

I ask Miss Wolstenholme for one last favour. As I am going away, I want Michael to carry on with his piano lessons, and I can't think of a better teacher. She is so happy to be asked, accepts the challenge, and laughs that 'I'll come out of retirement and it will keep me young.' I walk home with a spring in my step. Today is going well, and I am making my own decisions.

Donna looks pleased to see me. She pulls me close for a matey hug. 'All good?' I tell her I would like to take up her offer on the flat. I cleared it with Dad last night.

'How did Ruby take the news?'

I say I think she already knew. 'Maybe the witches had a premonition?' She smiles, I'm sure those three were talking about me and arranging things behind my back. Mum comes in, and I shout out my news. I am going back to finish my degree, and moving into Donna's flat. I'm going to get my head down and work harder than ever. She looks ecstatic. She can see I am happy with the decision.

The four of us have a late roast and talk about the future. Donna tells them all about our gigs in New York and how she is looking forward to moving there in August. She and Dad go to the turntable and talk jazz. He loves having her around the house.

I wash up as Mum clears. She puts her arm around me. 'You ok?'

'Yeah, it was a pretty good day, considering.' I think of Ruby, all that she has done for me over the years, and I still don't feel like I was caught up in anything. It was a roller coaster of a ride all the way to London. I was happy to be in the front seat.

CALL ME

WEDNESDAY 26 APRIL 1978

Dad takes the day off, and we speed towards London faster than we legally should. Donna is so excited about her New York plans, and there's not a moment's silence in the back of the Jag. She says she's happy I am back on track and plans to move her stuff to Stevie's to give me some space. Dad helps me in, and Donna disappears to leave us to chat.

'Take care, Sonny.' He's so close to me. 'Grief can creep up at any time, cutting your legs off when you least expect it.' He says keep talking to anyone who will listen and if I get stuck, call him.

'Is that what it was like for you?' I've never asked him such a personal question.

'Yes and no.' He fishes for his wallet, and he removes a folder with three photos of Maisie. 'In my day, you didn't talk about it.' Twenty years of bottled-up emotions come flooding out. 'I lost myself in work and booze and didn't even speak to your mum about it.'

'Hey.'

'I was so bloody stupid, wasn't I?'

I hug him tight. 'Not really.'

'The thing is, I had all this love, all these dreams for Maisie and bang, they had nowhere to go.'

I can't leave him like this, so I rush into the kitchen and tell Donna we're off for a quick bite to eat. 'Dad's finally opening up.' We sit in a pub garden and chat for a couple of hours, the longest time we've been together on our own since I was a child. It feels natural, and he dispenses all sorts of advice, just like dads do. Two years ago I'd have bitten his head off, but today it's good to talk.

We wave him off, I lean in through the window. 'Thanks for the money, Dad. Have a safe trip back.' I'm running late for my appointment at college. Donna asks me if I am going to be alright, she's mothering me again. I charge out. I have already missed two weeks study after Easter and have to meet with the head of jazz before returning to the classroom. I'm not looking forward to the meeting but can't wait to get playing again. I dash into reception, Alice looks up and asks, 'Is he expecting you?'

'Yes, about five minutes ago.' I wipe the sweat from my face and take the short walk to the office. To my surprise, Mrs Challinor is sitting alongside Alphonso. They both jump up when they see me, and Mrs Challinor says, 'I was so sorry to hear about Julia.' She recalls her as a model pupil, and she gets teary when I talk about the funeral service. I'd always looked at her as quite stern, but she seems stunned at the loss of one of her favourite students and adds, 'Thank you for being with her in that last week, Alphonso told me about you playing as ...' She can't say anymore, she grips me, wipes away her tears and leaves the room. Alice brings a tray of coffee in, and as she leaves, she caresses my shoulder. Everybody is being so nice.

Alphonso stirs forever, adds milk and sugar, and stares out

of his window. 'You know when you first came here, and we said you had to go through the hoops.' I do remember. I was so annoyed that I didn't pass my first audition, I thought I had failed. But Ruby and Alphonso believed in me, and they got Julia on board to direct me. 'You came back stronger. You were a force because Julia inspired you.' He gesticulates wildly. He turns to face me. He says that now I am back, 'You have to go through the hoops again.' I am shocked, and I can't hide it, and then he realises he has made a big mistake. Alphonso laughs. 'Excuse me, I mean challenges, not hoops, you have to come through these challenges, excuse my English.'

He explains that grief challenges me, not music this time. It makes sense now. They are trying to help me back into college because I have lost a friend. We sip our coffee and move on, and it's much easier talking about music. 'Tommy called me.' Alphonso talks about our little show at Blue Note, New York. 'It sounded stunning.'

'It was so good. We put so much hard work in, and it paid off.'

'Good, you are learning.'

'I know, I know.'

We're back on steady ground, he understands I have changed. I take him through the gig, the students we met, the fun at Juilliard and the joy of playing with Donald Byrd. He leans forward. 'Put the hours in, Sonny, come back to the music, listen with new ears, and you can make Juilliard too.' I'd not really thought of it seriously, but that would be so much fun, meeting up with Donna and Stevie a year from now. He sits back in his chair, we've made our peace without mentioning Ruby once, but I know he knows. And he knows I know he knows. 'I'm on your side, Sonny.'

I stand up and offer my left hand. 'I know you are. I will get my head down.'

'What have you done?'

'I've been very stupid, that's what I've gone and done. Give me a few weeks ...'

'From the very first time I heard you at Freddie's piano, I knew. Don't let me down.'

We part as friends. I walk out of the office and head home. As I'm passing reception, Alice looks up smiling. 'Welcome back, Sonny.'

I smile in return. 'It's good to be back.'

Donna's moved out of her bedroom already. She shows me around, empty wardrobes and drawers ready for my stuff, clean sheets and pillows. I can tell she pities me. She makes me promise her I know how to wash, clean and look after myself. 'You've never been on your own, have you?' She cries fake tears until I whack her with one of the pillows. She makes me follow her around, so I understand everything about the flat, even letting me know there is a 'flat book' by the phone for emergencies. I tell her she's worse than my mother, and she takes it as a badge of honour. 'I've let everyone know the flat phone number so they can call you.' We shop together, and I get everything I need in for a few days, and I agree to cook tonight for her and Stevie.

'Donna, thanks for being there for me.'

'Sonny, you saved me once, remember. Physically saved me. With Julia, and Ruby, of course.'

'That was some night.'

'I'll never forget it, and I'll never forget Julia.'

'Thank you.'

I'm so full after our meal, Donna has long gone, and the telephone rings. It's Ruby.

'Hello Sonny, are you ok?' Our new life begins, a new relationship with Ruby, mainly based on the phone, but to be interspersed with gigs, theatre and meals. With love and respect. We agree to meet at the weekend to collect my things. 'Goodnight, Sonny.'

'I'll always love you, Ruby. You know that.'

She breathes so deeply, the air whistles on the way in. 'I can feel it. Thank you.'

I like being on my own.

Jack calls. 'I want to see you at the London Palladium one day.'

Mum calls me. 'Dad is home safe and sound, and we both say hi and good luck with this term.'

Marj phones. She wishes me good luck finishing year two and thanks me for caring so much about Julia.

Donna phones to check up on me. 'We all love you so much and we are with you every day.' I get ready for bed in my own little world for the first time.

I am about to turn out the light when the phone rings again. It's Stephen. 'Sorry this is so late,' and he lets me know about his day and how he is coping with childcare. Michael has had his first lesson, and I smile as we talk about Julia.

'Thanks for taking the time to call. I think about her every day.'

'So do I. Keep moving forward with her in your heart. Goodnight, Sonny, there is a little surprise for you under your pillow.'

Donna has hidden a present. I open the envelope, and there is a card from Michael, with a picture of a piano on the front and two people sitting on the stool playing, one tall, one small. High above us, Mummy is looking down as we play, an angel on the clouds. Inside there is a photo of Julia, a big kiss from Michael and a beautiful message from Stephen that says the next time he comes to London will be for my graduation.

GIANT STEPS

THURSDAY 31 AUGUST 1978

The taxi rattles and rolls as we pull away from Hammersmith towards Heathrow, I look across at Ruby and tell her we should have taken the tube. 'That suggestion is not helpful.'

She checks her watch for the fifth time in as many minutes. Despite going out last night, Donna insisted we were there to wave her and Stevie off on their big adventure. I check my watch, two hours till the gate closes, I hope they have not gone through yet. It's my fault we are late. I missed my alarm, which is why Ruby had to call me and say she was on the way and then she pulled up and told me to jump in. And here we are. 'I'm sorry. Alright, it's my fault.'

'You can tell that to Donna – if we see her.' Ruby does not forgive me just yet.

We run in and spot them hovering with their passports looking anxious, 'Sorry, guys, my fault.' Donna eyeballs Ruby, and there is a silent agreement between them that it is par for the course. Ruby gives Donna a list of must-visit places and me and Stevie talk about the last time we were there. He is trying to get me to agree to visit at Christmas, and I'm up for it, but

I'll have to see if I have to go home first. I have just spent quite a few weeks teaching Michael, and it was fun so I might spend Christmas in Manchester. Stevie says if I come he'll get me a gig with Vincent and Martha again, that's a good a reason as any to plan a visit. We don't even have time for a coffee. I apologise again, and Donna says not to worry.

'I'm going to call you, Sonny, every week, and you'd better pick up.'

I promise to and tell Donna 'I'll visit soon.' We watch them walk through, and they turn and wave.

Ruby says, 'Relax, I'm going to look after you today,' and she takes my arm as we descend into the dark recesses of the underground. Since April we have met most weeks, usually for a coffee or a meal at Ruby's, sometimes for gigs in town. I'm playing far more now, and she often pops along and supports me, which is nice. I'm daydreaming about Waverly as we wait for our train. I did so much practice in the summer. I've still got my key, and I could go and visit anytime, which was lovely. I stayed at Mum and Dad's, but they don't have the piano anymore, so I would mooch along to Ruby's. On a few occasions, Mum came with me, and they sat and chatted or went out, and I cracked on. Most days I would catch Stephen and Michael, and we would have a little fun lesson; he is coming on so well. Ruby encouraged me to invite Jack and Karen round, and even Debs and Hamish came to stay, and Ruby and I played host and showed her new boyfriend around town. It was like having a best friend always on hand, and not once has it been difficult to navigate our new relationship. One weekend Alphonso came to stay, and when he asked me how I was getting on, he was surprised when I said, 'Let me show you.'

We spent two days going through Freddie's collection and playing and chatting. Ruby kept asking if were finished and bringing more tea and cakes and listening to us. Alphonso showed me how good he was on piano and pushed me harder and harder into technical areas. He then surprised me by coming on one of my walks to Stephen's, and he was so gentle with Michael and played along happily. He spent ages with Stephen telling him why Julia was his favourite student. It was lovely to listen in, and we meandered home, talking about his childhood in Italy. We passed June's, and as usual, she shouted as we passed. I stopped to chat and June said to Alphonso 'You wanna watch this one he's going to be a star.'

He agreed with a huge bow and said, 'You are correct, young lady. I am his tutor in London.' His accent and the use of 'young lady' meant June blushed and I am sure she tried to curtsy, I've never seen her so quiet. Alphonso took pity and bought a bouquet of flowers from her.

Ruby nudges me as the train hurtles into view and the whoosh of air wakes me from my dreams. We jump on together and get a seat.

'You were miles away.'

'I was thinking of a few weeks ago when Alphonso and I did that jazz marathon.'

'He's as crazy as you.'

'He's very fond of you. You know that?.'

Ruby smiles and pats my arm. 'Do you mind?'

I think for a few seconds. 'Not at all.' I run the idea around my head before adding, 'I really don't.'

'And I don't mind about Alice.'

'Alice. From the reception at college?'

'Yes, the young girl who turns up at all of your gigs and flutters her eyes at you.'

'Really? Why haven't I noticed?'

'Because you've never asked a lady out, have you?'

I guess I haven't, and all those thoughts of nervousness when I was at school come back to me, how shy I was, how I never approached girls and I stumble using the right words. Alice, she's gorgeous, I'd noticed that but …

'What are you smiling at?'

I was about to say Alice, but even I know that would be wrong. 'You giving me dating advice.'

We travel on, lost in our thoughts, and I drift from Ruby to Alice and back again. I promise to be braver.

Ruby's flat is perfect, and we have croissants and coffee, and a little while later we have eggs and toast, and I tell her that I am so grateful for all she has shown me. Ruby passes my thanks down the line to Freddie and says he taught her everything. And we raise our glasses of orange juice to Freddie. 'Can you swim?'

'Yes, of course. Why?'

'You laugh when I go to all the old places so today I am going to be spontaneous.' She gets excited and says there's one thing she's always wanted to do.

She takes me shopping for what seems like hours and then a long walk towards the heath. Ruby shouts, 'Be brave,' and we jump in together and we're floating in Hampstead Heath Ponds in our new costumes that she made me buy. Ruby splashes me and says she would never have done this on her own. It feels refreshing to be moving from the familiar to doing something new with Ruby. This is us, this was a first for just us. She looks at me. 'Thank you, Sonny. I need to move forward and discover new pleasures.'

We dry ourselves and walk from Hampstead towards Mayfair through Regent's Park, where we stop for ice cream. It feels like our summer is coming to an end; I am going into my final year, Ruby into year two of her studies. But more than that, we are learning to co-exist, to be comfortable around each other with our shared history. We discuss college and courses and galleries and gigs. It's going to be busy right up until the end of term. I think Ruby was worried about me saying bye to Donna today, but I'm good, I'm in a nice place. We hold hands for the last few minutes, the sun on our faces. Ruby checks her watch, 'I've got to go.' She jumps up, grabs her swim bag and kisses me on both cheeks. 'Continental.' She marches off, turns and shouts, 'Let's do this again, it was fun.' I get a coffee and sit back and think. And think again. Over and over, around and around, what did Ruby tell me?

College starts in a week, so they must be open, prepping for the new term and setting up. I take the familiar paths, my pace quickens, and my heart skips a beat. I want to turn back a hundred times but today is the day for trying new things and being brave. I push the door open and look in reception. No one is there. How stupid do I look? What was I thinking?

There's footsteps from my left, 'Hello, Sonny,' and I turn to face Alice. 'You're early. We don't start until next week.' I take a huge breath, and remember what Ruby said before she jumped: 'Be brave.'

'Hi Alice, do you fancy going for a drink later?' She looks

startled, and for a second I think I have got this so wrong. She gulps. Her mouth widens in slow motion, before she smiles.

'What took you so long?'

I have my first proper date.

St James Infirmary

MONDAY 8 JANUARY 1979

The alarm goes off at seven-thirty, and I hear Alice get up and go to the bathroom. I turn over and shut my eyes. This is way too early for my second morning back in the UK. Still jet-lagged, my return to college is a week away, but it's open, so she's going in.

Half an hour later she wakes me again and kisses me goodbye. 'Sonny, you look like shit.'

'I feel like shit.'

'Well, I'm off. Rest up won't you?'

'I'll try.' I cough lumps up and my ribs ache. I manage a wave as the room spins. I was so good at Christmas in Manchester with Alice and then the sickness started after I flew to America for New Year to meet up with Donna and Stevie. I played so much music in five days, it was insane. We stayed up all night and slept all day. Alice was miffed I didn't invite her, but she wouldn't understand my topsy turvy world. I turn over and sleep for another few hours until the bed is soaked with sweat and I'm desperate for a pee. I wobble to the bathroom and feel nauseous walking.

I slouch in the chair with a strong coffee to fight my tiredness and aching body. Ruby calls to invite me over – she's back in town too. I shower and head out. I'm grateful it's warmer than New York.

The first term of my final year couldn't have been better. I have a keyboard in the flat, I can go to Ruby's if I need peace and quiet, and there's any number of practice rooms at college. I get to play so much. I usually go to Ruby's on my own, but Alice has joined me a couple of times. She finds it awkward, and so do I. I'm not my usual self. When it's just the two of us, we're fine.

Ruby lets me in, and I shuffle up the stairs. The door is open, and I enter the kitchen to beautiful aromas of home baking. I sneak up behind the cook and give her a cuddle and a kiss on the neck. She turns rounds, kisses my cheek and threatens me with both hands covered in flour. 'Good to have you back.'

I shiver. 'I'm knackered, but it's good to be back in London.'

'How was New York?' I go through all of my travels and hangouts from Brooklyn to Manhattan, and she nods and knows them all. I tease her, 'You may be able to visit me next year.'

'Fantastic, I thought you might apply. How's Donna?'

'She loves it,' and I tell her all about the college, about Stevie, the friends they've made and the club scene. Ruby says she used to love New York, especially the diners and the shops. I get through a pint of water. I'm feeling terrible and shaking.

'Sonny, are you okay?'

'Not really, I think it's jet-lag.'

'How's Alice?' I talk her through the Christmas break, but my enthusiasm levels drop, and it's obvious. I can't talk to Ruby about another girlfriend, and Alice distrusts Ruby when we are together. It's just one big mess. We talk around the subject, about Mum and Dad and Waverly, and she asks after Stephen and Michael. We're going through the motions today and Ruby seems distracted.

I stand to leave, and I find out why.

'Sonny, I want to tell you something before you hear about it from anyone else.' She sits me down on the sofa, pours me another strong coffee. She's loud and clear. 'Alphonso has declared his intentions – I think we may become a couple.'

'He's quite old, isn't he?'

'He's fifty, fourteen years older than me.'

'Wow, nearly thirty years older than me.'

She's tetchy. 'Is age a defining characteristic in a relationship?'

Point made. 'No, of course not, that was unfair, sorry.' My head spins, I'm sweating, and I need to get out of the flat as fast as I can.

'You've got Alice.'

'Yes, but ...'

'But what?'

'I need to go.' I get up and leave, stumble down the stairs, press the buzzer and try to catch my breath. I can't. It's freezing now, maybe the flat was too hot, but the difference chills me to the bone. I walk the streets trying to work out my feelings. I thought all of this was in the past, but it's strangling me, my throat is tight and my heart is racing. I try hard to think, but I don't recognise the streets. I can't read the signs.

I open my eyes in the back of an ambulance. Then nothing.

I come round much later, drip in my right arm and with a mask on my face. I can't see anyone.

'Ruby?' Alice comes into view, shakes her head, and I know in that instant that we're through. I see the disappointment in her eyes. Someone holds my left hand. 'It's okay, Sonny, you've got pneumonia.' Mum squeezes my fingers, 'You're in the right place now.' She explains the nurses had said I'd probably started it in New York, but the flight has made it worse. They also suspected I had overdosed on coffee as I was shaking so much.

I remove my mask. 'I had drunk a lot of on the flight back, two more cups at home to wake myself up, and then Ruby served me a really strong coffee at lunchtime, and that's the last thing I remember.'

Alice is angry. 'So you were around at Ruby's again? I waited all night, worrying about you.' She picks up her coat and leaves, heels clicking goodbye. Mum calls her, but she doesn't return.

'How did you get here so soon?'

'They looked through your wallet and called home. I phoned Ruby, and she said that you were upset when you left the flat.'

'So you put two and two together and ...'

'Sonny, I thought that ... Jack told me about the bath incident in Edinburgh and ...'

'Mum, it's not like that.'

She bursts into tears, and I am left gasping for air. I suck in some oxygen.

'Mum, look at me.' I breathe in, my ribs burst. 'I promise I will never, ever do anything like that.'

'Sonny, you're all I've got left.'

Maisie comes into my thoughts, Mum's lost so much. I take Mum's hand. 'I'm going nowhere. Promise.'

'I need to stay and look after you. Your dad will have to fend for himself.' She goes to find a phone, and when she returns, she looks calmer. 'I called Ruby. She said I can stay with her for a few days until you are back on your feet.'

'Thanks, Mum, love you.'

She does that thing she always does when we go to see Maisie.

She kisses her fingers and taps me on the head. 'And I love you too.'

She holds my hand as I drift off, and I feel the sheets being tucked in and my hair being brushed off my face.

Lean on Me

Saturday 13 January 1979

I am so weak. I hear the birds tweeting but I can't seem to fully wake up. I was in hospital for five days, and when my temperature dropped to normal, they let me leave. Ruby and Mum took me back to her flat in a taxi, and I am still here. I know I am due back at college on Monday, but I won't be ready, I've lost too much weight and strength. Two more weeks of antibiotics should do the trick. I toss and turn and can't get comfortable, but at least the night sweats have gone. I called Donna, and those guys have been ill as well, so I guessed we all burned the midnight oil too much and then the flight home finished me off. Alice came round on Thursday, and we finished our short-lived relationship. She knew it would happen, of course. We said a friendly goodbye, but she was right when she said, 'I can't compete with Ruby can I?' I couldn't disagree.

The door creaks. 'I can hear you.'

Mum comes and sits on the bed. 'How are you feeling? I've got the porridge on.' Ruby has been staying with Alphonso and me and Mum have had the flat, but she's leaving tomorrow to resume her studies. I walk into the kitchen and Mum's lining up boiled eggs and toast as well.

'I need to know you're going to be okay. You had me worried for a while.' She fills me beyond full, and makes me drink juice too. 'No more coffee.' I waddle back to my room, shower and shave and feel a hundred times better.

Ruby has come round. She hugs me. 'How are you doing?'

'Full to the top.'

'Mum's love.'

'The best. How are you?'

'I'm getting used to being in someone else's apartment.'

'And ...'

'It's ok, just ... Ok.'

We had 'the chat' on Wednesday about how she thought my collapse was due to her news, but even though I thought the same, the doctors told me that I was ill, very ill, and I would have collapsed anyway. The dash into the cold air did tip me over the edge, so Ruby is off the hook and I said she and Alphonso have my blessing. She said he was worried about me completing this term, but I tell Ruby to tell him I'll work the hardest I have ever worked to finish. 'I haven't got Alice to distract me anymore.'

Ruby looks at me. 'Ohhh, tell me more.' She says she knew Alice wasn't right for me and when I find the right one she'll tell me. Ruby offers to look after me for a few weeks, making Mum happy as she plans to go home. For the first time in a week, I have a little tinkle on the piano, but I am soon tired and flop onto the sofa. I can hear Mum and Ruby talking away in the kitchen, best friends enjoying each other's company. I put my head back for five minutes to relieve my tired eyes.

'Sonny, Sonny. Are you with us?' Once again, I have to fight to remain in the room. I slept for two hours and I'm desperate for the loo. I can feel their eyes are on me as I edge across the room. I'm steadier on the way back, and more food awaits. Mum forces my tablets on me. Ruby has to promise daily updates for Mum, and I promise to be a good patient until I am strong enough to return to college.

'After all the hard work, you can't miss out now. We'll be here for you.'

'I know, Mum, don't worry.'

'Mums always worry, Sonny, but I'll be here every day to keep an eye on you.' They look at me like I am five and watch as I take more tablets and eat another huge meal.

'That's a good boy.' I do Scout's honour and they laugh.

Both Sides Now

Ruby's gone to meet my mum and dad who are visiting me for the weekend. Donna runs into the flat and screams when she sees me. It's so good to see her. Juilliard have let her finish at Easter in her first year as her mum has been quite ill.

I ask Donna, 'How's your mum?'

'She's on the mend but never mind her, how are you?'

I tell Donna I'm feeling a lot better. The pneumonia weakened me so much, and I have been holed up at Ruby's ever since. She can't believe I haven't been to college since December and asks me about graduating in May. We take a walk outside. It's so good to get fresh air, and we update each other on what's gone on. She quizzes me on Alice and the breakup and lots of questions about Ruby of course.

'But what about your graduation?'

'Well, you are not going to believe this.' I dive into the details of how ill I was, not concentrating and sleepy all the time. Alphonso wanted to boot me out of college, saying I should come back and repeat year three. There was a meeting and Ruby had to attend because of the money, and he completely lost it.

'That doesn't sound like Alphonso.'

'I know, he even had photos of you and me from the lost weekend, Jimmy had got them printed.'

'Bloody hell.'

'He was threatening me and then Ruby stepped in and reminded him.'

'What?'

'Let's just say, Jimmy had tried to bribe Alphonso many years ago, a story about a young student.'

'I'd never heard that.'

'No one has, it was hushed up. Nothing inappropriate but guess who his lawyer was?'

'Freddie?'

'Got it in one.'

'Ruby told him we all make mistakes, and that he better back off.'

'And did he?'

'Yes, and then the most extraordinary thing happened. Eloise came round.'

'Who's Eloise?'

'You know, Mrs Challinor.'

Donna is shocked. 'That old battle axe. She tried to kick me out once.'

It turns out Ruby had told her at the meeting I was ill because of Julia, that it had affected my health.

'And the pneumonia.'

'From that moment on she couldn't do enough for me.' She drops off worksheets, music, plays for me and, 'She's inspired me to start writing my own material.'

Donna's mouth is wide open. 'So you can teach an old dog new tricks.'

I laugh. 'Maybe she's just benefited from some of my Sonny charms.'

'Bloody hell, it sounds unreal. And the photos from the lost weekend?'

'All copies destroyed, so he says.'

We take a stroll, find a cafe and talk for hours. We make plans for Donna and me to move back into her flat, she'll set up a bed in the lounge, and I want to return to college next week. I need to graduate. Eloise has been brilliant, and I have almost caught up with the course work. In fact, I am way ahead in specific modules, especially the history of jazz and composition. Being so well looked after and not in college has meant I have got my head down without distractions.

'Is it weird living at Ruby's?'

'Yes and no.'

'What do you mean?' I explain it's been good because I always had someone to talk to, someone to cook for me when I was most ill and of course the piano. But it has been weird being the ex-boyfriend.

'It's difficult when Alphonso stays over.'

Donna pulls a face. 'Nooooo. Don't go there.'

'It's alright. I've got used to it now.'

'Is he okay with you?'

'Yes, he went quiet for weeks, but Ruby worked on him and he came and apologised to me. We're good now.'

We agree to tell the others that I will move next week. I've got one more session with Eloise to get through. We walk via the park, and I gulp in the fresh air as Donna updates me about New York. It seems like they have settled in well.

'Do you want to come and study with us?'

'I do, but no flying allowed for a while.' Donna says they are doing London auditions in late April and she may be able to call in a favour. She says she'll borrow a bass and we can start work next week, get a little trio together just like the old days. Seeing Donna and getting a little sun has me feeling so much better as we head back.

Mum and Dad are sitting in the lounge, and both jump up to greet me. Mum sees I have put on weight and gives me a cheeky pinch around the middle. Ruby has got her friends, I suspect she means caterers, to drop off a full tray of chicken and veg, and we sit down to a beautiful meal. Ruby tells everyone I have been a model patient and Alphonso says I have been a model student. It's all going so well until I mention I may be moving back to Donna's flat next week.

Mum jumps in. 'Are you sure it's not too early?'

Ruby adds, 'What about meals?' They all look petrified that I'll go downhill.

Donna reassures them that she will be in charge of me, for food, water and music. She adds, 'I'm going nowhere till September.'

'Hello, hello. You are all talking about me. I can hear you.'

Dad smiles at them. 'Can I just say? It was the women who jumped in then, Sonny.'

Alphonso agrees. 'I am sure Donna will take good care of you.' I think he may have ulterior motives for getting me out of Ruby's flat, but I keep quiet.

'Can I just say?' shouts Ruby. 'I was only thinking of your health, but now Donna is on board ...'

'He'll be fine,' says Donna. 'If not I'll ship him right back where he came from.'

Ruby frowns. 'Once discharged, the patient never returns.'

Mum joins in. 'You can send him back to me, Donna.'

They finish talking about me, and we have a lovely evening, the first whole day I have felt normal. It helps that spring has arrived, and I can get out now, and it is a massive bonus that Donna is back. Mum and Dad leave for their hotel, Ruby and Alphonso go with them, I think it's an excuse for a nightcap as I am not allowed to drink. Donna and me sit on the sofa chatting. I ask her if she could make that call for me about the audition but not to mention it to anyone as I don't want to get my hopes up.

'You'll be fine.'

'The biggest thing I missed when laid low was ...'

'Me. Go on, say it. I know you want to.'

'The biggest thing I missed was you, followed by playing the piano.' I wallow for ten minutes in self-pity about how I used to be a lazy sod who thought it would all come easy and now I realise that I have to put the work in otherwise I go backwards.

'They drill that into you in New York, incremental achievements.' She says they have a saying that once you have mastered something, it is 'in the bank' and that you don't sit back and congratulate yourself, you just look at the next hill and start climbing again.

'That's what Julia used to say too.' We spend a while talking about Julia and how cruel life can be. 'Let's play.'

'How's your hand?'

'Pretty much back to its best.'

I take Donna to the piano and place her on the left side of the stool. I reach into a folder and retrieve a piece of handwritten music. On the top is written, 'Nowhere To Go'. The composer is Sonny Jackson. I have never shown anyone one of my tunes before. Donna says she's heard the phrase somewhere. I'm nervous as I play the tune, gaining confidence as I return to the top and start again. Donna picks ups the bass line and adds some deep notes and chords with her left hand, and I hear what I have written take on a life of its own. I know this will now work in a band situation. We look at each other, smiling as we play through again and this time I add some improvised melodies over the top. Donna puts her arm around me as we finish, and it feels so good. Applause comes from the sofa, and we turn round to see Ruby sitting there and Alphonso approaching us.

He picks up the sheet. 'Composed by yourself, I see. Very nice.'

'It's something I've been working on with Eloise.'

'I can tell, that was beautiful, Sonny. What inspired you?'

I start to tell him about Maisie and a conversation I had with Dad, and I find myself in floods of tears. 'I'm sorry, this isn't like me.' My emotions crash, I am so devoid of energy. I look up, but I can't go on. Ruby comes to the rescue, takes my hand and leads me to the kitchen.

She puts the kettle on. She says she understands. 'I know that story too, the love never stops, the thoughts don't go away. You're brave for using Maisie and Dad as inspiration for new music.

'Or stupid.'

'Hey, look at me.' She snaps her fingers. 'One thing you're not is stupid. That song is beautiful.' She makes me a hot toddy with lemon and honey and says I am just getting back on my feet and not to be too hard on myself.

We join the others, who are still talking jazz. Donna has persuaded Alphonso to let us use the practice rooms, and he's going to get me a young drummer from year two so we can form a band for my graduation concert. He waves the sheet music. 'And I expect this tune to be in the show.'

I am so tired. I start closing my eyes during conversation. Donna lifts the mug from my hand and says, 'Bed,' and she directs me to the bathroom. She promises to look after me for the next few months and says, 'No drink or drugs.' I lay back, thinking I'll never be able to stay up late again, let alone drink. Donna lies down next to me. 'Have I ever told you about your dad and I sifting through his music in Manchester when I came to stay?' I remember them getting close. 'He spoke about Maisie, and he told me that if she'd have turned out like me he would have been so proud.' Donna wipes away a tear. 'I was so grateful he said that to me, he didn't have to.'

'That's nice.' I am drifting off.

'He told me the same thing he told you. He felt he had nowhere to go after Maisie died.'

'So now you know.' My eyes are heavy. 'Dad inspired me to write my new tune.'

'When you were talking to Alphonso … The words came flooding back. "Nowhere to go". The song is so beautiful.'

She holds my hand, and I mumble, 'You are like a sister to me, Donna. I love you.' I dream of ice cream castles and Mum and Dad and Maisie and me going on holiday together.

Detour Ahead

There are three audition rooms set up in central London. We are in number two. Three tunes and fifteen minutes for an interview, that's it. New York is my dream, and we have rehearsed so much, the same three songs I am doing for my graduation concert. We've roped Tom in, a young drummer from year two; it's a tight little trio.

We finish playing the last tune, and Donna punches the air.

'Thank you,' says Mr Amato. 'Take five and we'll see you for a chat in the suite next door.'

I think it went well. I know it went well, we were on fire. Tom is packing his kit away, Donna's bass already in its hard case.

'That was brilliant,' says Donna. 'Well done, Sonny.'

'I couldn't have done it without you guys, thanks.'

I wipe my face, still sweating from performing. I agree to meet Donna in college in half an hour.

'Good luck, looking forward to having my buddy in New York.'

I'm happy. 'Thanks, guys, I really appreciate it.'

I look up at the double doors. This reminds me of my first

trip to the jazz college all those years ago. I was so naïve. But this time I know what I am doing, I'm ready for the next steps. I take a deep breath and knock. There are three of them. Why is it always three? Safety in numbers I guess.

Mr Amato is the lead. 'Beautiful playing, Sonny. Bill Evans a favourite?'

'Absolutely, one of the very best for me.'

The lady to his left smiles and her slight nod tells me she agrees. 'That was brave to put in an original.'

'I have been working hard on my song-writing with Mrs Challinor, I need to stretch myself.' I hope I don't sound too cocky.

'Well, you pulled it off, well done.'

Mr Amato is opening an envelope, and he frowns as he reads it.

He passes it on. 'No problem with the playing, tell me about your recent illness.'

This throws me, I didn't realise they knew this, and why does it matter? I try to read the papers upside down, all I can make out is the jazz college logo.

'Sonny? Is it a problem.'

'No, I just didn't realise we were discussing it today. It's not relevant, I was in hospital with pneumonia but I am back to my best.' I feel a bead of sweat running down my face and turn sideways to move it out of shot.

'It is relevant if you fail to graduate this year – we will have to defer.'

'I will graduate this year.'

'It says here,' he turns more pages. 'It says here, and this is from the head of jazz, that you are unlikely to complete your studies due to having missed three months of study.'

The bastard, the absolute bastard. He's knifed me in the back and left me to die. He flicks his papers back and forth, searching for something. I'm lost, I need this, I have to get away from London this year. It must be a mistake, we have been getting on great lately.

I blurt out. 'What's the date on that note?'

He licks his finger and pages back. 'March.'

I dismiss it. 'That was months ago. I only applied in April. I have completely caught up. I am graduating on the first of June.'

'There's nothing I can do, I'm sorry. Your college has to approve your application in writing.'

'But … I have to go this year. I need to go this year.' I sound desperate because I am.

'Sonny, I'm Miss Shelley. Your playing was exquisite, but you can only come to Juilliard if you graduate, and your college don't think you will. Now, if you excuse us, we have more students to see.' They stand up and close their files.

I want to scream, my dream is in tatters because of one suspicious man. The one thing I want is out of my hands, fading to nothing.

'The reason I got pneumonia was because I was in America in December. What about last April? Does that count for nothing? I was at Blue Note with Donald Byrd. Even Tommy Flanagan loved the show. Ask Martha and Vincent, your students.' I'm pleading with no one in particular, talking out of turn. Miss Shelley pauses at the doors.

'That was you supporting Donald Byrd?'

It's now or never. 'It was, with your students in my band.'

'Well, you listen here, young man, get your sassy ass down to college and get an updated referral.' She hands me a card. 'We are in the UK for one more week, staying at the Grosvenor.'

'And then what?'

'Currently, we have you pencilled in for September 1980. You would have to re-apply, unless we could …?'

'Bring it forward?'

'In exceptional circumstances, yes.'

I look at the card: Miss Cecile Shelley, Head of Piano Studies. 'You know Martha?'

'Of course, and that was some gig by the way. You have one week.' She's gone.

I run all the way to college, and dive into the common room. Donna whoops in delight.

'Alphonso has stitched me up; he says I won't graduate. I'm not coming this year.'

Donna looks more shocked than I feel. 'Is there any way you can overturn it?'

I hand her the card. 'She says I have one week to try and get a new reference, plus I need to graduate, and I don't think he's going to allow it.'

'We'll see about that.' Donna drags me along to reception. Alice informs us that Alphonso has gone to Italy for a family bereavement and he won't be back until after the bank holiday. That's ten days away. We retreat to the common room.

'Well, at least you are ok for next year.' Donna tries to lift my spirits.

'But I have to do it this year, or never at all. That's it.' I pick up an ashtray.

Donna screams. 'Sonny, not again …'

'I'm just so angry ...'

Alice interrupts. 'Mrs Challinor will see you now, I told her how upset you were.'

'You said she wasn't in.'

'She wasn't, but I had to call her about something else, so I may have mentioned your predicament.'

'Thank you, Alice.' We rush to her office and I am trying to stay hopeful. I have never wanted something so much in my life. I knock.

'Tell me in your own words what they said.'

I rush through the story, saying it's not about the audition, it's about the referral. Alphonso said in March I couldn't possibly graduate this year. They believe him as it is in writing.

Mrs Challinor reads a report and looks over her glasses at me. 'He's sent the wrong one, this is the Easter end of term report.' She explains that they are internal documents unless affiliated colleagues request them. 'You also know that our head of jazz and I differed on how to get you through this year.'

Donna joins in. 'Sonny is so grateful for your personal tuition.'

'Thank you, Donna, that may be the case, but it doesn't help here I'm afraid.'

I plead my case but, 'The only answer is to get a written update from Alphonso, and that is going to be very difficult indeed.'

'I've got a week, and I am meant to be rehearsing for my finals.'

'Listen, Sonny. I'll do my very best to get this sorted. Don't kick off. I'll work on this, you work on your music. Agreed?'

We hit the pub, and my doubts about being good enough,

about deserving it resurface and Donna fails to lift me. I am rubbish company and I think that it has all been one big tease. Donna is off to see her mum for the weekend so she leaves me at the flat all alone. It is probably my comeuppance for all the luck I had, for all the good things that dropped into my lap too easily. I lie on the bed and wallow, and think about Freddie's funeral, then Ruby and of course my introduction to Julia. I was so in love with her, we both knew it, we were musical soul mates. God, she was beautiful and I think it was she who sent me Eloise to get me though these last few months. I fall asleep and wake and repeat it all until dawn, dreaming of Julia and the fun we had on piano.

Darn That Dream

MONDAY 21 MAY 1979

I am back in college, music room number two. I can see the dots on the page, and I try and infuse them with feeling, but I fail. Donna calls it. 'Come on you two, that's enough for today.' No one disagrees or fights for another run-through. I head for the flat. Donna says she'll catch me later on. I don't see the point of practising if my end goal has disappeared. It's raining, and I dodge the puddles and pull up my hood. I have to come up with a plan. I can't rely on others to get me through this.

I ring the buzzer and Ruby answers immediately, and I climb the stairs hoping she can help.

'Come in, Sonny. Coffee?'

'Not after last time. Tea please.'

She smiles. I think she's teasing me. I explain about the last few days, the audition followed by the rejection. Ruby is surprised, 'I thought Alphonso had got over it.'

'What do you mean?'

'He is hot headed and at one point he thought you were working your way back in to my life after you collapsed. Especially when I offered you my flat.'

'Was he jealous?'

'Of course. You men are so insecure.' It's my turn to smile.

'I need to speak to him.'

'You can't, not right now. His sister is being buried tomorrow.'

'Ruby, I have to speak to him – this is my future we're talking about.'

'Stop being so dramatic, Sonny.'

'They are taking his March report as accurate, you know how much effort I have put in since then.'

'Thanks to Eloise.'

'It's her teaching me, but it's me doing the graft. It's me putting in the hours after she's gone. You've witnessed it yourself.'

'That's true, but still, you can't call him.'

She doesn't get it, why doesn't anyone see that this is my dream? After all the years of messing about, being the lazy sod that my dad used to call me, I have worked my butt off these last few months since coming out of hospital. This is the first thing that hasn't been handed to me on a plate, the one goal I set myself. And now, Alphonso, the jealous boyfriend, has killed my aspirations.

'So you're not going to help me?'

'I didn't say that.'

'You did.'

'Sonny, listen. I said you can't call him. But when he calls me tonight, I can relay a message. What do you want me to say?'

I calm down and say tell him I think he has made a mistake, sending in an earlier report, and not the latest update. We part on friendly terms, and I feel a little better, but there is more I can do.

I walk towards the Grosvenor and ask for Miss Shelley at reception. She appears in a few minutes, says 'Call me Cecile,' and is warm and friendly. I go through the last year, visiting Juilliard, being inspired, losing a dear friend, playing at Blue Note and then falling ill. I tell her that Alphonso has sent her an old assessment by mistake from when I had just left hospital, but since then Mrs Challinor has tutored me and I am fully up to speed and graduating in two weeks. She writes down the details.

'Can you get Alphonso to send me a new report?'

'It's difficult as he is in Italy for his sister's funeral tomorrow, but we are speaking tonight.'

'You are keen.'

After the year I've had, music is my salvation. 'I really want to be with Donna, Martha and Vincent.'

We spend fifteen minutes going through my musical inspirations, and hers, and we are on the same wavelength. She stipulates Mr Amato has the final say.

She shakes my hand. 'I appreciate you coming to see me. I love your attitude.'

I wander the streets thinking over the conversations, trying to find a glimmer of hope. Donna is cooking dinner when I get back.

'You ok?'

'A little better. I went to see Ruby, and then I went to the hotel and chatted to Cecile.'

'Sonny, you are going for it. And …?'

'Ruby is speaking to Alphonso tonight, and Cecile was really nice but says she doesn't have the final say.'

'Well done you, let's hope the situation changes.'

We are just about to dive in when the phone rings, and I dash to the hall. It doesn't take long.

'That was Ruby. She said Alphonso is very sorry, he wasn't being spiteful, he just rushed off an existing report when they asked for it.'

Donna looks set to explode. 'Not good enough. You applied in April, and he sent a report nearly six weeks out of date.'

'He's busy tomorrow, he'll look at it on Wednesday. Ruby thinks it's a genuine mistake.'

'Come here.' Donna gives me a cuddle. 'Let's just carry on rehearsing, He'll do the right thing.'

'What if he doesn't?'

'If you can get a visa you can come and stay with me, there's plenty of gigs.'

Autumn in New York

Thursday 24 May 1979

We eat breakfast in the flat and get our folders ready to go to college. Tom is available for two hours today so we are having a run-through the graduation pieces. I wanted an answer yesterday, but it didn't come. I rang Mum last night and poured my heart out. She reminded me of the time difference between Italy and New York, and told me not to worry. It didn't make me feel any better. She said she was looking forward to my concert next week, they are all coming to London to see it. I said it may be pointless now but she talked me round and left me feeling much better about my degree. I'm lost in thought, blowing bubbles in the corn flakes and sipping my tea.

'Hey, Sonny. We're off.'

'Yeah, yeah. I'll be there.'

Donna slips her arm through mine, and we fall in line. 'Remember when you came to college for the second time?'

'You and Fi scared the life out of me, so knowledgeable.'

'That's you today, think about how much you know. Tom said so on Monday, you're the best pianist at college.'

'Really?'

'Yes, Sonny. Even if this doesn't work out, you'll come next year. Be positive …'

'I know, it was just …'

'You are so impatient. Let's put on the best show we can next week, and see what happens.'

We breeze through the doors and Alice is smiling at me. It's way over the top and her greeting is too forced, something is up. 'Mrs Challinor would like a word in her office before you two use the practice room.'

'Any news?'

'Can't say. But the telex has been busy.'

We skip along the corridor, my heart rate soars and I spot two shadows sitting there. She's got company.

'Shall we come back later?'

Donna says. 'Don't be stupid, just knock.'

The door opens, and Cecile has the widest smile as she stands and shakes both my hands. She holds up a stream of paper. 'This came through last night. We can offer you a place this September.'

Donna screams, I burst into tears and we hug and kiss. Cecile asks Donna if she can show her the practice room, and she reminds me not to tell anyone just yet. 'You must wait until after you graduate,' and she winks at me. 'See you in New York.'

Those words sound fantastic.

I turn to Mrs Challinor, she's in tears too. 'New York, Sonny. That sounds good.'

'How did you do it?'

'It was easy in the end. Ruby told Alphonso to call me, and I told him to do this one last favour for …' she starts crying and fetches tissues from her handbag. 'I told him he had to do this for Julia. I knew you two were close and this is what she would have wanted.'

'Thank you, Eloise. That's perfect.'

She's made one last promise to Cecile, so we walk to the practice room where the guys have set up.

'I just wanted to hear that Bill Evans arrangement one last time before I fly home. Hope you don't mind.'

I jump on the piano, Tom counts us in and we are away. It's the best we've played all week.

'See you in New York.'

Shadows Who Dance

Friday 1 June 1979

I rush into college for my final practice. I'm excited but nervous too. Alice smiles at me as I go in and says, 'Good luck for this afternoon.' We went for a coffee a few days ago. I was so grateful to her for helping me. She was laughing when I told her she was the only girl I'd ever plucked up the courage to ask out. I ask her if she is coming to the show today; there are three final student recitals. She says, 'Would you mind?'

'Of course not. Mum and Dad will be there, you met them at Christmas.'

'Alphonso's back. He asked me to let him know when you were here.'

I run along to his office, best to get this out of the way. I knock and enter, and he looks at me over his coffee, there is a new photo frame on his desk.

'I'm sorry to hear about your sister.'

'Thank you, Sonny. Listen, I need to apologise to you. I messed up and caused you a great deal of worry, I'm sorry.' He gives me a bear hug. 'Enjoy today, no hard feelings?'

'None. All's well that ends well.'

'We'll catch up after your concert.'

I go to the main practice room. I'm first in on purpose, and I run through on my own before the crowds arrive. Donna and Tom are coming in for eleven, so I have a while. I'm running through my warm-ups when Eloise walks in.

She booms, 'Good morning,' as soon as she's through the doors, and asks, 'Are you ready?'

'I am, I'm there. I owe you a huge debt for helping me. Thank you so much.'

She blushes a little, and stumbles over her words. 'You know, I've always regretted not supporting Julia. I used to think students' lives were private and I shouldn't intervene, but Julia changed my mind on that score. I had her down for post-grad studies and she was going to work with me on her piano and singing career, but she was so traumatised I couldn't persuade her to return.' She adds the college was less than supportive and shouldn't have gone anywhere near Jimmy the Drums ever again.

'Well, I benefited from your help for sure.'

'That's nice of you to say so, Sonny.'

'And if you stick around after the concert I'll introduce you to Julia's son. He's got the day off school.'

Her face lights up. 'I'll see you later,' she says, and then she touches my shoulder. 'And good luck.'

The room is silent, and I think back to December 1975, over three years ago, when I first stepped into college for my audition. She was a battle axe, Donna is right, but people change don't they? I mean, look at me. I was so green back then. I had only just started, then I got lucky with one night in the music room at Waverly. One night has changed my life, and one man backed me to become a pro.

Alphonso was brave to take a punt. In reality, it was another man who made it all possible, because none of this would have happened without Freddie, well Freddie's demise if truth be told. I sit on my stool and think how weird life is. I am twenty-one now, I am going to America in two months, and I haven't told anyone yet. I need to get today over with. So many people are coming to the show and are then crashing for the weekend in London. Donna has taken on the role of social secretary so I can concentrate on my music. After all the lows of this year, I am ready to play in public. The degree is in the bag, but the pressure is on to perform, the reputation of the college is on turning out professionals. That is why we are encouraged to invite all our family and friends to mirror a gig. Eloise has inspired me to write a bunch of tunes, but I'm only playing one today.

I sneak along to the hall and peep in, the techies are setting up, and everyone is in a good mood. There's a couple of hundred chairs out, and they are lighting the main stage. We have one practice after lunch and then doors open at three. I walk back to the common room for a tea and Donna and Tom are already there.

'Nervous?' asks Tom.

I shake my head. 'Not really, excited.'

'You?'

'It's not my recital.'

Donna gives me a boost, in her best MC introductory voice. 'This man has played at Blue Note New York, he doesn't get nervous.'

'So I've heard,' says Tom. 'Thanks for booking me for the gig, I feel honoured.'

'Alphonso says you were the best.' He looks smug. 'In your price range.' His smile disappears.

'You're not paying me.'

'Maybe a beer later.'

We sit around and chat, avoiding talking tempo and tunes. We have been doing this for a week now; we just a need to get on with it. Donna calls us to order. 'Come on boys, one last run through.'

After lunch, I change backstage into the snazzy suit Ruby bought me in Manchester. I can hear the band before us killing it, beautiful Sonny Rollins blasting out of Richard's saxophone. We've got thirty minutes to go. Donna gives me a pep talk, telling me to remember I am getting marked on everything, so make sure I talk well, count us in loudly, introduce the tunes and thank the musicians. I check my music. Reminders are in pen and underlined. She leans across the table. 'I can't wait to show you New York. Mum's the word.' She blows me a kiss. We hear huge applause and Richard's trio walk in, sweating and smiling. I jump up and shake his hand and Sophie and Ben too.

Sophie says, 'You'll love that piano, it's spot on,' and Richard says, 'Good luck.'

I take deep breaths and make sure my music is in order. It's my turn. I can feel the ruby in my trouser pocket, and I think of Julia and Ruby and Granddad who got me started and …

'Ladies and Gentlemen, will you welcome our third band of the day, led by Sonny Jackson.'

I lead our trio to the stage. All thoughts cut short as I look out, and the lights blind me. It helps that I can't see anyone. I take the music out of my jacket pocket, and a piece of paper flutters to the floor. I bend down. It is a note from Ruby, 'To Sonny, enjoy tonight, I love you so much, Ruby X'. I'm trying to take it all in when Donna coughs and brings me back to my senses. It's from a previous gig. For a moment I thought … Right, concentrate.

Music out. On the stand. Large letters at the top say BREATHE. And then underneath, INTRODUCTION.

I take a deep breath, I exhale too fast, and the music flutters on the stand, I hear a little murmuring. I breathe again and lean into the microphone. 'Welcome all, this tune was the first song I ever played in front of an audience, and it's the main reason I am here today. This one is for Freddie and Ruby.' I count us in, and we play the Bill Evans arrangement of 'Time After Time', the tune that Syd Lawrence blew so beautifully at the church and then with me at Waverly all those years ago. I don't know how long we play for; we add and improvise and have so much fun it may be ten minutes. I look across the stage, and Donna signals me to wrap it up, so the guys turn it around, and we close together. The applause brings me right back to the moment, and I sit back on the stool and wipe my face.

'The second tune I have chosen for you this afternoon is …' my mind goes back in time, and my voice sounds squeaky. I think of the day Eloise introduced me to this tune in Ruby's flat, but I lose my way. Donna puts her bass down, walks over and makes me drink some water, and she pinches my arm until I react, and I'm back. 'The second tune originally featured the piano playing of Franco D'Andrea.' I hear a shout of 'Bravo' from the crowd. It settles me. 'Earlier this year I was out of college with pneumonia. I am very grateful to Eloise Challinor for continuing to teach me and for letting me know that Franco is a favourite of our esteemed head of jazz Alphonso,' and the place erupts with cheers. 'This is "Last Tango in Paris – jazz waltz".' We nail it, and I hear another 'Bravo' and 'Bellissimo' as we finish.

It's my last ever tune at college. I look at my notes. They make sense, but I know I can do better. I take my jacket off as Ruby taught me, pick up the mic and stand up and turn to the auditorium. As I am about to speak a little voice shouts, 'Piano,' at me and everybody laughs. I wave to Michael and tell everybody how we lost one of our former students just over a year ago. I introduce Michael as Julia's son, and he gets the loudest applause of the day. I tell them how I almost gave up but was persuaded by so many people around me to continue, and I am very grateful. I remember to introduce the band and give a special mention to Donna, 'Who graduated last year and is now a student in New York doing her master's degree. Finally, I must thank Mrs Challinor once more, someone who inspired me to write my own songs.

'So forgive me, this is one of my compositions, and it is the first time we are playing it in public. This song is about love, about regrets, about time passing you by and how your memory plays tricks on you. It's about meeting someone so special in your life that you never forget; it's written for my dad about my sister Maisie. It's called "Nowhere To Go". I hope you like it.' They whoop and cheer as I take a few paces across to my piano stool and make my debut as a songwriter. The performance is flawless. We are at the top of our game not thinking about the song's structure, just the emotion connected with playing it. Halfway through, the stage lights are dimmed, and the house lights come up, and I see a packed room standing and clapping along. I eyeball so many people, and I feel the love coming right back. Michael is held aloft by his dad, and I signal for him to come up and join us. I lift him onto the stage, and he feels right at home as he waves to the crowd. He joins me on the piano stool as he has done so many times before and we finish the tune. He never stops smiling.

We take a bow, the four of us, and that's it. I look out for the last time, and I see Ruby cheering for me. I blow her a kiss and mouth a 'Thank you' and then I see Dad with tears rolling downs his face and Mum searching for a hankie. I look left to the teachers on their raised dais. Alphonso gives me a thumbs-up, and Eloise stands and applauds. She's wiping her eyes too. Jack and Karen, Debs and Hamish have made it.

Stephen approaches the stage and I bend down and whisper to Michael, 'This is where your mummy came to jazz college.'

He opens his mouth in awe. 'Wow.' I tell him I will see him in a few minutes as I hand him down to his dad, who shakes my hand and says, 'I am so proud of you.'

We go backstage and us three final year students scream and shake hands and pat each other on the back. The relief is palpable. I hug Tom, thank him and tell him he'll be doing this one year from now. Donna squeezes me so tight I struggle for breath. 'Well done you. I'm glad I was here to witness that.'

'What's all this noise for?' I turn around, and Alphonso is approaching hands raised, he clasps them around my back and his voice breaks. 'I am so very proud of you, Sonny, so very proud.'

'Thank you, Alphonso, for everything.'

'Sonny, you were right to finish your degree this year. I was wrong, I'm sorry.'

I tell him I am on my way to New York and he smiles, he knows it already. 'You deserve it.'

Ruby enters the room, and she looks at me like I am her flesh and blood. Whatever she did for me, her pride at what I have achieved today is written on her face. I take her hand and lead her to the dressing room, just me and her. I give her a bag that contains a gift I have been thinking about for weeks. What do you give the woman who has everything? Someone who gambled on your ability when it was raw, and loved you as you changed from boy to man. I have returned the gemstone, the original ruby from which she took her name, and she opens the card and reads aloud.

'Dear Ruby,

When you were lost, you found me. And when you found me, you gave me love and hope. Thank you for everything you have ever done for me. I am forever in your debt. This gemstone brought me love, passion and motivated me to find my true path.

I will always love you,

Sonny Jackson, June 1979.'

She plays with the stone, 'One day I will tell you the story …' She stops herself. I never did tell her that Phil the driver had let me in on some of her secrets, there's no point. I love her for who she is.

'I am going to New York soon,'

'I knew you would.' She smiles at me. 'You're the only …' Tears begin to fall. 'The only one who always mentions Freddie, and that means so much to me. Even today you had the guts to dedicate a song to us.'

'I'm sorry I can't ever thank him, but at least you know how …'

She raises her hand. 'He helped us both. More than he'll ever know.' Her eyes are misty, mine too.

I have an urge to kiss her, to smother her in my love, to say I'm sorry we didn't work out. She knows it. She has that look I have seen a thousand times before. She has strength.

'I'll see you at the party, young man.'

No Greater Love

Donna has arranged a party for the bands later on, but my guests are having a meal first. We leave college together and head for the hotel where Mum and Dad are staying. In reception someone calls my name, and I look up to see a shadowy figure with a baseball cap pulled down low over his eyes. I'd recognise that stoop anywhere. Twenty years of heaving drums around. I send Donna ahead.

'Jimmy?'

'Sonny.' He holds out an envelope. 'You don't have to worry.'

I peer inside, film negatives. The lost weekend. 'Why now?'

He looks forlorn. 'I'm clean now, done the programme. My way of saying sorry.'

'Is that all?'

'That's all. No hidden agendas.'

'And Ruby?'

'Been there. Done that.'

'Really?'

'Really. Months ago.'

'She didn't say.'

'She's a mysterious woman.' His face flushes.

'What is your problem with Ruby?'

He take his time, 'No problem now, but back then … Let's just say we both loved the same man.'

'And you both lost him.' He nods.

'I never looked at it like that. I was too stupid and too arrogant, stuck in my own world.'

'And?'

'We've made our peace, Sonny. It's finished.'

'Julia?'

It hits home. He shrinks before me, his eyes drift downward and he shuffles back. He shakes his head from side to side and when he finally meets my gaze, there are tears in his eyes. The scar on the side of his head pulses. 'I'm sorry, I'm so sorry. I've done my time.' He fades away. I go to the gents, flush the negatives down the toilet and then splash my face. I look in the mirror. I'm desperate to be in New York, away from this turmoil.

I walk into the bar to all of them drinking and chatting, and for the first time today, I relax. I feel the nervous energy leave my body. I want to get to Mum and Dad, but it's difficult with all the arms patting me and wanting to shake my hand. I need to tell them before they hear it second hand. I order a beer from Jack and tell him I'll be in the corner. Dad jumps up when he sees me, and I get a hug like no other. He can't speak, but there's no need.

'Mum, Dad, I've got something to tell you.' I say I didn't want to jinx it, but I applied to Juilliard a few months ago. 'I'm moving to New York for two years.' Dad's arms shoot up and sends my beer flying out of Jack's hand.

'He's going to New York,' is his way of apologising to Jack and he stuffs some notes into his hands and says get a drink for everyone. Dad whispers to me, 'Do not let Ruby pay for this, tonight's on me.' Mum cries for me, she cries with me and tells anyone who will listen how proud she is. The party has started.

Little Michael jumps on my knee, and I ask him how old he is. 'I'm five, nearly six.'

'Have you got the day off school to come and see me?' He nods. I thank him and tell him I want to see him on the same stage one day, just like his mummy and me. He accepts the challenge and asks his dad for the photo. Stephen gets it out of his wallet. It's a smaller copy of the one I got for them. 'That's my mummy at Ronnie Scott's.'

'I know, I was there that night. Your mummy is a big star.'

Stephen shakes my hand and says, 'Thanks for everything. I wouldn't have missed this for the world.'

Donna squeezes in next to Dad, and I remember what she told me. She smiles. They are happy in each other's company. Mum doesn't let go of my knee. 'This will be you next summer, Mum. You know I'm coming home for your graduation party.'

'Don't be so stupid. They don't do this at my age.'

'I hope they do.' She huffed. 'Life's weird isn't it, Mum?'

'What do you mean?'

'It's just that we seem inbuilt to find the happiness, the light after the dark.' We have a philosophical five minutes as I down my pint, and we go through all the people we've loved and lost, including Granny and Granddad, Maisie, Freddie, Julia, Matilda.

'And yet, we come out of it somehow with hope.'

'But we don't forget, do we?' says Mum, and adds, 'Have you ever considered all their love has worked its way into you?'

'That sounds nice. Weird, but oddly comforting.'

Mum raises her glass of martini. 'To absent friends.' Dad

hears, he looks across at us both and raises his glass too. He never forgets. Ruby looks over. 'To absent friends.'

The restaurant calls us through. I am starving, that performance has taken it out of me. I sit at the young end of the table, Jack and Karen, Debs and Hamish, Stephen and Michael. We chat about movies, emigrating and travelling, anything but music. It's so good to have my best friends here with me. After the main course, I change seats and take Michael to sit with Eloise and Alphonso and thank them for all the help, especially after my illness. Michael jumps on to Eloise's knee, and when she says she knew his mummy, he is transfixed. He shouts to Stephen for the photo and asks for stories about her, and she relaxes into her new role. I sneak a 'Thank you' to Eloise, and she thanks me in return and cuddles Michael as tears roll down her cheeks. Alphonso winds her up and says she'll be too old to teach by the time Michael joins the college. I look around the table, full of smiles and happiness. Ruby sneaks away, and I watch her as she approaches the bar, I sneak up. 'Do not let this lady settle the bill.' She reels around, I know what she is up to. She protests, but tonight, no means no. We lean on the bar surveying the room. 'In one way or another you are responsible for all of this, Ruby. Everybody is happy because of you.'

She looks delighted. 'Freddie used to say that.'

'It's true. If both of us have said it, it must be true.'

'Can I have that as my epitaph, please?'

Rise

Thursday 30 August 1979

Tonight is the opposite of my graduation party, quiet and refined. Donna, Stevie and I are dining at the Mirabelle care of Ruby. She insisted. I tried to wheedle my way out of it but as Donna said, 'After all she's done for you, what's one more night?' We are packed and ready to go, tomorrow I begin my new life in New York hunting for some student digs. I've been back in Manchester all summer, saying goodbye to friends and family. I've enjoyed teaching Michael and have looked after him on a few nights as Stephen is dating a young lady called Vicky. He seems quite smitten but hasn't brought her home yet. Jack and Karen were an absolute hoot. Karen has moved in with Jack, and they are saving up. I even managed to get up to Edinburgh for a week with Debs and Hamish. They all spoke of the best party in London back in June. It seems so long ago, and it was a hell of a send-off after three years at college.

I've put my suit on again. It has been dry cleaned. Stevie takes the mick but Ruby will understand the significance of it. She insists I sit next to her. Alphonso is to her right and then Stevie and Donna. For once in my life, I am a little lost for words. I stare at the wine list, but I don't read it. I am deep in my thoughts. Here is my mentor, who became my lover, who sponsored my degree, who has set me up for my next journey. I owe her so much, and despite highs and lows, we have remained the best of friends. I search for her hand under the table, and it feels so natural as our fingers intertwine and I give a little squeeze to say, 'I'm going to miss you.' She squeezes me back, and we sit there like teenagers daring each other to make the next move. Alphonso chooses a Chianti of course, and Donna selects a Blue Nun. Ruby squeezes me again and unlocks her hand from mine and picks up her menu. She leans towards me. 'You'll be fine, Sonny.'

'I know. I was thinking about when we …'

'That was a long time ago.'

'It was, wasn't it?' She lets me know that tonight isn't for reminiscing.

'It's your time to shine now.' She slips me some song lyrics, just like she used to do when I first moved to Waverly.

I unfold them slowly. It's Julia's handwriting from that night at Ronnie's.

She smiles, and I understand she's telling me I am going with her blessing. 'It's your time to rise, Sonny.' Her lips tremble and she leaves the table and rushes to the ladies, followed by Donna. Alphonso looks at me, Stevie looks at me. I shrug my shoulders. We drink our wine and say nothing. The ladies return. Ruby has fresh lipstick on. Donna smiles at Stevie. Ruby finds my hand again and grasps me and then Donna does the same. I am sitting in a restaurant, both hands are held in vice-like grips under the table. I feel like a hostage. My escape comes when Alphonso raises his glass.

'Congratulations, Sonny, *alla prossima*.'

Ruby translates, 'Till we meet again.'

This breaks the spell. Donna says, 'Not to worry,' and we order our food.

We have an evening full of laughter and anecdotes and New York tales, Alphonso is on sparkling form and weaves his way around international connections. He knows everybody. When we finish talking and look around, we are the last ones in the restaurant. Ruby goes off to settle the bill.

We stand together, and I say goodbye to Alphonso. 'I think we may see you soon, Ruby is desperate to revisit New York.' Alphonso puts his arms out and holds me by both elbows. He's like a favourite uncle, looking at me with pride. 'Charlie bloody Watts.'

We burst out laughing. 'Thank you, Alphonso, for looking out for me, then and now. I mean it.'

He waves his arm. 'N*on era niente*, it was nothing.'

Ruby is at the door. 'Come on, boys, home time.'

She takes my arm as we walk towards Blenheim Street. 'Nice suit.'

'It's my favourite.'

She reaches into her handbag and pulls out an envelope. 'This is for you, please don't open it until you are on the plane.'

'What is it?'

We stop walking. She is desperate to tell me something and for the briefest of moments she lets her guard down. 'I used to be a singer you know.'

I feign surprise. 'Really?'

She pushes the envelope on me. 'You'll see.'

Ruby kisses me on the left cheek, then the right. 'Continental.'

I look back as we head home. They are arm in arm on the steps, and they look good together. I can see that. Ruby is crying, I wave one last goodbye, and she leans on Alphonso's shoulder. He comforts her, and now I'm crying too.

Donna puts her arm around me. 'You big softie, we're going to America.'

I wipe my eyes. 'If I can make it there, I'd make it anywhere.'

The three us frighten the sleeping birds. 'New York, New York.'

Here's to Life

I check my iPhone for the twentieth time. The sun is shining as the hearse pulls up outside Waverly. I shout to Sylvie, my wife, 'She's here.' We watch from the front door as the limousine reverses in to collect us. Sylvie looks at her watch. 'It's ok, we have plenty of time.' After thirty years in England, she still has the American twang that I fell in love with. I tell the funeral director we will be five minutes and I pull the door to.

My daughter Maryanne is coming downs the stairs. She looks as though she has been crying. I hug her. 'Will you fetch Granddad from the front room?' Sylvie reappears, carrying our granddaughter. Little Georgie is asleep, nestled into the baby seat.

Dad shuffles along, a little stooped and hanging on to Maryanne for support. 'Ok, Sonny, are we ready?'

'Yes, I think we're all set.' He's eighty-four now, sharp as a tack, but hard of hearing and wobbly. Maryanne's husband Tony is outside waiting for the baby seat to go in their car. Sylvie puts her shoes on and picks up Georgie. We stand in the hall, composing ourselves. I open the door, look at my daughter. 'Let's do your godmother proud.' Dad and Maryanne take the back seats, Sylvie and I in the middle, and we follow the hearse for the short journey to St Mary's.

It's nearly forty-four years since Dad and I drove here in the Ford Escort to Freddie's funeral. I didn't have a clue about life and death and the passage of time, about families and support structures and rituals that help us get through days like these. I'm sixty-one now and have spent the last twenty years in Manchester working as a professional musician. Forty-four years, that's gone so fast. Too fast. The city I grew up in has changed so much. There are so many planes and trams and bistros and restaurants. I'm daydreaming again as we pull up. Dad leans forward and pats me on the shoulder. 'Do you remember that trumpeter at Freddie's funeral? He was amazing.'

'I do, Dad. It was Syd Lawrence. I got to know him very well.' I even played in his orchestra for a while.

'And the string quartet. Remember them?'

'They played Puccini.'

'You've got a good memory, Sonny.'

We approach the church and at the final roundabout, Dad taps me on the shoulder. 'Turn right, Sonny.' I glance back and he's smiling at our in-joke.

We sit still until the funeral directors open the doors. The tinted windows give way to brilliant sunshine, which blinds me for a while. I look up, shielding my eyes, I recognise Debs and Hamish, and we acknowledge each other. I make sure Dad is ok, Maryanne is holding onto her granddad and Tony and Georgie join us. We are the funeral party. No relatives, no London contingent today, just her adopted family, and her much loved goddaughter, Maryanne. We follow the coffin into the church. As I walk down the aisle, I recognise a few faces. Jack and Karen are over from Australia visiting, Stephen and Vicky wave, some of the people Sylvie knows from the choir she runs have come to support her. Donna and Stevie nod as I pass. And right at the front, on a keyboard set-up for today, Michael is playing Chrysanthemums as they place Ruby at the front of the church.

We take our seats. Just as all those years ago, my mind wanders as the service begins. Ruby called me six months ago to tell me she was dying and I knew what I had to do. We drove to London and stayed with her and discussed everything. She was on her own since Alphonso had passed away six years before, just after Mum, and she loved her flat with the terrace on the first floor and its light, airy rooms. I invited her to return to Waverly, to the house I had bought from her with my first big pay cheque over thirty years ago. At first, she said she couldn't possibly be a burden to us, but Sylvie and I worked on her. We stayed for a week in early December, and we took her to the theatre, to Ronnie's and back to the Mirabelle. We sat around chatting and watching the world go by from cafe windows. When we left I said I would come and pick her up for Christmas. Maryanne was staying, and would love to see her, and she would enjoy seeing Georgie, our only grandchild. That clinched it. She always enjoys chatting with Maryanne, and since we had got her a mobile phone, she was forever sending texts and watching videos.

I got the Jag checked and cleaned and drove to London three days before Christmas thinking it would be an additional surprise. It was me who was in for the bigger shock. She had gone downhill so fast and was very frail. I scooped her up and put her in the car as gently as I could, and she instructed me to fetch a pile of things from the front room, boxed up and ready. I took one last look around the flat, stacks of envelopes with friends' and neighbours' names beautifully written on the front, final farewells. I knew then that she would not be returning. She tried to apologise to me, but I wouldn't accept it; it was my mistake for leaving her alone. We shot off, stopping on our way out of London for some tea and toast. Some colour returned to her cheeks and she slept most of the way to Manchester. We had a great three months full of laughter and old stories, and I didn't mind giving up some work and helping out. She told me she loved being back at Waverly, and now and again we'd ride out in the Jag and see some countryside.

As spring arrived Ruby began to fade. Some days we managed to make it into the garden as the crocuses and daffodils began to show. She loved it when the girls visited, and Georgie would jump up on her lap. She gave me a box with my name on it and I read all of her diaries, and we talked and talked and talked. All of the old familiar places. Ruby was seventy-seven on the fourth of April. We celebrated with some Champagne and scones, her favourite.

Sylvie taps me, and I stand up and walk to the lectern. The church is silent as I take out my notes.

'Ruby Wilson was an extraordinary woman. Born seventy-seven years ago into poverty and with both her adopted parents dying before she was fifteen, she became a force for good. No one benefited from her generosity more than me. Not many people are aware she was an aspiring singer when she met Freddie Wilson, and her life took an amazing turn. For someone who grew up with nothing, she gave unconditionally. She loved without judgment, and she lived life to the full. Sylvie and I are proud to have cared for Ruby for the last six months. We are proud she is godmother to Maryanne, our daughter. I knew both Ruby's husbands, and I can tell you she enriched their lives. As she did mine. Once, I was having a chat with her, and I told her, "You make everybody happy." She said that was what Freddie used to say. She asked me, "Can that be my epitaph?" I can think of no better sentiment. She was a bringer of joy, of laughter, music and love. I still see her everywhere I go, theatres, clubs and restaurants. All the places that became familiar in my life.'

The service finishes and Michael plays 'Nowhere To Go', the song I wrote for my graduation. Sylvie walks to the microphone and sings as they carry Ruby out. This is the song that gave me enough money to buy Waverly. It was written about love and loss, it was for my dad and Maisie, but it was also about Ruby and Matilda. The song is Ruby's words, her lyrics, her poetry to my music. That's what was in the envelope she put in my pocket forty years ago; she could have been a songwriter herself, but she gave it up for love. It was her parting gift to me as she let me go. I read it for the first time on that flight and cried all the way to New York.

Ruby's coffin is lowered into the soil above Freddie.

Dad turns to me. 'I am so proud of you, Sonny.'

'That's all I ever wanted.'

The End.

Epilogue

Forty-four years in the blink of an eye. You hear people say, 'If I knew then what I know now ...' but I guess the real fun lies in making our own mistakes with new friends. I think Ruby and I grew up together in some ways, which sounds strange given our age difference. We spoke about it many times. She was a brilliant godmother to Maryanne. I can't tell you how she loved having the word 'mother' in her title. She talked about Matilda and Freddie until the very end. Her long marriage to Alphonso and their constant globe-trotting brought immense joy to her. When I first went to New York, they would come and visit, and we would hit the jazz bars. I never did tire of hearing her stories. I told her about my conversation with Miss Wolstenholme, who said her love for Bert sustained her throughout her life. Ruby replied in a flash. 'Well then, I must have been lucky, I've had three lovers.' That was Ruby. Straightforward, honest, a lover of life.

In my third term, I got together with a beautiful bass player called Sylvie, and on one of Ruby's visits she took me aside and said, 'She's the one.'

'How do you know?'

'She adores you,' was the response, and that was enough.

She was correct, of course. Sylvie loved her the minute she

met her. We had just one difficult weekend when I shared the full history with Sylvie, as I had to. At Ruby's suggestion, she took Sylvie out to dinner. I still don't know what they discussed, but they returned the best of friends, and all Sylvie would say was, 'Charlie bloody Watts.' I think it was Ruby's way of saying 'carpe diem'. Seize the day. Sylvie seized me, and she's never let me go.

When we started a family, my wife suggested Ruby for godmother, an inspired choice. And we purchased and settled at Waverly. Ruby's best friend, my mum Jess, died in 2013. She and my dad were brilliant grandparents, always on hand for us. Just a short while later, Alphonso passed away. That was a tough year for all of us, but we got through it together. She came back to Waverly for a few months and she and Dad would visit galleries and cafes. They helped each other through their grief. Maryanne was at school, and she and Ruby would sit and chat over homework. Then Ruby would say, 'It wasn't like that in my day,' and she would paint beautiful pictures of concerts and dances and jazz clubs and romance. One weekend Michael came to see us, and he brought round his framed photo of Julia on stage at Ronnie Scott's. Julia's story entranced Maryanne, the audience waiting in anticipation as Julia walked to the front, and how they moved from hushed respect to rapturous applause. I scanned the photo, and it now has pride of place in my music room, Freddie's music room. Not one image has been removed. Ruby loved being in the room right up to the very end. She would take tea on the chaise longue, and I would play for her. Sylvie would join us, sing the old show tunes, and Ruby would sing along. I made sure everyone visited during that last six months. All of my friends became family to Ruby, and we loved and cherished her with all of our hearts.

Jack and Karen got married and are now Australian citizens, with three children. Vera and Fred moved there too, sadly passed away now. Debs and Hamish have two boys, and we visit them in Edinburgh. Mr Potter left teaching and ended up being a karaoke star in Manchester; he could impersonate anyone, but perhaps he was most famous as Elton John. Jack and I dropped in on him once and requested Crocodile Rock on the sly. Cindy stayed at the record shop, and I spent so much money there over the years, and often had a cup of tea with her. I used to phone Marj from all over the world when I was gigging, and she and Michael had this extraordinary lifelong bond. Miss Wolstenholme passed away, and I saw her several times on my visits home. We always had a coffee and cake, and I insisted on playing her a tune and talking about Bert.

Ruby became a respected counsellor as Mum predicted she would, and she practised for nearly thirty years in London.

I did return home for Mum's graduation, and she did become a social worker in Manchester. Dad is proud of her to this day. And Fred looked after Ringo for the rest of his life. He never missed a walk.

It's been quite a story, and I think back to that first night at Waverly like it was yesterday.

We wave Maryanne and Tony goodbye. They have strapped Georgie in. We are both frazzled. I walk into the kitchen, and Sylvie is opening a bottle of white wine. She pours me a glass. That was one heck of a day. We wander into the music room, it's our sanctuary now.

'It was a good day in the circumstances.'

'It was. You Brits say the funniest things.'

'I love you, Sylvie.'

'I love you too.'

She looks up, and spots one of the photos is off centre. She gets up to straighten it as I feel a shiver run down my spine and a white feather flutters into my lap. I sense it is Freddie, thanking me for taking care of his beloved wife.

'Who is it in this photo?'

Without looking, I know.

'Charlie bloody Watts.'

PATRONS

Many thanks to hundreds of jazz fans who invested in
advance,
I really do appreciate your trust. I hope you enjoy the story.

WORDSMITH PATRONS

Charles Ledigo
Charlotte Keech

BETA READERS

Thank you so much for your feedback over the last two years,
for your time and dedication in improving my story.

Enid Shelmerdine
Anne Earley
Steve, Josh, Anne

EDITOR & MENTOR

Thank you to Cornerstones Literary Consultancy for reading
my pitch and putting me in touch with Mark Leggatt, editor.
It is so nice to have someone on your side, believing in your
story, polishing and improving as you write.

www.emony.co.uk